JWI
JWO.
AA.

GAITS OF HEAVEN

A DOG LOVER'S MYSTERY

GAITS OF HEAVEN

SUSAN CONANT

THORNDIKE PRESS

An imprint of Thomson Gale, a part of The Thomson Corporation

Detroit • New York • San Francisco • New Haven, Conn. • Waterville, Maine • London

ALL RIGHTS RESERVED

Thorndike Press® Large Print Mystery.
The text of this Large Print edition is unabridged.
Other aspects of the book may vary from the original edition.
Set in 16 pt. Plantin.

LIBRARY OF CONGRESS CATALOGING-IN-PUBLICATION DATA

Conant, Susan, 1946–
    Gaits of heaven : a dog lover's mystery / by Susan Conant.
      p. cm. — (Thorndike Press large print mystery)
    ISBN-13: 978-0-7862-9281-3 (alk. paper)
    ISBN-10: 0-7862-9281-4 (alk. paper)
    1. Winter, Holly (Fictitious character) — Fiction. 2. Cambridge (Mass.) — Fiction. 3. Dog trainers — Fiction. 4. Dogs — Fiction. 5. Psychotherapists — Fiction. 6. Large type books. I. Title.
PS3553.O4857G35 2007
813'.54—dc22   2006034885

Published in 2007 by arrangement with The Berkley Publishing Group, a division of Penguin Group (USA) Inc.

Printed in the United States of America on permanent paper
10 9 8 7 6 5 4 3 2 1

In loving memory of my own Rowdy,
Frostfield Perfect Crime, CD, CGC,
ThD, WPD
(November 29, 1993–
November 29, 2004),
my perfect girl.

ACKNOWLEDGMENTS

I am grateful to Phyllis Hamilton for allowing me to write about her majestic Monty, Alaskan malamute Ch. Benchmark Captain Montague, ROM, a legend in the breed.

For answering my questions, I am grateful to James Dalsimer, M.D., and Michael Glenn, M.D. Special thanks to Carter Umbarger, Ph.D., for discussing hypothetical cases with me. Any errors are mine alone. Roseann Mandell, please accept my thanks for your help with the manuscript. Profuse thanks, too, to Jean Berman, Lynn Madar, Pat Sullivan, Margherita Walker, Anya Wittenborg, Suzanne Wymelenberg, and Corinne Zipps.

For companionship and inspiration, my thanks to Jazzland's Got That Swing, my beloved Django.

CHAPTER 1

The first step in recovery is to admit that you are powerless — your life has become unmanageable. Second, you need to believe in a power greater than yourself that can restore you to sanity. When I first met Ted and Eumie Green, they were indeed powerless. Their dog, Dolfo, hadn't exactly become unmanageable; he had never been otherwise. As to restoration to sanity, I, Holly Winter, intended to become the Higher Power: I wanted to rid poor Dolfo and his owners of their multitudinous defects and shortcomings, thus inducing in all three a spiritual awakening that would free the dog from his seemingly incurable addiction to canine bad citizenship and simultaneously cause Ted and Eumie forever after to practice the principles of responsible ownership.

Having mentioned sanity, I feel compelled to defend myself against the potential psychiatric insinuation that I was suffering from delusions of omnipotence. I intended to become a Higher Power only with respect to *Canis familiaris:* I never imagined that I had created the world or had the power to change it except in one limited sphere, which was, is, and ever shall be the behavior of dogs. Even so, such chutzpah! The word was a favorite of Ted Green's. In his devotion to Yiddish expressions, he pronounced the *ch* with a deep gurgling in his throat. Shikse that I am, I settle for a WASP's *h.* Still, no matter what your ethnic origin, you'd readily admit that when it comes to dogs, I have a lot of nerve. *Chutzpah:* nerve, gall, moxie, as opposed to the ancient Greek *hubris,* pronounced "Hugh Briss," as if it were a normal first name followed by the term for a Jewish circumcision ritual. Anyway, chutzpah can be bad or good, whereas in ancient Greece, *hubris* referred to considering yourself on a par with the gods, an act of arrogance that invariably led to divine retribution. In this story, fairly or unfairly, the person who suffered the ultimate fatal fate was not she who set herself up as God's gift to horrible-acting dogs. Rather, it was Eumie Brainard-Green.

To begin: I first met Ted, Eumie, and Dolfo at 6:15 on the evening of Thursday, May 26, in front of the Cambridge Armory, where the Cambridge Dog Training Club holds its classes. The armory is a low, unprepossessing brick building on Concord Avenue near the Fresh Pond rotary and the LaundroMutt self-service dog wash. The club's classes take place in the big hall that occupies most of the armory's interior, a space big enough for the club to run three classes simultaneously and blessedly free of those damned supporting columns that handlers are always smashing into when they're zeroing in on their dogs rather than on the risk of bruises and concussions. From my viewpoint, another advantage of the armory is its proximity to my house, which is the barn-red one at 256 Concord Avenue, on the corner of Appleton Street. My husband and I, together with two of our five dogs, were making our way along the sidewalk by the little fenced playground that abuts the armory grounds, and both dogs, Rowdy and Sammy, father and son, the two most breathtakingly beautiful male Alaskan malamutes ever to set big white snowshoe paw on the lucky planet Earth . . . Sorry. I seem to have drifted Arcticward.

Anyway, as Steve, Rowdy, Sammy, and I

approached the armory, I got my first glimpse of Ted, Eumie, and Dolfo, and without even knowing who they were, I knew they were rank beginners, and I knew they were trouble. The club's current beginners' class had started on the first Thursday in May, and this trio wasn't enrolled. Ted Green, whose name I didn't yet know, was a tall, slim man dressed in crisply creased dark-navy jeans, a cotton pullover in the shade of periwinkle that L.L.Bean considers unsuitable for men and offers only in women's sizes, and leather loafers rather than Cambridge-ubiquitous Birkenstock sandals or the sensible dog-training footwear that most of us wear, namely, running shoes that give good traction. His black hair was so short that if it hadn't been for the presence of the woman and the dog, I might have overlooked his age — midfifties, at a guess — and assumed that he was at the armory for a National Guard or army recruiting event rather than for dog training. The woman, in contrast, had lots of hair that had been skillfully tinted in shades of light brown and blond. The effect of the colorist's art was expensively naturalistic or even hypernatural; art imitated nature with no intention of fooling anyone. She wore unflatteringly cropped khaki pants, a blouse in a sickly shade of yellow-green, and dainty leather sandals that revealed pedicured feet with bright pink toenails.

I soon had the opportunity to observe details such as the woman's nail polish, as well as the man's receding chin and the reflection of the yellow-green blouse on the woman's face, because having sized up the situation, I handed Rowdy's leash to my husband, Steve, and dashed ahead to offer my help. The armory, I should explain, has a front lawn with a concrete walk that leads to the doors. The fencing on either side of the walk turns it into a sort of chute, capering about in which was one of the most peculiar-looking animals I had ever seen. His size was ordinary: I guessed his weight at sixty pounds. His coat, however, was a motley assortment of colors and textures, and consisted of uneven patches of gray and yellow, some long and silky, some short and wiry, as if his body had been inexplicably carpeted with a dozen or more ill-chosen remnants. His floppy ears and exceptionally hairy feet, in combination with his goofy smile and his long, heavily furred tail, gave him a clownish appearance. One of his eyes was hazel, the other deep brown. So odd was the creature's appearance that to the casual observer even his membership in *Ca-*

nis familiaris might have been open to question. I, however, had been raised not merely by golden retrievers but as a golden, and had spent the rest of my thirty-plus years with dogs. I train dogs, I show dogs, I earn my living by writing about dogs, and I live with my two Alaskan malamutes, Rowdy and Kimi, my husband's German shepherd, India, his pointer, Lady, and the aforementioned Sammy, Rowdy's son and the household's third malamute, the only one of the five dogs Steve and I co-own. The previous October, I'd added a new credential by marrying not just any veterinarian, but my own veterinarian, Steve Delaney. In brief, I was in a position to conduct an expert assessment of the bizarre-looking animal running from one end to the other of the armory's front walk, with pauses to leap on the man and woman who accompanied him, and authoritatively to reach the counterintuitive conclusion that he was most definitely a *dog.*

I learned his name, Dolfo, from his strikingly coiffed and dressed owners, who were uselessly repeating it, the man in a deep, pleasing voice, the woman in a high squeak. "Dolfo! Dolfo, good dog! Good Dolfo! Good, good boy!"

In violation of the Cambridge leash law and the rules of the Cambridge Dog Training Club, Dolfo was off lead. When I had pulled a spare leash from my pocket and brushed past the woman, who was blocking the dog's access to the traffic on Concord Avenue, I discovered that he wasn't even wearing a collar. Having applied my expertise in dogs to identifying Dolfo's subspecies, I should have gone on immediately to apply my knowledge of Cambridge and, in particular, my familiarity with Cambridge psychotherapists to the simple task of realizing that the absence of a collar was a sign of owner lunacy and therefore a sign that Dolfo's owners were probably psychotherapists. As it was, I naively assumed that Dolfo had slipped his collar.

My spare leash was a four-foot leather obedience lead with a snap at one end and a loop handle at the other. When I reached the dog, felt for his collar, and found none, I ran the length of thin leather through the handle and slid the resulting noose over the dog's head and around his neck. Pleased with the success of this makeshift arrangement and the dog's consequent protection from the cars on Concord Avenue and in the nearby rotary, I smiled at the owners and said, "He's safe now!" As I awaited their thanks, the dog jumped on me, but I didn't correct him and didn't really mind. After all, if a guy walks into a psychiatrist's office and faints from a panic attack or announces that he's Jesus, the shrink's task isn't to criticize and complain, is it? So, my principal reaction was happiness that the dog had arrived where he belonged, namely, at a psychoeducational facility where he could gain control of a symptom that irritated people and could go on to master skills that would transform him into a delight to himself, his owners, and the community as a whole. Also, I was wearing old clothes that had been ruined, in part, by dogs a lot bigger than Dolfo. My female malamute, Kimi, was seventy-five pounds, Rowdy was a lean eighty-five, and his young son, Sammy, was eighty-two pounds and still filling out. India, Steve's shepherd, was a big girl, but she was too perfect ever to have ruined a piece of clothing, and Steve's pointer, Lady, was small by my standards and too gentle and timid ever to have done any harm at all.

Anyway, instead of thanking me for capturing their loose dog and instead of apologizing for his uncivilized behavior, the couple exchanged knowing glances. Clearing his throat, the man said in that strikingly pleasant, deep voice, "*Oy vey!* It's hard to explain. Let's just say that we don't believe in leashes."

Evidently feeling that her partner had failed to express himself properly, the woman confided in a soft squeak, "Dolfo isn't really a dog, you see. He's a fur person."

I came close to welcoming her to the Cambridge Fur Person Training Club. What stopped me was the realization of who these people were and the concomitant understanding that their presence here was my fault.

As I heard the woman, she uttered two personal pronouns: "You me." When she held out her hand, I understood that she was saying her name. "Eumie Brainard-Green. And my husband, Ted Green. And Dolfo, of course."

Still holding Dolfo's makeshift leash, I shook Eumie Brainard-Green's hand. "Holly Winter. And you won the Avon Hill auction."

Several months earlier, my cousin Leah, who had taught at the Avon Hill School's summer program, had persuaded the board of the Cambridge Dog Training Club to donate training classes to the school's benefit auction. Leah, a Harvard undergraduate, had insisted that she was too busy to act as the liaison between the club and the elite private school. Consequently, I'd volunteered and had dutifully sent the auction chairperson a write-up of exactly what the club was offering, together with instructions for the high bidder and a brochure about the club. The most important instruction to the winner had been to call me to register for a class. The information packet had explained the need for preregistration and had contained a list of rules, including the requirement that dogs arrive on leash. So, it may seem as if the fault lay with Ted and Eumie, but it didn't. I knew better. Pop psychology would, of course, urge me to soften the statement by saying that Eumie, Ted, and Dolfo's presence was my responsibility rather than my fault. In reality, it was both. When I'd convinced the club to donate dog training to the Avon Hill School, I'd made the mistake of listening to my cousin Leah and ignoring the possibility — worse, the likelihood — that we'd end up with rich Cambridge lunatics who'd feel entitled to show up at the club whenever they felt like it and to violate the club rules in exactly the same fashion they violated the Cambridge leash law and, for that matter, all other rules and regulations written and enacted for ordinary human beings and irrelevant to special people like them. And special dogs, too.

As if reading my thoughts, Eumie said, "We were going to call, but Dolfo is a very special dog, you see, and we're in a crisis. We need help now."

My pockets are dog training kits. After raiding my supply of Gooberlicious peanut butter–flavored treats, I'd lured Dolfo off me and was helping him to love the feel of concrete on his paws. He was licking my hands and bouncing around. He didn't try to force the treats out of my hand, and he didn't growl at me. Furthermore, although Steve, Rowdy, and Sammy were now approaching, Dolfo stayed focused on the food in my hand. If a dog is going to display aggression toward any other dogs, he'll usually show it to Alaskan malamutes. The stimulus isn't malamute behavior but what's called "breed type": as big dogs with ears up, plumy tails waving over their backs, and thick coats standing off their bodies, malamutes register as potential threats even when they are behaving like ladies and gentlemen. But as I've said, Dolfo didn't react.

"Beginners' classes start on the first Thursday of the month," I said, "and it's too late to enter the one that's already begun. You've missed too much, and it's full, anyway. There won't be another beginners' class until September. I'm sorry. But you're welcome to come in and —"

As I'd been apologizing, my dog training buddy and my plumber, too, a guy named Ron Coughlin, had opened one of the armory doors. The club was lucky to have the use of the parking lot behind the armory. People who parked there entered through the back doors, as Ron had done; I'd noticed his van turning in. Ron was a nice guy and an excellent plumber. I'd known him for ages. We'd both served on the club's board, we'd trained dogs together, he owned a perfect male golden retriever I'd helped him to adopt, and we'd hung out together at obedience trials. He'd recently done a lot of plumbing for Steve and me when we moved my friend and second-floor tenant, Rita, to the third floor and converted her second-floor apartment and my original ground-floor apartment into one big unit for ourselves. Still, when I ran into Ron, I didn't fly up to him and give him a hug, and I didn't shriek.

That's just what Eumie Green did. "Ron!" she squealed. "What a surprise! What are you doing here?" When he finally escaped, his normally ruddy complexion was outright red, but he managed to mumble the obvious, namely, that he was training his dogs.

"The Greens won us at the Avon Hill auction," I told Ron. "Their dog needs a collar and a leash so they can come in and observe. Do we have —"

Ron was now expressionless. "Dolfo," he said, "doesn't wear a collar."

"Ron, *vee geyts?* Ron does our plumbing." Ted spoke with just a hint of a southern accent. "He's one of the family. He and Dolfo are old friends." Ron later told me that Ted and Eumie had waited six months to pay the last bill he'd sent them. Ron was a friend of Steve's and mine, too, but he wasn't one of the family. Consequently, we always paid him promptly.

"Well," I said brightly, "tonight is going to be a new experience for Dolfo." The dog, I should say, was perfectly happy on leash. In fact, he was always happy. Bizarre-looking, yes, and uncivilized, but wonderfully cheerful.

Ted and Eumie exchanged glances and then reluctant nods. *"Nisht gut,"* said Ted. "But we'll try it for a few minutes."

By then, handlers and dogs were arriving, so I hustled Dolfo into the entrance hall,

21

where people were checking in and paying, but before Ron even had time to borrow a collar and leash from the club's equipment box, the Dolfo experiment failed. To avoid getting graphic or disgusting, I'll just report that right there in the middle of the entry-way, Dolfo staged a large and smelly demonstration of what happens when owners fail to housebreak a dog. Instead of apologizing, cleaning up after their dog, or helping me to get him outside, Ted and Eumie decided that Dolfo was responding to stress.

"This whole situation is traumatic for him," Ted announced.

Far from acting traumatized, Dolfo was merrily sniffing the evidence of his crime.

"Good boy," Eumie told him. "We'll take you home right now."

"Eumie," said Ted, "you're forgetting the crisis."

"We'll find another housekeeper," she replied. "We always do."

"And she'll quit, too."

"We need to discuss this matter outside," I said in my dog-trainer voice. As I led Dolfo out, he raised his leg on a doorjamb. Then he turned around and jumped on me. When I'd finally lured the Greens all the way to their brand-new silver Lexus SUV, which was parked in an illegal but nearby spot on

Concord Avenue, I again apologized for what I called the "misunderstanding" about the auction item. "You probably paid a lot of money for dog training classes, and we can't offer you anything until September. And Dolfo really can't be loose. I know you don't like to restrain him, but it's a club rule. And it's necessary. For the safety of all the dogs." Ted opened the door to the backseat, and Dolfo jumped in. I reclaimed my spare leash and rubbed his ridiculous ears. "He's really very cute," I said.

"I'll bet you don't know what breed he is!" Eumie exclaimed.

"I can't begin to guess," I said truthfully.

"You probably thought he was a mongrel," she said. "Or a Goldendoodle. We hear that a lot."

There were so many Goldendoodles, Labradoodles, and cockapoos around these days that I'd learned to identify them, but my new skill hadn't convinced me that they were anything other than costlypoos. Still, I said, "People always think that my malamutes are Siberian huskies."

"Dolfo," said Ted, "is a golden Aussie huskapoo. We found him on the Web." With warm condescension, he added, "It's a new breed."

I refrained from asking how much Dolfo

had cost. My bet was at least twice what Steve had paid for Sammy, who was a show-quality puppy out of a champion sire and dam, my Rowdy and American and Canadian Ch. Jazzland's Embraceable You. I later learned that the Greens had actually paid four times Sammy's cost, which goes to prove that I know less about dogs than I like to imagine. "Golden retriever, Siberian husky, poodle, and Australian cattle dog?" I asked. Because of my heritage, I can usually spot even a trace of golden retriever in a mixed-breed dog. I couldn't see or sense any golden in Dolfo, but I wouldn't have guessed the other parts of the mix, either.

Ted was delighted. "Australian shepherd," he corrected. His face fell. "But the breeder told us that they practically house-train themselves."

"The crisis," I said.

"Our housekeeper quit," he said.

"We're well rid of that one," Eumie said. "She really wasn't very nice to Dolfo. Not that she was mean. We wouldn't have allowed that. But she just didn't give him the affection he needs. And she complained about him. She was not a self-reflective or self-actualizing person."

Horrors!

"All she ever did was kvetch," Ted agreed.

"But we have to have someone."

Job description: *Help wanted: self-reflective, self-actualizing housekeeper willing to give affection to unhousebroken dog.*

"We lead very busy lives," Eumie said. "We work a lot. We're both therapists. We have patients to see."

Rita, our tenant and friend, is a psychotherapist. Consequently, I was wary of raising a matter to which Cambridge psychotherapists pay what strikes me as pitifully little attention. The small matter was reality. "Housekeepers," I said bravely, "aren't going to keep cleaning up dog urine and dog feces. So, you've got a choice. Either you can get by without a housekeeper, or you can teach Dolfo to go outdoors. Which is it going to be?"

A word about my courage. The Alaskan malamute is universally considered to be a challenging breed. I not only lived with Alaskan malamutes but showed them in obedience. The dogs and I didn't get the high scores that I used to get with my golden retrievers, but we did get titles. More to the point, as does not go without saying, after repeated experiences of entering American Kennel Club obedience rings with malamutes, I was still alive, a condition I attributed more to God's mercy in forgiving my false promises than to the behavior of the dogs. Again and again as I'd waited outside the ring, I'd vowed that if God spared me the heart attack I was about to suffer, I'd never enter a malamute in an obedience trial again. I'd lied. And been forgiven, doubtless because even God had to admire a woman with my guts. In the past few months, my ring nerves had been acting up, and I hadn't shown a dog in any competitive event, but when it came to speaking up, I was as bold as ever.

Ted, being a Cambridge therapist and therefore phobic about reality, evaded my question about housekeepers versus house-breaking. "I have to tell you that I am feeling disillusioned. Really, what I'm feeling is anger. When Eumie and I bid on dog training, we were told that the methods here were positive."

"They are."

"Leather straps are not positive."

I quoted the bumper sticker. " 'Love is a leash.' That's another way to look at it."

"The atmosphere did not feel positive," Eumie complained.

"Look," I said, "there are ways to train dogs totally off leash using completely positive methods, but a big dog-training club with group classes doesn't lend itself to that kind of approach. Among other things, we'd have dog fights. We use lots of food and lots of praise, but we can't take the chance of having untrained dogs or aggressive dogs starting trouble or getting themselves in trouble. We don't want anyone to get hurt. Besides, we'd get sued."

"I have to say that I feel that we were misled," Ted told me.

As I've mentioned, the presence of Ted, Eumie, and Dolfo was my fault. And my responsibility. "I can't train Dolfo for you," I said. "But I can get you started. We can work on housebreaking. Is your yard fenced?"

They nodded.

"Then we can do it off leash."

The real reason I offered was neither guilt nor responsibility. I didn't do it out of loyalty to the club or a desire to protect the club's reputation. The real reason was that I hate to see a dog do bad things only because no one has taught him to be good. In other words, I'm a total sucker for dogs.

CHAPTER 2

In my mind's eye, I see relief on Eumie's face as Ted steers her new SUV into the traffic on Concord Avenue. The source of the relief, which is to say, the relief I imagine Eumie to feel, is not Ted's miraculous luck in escaping an accident: she is so used to his terrible driving that she barely notices it. If he had in fact sideswiped the little Saab he'd missed by an inch or two, her luxury truck would have kept her safe — it is only slightly smaller than a Hummer — and if he had totaled her car, she'd have bought a new one. Because Eumie died an unnatural death on the Monday night following her brief appearance at the armory on that Thursday evening, my imagination tempts me to attribute at least a little of the relief to a sort of emotional precognition, a fleeting feeling of happiness that she is not going to die right now, but I don't believe that Eumie glimpsed the future. As a general principle, I reject the notion of fortune-telling and thus won't allow it in what is, after all, fantasy, albeit fantasy that is as realistic as imagination can make it. No, the source of Eumie's relief is the sense that her beloved dog, Dolfo, is going to be in capable hands, which is to say, my hands, and that she is thus going to be able to hire a house-keeper who won't abandon her the way the last one did. Eumie would, I think, have agreed with this portrayal of her. She'd have acknowledged that safety and money were important to her.

"Dolfo developed an immediate bond with Holly, don't you think?" she says to Ted in her squeaky but weirdly sweet voice. "A special bond. There was something so tender about the way he looked at her."

In the backseat, Dolfo responds to the sound of his name by beating his bizarre tail on the leather upholstery. His face wears the smug look of a dog who understands that life has landed him in an altogether cushy situation.

"I know who she is," says Ted. "Holly Winter. She's married to the ex-husband of one of my patients. Anita Fairley. Anita's that lawyer I told you about. Beautiful woman. Very traumatized. The ex-husband must be that guy with the huskies."

"The hunk."

"He's a vet."

"Gulf War?" Eumie asks.

Ted smiles. "Veterinarian."

CHAPTER 3

I had no opportunity to talk to Steve during our class, which was the second in a series of four workshops on rally obedience. By comparison with the rigid formality of traditional obedience competition, rally-O was relaxed and easygoing. Obedience zealot that I am, I'd initially assumed that since rally failed to demand precision heeling, there was something morally suspect about it; and when I'd learned that rally handlers were supposed to talk to their dogs during the exercises, I'd decided that it was outright heretical. Imagine a Roman Catholic of fifty years ago who dutifully attends mass only to be told that there's no need to go to confession and that it's fine to eat meat on Fridays. The new sport turned out not to be sinful. For one thing, I'd found it surprisingly difficult. I was used to having a judge give orders, whereas in rally, the handler receives directions from a series of signs that mark a course. Some signs were readily interpretable: Halt. Others consisted of lines and arrows depicting, for instance, the route to follow around orange traffic cones or the manner in which the team should execute an about-turn. For another thing, rally classes turned out to be fun, and I'm convinced that the heavens smile on any sport that makes handlers laugh and dogs wag their tails. But would the light-hearted atmosphere of rally cure my ring nerves? I had no idea.

For the first rally workshop, which I'd attended a week earlier, I'd taken Rowdy, who was an experienced obedience dog and as such had left me free to concentrate on decoding the cryptic signs. Steve had been absent because of an emergency with one of his patients, a dog that had been hit by a car after running away from an off-leash playgroup. Tonight, Steve had intended to take India, his highly accomplished German shepherd bitch — a clean technical term here in the dog world — but she'd developed a limp at the last minute, so he'd ended up with Rowdy, and I'd boldly decided to take Sammy, whose only qualification for rally was that he and the sport were both about play. At the age of about sixteen months, Sammy was an adolescent puppy, and even for a young Alaskan malamute, he was wildly exuberant and thoroughly exhausting.

As Steve, Rowdy, Sammy, and I left the armory for home, I said, "Rally is perfect for Sammy. It's high energy. Do one exercise, rush to the next one, zip through that, lots of bounce and chatter. The one thing that bothers me is that no one ever comments on how good Sammy is. All anyone ever says is, 'Wow! What a beautiful dog!' "

"He is a beautiful dog," Steve said.

Sammy had started out as Steve's puppy. A few years earlier, Steve and I had split up, in part because I'd repeatedly refused to marry him. He'd soon married someone else, Anita Fairley, the human fiend who, in my opinion, had been incapable of loving Steve or anyone else but had wanted a husband as good-looking as she was. And for that matter, still is. The bitch. Nontechnical term. Not that I myself objected to Steve's appearance. He's tall and lean, with wavy brown hair and eyes that change from blue to green. So, it's my view that Anita the Fiend had made what Rita, my psychotherapist friend and tenant, calls a "narcissistic choice," meaning that Anita had wanted a husband who enhanced her already spectacular looks. But perhaps I'm in no position to criticize the Fiend on that account. After all, I believe in the old maxim that it's just as easy to love a beautiful dog as it is to love a homely dog, and if Anita felt the way about husbands that I do about dogs, so what! So what? The difference between us is that Anita is incapable of loving anyone except herself. In other words, she is a person of bad character, by which I mean that she hates dogs and, worse, instead of simply avoiding them, goes out of her vile way to be outright nasty to them. During her brief marriage to Steve, she'd known better than to target Steve's shepherd — GSD, German shepherd dog — India, but had directed her venom at his timid, vulnerable pointer, Lady, whom I had actually seen her kick. So, India and Lady had immediately caught on to Anita, but Steve hadn't been all that far behind them. To his credit, having married in haste, instead of repenting at leisure, he'd separated and divorced in haste, too. It was during his separation from Anita, and from me as well, that my Rowdy had been bred to American and Canadian Ch. Jazzland's Embraceable You, the beauteous Emma, who had produced a splendid litter of puppies, one of which Steve had bought. And that's how Sammy — Jazzland's As Time Goes By —

had entered our lives: by bringing us back together. So now you know how *Casablanca* should really end: instead of packing Ilsa onto the plane with boring, noble, sexless Victor, Rick entices her to stay by buying a malamute puppy. Rick goes to veterinary school, Ilsa joins the Dog Writers Association of America, and they get married and set up housekeeping in Cambridge, Massachusetts, where Ilsa becomes the dog's co-owner and foolishly persuades the Cambridge Dog Training Club to donate lessons to the Avon Hill School's auction, and . . .

"So, Steve," said Steve pointedly, "how did you like rally?"

"You liked it," I said. "I knew you would."

"And you," he said with a glint in his eye, "like a challenge. This time, you might've taken on more than you can manage."

"Dolfo. Dolfo, I'll have you know, isn't a dog."

"I know. I'm a vet. Remember?"

"He's a fur person. Therefore, he doesn't wear a collar, is never on leash, and, as you probably noticed, isn't neutered, and, more to the point, isn't house-trained, the point being that his owners, Ted and Eumie, are frantic because it's impossible to keep good help these days if one of the requirements is

35

cleaning up after the dog. Except that Ted and Eumie are not frantic. They are having a family crisis."

"And you're going to rescue them."

"Steve, I couldn't sic them on the club! They're impossible. It was my fault they were there. They won us at the Avon Hill auction."

"I kind of liked seeing them there. They reminded me of the birds at my feeders. One or two cardinals for every five hundred house sparrows. Colorful."

"That's one word for it."

"I wonder if Rita knows them."

She did. When we got home, Rita was in our little fenced yard with my cousin Leah and our third malamute, Kimi, one of my original two. Kimi was dark, intense, and tough. Although Rowdy and Sammy were also dark gray and white, Kimi had a "full mask," as it's called, with a black cap, a black bar down her muzzle, and goggles around her eyes. The boys, Rowdy and Sammy, had white faces with no dark markings, and both were far more lighthearted than my fundamentally serious Kimi. As to toughness, if (doG forbid) she'd gotten into a major fight with either of the males, she'd have inflicted more damage than she'd have sustained. Fortunately, she and Rowdy were old friends, and she adored Sammy, who was as close as she'd ever have to her own puppy. That's not speculation. I left Kimi intact so that my cousin Leah could handle her to her breed championship. (Breed: conformation, the judging of the extent to which a dog or bitch, technical term, conforms to the breed standard, and, in that respect, more than just a beauty contest.) Last winter, Steve had spayed Kimi, who could still be shown in obedience and in other performance events, but was now ineligible for the breed ring. As a show dog, she'd been good, but not up there with Rowdy. As for Sammy, he lacked only one major (let's just say one big win) to finish his championship. Was he better than Rowdy? Two judges had thought so. My own opinion? It depended on which of the two I happened to be admiring at the moment.

So, when we got home, Kimi was in the yard with Rita and Leah. If you know Cambridge, you've probably walked by the yard, which is on the Appleton Street side of my house. *Our* house. Marriage changes everything. Possessive pronouns. Possession itself. As I was saying, Steve and the dogs and I live in the barn-red house at the corner of Appleton and Concord. On the actual corner is what's called the "spite building," a long, narrow one-story structure presumably built as an act of revenge in some forgotten real-estate dispute. Far from resenting the spite building, I love it, mainly because its brick wall helps to fence my yard, as does my house itself. The other possible avenues of escape into traffic and death are blocked by ordinary wooden fencing that's less attractive than the ivy-covered brick of the spite building. In contrast to the brick, the yard itself had disappointingly little vegetation. Having repeatedly failed in my efforts to grow plants, I was trying to cultivate a Zen-like attitude toward what an unspiritual person would have seen as the dogs' warmongering determination to despoil this peaceful little spot of urban greenery. India and Lady were blameless. Rowdy would have abided by our Malamute Nonexcavation Proliferation Treaty were it not for his political alliances with excavating nations, namely, Kimi and Sammy, who were born to dig.

At the moment, Kimi was not digging, mainly because she was lying on her back with her white legs and feet tucked in and her white tummy exposed for the rubbing Leah was delivering to it. Leah was kneeling next to Kimi on my latest effort to pacify the war zone, which is to say, a thick layer of fir bark mulch that had been a mistake. Literally. The malamutes had mistaken it for dog food. (Deleted: graphic description of consequences of malamute mistake.) Happily, Leah may be described in attractive terms that will, I hope, divert attention from the nearly omnipresent topic of canine digestive malfunction. Leah had masses of red-gold curls that were spilling from a knot on top of her head. Although she is the daughter of my aunt Cassie, my late mother's sister, I have no idea where she came from except with respect to the red hair that runs in the family and bypassed me. The family breed should be the Irish setter but is the golden retriever, which is what I resemble, and not a show-quality golden, either, but a decent-looking family pet. Leah, however, is showy: voluptuous and flamboyant. Even there on the dog-tilled fir bark, she looked romantic and otherworldly. Looks deceive. Having just finished her exams at the second most famous local institution of higher learning, the most famous being the Cambridge Dog Training Club, she was about to move in with us for the summer and to begin working for Steve in the unromantic and worldly position of veterinary assistant.

Rita was seated at the L.L.Bean picnic table we'd been given as a wedding present. Sammy had sculpted it in a few places, but my efforts to train the dogs to lift their legs elsewhere had been remarkably successful, and just to make sure that the table was fit for human use, I routinely washed it, as Rita knew. She is not the sort of person who places anything but the soles of her high-heeled shoes on the ground and is definitely the sort of person who cares whether or not her Ann Taylor and Eileen Fisher outfits come in contact with canine bodily fluids. She doesn't actually get her hair streaked and trimmed every week, but you'd never guess it, and she uses makeup and hair spray and other foreign substances that the American Kennel Club wants removed before dogs enter the show ring. Dog makeup? Human mascara covers pink spots on dogs' noses, not that Rita blackens her nose, of course. There is nothing outré about her. She is very New York and, if I may use an old-fashioned word, very smart.

In more ways than one. While Steve was inside checking on India's limp, I poured out my story of Ted, Eumie, and Dolfo, and

Rita said, "Them!"

"We wondered whether you knew them." To Leah, I said, "They're therapists." In normal places, *therapist* might mean a physical therapist or some other kind of therapist. In Cambridge, *psycho* goes without saying.

"They're crazy," Leah said.

With Rita right there! "Leah, really!" I said. "Rita is a therapist, and she —"

"I know their daughter. Not their daughter. Hers. Caprice Brainard. She was in one of my classes this year. She's a freshman. She used to come with us to Bartley's, which is the last place she ought to go. Caprice has a major weight problem."

Harvard College was founded in 1636. The Cambridge location was chosen because of its proximity to Bartley's Burger Cottage, which was already producing the gigantic, greasy, delicious hamburgers and sandwiches for which it once received an official certificate of condemnation from no less a person than the late Dr. Atkins himself.

"Is that all you have to say about her?" I asked.

"No. Not at all. I like Caprice. It's just that she's very needy. What she is, is unhappy. And obsessed with her parents. That's why I know about them."

I was suspicious. "Was this a psychology course you were in together?"

Simultaneously, Leah said, "Yes," and Rita said, "What's wrong with psychology?"

"Nothing's wrong with psychology," I said. "What's wrong with Ted and Eumie Green?"

"Brainard-Green," Rita said. "He's Green. Her previous husband was Brainard. Ted Green is a psychologist. Eumie is a social worker. She was his patient, and he left his wife to marry her. After she divorced her husband. That was in New York. They moved here maybe four years ago."

Until I met Rita, my image of social workers was based on Jane Addams, Hull House, and genteel ladies who delivered baskets of food to the poor. Rita, however, explained to me that clinical social workers do therapy, sometimes with the poor, sometimes with the prosperous, the latter presumably on the grounds that the rich deserve help, too.

"With his awful son," Leah said. "Wyeth. He goes to Avon Hill. I think he's a junior. Caprice says he's a spoiled brat. She can't stand him. She's living with them this summer."

"Where's her father in all this?" Rita asked.

"New York."

I asked, "Why is she spending the summer with Ted and Eumie and this stepbrother if she can't stand them?"

"It's just Wyeth she can't stand, really. With her parents and Ted, she's overinvolved."

"Enmeshed," Rita said.

"Preoccupied. Just because Ted and Eumie live in Cambridge, it doesn't mean that Caprice has to go there all the time, which she does. She should've gone away to school." Leah paused. "She could've gone to Yale." Then, with profound Harvardian doubt in her voice, she said, "Or Princeton, I guess."

Rita rolled her eyes. "Princeton," she said. "Otherwise known as the University of Outer Mongolia."

"Also," said Leah, "Caprice's therapist is here."

"Who's her therapist?" Rita asked.

"Missy something. Zinn. That's it. Missy Zinn."

"She's quite good," Rita said. "At least someone in the family is getting help."

"They all are," Leah said. "They're all in therapy."

The door to the house opened, and Rowdy, Sammy, and Lady ran down the stairs. Steve followed. When I was alone with the dogs, there were strict rules about who was allowed to be loose with whom. Rowdy and Kimi were fine together if there was no food around. Lady, who was no threat to anyone, got along great with all the other dogs, but under no circumstances were Kimi and India to be together unsupervised, and the same went for Rowdy and Sammy. Kimi and India had never actually had a fight, but I'd seen Kimi deliberately provoke India, who was capable of retaliation. As for Rowdy and Sammy, they were both intact male malamutes, and dog aggression certainly does occur in this breed, especially same-sex aggression. Under my tutelage, Rowdy had learned to behave himself with other dogs, but his bred-in-the-bone inclination was to tolerate no disrespect from anything canine. Sammy, however, even in the throes of raging adolescent hormones, was one of the few malamutes I'd ever known who acted oblivious to challenges. If other dogs barked or growled at him, his first response was to throw me a bewildered look that asked, *Why don't they want to be friends?* This from Rowdy's son! I couldn't get over it. I mean, who expects Tony Soprano to sire a pacifist? Not me. Consequently, I kept a close eye on the boys. Steve, however, habitually let the pack loose together, possibly because he trusted himself to repair any injuries the dogs inflicted on one another. I'd quit warning him to be careful. For one thing, he was careful. For another, the dogs responded to his expectation of good behavior by being good dogs.

After Steve, Rita, and Leah had greeted one another, and after Leah and I had gone into the house and returned with a bottle of wine and four glasses, Steve asked, "Has Holly told you about her new job?"

"Yes, I have. And it's not a job. Rita knows Ted and Eumie, and Leah knows Eumie's daughter, Caprice. The consensus is that this family is not a model of mental health."

"I don't know them well," said Rita, accepting a glass of red wine from Steve. "I've met them. I know them by reputation."

"Which is?" I asked.

"Within their field, it's okay, as far as I know."

"And their field is?" I prodded.

Rita was expressionless. "Trauma. Ted wrote a book called *Ordinary Trauma*. Lots of people find it helpful." She sipped from the glass Steve had handed her.

"And that's all you have to say about it?"

Leah demanded.

"What I said is perfectly truthful. Lots of people find it helpful. Some of my clients have read it."

Steve was watching her.

"And," I said, "have found it helpful. Don't tell us again."

"It isn't a bad book," Rita said. "Really, it isn't. It's just that Ted has a very inclusive definition of trauma. But he's perfectly sincere about it. And he's connected to a place in western Massachusetts that's, uh, in line with his thinking."

"Is that the place you tried to send Kevin to?" Leah asked.

Our next-door neighbor, Kevin Dennehy, is a Cambridge police lieutenant. One time when the chronic stress of his job had become acute, Rita had tried to persuade him to spend some time at a retreat center of some kind. Her plan failed when Kevin discovered that one of the stress-reducing activities consisted of learning to feel at one with nature by developing the ability to identify wild animals by their spoor. He'd accused Rita of trying to send him to the woods to find raccoon dung, and there had ended her attempt at intervention.

"No," Rita said. "This one is called CHIRP."

"Birds," I said. "Instead of raccoons."

"Not at all. Center for Healing, Individuation, Recovery, and Peace. CHIRP."

"Oh, God," Steve said.

"Yes," said Rita, "except that it's more spiritual than outright religious. It's a sort of spa, I think, oriented toward personal development. Retreat center. And a detox facility for people who need support rather than actual detox. Twelve-step programs, yoga classes, meditation, steam baths. For all that it's focused on construing almost everything as trauma or addiction, hence Ted Green's involvement, it's supposed to be quite luxurious. Maybe that's part of the recovery. I don't know."

"Steam baths," I said. "That sounds wonderful."

Leah was skeptical. "How much do you want to bet that dogs aren't allowed?"

"I think Leah's right," Rita said. "There's probably a concern about allergies."

"What's it called again?" I asked.

"CHIRP," Rita said. "I assume it's intended to sound upbeat."

"Center for . . . ?"

"Healing, Individuation, Recovery, and Peace."

"With no dogs allowed? Healing, individuation, recovery, and peace — the very definition of the magical powers of dogs. You know what, Rita? Steam baths or no steam baths, that place is no retreat center. What that place is, Rita, is a scam."

"You're so quick to judge," said Rita. "It's a good thing you didn't become a therapist."

"I am a therapist," I said. "Remember? I'm the one who's going to save Dolfo."

CHAPTER 4

In my mind's eye I see Eumie and Ted on that same Thursday night as they prepare for bed. They are in the sumptuously renovated bathroom that adjoins the master bedroom of the Greens' big house on Avon Hill. The neighborhood is perhaps a ten-minute walk from my house and, like mine, a twenty-minute walk from Harvard Square. Less grand than Brattle Street, the area looks misleadingly suburban and affordable. A newcomer to Cambridge, Massachusetts, someone unfamiliar with real estate values in the vicinity of Harvard, having taken into account the spaciousness of the houses, the well-kept appearance of the lawns and shrubs, the aura of comfort and prosperity, and the absence of commercial establishments and multifamily dwellings, would guess the average price of a house on Avon Hill to be between one-tenth and one-fourth the actual market value. Four years earlier, when Ted and Eumie had reluctantly realized that Brattle Street was beyond their means, as was the area near the Cambridge Common and the delightful little neighborhood between Kirkland Street and the American Academy of Arts and Sciences, they reconciled themselves to the comparatively unpretentious pleasures of Avon Hill by resolving to invest in their newly acquired eighteen-room house all the money they'd saved by not buying in a neighborhood they'd have preferred, which is to say that they agreed to spend a great deal of money that they didn't have.

The results so far had been satisfying. The master bath, in particular, was sybaritic beyond their dreams and, in fact, beyond the desires of most of the old-time residents of the gigantic and unaffordable colonials and Victorians that Ted and Eumie coveted. Whereas many houses on Brattle Street itself had bathrooms with ineradicably stained sinks and the original claw-footed tubs, Ted and Eumie's master bath had a Jacuzzi, an enclosed shower with steam, and what was known as a double vanity, two sinks, each with its own mirrored medicine cabinet.

This Thursday evening, I see in my mind's eye the masters of that palatial facility as they stand before the open medicine-cabinet doors of the double vanity and prepare for sleep by selecting from among a tremendous variety of soporifics, mood stabilizers, selective serotonin reuptake inhibitors, and neuropsychiatric medications presumed to have beneficial effects even though no one quite knows what those effects are or why the preparations should produce them.

"Ambien is safe with anything, isn't it?" Eumie wonders aloud. "It's fine with Prozac. And Neurontin is really compatible with everything, I think. So is lithium." She shakes two capsules into her hand and washes them down with the remains of her gin and tonic. She then drinks a small glass of soy milk and a small glass that contains a concoction of herbs and vegetable juices.

Ted, who has been peering at the plastic bottles in his very own medicine cabinet, selects one and tenderly offers it to his wife. "Do you want to try Sonata?"

"Thanks," says Eumie, "I've tried it before, and it just doesn't work for me." Studying the vial she is holding, she asks, "What's Paxil? It's an SSRI, isn't it? Something like Zoloft."

"Eumie, those things take time to kick in. They aren't going to do a thing for you tonight."

"Depakote," Eumie says. "Is that slow, too? I'm a little volatile. Maybe that's —"

"Have you asked Dr. Youngman about sleep? Addressing the, uh, sense of volatility is one thing, but you need something for sleep."

"What are you taking?"

With heartfelt affection, Ted says, "Good old Valium."

"Valium! I'd almost forgotten about it. Can I have some?"

Wordlessly, Ted shakes three yellow tablets into the palm of his hand, gives one to Eumie, and dry swallows the other two. After closing the cabinet doors on what are almost like twin wine cellars, Ted and Eumie companionably brush their teeth and enter the bedroom, where Dolfo occupies the center of the king-size bed. Like Dolfo, the comforter is multicolored and expensive. The resemblance is no accident. Eumie chose the comforter to match the dog's coat. At the sight of Ted and Eumie, Dolfo beats his peculiar tail, leaps to his feet, bounds off the bed, sniffs a corner of it, and, with a goofy smile on his face, lifts his leg, and empties his full bladder on the comforter.

Ted and Eumie exchange little smiles and shakes of the head. Eumie reaches for a spray bottle of odor-neutralizing enzyme solution that sits ready on the top of her dresser, sprays the drenched corner of the bed, returns the bottle to the dresser, and settles herself in bed. Ted is already under the covers. Dolfo jumps onto the comforter, turns around twice, and lies down between Ted and Eumie, who turn out their lights and wait for their medications to act. Dolfo, however, falls immediately to sleep. Or so I imagine.

CHAPTER 5

At three o'clock on Friday afternoon, I managed to find a parking space only a half block from the address Eumie Brainard-Green had given me that morning when we'd set the time for our meeting. I'd spent the day indoors working on a reminiscence of my late mother for the official publication of the American Kennel Club, the *AKC Gazette,* which was planning an issue focused on the golden retriever. Both of my parents bred and showed our goldens, but my mother was a grande dame of the breed. My father, I thought, would be pleased with what I'd written about Marissa, and I'd tried to avoid saying anything that would distress his second wife, Gabrielle, whom he'd married only a few years earlier. As I'd taken pains not to mention in the article, my mother was a hypercompetent martinet who set high standards for her dogs and for me, and who vigilantly monitored our performance with the intention of correcting deviations from perfection. In contrast, Gabrielle was warm and easygoing. I not only adored her but felt grateful to her for marrying the most impossible person I've ever met, thereby relieving me of the burden of worrying about him all alone.

Anyway, I'd squandered a beautiful spring day by spending it indoors, and as I took care not to trip on the uneven brick sidewalk, I mulled over my goals for the meeting with the Greens and Dolfo, the principal goal being to do whatever we did outside in the sun and fresh air. In the universal manner of overconfident fools, I assumed that my experience and expertise would carry me through; except to pack a tote bag with a collar, a four-foot leash, a clicker, and six different kinds of dog-delicious food treats, I'd made no preparations. If the animal-loving forces that govern the universe had wanted to reward me for my efforts to improve the lot of the creatures who had helped Homo sapiens to evolve, I'd have lost my footing on the rough sidewalk and taken the kind of hard fall that might have warned me of the consequence of pride.

As it was, I walked smoothly and confidently past a parking area paved with cobblestones to the steep flight of steps that led up to the Greens' house, which was a big, rambling brown-shingled place with a rose-covered fence, bright flowers, and a charming veranda. The fence, the steps, the porch, the shutters, and the other trim were neatly painted in cream. Arrayed on the veranda were wicker chairs and end tables, and from the beams hung baskets of flowering plants and ivy that were being tended by a well-muscled, dark-haired young man in a T-shirt printed with words that I'd just read on a van parked on the street: *Year After Year: Perennial Care for Perennials.* The front door had a shiny brass knocker and matching doorbell. Mounted on the frame was a little brass cylinder that I recognized as a mezuzah, a container for a tiny scroll, a fixture of traditional Jewish households. A Jewish friend had explained to me that the mezuzah was a reminder of God's presence and commandments. Had I known what I was in for, I'd have paid attention to the mezuzah and found comfort in the knowledge that if my own efforts failed, I could turn to a truly High Power for help with Dolfo and the Greens. In fact, after giving the mezuzah no more than a glance, I rang the bell and, as I waited, made unproductive use of my brain by wondering why Year After Year was taking care of the lobelia, nasturtiums, and other annuals in the baskets. The answer should have been obvious: because the company was paid generously. Had I put my mind to work, I'd have focused on the row of shoes and rain boots to the right of the doormat. What's more, when Eumie opened the door, I'd have taken in the rows of shoes and sandals in the foyer, realized their significance, and wondered how any sane person could exist in a shoeless house with an unhousebroken dog. That answer, too, should have been obvious: chez Green, sanity had nothing to do with anything.

That's not what Eumie said when she greeted me, of course. And *greeted* is an understatement. Just as she'd done with Ron, she squealed, threw her arms around me, and welcomed me as if I were a beloved old friend she hadn't seen for years. "Holly, come in!" Gesturing to the footwear on the floor, she said softly, as if confiding a secret, "This is a shoeless house. You don't mind, do you." It was a statement or perhaps an order or even a commandment. "We have socks and slippers you can use."

Reminding myself to watch before I stepped, I eased off my running shoes and said, "I'm wearing socks. I'll be fine." Actually, if it hadn't been for Dolfo, I'd have been delighted. The phenomenon of shoeless houses fascinated me, mainly because everything about the concept was not just foreign to the way I lived but entirely incompatible with it. I'd been in two shoeless houses before this, and both times, I'd tried to imagine explaining to my husband, my friends, and my relatives that henceforth they were to remove their shoes at the door and walk around in slippers or stocking feet. That's about as far as I'd gone with the notion, since it was clear that my husband, my father, and Kevin Dennehy would have been unable to comprehend what I was saying; they just plain wouldn't have understood. The same went for the dogs, who didn't wear shoes, of course, but who'd somehow have been mystified by the ban anyway.

"Ted is dying to see you," said Eumie, who was wearing loose, flowing white garments, white slippers, and large silver earrings. On her left wrist were six silver bangle bracelets. I wondered whether the peasant-priestess garments and the artisanal silver represented an effort to adapt to Cambridge, which favors natural fibers, ethnic or handcrafted accessories, and shoes too hideous to deform the feet. As on the previous evening, Eumie's hair was, however, artfully blond and her makeup copious and colorful. "We both feel awful that we've waited so long to get help for Dolfo," she said. "It's not like us. We are *not* help-rejecting types."

By now, we were in the front hall, which was redolent of freshly applied Simple Solution, an enzyme product that neutralizes dog urine. Although Dolfo was not in sight, his presence was visible on the chewed rails of the graceful staircase and on the gnawed fringe of an otherwise lovely Persian rug.

"I thought we might work outdoors," I suggested, not only because I wanted to enjoy the spring day but because Eumie and Ted might expect me to clean up after Dolfo if — when — he messed in the house. As Eumie had just said, she was not a help-rejecting type. Visible through the archway to the dining room was a barefoot woman energetically polishing a banquet-size table. Another woman, this one wearing slippers, was dusting a menorah that sat on a buffet. Glancing at them, I asked, "Your housekeepers?"

"They're from Maid for You. They're just

tiding us over. We really prefer to have people who become part of the family. Ted should be free in a few minutes. Where on earth is Dolfo?"

Eumie set off on a Dolfo hunt with me trailing behind. We passed through a large living room, an even larger family room with massive leather furniture and a wall of glass doors, and a kitchen that was all cherry, granite, and stainless steel. All three sinks were piled with dirty dishes, and there were crumbs scattered on the hardwood floor. "Dolfo! Dolfo!" Eumie kept squealing. From behind a door in a corridor off the kitchen came the sounds of scratching and retching. Eumie opened the door to reveal a pink-tiled powder room and the clownish dog, who greeted us by dropping the bar of soap in his mouth into the puddle of soapy saliva at his feet. Bubbles dripped from his mouth and his tongue, which was the correct size for an Irish wolfhound, perhaps, and, being far too long to fit in Dolfo's mouth, was doomed perpetually to loll from his mouth. Neither his tongue nor the taste of soap appeared to bother him at all. On the contrary, he wagged his silly tail and, catching my eye, gave what I thought was a smile of happy recognition.

Eumie was furious. "Those damn cleaners! They shut him in here like an —"

"Animal," I finished. "He doesn't seem to have swallowed much of the soap." Blocking his exit, I said, "Eumie, if you'll get a couple of paper towels, I'll swab his mouth out, and he'll be fine."

Before I had malamutes, I might mention, I was a straightforward person. Now, thanks to Rowdy and especially thanks to Kimi, I'm manipulative and opportunistic. During Eumie's brief absence, which I'd engineered, I reached into my tote bag, got a thin collar and a short leash, and had Dolfo dressed for the day by the time she returned.

"Dolfo's school clothes," I told her. "Ninety-nine percent of housebreaking is preventing accidents."

Ted appeared in time to hear the statement. Dolfo, I might brag, didn't jump on Ted. Rather, he obligingly looked at my face, and I fed him a treat. Dog training defined: you get the dog to train you to do what he wants when he does what you want. And people training? Oh, my. The next forty-five minutes could have served as a demonstration of how not to do it. We moved into the family room, which was at the back of the house. It had a floor of terracotta tile, a fireplace, big, comfortable leather couches and chairs, and a wall of glass doors that opened to a wide deck. Visible through the glass was a yard ten times the size of Steve's and mine with a new wooden fence, teak benches, and an extraordinary number of large and expensive-looking bird feeders. There were glass-walled copper feeders on poles, hanging globes and elaborately designed suet baskets suspended from tree branches, and two platform feeders mounted on the railing of the deck. The first of my many therapeutic errors was to allow myself to be diverted from the task of housebreaking Dolfo by asking about the feeders, which were being cleaned and filled by a man who wore white coveralls with a company name embroidered on the back: On the Wing.

"Birds are special to us," Ted said. "Eumie and I deal with trauma in our patients and" — he lowered his mellifluous voice — "in our own lives. The concept of flight as a beautiful adaptation has special significance for us."

I'd intended to say that Steve was slaving to maintain a couple of feeders that were being raided and ruined by squirrels, but I felt almost ashamed to admit that winged creatures had no great symbolic meaning for my husband, who, in ordinary fashion, wanted to feed birds because he enjoyed watching them.

"Our own trauma histories," said Eumie, "are probably what accounts for this delay in connecting to Dolfo's needs, and —"

"Speaking of Dolfo," I began.

"Oh, we are!" Eumie squealed. "You see, just as birds represent the healthy, adaptive flight from overwhelming experiences, Dolfo represents grounding in the safe sensations and perceptions of the here and now."

My second major mistake: instead of zooming in on my area of expertise, namely, dog behavior, I got sucked into Ted and Eumie's anthropomorphic perspective. Simultaneously, I made my third big error, which was to ask a routine question about Dolfo's history. "Dogs certainly are the ultimate in the here and now," I agreed in an effort to form an alliance with Dolfo's owners. "But they have histories, too. Maybe you could outline Dolfo's for me."

Eumie smirked at Ted. "Isn't that cute! She's doing just what therapists do. Most therapists. Dr. Needleman spent our first two sessions on it. She is not gestalt at all. She's an analyst. You know, Ted, now that I think about it, Dr. Foote hasn't delved all that deeply into our individual narratives, has she? She's more oriented toward our dialoguing, isn't she?" To me, Eumie said, "That's our couples therapist. When you're dealing with two people with our kinds of histories, well —"

I knew exactly who Dr. Foote was. In fact, I'd "seen" Vee Foote, in the expensive sense of the word, after the combination of a head injury and Steve's marriage to Anita the Fiend had left me . . . But that's another story. Rita, who had referred me to Dr. Foote, now considered her greedy and incompetent. I, on the other hand, pitied Vee Foote just as I pitied everyone else afflicted with a pathological fear of dogs, which is to say, a paralyzing fear of life itself.

"The whole issue of time orientation in therapy is interesting," said Ted. "I'd be curious to know how Missy Zinn handles it with Caprice . . ." And he was off. His own individual therapist was a Dr. Tortorello, Eumie's was named Nixie Needleman, Caprice's was the aforementioned Missy Zinn, and Wyeth's was Peter York, who, as I didn't say, was a young psychologist whom I knew because he was a friend of Rita's and was about to go into supervision with her. Ted and Eumie shared a psychopharmacologist, Quinn Youngman, whom I knew because Rita was dating him. In addition to the traditional shrinks, there were herbal-ists, acupuncturists, massage therapists, Reiki healers, hypnotherapists, and experts in guided imagery, and there must have been primary-care physicians and dentists as well.

"Dolfo," I summarized, "clearly inhabits a richly populated environment. So, all the more need for him to learn the skills required to be a valued member of this, uh, complex support network." Having staked my claim to the conversational field, I consolidated my position by demonstrating clicker training, which is good old operant conditioning with positive reinforcement for desired behavior. The sound of the clicker gets paired with food and thus becomes a secondary reinforcer that precisely marks behavioral perfection, so to speak. Dolfo did great. By the tenth time I'd "charged the clicker" by clicking and giving a treat, he was watching me with an expression that said, "Ah-hah! Click means that food is coming!" I went on to explain that we'd click and treat when Dolfo produced outdoors.

"You see what Holly's doing?" Ted asked Eumie. "Instilling hope! Showing that healing is possible."

Heeling with two *e*s was possible, if a bit advanced for Dolfo and his owners, so my misunderstanding was inevitable. Fortunately, I caught on when Ted said something about recovery, and instead of sounding stupid or ridiculous, I said that we had every reason to feel hopeful. The bird feeder professional having finished his work, we then spent about ten minutes outside in the fenced yard, where Dolfo cooperated by lifting his leg on trees and shrubs, thus giving Ted and Eumie opportunities to click and treat.

If reinforcing desired behavior were sufficient to housebreak a dog, we'd have been all set. As it was, I had to harp on the need to prevent accidents indoors. When we were back in the family room, where I sat on a couch with Dolfo lying at my feet and studying my face, I said, "We have to remember that Dolfo can't be given the chance to practice the behaviors that we don't want."

"Oy vey!" said Ted. "Where to begin? You have to understand that we are a merged family. We have a daughter, Caprice, from Eumie's previous marriage, and a son, Wyeth, from mine."

"And Dolfo," said Eumie, "is the child we have together. We are deeply committed to providing him with unconditional love."

Oy vey! Where to begin? Operant *condition-ing* is about as *conditional* as you can get.

"You see," said Ted, "communicating negative emotions can give the child the message that he is globally bad. So, he adapts by splitting off that part of himself. And what began as a whole, unified, healthy organism becomes divided." He paused dramatically. "Divided against itself."

"And what are possessions, after all?" Eumie demanded. "Things! Objects!"

"Maybe we can agree," I ventured, "that soiling outdoors is preferable to soiling in-doors."

On that point, we did agree. Ted again mentioned the dog's breeder, who claimed that golden Aussie huskapoos housebreak themselves. It said so on her Web site.

"The Web site lied," I said. "Furthermore, Dolfo has had the chance to practice going in the house. He thinks it's just fine. The behavior has become a habit, and unless we can break the habit, he's going to keep on doing it."

Their faces fell. "You want us to lock him in a cage," Eumie charged. "That's what the vet said to do. Dr. Cushing. We need to find someone else."

"She has an excellent reputation. But there are alternatives to crate training." I mentioned some: keeping the dog on leash every second, confining him to the little powder room near the kitchen, and so on.

Far from recognizing my advice as emanating from a Higher Power, they continued to regard me with suspicion and took turns explaining that my suggestions translated into making Dolfo feel cut off, rejected, frustrated, and unloved.

To borrow a word of Ted's, *meshugass!* Madness! If it hadn't been for Dolfo, I'd have walked out. But the foolish-looking dog got to me, in part because his background and experience predicted a disaster I just wasn't seeing, namely, a horrible case of aggression. He'd been bred, I suspected, for nothing but money, sold to people who knew nothing about dogs, and taught nothing about the rules of canine conduct, yet far from becoming a danger, he was sweet, zany, weirdly loveable, and touchingly eager to learn to be a good boy.

"Let's give ourselves some time to mull matters over," I suggested. "You can use the clicker and treats when you take Dolfo out. But you have to *take* him out and not just let him out. And we'll schedule another meeting. Monday is Memorial Day. How would Tuesday be?"

Ted gave a strange nod, but Eumie, as if translating from a foreign language I was too dense to understand, said, "Tuesdays are my special days just for myself."

"If you love Dolfo," I pointed out, "then he is part of yourself. I'll be here at nine on Tuesday morning."

Somewhat to my surprise, Ted and Eumie both thanked me. Armed with his clicker and treats, Ted took Dolfo outside to the backyard. It was Eumie alone who showed me to the door. When we got there, she spoke in a voice far softer and gentler than her usual squeal. "You're anxious about something," she said, "something that has nothing to do with us. I have the feeling that you're panicking about something."

To my amazement, I found myself telling her what it was. "Showing my dogs," I said. "I've always had ring nerves. But it's all much worse. I haven't been showing in obedience at all."

"I can help you with that," Eumie said. "And I will."

Oddly enough, I believed her.

CHAPTER 6

On Saturday, while Steve and Leah were at the clinic, I show-groomed Rowdy and Sammy, who were entered the next day, both with professional handlers. I'd almost always used a handler for Rowdy, who'd finished his championship easily and had thereafter been shown occasionally as a "special," a champion competing for Best of Breed and, with luck, for a placement in the group to which the breed belongs. A *show,* as maybe I should mention, is a *conformation* event, as opposed to performance events like obedience and agility trials: in conformation, the judge evaluates the extent to which the dogs *conform* to the ideal image spelled out in the breed standard. The Best of Breed winners then compete within their respective groups, and the first-place winners in the groups compete for Best in Show. These days, when I entered Rowdy, I was interested in a group placement, that is, in having him take first, second, third, or fourth place in the Working Group, the one to which the Alaskan malamute belongs. Well, at Sunday's show, Rowdy never made it to the group because the judge overlooked him in favor of Sammy, who went Winners Dog and Best of Winners, and then BOB over specials, including, of course, his own father. Naturally, Steve and I were thrilled about Sammy, and neither of us was surprised when he went nowhere in the group, mainly, we thought, because he was still a puppy and looked immature next to the competition.

On Monday morning, Memorial Day, Steve devoted an hour to taking down his bird feeders and remounting them on poles equipped with new squirrel baffles. When he finished, he came into the kitchen and looked out the window above the sink as if he already hoped to see cardinals and chickadees devouring sunflower seed and goldfinches scarfing up expensive thistle. The feeders, I might mention, were not in the fenced yard but on the opposite side of the house, where any birds they might attract would be safe from Rowdy, Sammy, and Kimi. It was Kimi who'd delivered the coup de grace to my previous bird-feeding efforts by interpreting the term *bird feeder* as a personal invitation to feed on birds. Feed on them she had. I'd given up and given the feeder away. The dogs, however, never entered the area on the opposite side of the house, and Steve was optimistically convinced that his magic touch with animals — he truly has one — would enable him to devise a system for foiling the squirrels.

"Maybe we should get a squirrel feeder," I suggested. "People do that. They put out dried ears of corn. The idea is that the squirrels prefer the corn and leave the birdseed alone."

"Unlikely," he said.

"It isn't as if we have ordinary squirrels. The black ones are special."

Cambridge abounds in what Steve calls *melanistic individuals* or *black morphs,* which is to say, black squirrels. When I first lived here, I was convinced that some Harvard lunatic who'd spent a year in a place like Ceylon or Java had brought home a breeding pair of exotic squirrels that had filled Cambridge with pigmented progeny. As it turns out, our Cambridge black squirrels are probably descended from a colony in plain old ordinary Westfield, Massachusetts, a colony descended from black squirrels imported from plain old unexotic Michigan. Fantasy is often better than reality.

"An attractive color variant," Steve agreed.

"Ted and Eumie don't have any squirrels," I reported.

"Then they don't feed birds."

"Oh, but they do! They must have a dozen feeders. Maybe more. Including right on the rails of their deck. There's a company that comes to clean and fill the feeders."

"What kinds of baffles are they using?"

"None. None that I saw. But the feeders weren't damaged at all."

"Impossible," Steve said.

"Fact. Tons of feeders. No squirrels."

"You just didn't see any. Where there are feeders, there are squirrels. It's a law of nature."

"Not on Avon Hill."

"Everywhere." He paused. "Unless someone's killing them."

"Don't say that," I said. "Ted and Eumie are . . . they're not monsters."

That afternoon, we had a little Memorial Day barbeque that left me regretful that Steve and I hadn't taken all five dogs for a hike instead. Everything was going well until Rita showed up with Quinn Youngman, who made himself mildly obnoxious by droning on to Leah's friends from school with stories about his wild youth of sex, drugs, Bob Dylan, and radical politics. When Rita had started to date him, I'd tried to support her by concentrating on their shared professional interests and ignoring their age difference. My reaction after the barbeque was, so what if she was a psychologist and he was a psychopharmacologist? He was twenty years older than she was, and a bore to boot, albeit a tall, striking, and fairly good-looking one. On reflection, it seems to me that my annoyance at Quinn Youngman stemmed in part from knowing that Ted and Eumie were his patients and knowing equally well that professional ethics would prevent him from satisfying my idle curiosity about what he prescribed for them and why.

On Tuesday morning, I was tempted to cancel my appointment with the Greens and Dolfo. Steve and Leah had taken India, Lady, and Sammy to work with them. Steve's old apartment over his clinic was still furnished, not that the dogs cared; and except for occasional canine tenants, it was vacant, so when he took dogs to work with him, they occupied the apartment and didn't have to be kenneled at the clinic when he and Leah were busy with clients. At eight o'clock I was settled at the kitchen table with Rowdy and Kimi snoozing on the floor and a cup of good coffee, a yellow legal pad, and a pen in front of me. The traffic on Concord Avenue was low background noise that I tuned out. Thanks to the squirrels that had emptied the feeders outside the kitchen window, there wasn't even any chirping to disturb me. I could've spent the morning dreaming up a topic for my *Dog's Life* column, making notes, and starting the first draft. As it was, the prospect of breaking up my morning ruined my concentration. After wasting forty minutes, I gathered my Dolfo-training supplies and drove to Avon Hill. This time, there were no service agency vehicles and no service providers in sight. When I rang the bell, Ted opened the door, and before I could even remove my shoes and walk in, Dolfo jumped on his back and almost knocked him down. "Dolfo, *genug!* Enough already!" Ted exclaimed.

The immediate cause of Dolfo's excitement was my arrival. His eyes — the hazel and the brown one — gleamed with happiness, and he quivered from funny-looking head to silly-looking tail. Possibly because of a certain authoritative gleam in my own eyes, however, he did not jump on me but loped out of the hallway toward the kitchen. Among his many oddities was a strange gait. I took comfort in the thought that if Dolfo suffered from a major structural flaw, at least his owners could afford orthopedic consultations and surgery.

After Ted and I had exchanged greetings, he informed me that he was expecting an important phone call from a patient at nine-fifteen and that he had patients scheduled after that. Because of the way he and Eumie had conspired to thwart my efforts during our previous meeting, I was actually glad that only one of them was available: divide and conquer. As it turned out, Eumie, however, was still in bed. "I moved to the guest room in the middle of the night," Ted informed me. "I haven't seen her this morning except when I let Dolfo out at seven. She was asleep then. But she's probably getting up now. She has a pedicure appointment, and she won't miss that. You can get started with Dolfo."

Embodiment of positive training that I am, I said, "No. Our agreement is that I get *you* started, and I can't do that if you're working and Eumie's in bed, so I'd suggest that you go and get her, or we're going to have to forget about the whole thing. Dolfo can keep soiling in the house, and you can keep losing housekeepers, and, I might add, I don't particularly like it that both of you apparently forgot about your appointment with me but that Eumie certainly wouldn't miss her pedicure. So please go and get her and ask her which she loves more, her dog or her feet."

After glancing at his watch, Ted complied to the extent of going halfway up the stairs and calling, "Eumie! Eumie, the dog maven's here." After waiting a moment he said to me, "Maybe she's in the shower. Look, I can't miss this phone call. Why don't you go on up and find her. It's the door straight ahead at the top of the stairs."

Perhaps I should explain that I had occasionally taught people to train their dogs and had coached obedience handlers to show their first dogs. On rare occasions, I had even trained people's dogs. Never once had my duties extended to dragging lazy owners out of bed or out of the shower, and I was not about to start redefining my obligations now. I was taking time from my own work out of loyalty to the club and sympathy for Dolfo. If the Greens had been paying me, instead of speaking my mind, I'd have quit the job. I settled for using a favorite word of Rita's to justify my refusal to barge in on someone I hardly knew: "It really wouldn't be *appropriate*," I said, "so please just take a few seconds to go and get her." I paused and added, "And I'm sorry I was so sharp. It's just that Dolfo really needs help, and so do both of you."

This time, Ted hustled all the way up the stairs. Dolfo chose to remain with me, either because he at least recognized my potential as a Higher Power or because he smelled the roast beef and cheese in my pockets, not that there's all that much difference from a dog's perspective. Having nothing better to do during Ted's absence, I whiled away the time by pursuing my mission in life, which is to say that I used a tiny piece of the roast beef to lure Dolfo into a sit, and then sounded my clicker, fed him the treat, and told him what a good dog he was, as was certainly true. The experience of replacing barbarism with one small element of civilization was so satisfying to both of us that we repeated the exercise several times and might, in fact, have kept on training for quite a while if Ted hadn't interrupted by running down the stairs in a panic and shouting, "She won't wake up! I shook her, and she wouldn't wake up! Help me!"

Ted's show of alarm registered on me as nothing more than a manipulative ploy to get me to do exactly what I'd refused to do, namely, to act as Eumie's maid by dragging her out of bed for the day. The thought crossed my mind that if Ted kept trying to force me into the role of lady's maid, I'd empty a bucket of water on Eumie's head and subsequently inform her that I'd merely been following Ted's orders. "Should I call an ambulance?" I asked coolly.

Taken aback, he said, "Let's keep it quiet. Eumie uses a lot of sleeping medication. I keep warning her to watch what she's taking when she gets up at night. She loses count of what she's already had. Maybe she's just sleeping it off."

"Ted, if she's taken an overdose —" Breaking off, I dashed upstairs and through the open door of the room that lay straight ahead. The room was almost totally dark; the only light came from the hall. The stench was nauseating. Despite my sudden realization that something might actually be wrong, I now had the sense that my presence was genuinely inappropriate. Still, I ran my hand over the wall near the door frame, found a light switch, and flipped it. Two lamps with low-watt bulbs came on, one on a dresser and one on a small desk. Ahead of me was a king-size bed with a duvet so heavy and rumpled that it was at first hard to see that the bed was occupied at all. Fighting the awkward sense of being an intruder, I spoke Eumie's name as I moved toward the left-hand side of the bed, where masses of streaked blond-brown hair were almost camouflaged by the multicolored duvet cover and matching pillows. "Eumie!" I said loudly. "Eumie, wake up!"

My first physical effort to rouse her was tentative: I lowered one hand to what I guessed was the vicinity of her shoulders and patted gently. Nothing whatever happened: there was not the slightest sign of movement, not the faintest sound of breath. After that, I was all action, ripping the comforter off, rolling Eumie onto her back, pushing up one sleeve of her pink silk pajamas to check for a pulse, feeling the cold of her skin, observing the rigidity of wrist and elbow, and yanking the cell phone out of my pocket, pushing the button that brought it to life, and punching the emergency number. Struggling to speak clearly, I gave the Greens' address and had just finished saying that Eumie was dead when a young woman burst into the room and came to an abrupt halt.

I recognized Caprice Brainard immediately. My cousin Leah had said that Caprice had a major weight problem. The problem, as I now saw, consisted of distribution as well as of simple obesity. Bad genetic luck or some vicious force of nature had forced excess pounds upward to her face and neck. What looked like separate pockets of fat seemed to have been cruelly inserted on the upper and lower lids of her blue eyes, on either side of her mouth, on her cheeks, and even on her forehead; and distinct rolls encircled her neck. Her body was heavy, but her torso was mercifully rounded, and she wore a long denim skirt that hid her legs and feet. Her beautiful hair seemed to mock the disfigurement of her face. She had the blond ringlets of a cherub.

Still holding the cell phone to my ear, I used my other hand to gesture to Caprice to stop where she was. Simultaneously, I shook my head. "Wait outside," I told her.

Unfortunately, I was too late. Caprice's eyes were fixed on her mother's body. Frozen in place, she began to scream. Having finished reporting the essentials of the emergency, I gave up on the 911 call, put the phone back in my pocket, and was moving toward Caprice when Ted appeared. Instead of checking on his wife or attending to his stepdaughter, he rushed past Caprice and through the open door of what proved to be a large and luxurious bathroom. When he put the lights on, I could see tile, marble, and mirrors. Noticing my gaze, Ted hastily shut the door.

The bang of the door silenced Caprice, but before I had the chance to lead her out of the room, a teenage boy staggered in and began shouting, "Caprice, for Christ's sake, shut up! All I'm trying to do is get some sleep. Now shut your fat mouth!"

His eyes were heavy, and he was naked except for a white towel wrapped around his waist. His sandy hair formed a thick mat of wiry curls, his face was pale and blotched, and his body was so pitifully lacking in muscle tone that he was at once thin and flabby. The combination of visible ribs and a swollen belly suggested some form of malnutrition more prevalent in Third World countries than on Avon Hill.

"Wyeth, get out of here!" Caprice told him. "My mother is dead. Now, leave!"

Simultaneously, Ted emerged from the bathroom, and Dolfo rushed into the room and leaped onto the bed.

"It stinks of shit in here," Wyeth said.

"Eumie is very sick," Ted told him. "I need to call an ambulance."

"She's dead," Caprice corrected. "Look at her elbow. That's rigor mortis." Seconds earlier, Caprice had been wailing. Now she was coldly clinical.

"Dummkopf," he said. "She's overdone her meds."

Heading for the door, Wyeth said, "If she's dead, so what? Selfish bitch. Good riddance. I'm going back to sleep."

The fundamental indecency of the entire scene hit me all at once. I had the power to restore decency to only one aspect of it: I could remove the dog from what was certainly a deathbed. Pulling a slip collar and leash from my pocket, I edged to the foot of the bed, where Dolfo had turned onto his back and was scent rolling in a fashion that might have been cute in a different setting but was now revolting. On the verge of gagging, I summoned the reflexes built up over a lifetime and soon had Dolfo restrained, off the bed, and out in the hall, where Caprice and Ted had moved to continue their quarrel.

"Her trauma history," Ted said. "The underlying suicidality! I warned her and warned her about mixing her meds. She must've stumbled to the bathroom and grabbed something from the medicine cabinet."

"My mother was *not* suicidal," Caprice insisted.

"I didn't say she —"

"Yes, you did."

"I did not. And there's no reason to assume she's beyond help. Why are we wasting time? I'm calling an ambulance."

By then, Dolfo and I had reached the bottom of the stairs. I'd survived Dolfo's descent by clinging to the banister and considered myself lucky not to need the ambulance I'd already called and that Ted was unnecessarily summoning on his cell phone. Pausing to get both hands on Dolfo's lead, I heard a door bang in the upper hallway. Once again, Wyeth began to holler at Caprice. It seemed to me that when the police arrived, they'd be justified in assuming that the emergency consisted of the kind of domestic disturbance that cops hate. My cop friend and next-door neighbor, Kevin Dennehy, for example, was practically phobic about the sight of a domestic partner armed with a cast-iron frying pan, mainly because he was convinced that the weapon was inevitably going to be smashed down on his own head.

What drove me out of the Brainard-Greens' house wasn't a sense of vulnerability to physical violence. Rather, the physical and emotional atmosphere of the place felt so toxic that I simply had to escape from the urine-scented air, the angry voices, and the ugly sense of contamination. I took the nearest exit, which was the front door and, by reining in Dolfo and forcing him to remain at my left side, managed to make it safely down the steps and reach the sidewalk, where I was surprised and relieved to see someone I knew and liked, a woman named Barbara Leibowitz. Barbara and her husband, George McBane, had taken their dog, Portia, through the beginners' course at the club the previous fall, and Steve and I had sat with them at a fund-raising dinner for the MSPCA a few months earlier. Although Barbara and George were both psychiatrists, they had a tendency remarkable in the helping professions to talk about matters other than mental health. Barbara was a tall, striking woman with brown-black skin and black hair in elaborate cornrows. Leibowitz was, she'd told me, the name of her adoptive parents, who were white, and she'd kept it when she'd married George, all of whose grandparents had been born in Ireland. Maybe I should mention that this isn't a story about Barbara's search for her roots. I don't know what they were or whether she had any interest in them. The interest of hers I knew about was animal welfare. Besides attending MSPCA events, she helped organize them and was known as a generous supporter of animal welfare groups. Her dog, Portia, who was with her in front of the Greens' house, had come from the MSPCA shelter in Jamaica Plain. Portia's roots did interest Barbara, who guessed that the little dog was half West Highland white terrier and half Heinz 57. In any case, Portia was entirely adorable. She had a pale, wiry coat, intelligent, snapping eyes, and a delightful habit of cocking her head when someone spoke her name.

Barbara greeted me warmly and said, "I was so glad when Eumie told me you were helping with Dolfo! It's about time someone did, and *'Tout comprendre, c'est tout pardonner'* and all that, but if you have any success with Dolfo, maybe you could tackle the son while you're at it." She gestured to a big yellow house next door to the Greens'. "That's our house, so we have something of a personal interest."

I had no idea what Barbara meant in saying with regard to Wyeth that to understand all was to forgive all. In ordinary circumstances, I'd probably have asked her, but as it was, I told her about Eumie's death and the imminent arrival of cruisers and medical vehicles.

"Are the children there?" she asked.

"Yes. Unfortunately. It's a horrible scene. I was the one who found Eumie. She was in bed. She apparently took an accidental overdose of something. If I'd known that the children were there, I'd have closed the bedroom door and kept them out, but it never occurred to me, and Caprice came in. It was terrible. She was screaming and screaming, and the son must've been asleep, and he came in and started yelling at her for waking him up. And Ted somehow has this crazy idea that Eumie may still be alive, and for God's sake, rigor has set in. Dolfo jumped on the bed and . . . it was more than I could take. I've called nine-one-one. They should be here any second. I am *so* glad to see you. I feel as if you're restoring my sanity."

"At the best of times, Ted and Eumie can be a little disorienting, and this sounds like the worst of times. Maybe we can get the children out of there. Not that they're little children, but they are, uh, vulnerable. Wyeth could go to his mother's. He splits his time between his parents. You might know his mother. Johanna Green? She lives somewhere near you. She has a papillon she walks a lot. Dainty little blond woman."

"I think I've seen her, but I don't know her."

"Let me go try to reach her. And Caprice. Let's mull that one over."

"Her father?"

"Monty Brainard lives in New York. She'll be lucky if he bothers to show up at all, but don't tell her I said that. It's not her view of him, and she's better off with the one she cultivates. Sad situation all around."

"Monty," I repeated. Say it ain't so! At the risk of leaving myself vulnerable to psychiatric insinuations, I have to confess that my immediate reaction to Barbara's negative assessment of Monty Brainard was that Barbara just had to be wrong. That's not exactly a confession, is it? The confession part has to do with the grounds for my skepticism, which were — here's the confession — not just religious but somewhat peculiarly religious, at least in the eyes of those who consider the faith handed down to me by my dog-worshiping parents to be odd, strange, weird, mentally unhealthy, or outright heretical, as it certainly is not. That being said, I was inclined on religious grounds to form a favorable opinion of Monty Brainard or, in fact, anyone else named Monty, because of the elevated position in the Malamute Pantheon occupied by a certain legendary Monty, namely, Ch. Benchmark Captain Montague, a justifiably famous Alaskan malamute bred and owned by my friend Phyllis Hamilton. Not that I imagined, of course, that every canine and human creature who shared the name Monty with the prototypic Monty simply had to possess the beauty, power, and strength of character so notable in Phyllis's dog. Well, not that I *exactly* believed that Monty Brainard absolutely *had* to be a good guy. Still, let's say that I was biased in his favor. And if my take seems irrational, let's just suppose that you hear someone make a negative remark about a person named Mother Teresa of Calcutta or Saint Francis of Assisi. Point made? Thus my readiness to assume the best about Monty Brainard.

Sirens wailed.

Gesturing in their direction, Barbara said, "Caprice doesn't need to see this. Can you get her out of there?"

Wanting to be as kind as Barbara expected, I said, "Yes. I'll go get her out of the house. And take her home with me."

CHAPTER 7

"I know who you are," said Caprice Brainard. "You're Holly Winter, and you're Leah Whitcomb's cousin. You train dogs."

It was less than a minute after I'd finished speaking to Barbara. Intending to leave Dolfo outdoors while I went upstairs to rescue Caprice, I'd entered the backyard through a gate at the end of a short driveway that also served as a three-car parking area. I'd found Caprice seated on a teak bench. Ignoring the sirens and the voices of the men and women responding to my 911 call, Caprice said, "Leah's bright, and she's kind. And she's so beautiful. At Harvard, everyone's intelligent, but Leah is special. She's a good human being. I'm Caprice Brainard. I'm Eumie's daughter. My mother did not kill herself."

I do train dogs, of course, but training is the least of it. My true vocation and avocation is dog watching. Indeed, so ardently have I watched dogs that I have half merged with my subject and thus lack a strictly human eye to cast on the behavior of my fellow human beings. Consequently, when I should perhaps have rushed to the bereaved and distressed Caprice and given her the human equivalent of the tail-wagging, face-licking comfort that my own malamutes would have offered, I took dispassionate note of the total absence of any such exchange between Caprice and Dolfo. Set loose in the yard, Dolfo returned to the gate, jumped up on it, popped down, and then sniffed his way along a well-worn dog path that ran parallel to the fence. Caprice, in turn, addressed herself exclusively to me, a stranger, and took no more notice of Dolfo than she did of the house, the deck, the fence, or the many bird feeders. Had my Rowdy been there instead of Dolfo, he'd have approached her, fixed his soft, dark eyes on her face, stationed himself within stroking distance, and probably raised a paw. Of my three malamutes, only Rowdy was a certified therapy dog; he'd been taught to wait for my permission or for a direct invitation before touching someone. Kimi would either have hurled herself at Caprice's feet or would have set herself the task of nuzzling and scouring the young woman's hands as if they were ailing new-born puppies in need of revivification. And Sammy? All exuberance, he'd have run up to her, leaned against her, placed a great white snowshoe paw on her arm or her lap, and treated her to a sparkly-eyed smile that radiated joy itself, including the sweet expectation of having the joy reciprocated in full. Although I liked to believe that I was half malamute myself, I lacked my dogs' unquestioning self-confidence. If Caprice had spurned Rowdy's offer of contact, he'd happily have turned to me. If she'd brushed Kimi off, the judgment written on Kimi's masked face would have been that Caprice alone was at fault for foolishly declining solace, and too bad for her! The whole point would've been lost on Sammy, who'd merrily have continued to assume that Caprice was just as thrilled with him as he always was with himself, and why not? He was handsome, charming, and happy; life in his vicinity was a delightful adventure; therefore, everyone else was as euphoric as he was. Being only half malamute, I felt inadequate and knew too well that rejection would leave me filled with self-blame. On the other hand — the big snowshoe-shaped one — I knew I had to try. Consequently, I took a seat next to Caprice on the teak bench and said, "Yes, I'm Leah's cousin, and I'm so sorry about Eumie."

"She *was* careless about her meds, but the worst that ever happened was that she was sleepy the next day. Lethargic. I don't care what Ted says! She was not self-destructive. Someone did this to her! She was not depressed. She was *interested* in things. Especially in people! Anyone who's depressed enough to commit suicide loses interest in everything, and my mother *had* to know everything about everyone. She wasn't *just* snoopy, which she was. She also had this passionate curiosity about people." Caprice fumbled in her pocket. I handed her a tissue, and she blew her nose. "People told her things. They confided in her. Her patients did, of course, and Ted told her everything about his patients, too. And she found things out, including things people didn't want her to know. And people resented her. Wyeth did. And Johanna. That's Ted's ex-wife, Wyeth's mother. Johanna blames Eumie for wrecking her marriage, and Wyeth takes his mother's side even though he doesn't exactly get along with her. Or anyone else, for that matter."

I said what I guessed Rita would say: "Wyeth seems very angry."

"Wyeth is a little bastard," Caprice said. "He's a spoiled brat. And that's not my mother's fault. It's Ted's. *And* Johanna's. I don't know which of them is worse. Oh, God! What am I going to do? Where am I going to go? I can't stay here. Not with Ted and Wyeth. My therapist is here. She's in Cambridge. I have to see her, especially now — I can't go to New York with my father. I have nowhere to go!" She burst into deep sobbing.

I put an arm around her. "Home with me," I said. "If you want a place to stay for a while, you're welcome at my house. Leah's with us for the summer. We'd be glad to have you."

Caprice was crying too hard to speak, but she nodded and gave me a big hug and then kept clinging to me. As I held her, I tried to think of ways to protect her. No matter what the need of the police for any information she could provide, I simply had to get her away from this lunatic household and especially from Wyeth, who, for all I knew, would repeat his insults to her and crow over her mother's death.

Somewhat to my astonishment, when I glanced toward the house, the row of glass doors to the family room revealed the hulking figure of my neighbor and buddy, Lieutenant Kevin Dennehy, who was the key element in my emerging plan to protect Caprice and thus seemed almost to have been conjured up by my imagination.

"Caprice," I said, "there's a cop in the family room who's looking out here. He's a friend of mine. My next-door neighbor. His name is Kevin Dennehy. I'm going to have a word with him, and we'll see if we can get you out of here. I'll be right up there on the deck or in the family room. Okay?" Hesitantly, I added, "Would you like Dolfo to come over and sit with you?"

The ridiculous-looking dog was curled up under a recently pruned forsythia bush. At the sound of his name, he roused himself and came loping toward us.

"Dolfo is an idiot," Caprice said.

In his defense, I said, "His intentions are good. And dogs feel grief, too. He could probably use your company."

Rolling her eyes, Caprice stretched out a hand to the dog, who took the gesture as permission to approach her. With a wry grimace, she tapped him on top of his head but didn't speak to him. With the sense that I wasn't leaving Caprice entirely alone, I hurried to the steps that led to the deck, ascended them, and beckoned to Kevin to join me.

His mother, who is the actual owner of the house next to mine, takes an ethnographic view of the human countenance: she always describes Kevin as having the map of Ireland on his face, by which she means that he has red hair, blue eyes, and freckles. Ireland is, however, a rather small country, whereas everything about Kevin is big: his head, each facial feature, his arms and hands, his torso, his tree-trunk legs, his mammoth feet. Furthermore, his oversized presence shoves him front and center. You could take a group photo of fifty people with Kevin standing on one side in the back row, and if you asked anyone to pick out the central person in the picture, the respondent would reliably point to Kevin.

"Hey, how ya doing," he said.

"Not too well, but better now that you're here. I had an appointment to help train the dog." I nodded in Dolfo's direction. "Eumie wasn't up yet." Giving Ted no credit, I said, "I'm the one who found her. Kevin, I need your help. That's Eumie's daughter down there on the bench. Her name is Caprice. I want *you* to be the one who questions her. Please don't delegate the job. She's very vulnerable."

"Mr. Sensitivity," Kevin said.

"And keep Wyeth, the son, away from her. He's her stepbrother. Ted's son. Ted is Eumie's husband. Anyway, I'm still reeling from the way Wyeth spoke to Caprice. When I found Eumie, it never occurred to me that the kids were in the house, and Caprice came in, and there she was, standing at the foot of the bed with her mother's body right there, and this kid, Wyeth, was unbelievable. Kevin, it was emotional abuse. The term gets tossed around a lot, but this was the real thing. I'm taking her home with me. She doesn't want to stay here with Ted and Wyeth."

"Ted," Kevin said flatly. " 'That'd be Dr. Green to you, boy.' "

"He didn't say that."

"Close to. Not in those words. What he says is it's an accidental overdose of prescription drugs."

"Not so long ago he was saying that Eumie was still alive, so I guess that in terms of his mental health, this is an improvement. Caprice says Eumie wouldn't have taken an overdose, accidental or otherwise. She thinks that her mother was murdered. She's very insistent."

"Hey, it's her mother." He shrugged.

"Do you really need to question her?"

"She was in the house, and like I said, it's her mother. Just a couple of questions, and then get her out of here."

Kevin followed me across the deck, down the steps, and to the teak bench where Caprice was sitting. Dolfo was on the grass a few yards away from her.

Kevin took a seat and said, "Kevin Dennehy, Cambridge police. You're going to be able to go home with Holly if that's what you want. Or somewhere else if you want."

"Another planet," Caprice said.

"Seeing that we can't manage a spaceship, will Holly's do?"

"Yes."

"She warn you about all the dogs?"

"I've met Kimi. Leah and I were in a class together. She brought Kimi with her a couple of times."

"There are four more at home. And a cat. You got any allergies?"

"No." She pointed at Dolfo. "It's just this one I don't like. He's ugly and demented."

I resisted the temptation to defend Dolfo. For one thing, Kevin wasn't just chitchatting; he knew what he was doing, and he was getting results in the sense that Caprice was visibly more relaxed than she had been. For another thing, Caprice didn't fit an idealized image of beauty any more closely than Dolfo did; the less said about appearance, the better.

With astounding disloyalty, Kevin said, "So is Holly's cat."

I said, "Tracker is *my* cat. She is a member of our family."

"Dolfo was Ted and Eumie's. Period," Caprice said.

"Slept in their bed," Kevin remarked.

"Peed on their bed," Caprice said. "And everywhere else. Both of them were disgusting about him." She eyed Kevin. "And if you're wondering whether Eumie killed herself, there's one reason why she wouldn't have. In her opinion, Dolfo needed her, and it would've been traumatic to him to lose her. Her patients needed her. She wouldn't have traumatized them by killing herself. More than anything else, she needed herself, if that makes sense. She was very narcissistic, and narcissistic people do not commit suicide. And if you're wondering about an accidental overdose, Eumie could be frivolous and silly, but she wasn't stupid. At one time or another, she took practically every prescription drug in existence, and so did Ted. Pills, capsules, liquid. And they shared. She talked about it all the time. But she was more careful than you'd expect. And lots of people had things against her.

Wyeth hated her. So did his mother, Ted's ex-wife. And she collected people's secrets. Her patients' secrets. Everyone's. And in case you wondered, the house is practically never locked. The door on the side of the house, the one to Ted and Eumie's waiting room, is almost always unlocked. We moved from the city four years ago. They thought Cambridge was safe."

"New York City," I translated.

"But they were wrong," Caprice said. "They couldn't have been more wrong."

CHAPTER 8

As I see her in my mind's eye, Anita Fairley sits at the desk in her room at CHIRP, the Center for Healing, Individuation, Recovery, and Peace. The room is all polished wood and natural fabrics. Its windows overlook fields and woods. The desk is bare except for Anita's notebook computer, a telephone, a sheet of paper with a rather long list of handwritten names, a box of thick cream-colored notepaper, and a Montblanc pen with blue ink. The notepaper and the blue ink are not figments of my imagination; they are facts. Anita, too, is a fact, as is her appearance: her long blond hair, her lovely features, her slimness, and the hauteur of her expression. She is wearing new and expensive clothes appropriate to the occasion and the setting. She always does; therefore she does so now. Consequently, I see her in a designer version of the loose, comfortable clothing invariably recommended for yoga and meditation classes. Although the diagnosis of global chemical sensitivity is now passé, having been replaced by unfortunate systemic reactions to mold, I see Anita in unbleached and thus off-white cotton: a loose long-sleeved top and drawstring pants that fall in flattering drapes.

Online, she looks up my address and makes a face. Still, she selects an envelope, addresses it to me, and, on one of the thick sheets of notepaper, pens a few sentences of apology for the pain she has caused. She is tempted to sign herself Anita Fairley-Delaney but reluctantly settles for Anita Fairley. Why the hell do there have to be twelve steps? she wonders. Eleven would more than suffice.

CHAPTER 9

"You haven't been married all that long," Caprice said. "Your husband probably won't want some stranger here."

We were drinking tea at my kitchen table. Steve's and mine. Our kitchen table, which I'd set with mugs, spoons, a saucer of lemon slices, and, after some internal debate, a bowl of sugar and a pitcher of whole milk. No one in the house drank low-fat milk, so I'd had none to offer, and although there was cream in the refrigerator, I couldn't bring myself to put it out. Anyway, the collectively owned object that was embarrassing the hell out of me wasn't the table but the jacket of the book Steve and I had written together. The book itself wasn't due out until October, but our editor had sent us a solicitation cover, as such a thing is called, the book jacket with no book inside. Delighted with this preview of our work, we'd pinned it on the bulletin board in the kitchen, where it now seemed to me to have grown to poster size and practically to thrust itself in Caprice's face — with special attention to disfiguring pouches of fat. The jacket art was in the style of Marcel Duchamp and consisted of a series of drawings that depicted the transformation of the obese dog on the left to the lean one on the right. The title was *No More Fat Dogs.* Professional dog writer that I am, I'd tried to inveigle Steve into selecting a cutesy, if derivative, title such as *Dr. Doggie's Diet Revolution* or even *The South Bitch Diet Book,* but in his amateur fashion, he'd insisted that the title should simply say what the book was about, and our editor had agreed, probably because ours was her first dog book. Because of Caprice, I now wished that I'd fought for a title that bewildered or misled potential buyers by making no reference whatever to weight loss. *Dogs Forever! The Happy Canine. Feeding Fido.* Anything but *No More Fat Dogs!*

"Steve isn't that kind of person," I said. "And Leah's with us for the summer. She has her own room here, and we have a guest room. Besides, with five dogs and a cat, we're never alone."

Rowdy and Kimi were with us in the

kitchen. Kimi, clearly remembering Caprice from the Harvard classes she'd attended with Leah, had greeted her with a peal of *woo-woo-woo*s. Rowdy had given her his winsome welcome of honor by fetching his favorite stuffed dinosaur, depositing it at her feet, vanishing briefly, reappearing with a fleece chewman, giving that to her, and then planting himself in front of her and offering his paw. "Which is which?" she asked. "They look so much alike."

Harvard or no Harvard, she had no eye for dogs. For that kind of tuition, you'd think they'd teach these kids something worth knowing! Then again, an eye for a dog is like perfect pitch, inborn, so perhaps Harvard had wisely decided not to offer instruction in the unteachable. Rowdy and Kimi are, admittedly, about the same color, dark gray with white legs and feet, and they both have plumy white tails, but they do not look *alike.* In deference to Caprice's bereavement, I'd contented myself with saying, "Kimi is the one with the dark markings, and Rowdy's the one with the all-white face. He's bigger than Kimi is." I'd been on the ghastly verge of saying that Kimi weighed seventy-five pounds and Rowdy about eighty-eight pounds, but I'd caught myself in time. I also refrained from pointing out obvious anatomical differences between males and females. Caprice would have understood, wouldn't she? Or did Harvard have to offer a course in remedial sex education?

Anyway, Caprice's response to Kimi's musical welcome and Rowdy's generous presentation of toys had been polite. She'd smiled at Kimi and taken Rowdy's paw. Kimi was now lying on the floor with her chin resting on one of the rungs of my chair. Rowdy, however, had assigned himself the task of keeping an eye on Caprice. Literally. He sat next to her with his dark, almond-shaped eyes on her face. His expression was calm and watchful, as if he wanted nothing from her and intended to offer her nothing except the solidity of his presence and the warmth of his gaze. Although it was one o'clock and time for lunch, the dogs showed none of the usual bouncy, ears-up signs that they were expecting me to produce food that they could share or steal. Kimi, my food lunatic, had all but convinced me that she could read the part of my mind devoted to thoughts of breakfast, lunch, dinner, and snacks. I'd been disconcerted to realize that when I rose from the table to get second or third helpings, she didn't bother to tag along, but when I'd finished eating and was taking my plate to the sink, she followed me.

At the moment, Kimi was probably contemplating with disdain my awkward bafflement about what to offer Caprice for lunch. Like many other writers, I usually settled for the skimpiest of midday meals: a hunk of cheese with bread or a small serving of leftovers that I ate while I kept working. Every sandwich filling in the refrigerator was outrageously fattening: tuna with lots of mayonnaise, sliced ham, and cream cheese and olives. Left from last night was a bowl of fettuccine Alfredo. The only yogurt in the fridge was Greek-style Total, which tasted as if it had been made with heavy cream. Steve and I were blessed with the same high metabolic rate; we could get away with eating anything we wanted. Leah watched her weight by limiting the size of portions. Salad? It was obviously diet food, wasn't it? I might as well serve two tablespoons of no-fat cottage cheese on a single lettuce leaf and try to pretend that it was what I always ate. It was not, of course, my job to help Caprice lose weight; it was presumably her own job and her therapist's. For all I knew, their task was to help her accept herself as she was. It was even possible that she already did. Still, as I looked at her, I couldn't bear to contribute to the disfigurement of her face.

I rationalized the decision to postpone the lunch dilemma by telling myself that it didn't really feel like one o'clock, as it, in fact, didn't. Oddly, it felt neither earlier nor later than one, either: the shock of Eumie's death, compounded by the weirdness and nastiness of the Brainard-Green household and my compassion for Caprice, had jolted me into some out-of-time state. Also, I'd lost track of time as I'd hung around waiting for Kevin to arrange to have Caprice pack the possessions she'd need to stay with us. After being accompanied to her room by a police officer, she'd emerged with nothing but her notebook computer, a small backpack, a large purse, and a small suitcase, all of which were now on the kitchen floor.

"I should call Steve and Leah, and let them know what's happened," I said. "And then we'll get you settled. Maybe there are people you want to call."

"I have my cell," she said. "I need to call Missy. That's my therapist. I need to see her. And I can try to call my father."

"Let me show you where you're going to stay. And where things are. And there are a few rules about the dogs," I finished. A few? There were hundreds, if not thousands, but I decided to let them wait.

With Rowdy and Kimi companionably accompanying us, we climbed the stairs to the second floor, which used to be Rita's apartment. We'd ripped out her kitchen but left the bathroom, which was newer and fancier than the one on the first floor because when I'd bought the house, I'd remodeled the rental apartments on the second and third floors, and economized on my own quarters. My office was still on the first floor, but my old first-floor bedroom had become a dining room, and Steve and I had moved to a newly redone version of Rita's former living room. The guest room was ready for occupancy. My stepmother, Gabrielle, had visited a few weeks earlier, and I'd vacuumed and changed the linens when she'd left. Gabrielle and her bichon frise, Molly, were exceptionally easy houseguests. Not only was Gabrielle a gracious, considerate person, but by my malamute standards, Molly the bichon didn't shed at all.

When Caprice put her suitcase and backpack down in her room, Kimi sniffed them with something more than her usual intelligent curiosity about new objects in her environment. "Kimi, leave it," I said softly.

Trying to sound casual and matter-of-fact, I addressed Caprice. "If you have food in your room, be careful because the dogs will filch it. In fact, unless you want company, you should keep your door closed. All the dogs are friendly, and if you want them in here, fine, but keep an eye on them. And don't let them jump on the bed. They're allowed on beds, but only if they're invited." I supplied Caprice with towels, showed her the bathroom, and said, "It's very important to keep the bathroom door closed. If you don't, the dogs will go in and steal things." That was a lie. The *malamutes* stole things. India and Lady never did. "They'll eat soap." I hesitated to elaborate, but anyone who stays here deserves fair warning. "And Sammy, my other malamute, is, uh, especially fond of makeup brushes." That was a gross understatement. Sammy was obsessed with the kinds of brushes used to apply blush. Did he have a not-so-secret longing for pink cheeks? Or did he perceive the soft bristles as the fur of small prey? For whatever reason, Sammy not only made off with the brushes but immediately chewed and swallowed so that nothing was left but bare handles. "He'll run off with paper, too. He looks grown up, but he's still a puppy."

As we were heading back downstairs, the phone rang.

"That could be my father!" Caprice's tone was indescribably eager. "Maybe he tried to call and Ted gave him this number."

And her cell phone? Her father wouldn't have tried it? I did not, of course, ask. In any case, the caller was not Monty Brainard but Ted Green, whose usually mellifluous voice was hoarse and strained. "I need this like a *loch in kop!* This *grosse macher* says . . . Caprice has to help me. Holly, put Caprice on. There's something I need her to do."

Having no choice, I handed the phone to Caprice, who, after saying nothing but hello, listened for what seemed like five minutes. Meanwhile, I let the dogs out into the fenced yard and put together a small lunch. I mixed a packet of water-packed tuna with much less mayonnaise than I usually use and put out bread, lettuce, and tomatoes.

Eventually, Caprice said, "Ted, there's nothing personal about it. It's the law." After listening, she added, "No, I am not calling anyone. It would be a waste of time. Besides which, don't you want to know? I do. And it's the only way to find out." Again, she waited. "Yes, I am fully aware of that, but it happened a long time ago, and my mother is beyond caring." After another wait, she said, "Being Jewish has nothing to do with anything, and as you perfectly well know, my mother wasn't Jewish. She grew up as some kind of Protestant, and she wasn't religious . . . Yes, of course she was spiritual, but she did not go to church. Your being Jewish has nothing to do with anything, and even if she had been Jewish, there would still have to be an autopsy. And there damn well should be one. I am not going to call anyone to object. In fact, if anyone asks me, I'll say . . . Ted, you know what? It *does* bother me to think about it, so thanks a lot for making me talk about it . . . Yes, she's here. Just a second."

The topic Ted needed to discuss with me on the afternoon of his wife's evidently unnatural death was, incredibly, Dolfo. In Ted's words, "Dolfo has grief work to do." For all that I am a dog-training zealot, it was clear to me that Ted ought to have other things on his mind. What's more, it's reasonable for a first-time dog owner to seek professional help in teaching sit, stay, and heel, but how could any human being, never mind a psychotherapist, fail to realize that a grieving creature, human or canine, has simple needs? Hold the dog, speak gently to him, keep life as normal for him as you can, not that poor Dolfo's life was *normal,* but it was the only life he knew, so, crazy though it was, it was normal for him.

"They can't cry, can they?" asked Ted. "It never occurred to me before. What a dreadful prospect!"

"Dogs grieve in their own ways," I said. "Crying isn't part of the repertoire. And there's nothing I can do to make things easier for Dolfo or to speed up the process. I'm sorry."

"You have to help," Ted pleaded. "Just come and take a look at him. Tomorrow? How's one o'clock? I've had to cancel my patients, but I might have to change the time. I have an urgent call in to my therapist, Dr. Tortorello, and he hasn't called me back, and I'm trying to reach our couples therapist, Dr. Foote, and I'm going to have to take any hours they offer because they're going to have to squeeze me in. But let's shoot for one o'clock. I'll let you know if that won't work."

I told myself that Ted was mad with grief. I agreed to one o'clock. Yes, indeed, which of us was truly meshugge?

Chapter 10

Although George McBane has never shared his wife's interest in animal welfare, he has always supported Barbara's good works. Lists of donors to the Audubon Society and the MSPCA include both names, George McBane and Barbara Leibowitz, and George has dutifully attended many fund-raisers, especially the ones that Barbara has organized. On a small and domestic scale, George has contributed by assembling and repairing the bird feeders in the backyard.

On the afternoon of Eumie's death, as Barbara fills her bird feeders, she can't help noticing the contrast between her squirrel-battered collection and the sparkling new avian dining establishments visible through and above the fence in the Brainard-Greens' yard. Her own classic pole feeder retains its built-in green baffle but long ago lost its perches to the squirrels, and the best that can be said about the chopsticks that

George cleverly substituted is that they are effective. The green paint is chipped, and the pole shows rust. George has performed many repairs on the platform feeder, which is a shallow wooden box with a screen floor for drainage. The birdseed stays dry, and certain ground feeders, including juncos, sometimes land on the platform and peck away in apparent comfort. It occurs to Barbara that none of the squirrel damage she notices today is recent. What's more, the thistle feeder is still half full of expensive thistle seed. In fact, as Barbara remarks aloud to Portia, who accompanies her, it's been a while since she has even seen a squirrel in the yard. Portia, despite her terrier heritage, takes no interest in squirrels. It is characteristic of Barbara to have a thoroughly peaceful dog; a predator wouldn't suit her at all.

Barbara doesn't exactly miss the squirrels, or at least she doesn't miss the gray squirrels. The distinctive black squirrels that inhabit Cambridge are another matter. They are somehow more attractive than their gray cousins. With a laugh, she says to Portia, "Black like me."

Chapter 11

Only when I was actually placing the serving dish on the dining-room table that evening did it belatedly hit me that the vegetable I had chosen for Caprice's first dinner at our house was none other than the traditional staple of canine weight-reduction diets, namely, green beans. Steve, seated at one end of the table, took a quick glance that darted from the green beans to Caprice and from Caprice to me. His face went blank. His handsome countenance was not, however, the family body part that worried me. No, what concerned me was Leah's mouth, inside of which were pretty white teeth that she chronically failed to use in the service of biting her tongue. In this case, my specific fear was that Leah would make the obvious association between the green beans on the table and *No More Fat Dogs*, in which Steve and I repeatedly and enthusiastically urged our readers to substitute that low-calorie legume for large quantities of fattening dog food.

"Leah," I said hastily as I took my seat, "would you pass the salmon to Caprice, please? Caprice, I hope that fish is all right. Not everyone likes it. If you don't want it, don't eat it."

"It's fine. Fish is fine," Caprice said. "It looks delicious. This is so nice of you to have me here. I'm sorry to impose. I just don't know where else . . ." Her voice broke off.

"You're not imposing," Steve told her, "and don't think about going anywhere else. You're welcome here."

"We want you here," Leah added. "And Holly and Steve have both had their mothers die, so —"

"We were older than Caprice is," Steve said.

"Holly wasn't all that much older, was she?"

"Leah," I said, "could we not argue about it? The point is that we're glad to have Caprice here."

"For as long as she wants," Steve said. "Speaking of which, we should go over the house rules about the dogs. If Holly hasn't already?"

"Steve, could you pass the green beans, please?" Leah asked. "Thanks. The first rule about the dogs is that the malamutes steal food. Sammy isn't too bad, but Rowdy and Kimi are awful, especially Kimi. And be careful about who's loose together. Kimi and Rowdy are fine together, and India and Lady are fine, and Rowdy can be loose with them. So can Sammy. But Rowdy and Sammy supposedly can't be left alone together."

"There's no supposedly about it," I said. "They're both intact male malamutes, and that's that."

"And," Leah continued, "Kimi and India really, really can't be alone together. Good salmon, Holly. Thank you."

"You're welcome. Then there's Tracker."

"The cat," said Leah. "She scratches."

"She doesn't scratch me," said Steve. "India, Lady, and Sammy are good with her individually, but not all three dogs together."

"It's Rowdy and Kimi you really have to watch out for," I said. "They weren't raised with cats, and they're predatory. But I'm working on it." Steve and Leah both laughed. "I am! My great strength as a dog trainer is persistence. We are making progress."

"And then there's Pink Piggy," Leah said. "We forgot him."

All color drained from Caprice's face. "You —"

In unison, Steve, Leah, and I assured her that our menagerie did not extend to a Vietnamese potbellied pig.

"Pink Piggy is Sammy's favorite toy," Leah explained. "Pink Piggy has a squeaker, so Rowdy and Kimi can't play with him because they'd tear him up and probably eat the squeaker. Sammy kills the squeakers, but they're replaceable. The point is, though, that Sammy loves Pink Piggy, and we're afraid that Sammy might defend him from the other dogs. *Any* of the other dogs. Except Lady. She'd never steal anything from anyone."

For some reason, Caprice was smiling. "I can't even tell all the dogs apart," she admitted. "India is the German shepherd, and Lady is the pointer, and the other three are malamutes."

"So," said Steve, "you're starting to be able to tell them apart."

"You know Kimi," Leah said. "You already knew her from school."

And to my amazement, Caprice gave an impish smile and said, "Sure. That makes it easy. Kimi's the one with the Harvard accent."

We all laughed. If Caprice was joking

119

about dogs, she was fitting in around here. Also, I have to admit I saw her in a new way. Before, she'd been an object of pity: a young woman whose face was distorted by obesity, a needy daughter whose mother had just died an unnatural death, the victim of her stepbrother's verbal abuse, and so on. All of a sudden, she was someone with a sharp wit. Furthermore, the little remark she'd made hadn't been about her obesity and hadn't been at her own expense; she hadn't played the role of fat clown. Anyway, the atmosphere abruptly loosened. Instead of issuing stilted, if genuine, assurances to Caprice that there was no need for her to return to Ted's house, we talked about summer plans. Steve later told me that he'd made the same naive assumption I had, namely, that Caprice was going to attend Harvard Summer School, had a job lined up, or was volunteering somewhere. Her only plan, however, was to see her therapist.

"All of us were going to go to Wellfleet in August," she said. "Everyone's therapist is away then, anyway."

"Rita says that they all go to Wellfleet," I commented. "Rita has our third-floor apartment. She's a psychologist. You'll meet her. Anyway, she prides herself in not always going to Wellfleet. Every so often, she goes somewhere else."

Caprice smiled. "Truro. It's the next town. But I'm not going with Ted and Wyeth. I don't know what they'll do. They're supposed to go to Russia in July. It's sort of a school trip."

I told myself that I'd seen Wyeth at his worst and that he must have redeeming qualities. Even so, it was difficult to imagine him reading Tolstoy and touring the Kremlin.

"That must be some school," said Steve, who'd had paying jobs practically since he'd taken his first steps.

"Avon Hill likes parents to take students to the places they're learning about. Eumie and I went to Greece the summer before last." Caprice spoke offhandedly, as if she were mentioning an outing to Salem or Plymouth Rock. "It makes everything real when you've actually seen the Parthenon and Delphi and so forth instead of just reading about them. My father was supposed to take me, but he couldn't. He had an important meeting."

"Is your father a therapist, too?" Steve asked.

Her eyes lit up. "He's a consultant. He's mainly in New York, but he travels. He's here pretty often."

I have never been able to figure out precisely what consultants do. Obviously, they consult. But about what? And how do they do it? I always imagine them strolling authoritatively past Dilbert-style cubicles or rows of machinery while making grand pronouncements. The only thing I know for sure about consultants is that they get paid a lot. It sometimes occurs to me when I'm writing my hundredth article about pet-stain removal or flea control that instead of making grand pronouncements on those topics (*Use enzyme products!* Or, in the case of fleas, *Infestation is easier to prevent than it is to cure!*), I, too, could meander through high-tech businesses or low-tech factories while exclaiming, *What this organization needs is an incentive plan!* Or possibly, *Responsive leadership is the key to productivity!* I have only the vaguest idea of what an incentive plan is, and for all I know, leadership is totally unrelated to productivity, but I've never been convinced that consultants know more than I do. In fact, they almost certainly know nothing about pet-stain removal and flea control, topics on which I am an acknowledged expert.

I kept my thoughts about Monty Brainard's profession to myself, of course.

Caprice went on. "He'll help me think about what to do now. He might e-mail me tonight. Or call. He just got back to New York today, so he's probably swamped."

"You can use my computer," Leah volunteered.

"Thanks, but I have my notebook."

"There's a phone jack in your room," I told her. We don't have phone jacks everywhere, but when Rita moved to the third floor, I hooked up my phone line to what had been her phone wiring.

The absence of dessert was normal enough; it wasn't part of some sneaky scheme to take weight off Caprice, who had eaten average-size portions of dinner, including only one piece of French bread with a small amount of butter. Furthermore, when she helped Steve, Leah, and me to clear the table and put away the food, she didn't dispose of small bits of leftovers by eating them as I often did myself. When the kitchen was clean, Leah invited Caprice to watch a video with her, but Caprice said that if we didn't mind, she'd just check her e-mail, take a shower, and go to bed. I was only a little surprised. She'd had a draining day. And I was happy to realize that if Ted Green called, I'd be justified in telling him that Caprice was unavailable. Shortly after

Caprice went upstairs, the phone did ring, but it was a friend of Leah's. Ten minutes later, he turned up at the door, and the two of them took Kimi for a walk.

Steve and I opened a bottle of wine and took it, together with two glasses and the remaining four dogs, out to the yard. Even though Caprice's room was on the opposite side of the house, we kept our voices low.

"I want to tell you," I said, "how good I felt today when Caprice had nowhere to go, and I knew I could ask her here without checking with you. I knew you'd feel the same way I did."

"The poor kid. What the hell is wrong with this father of hers? He just might e-mail her. If she's lucky. And he'll be swamped with work. What kind of bullshit is that?"

"Typical bullshit, I think. I ran into Barbara Leibowitz outside Ted and Eumie's. After I found Eumie. She and George live next door to them. She said that Caprice will be lucky if her father shows up at all but that Caprice is better off not understanding what he's really like."

"How could she miss it?"

"I don't know. At some level, she must get it. But with a family like hers . . . Steve, dysfunctionality would constitute a cure.

The scene this morning was more horrible than I can possibly say. And then this afternoon, Ted Green just had to call here and badger Caprice because he was upset about the idea of an autopsy. He was trying to enlist poor Caprice to object to it. That's nuts! Families can't just go around saying that they don't want autopsies. It's not like requesting donations to charity in lieu of flowers. The law requires autopsies in cases of unexplained death. Period. Plus, trying to involve Caprice? That's unpardonable."

"What did Eumie die from, anyway?"

"Oh, an accidental overdose, I imagine. Ted kept saying that her trauma history, whatever it was, had caught up with her, and Caprice insists that her mother was murdered. What child wants to believe that her mother killed herself? Even semi-accidentally. It sounds to me as if Eumie had a habit of swallowing anything that was in the medicine cabinet. If she took who knows what at bedtime, her judgment would've been affected, and in the middle of the night, she could easily have taken the wrong thing. Or taken two doses when she meant to take one."

"What kind of trauma was it?"

"I didn't ask. When I was there on Friday, Eumie said something about *their* trauma histories, and then today, of course, Ted kept mentioning hers, but somehow I just couldn't come right out and ask for details. I mean, trauma could be . . . well, except that Rita said that Ted's book defines *trauma* very broadly. His book is called *Ordinary Trauma.* So in his terms, it wouldn't necessarily mean sexual trauma, incest, something like that. It could be something less —"

"— traumatic," Steve finished. As Rita is always pointing out, he is quite unpsychological. Miraculously, they are good friends anyway.

"But it really couldn't be something trivial, either, could it?"

"It depends on what you mean by *trivial.* If the thesis of his book is that seemingly trivial events are actually traumatic, then it could be something that gets dismissed as trivial. I can't think of what that would be."

"Steve, when you're talking about Ted and Eumie, who knows? Take the way Wyeth treated Caprice today. Now, I wouldn't offhand consider his behavior to be traumatic. Abusive, yes. But maybe if she gets treated like that over and over, the result probably is traumatic or something close to it, anyway, especially if no one stops Wyeth from doing it. Here you and I are, taking the greatest possible care to make sure that our dogs can't hurt one another, and meanwhile, Caprice doesn't have the protection we routinely give our dogs. That's horrible. Maybe it's even traumatic. I don't know. What I do know is that the whole situation is enough to drive anyone crazy. Here's one more example. Ted and Eumie were going to Vee Foote for couples therapy."

"Her," he said.

"Her. Rita says that most of what Vee Foote does these days is diagnose everyone with depression and prescribe anti-depressants. With therapy, of course. Many hours of expensive therapy. Maybe she's redoing her bathrooms. It was her kitchen when I saw her. Anyway, seeing Vee Foote isn't even what's so weird, which is that they, Ted and Eumie, were seeing her for couples therapy, and now Ted says that he has to see her! And there is no doubt in my mind that she'll continue to see him for couples therapy for as long as he's willing to pay for it. When half of the couple is dead!"

"Holly, be fair."

"I always am."

He smiled. "Look, maybe the two of them, Ted and Eumie, were in the middle of something with her, and Ted needs to finish talking about it." It was one of the most psychological statements I'd ever heard him make.

"Okay. Fair enough. For one or two sessions. And then? We'll wait and see. But I'm telling you, Steve, it would be exactly like Vee Foote to build up a specialized practice in couples therapy that consists exclusively of treating widows and widowers. Couples bereavement therapy, let's call it. Now, don't you find that peculiar?"

"What's that old saying? All the world's crazy except me and thee." He paused and kissed me. "And sometimes I wonder about thee."

CHAPTER 12

Kevin Dennehy used to work out exclusively at the Cambridge YMCA, which is on Mass. Ave. near Central Square and thus conveniently near Cambridge Police Headquarters. In saying that Kevin worked out exclusively there, I mean, of course, that he worked out nowhere else; the Y is no one's idea of a la-di-da establishment. Under the influence of his girlfriend, Jennifer Pasquarelli, Kevin then expanded his fitness horizons by joining the Original Mike's Gym, which is on a little street off Concord Avenue beyond the Fresh Pond rotary, on the way to Belmont. Cambridge being Cambridge, the superficially unprepossessing Mike's Gym is highly exclusive in the sense that its membership is limited to persons who go there strictly to achieve strength and stamina and not, to borrow Kevin's words, to loll around gargling carrot juice and practicing heavy breathing.

The phrases, I might mention, irritate Officer Jennifer Pasquarelli, who regularly imbibes freshly extracted vegetable juices and dutifully performs the breathing exercises of various Eastern disciplines as part of a comprehensive program intended to keep her in the state of physical perfection that she obviously enjoys. She is strong and voluptuous. Unfortunately, the program she follows is less comprehensive than it might be: it has utterly failed to endow her with even the slightest trace of the most rudimentary sense of humor. But as I was about to say, the exclusivity of Mike's Gym consists only in part of excluding those whose purposes are frivolously nongymnastic. From Kevin's viewpoint, the important and winning aspect of exclusivity at Mike's is that it is populated only by town and gown, and not by newcomers who, in Kevin's opinion, have no business being in Cambridge at all.

I easily envision Kevin as he stands under the shower at Mike's Gym on Wednesday morning and vents his rage in an apparent effort to scrub the freckles off his face and wash the red out of his hair. My relationship with Kevin is, I hasten to add, such that I see him from the waist up and the mid-thigh down. Kevin's anger, by the way, has nothing to do with the mean-looking scar on his torso. Although he has listened to Ted Green blather on about trauma, it hasn't occurred to Kevin to apply the concept to his own experience in taking a bullet in the chest. In Kevin's view, if you don't want to get shot, you shouldn't become a cop, and there's no more to be said about it. Anyway, what accounts for his bout of matutinal fury isn't posttraumatic stress but the interruption of his workout by an urgent phone call about the results of the postmortem on Eumie Brainard-Green, who had taken a variety of prescription medications in quantities far too great to be consistent with accidental overdose. The substances identified by the medical examiner include Prozac, Ambien, Sonata, and various benzodiazepines, together with a moderate quantity of alcohol. The amounts and the combination are consistent with suicide. Or homicide, of course. She had also consumed a large amount of vitamin and herbal supplements as well as soy milk and the juices of raw vegetables.

Kevin disapproves of everything about the death of Eumie Brainard-Green. For a start, he hates weird food. He also disapproves of hyphenation. Although I have talked to him about Lucy Stoner, he disapproves of my having kept the name Winter when I married Steve. He disapproves of Eumie's neighborhood, too, not because Avon Hill is populated by the gown side of the town-gown split but because, like other gownish areas, so to speak, it has been invaded by the very rich, who flaunt their wealth and who, far from parading around in academic gowns and driving venerable Volvos, wear designer clothing and drive BMW and Lexus SUVs. He almost wishes that the dead woman had worn peasant garb, denim, and three hats at once, had driven some ancient and eccentric vehicle — an adult-size folding tricycle, for example — and had been getting a Ph.D. in some useless and probably unspeakable foreign language, which is to say that Lieutenant Dennehy wishes that she had been a familiar Cambridge type and not one of the new ones, to whom he objects principally because they baffle him. More than anything else, Lieutenant Dennehy disapproves of unnatural death or, indeed, unnatural anything else that occurs within the city limits and especially within walking distance of his own neighborhood and thus near his own mother. He feels particular rage at the young officer who was first on the scene and who was so intimidated by the Brainard-

Green house and the Avon Hill neighborhood that instead of immediately protecting the scene, he had allowed the surviving family members to meander around as they damned well pleased. Kevin Dennehy does not believe in policing by ZIP code. He does, however, approve of Mike's Gym. The invaders belong to overpriced tennis clubs with swimming pools. At Mike's, town and gown sweat together.

CHAPTER 13

On Wednesday morning, Caprice slept until eleven o'clock. Steve and Leah had left for work at six-thirty, and by the time Caprice staggered downstairs, I'd vacuumed up dog hair, unloaded the dishwasher, and written a four-page article, complete with sidebar, about pet-stain removal. Healthy people Caprice's age have an extraordinary capacity for sleep and can easily seem drugged when they finally rouse themselves. Caprice's mother had just died. Still, the young woman looked so abnormally out of it that I had to wonder whether she shared the family fondness for prescription medication. But what did I know? Damned little. And most of that damned little was, of course, about dogs. For as long as I could remember, veterinarians had been prescribing sedatives for agitated dogs. The old-time favorite was acepromazine, but these days, up-to-date vets prescribed some of the same drugs used for distressed human beings. According to Steve, all medications carried the risk of adverse reactions. He favored plain old over-the-counter Benadryl, an antihistamine that includes drowsiness among its side effects, but he occasionally prescribed tranquilizers, sedatives, and the same SSRIs, selective serotonin reuptake inhibitors, that Rita's patients used for depression. In fact, antidepressants were what had brought Rita and Quinn Youngman together. The circumstances were exceedingly unromantic. One of Rita's patients had a manic episode in response to Prozac prescribed by the psychopharmacologist to whom Rita was sending those in need of medication. Rita blamed the guy for starting the woman on too high a dose, and she was furious at what she saw as his lack of sympathy for her patient, who, among other things, talked nonstop for thirty-six hours, racked up gigantic credit card bills, and ended up in a hospital emergency room. So, Rita found someone else to do her meds, as the expression goes, and that someone else was Quinn Youngman. Anyway, I knew a little about psychoactive drugs from Steve and Rita, but all I knew, really, was enough to wonder about Caprice's grogginess.

It also concerned me that instead of eating what I'd have considered a nutritious breakfast, Caprice had nothing but black coffee and half an English muffin spread with peanut butter and jelly. When Caprice entered the kitchen, Rowdy and Kimi were there. Both leaped to their feet and, ever alert to alterations in pack membership, signaled their willingness to include her by pealing loud, friendly *woo-woo-woo*s. When she took a seat at the table, they stationed themselves on either side of her. The contrast between the young woman and dogs was heartbreaking. Caprice was still in a nightgown and robe, her eyes were puffy, her face blotched, her hair uncombed. Rowdy and Kimi had gleaming coats, and their eyes were clear and focused. Rowdy, I thought, shared my desire to rouse Caprice from her stupor: he knew better than to poke her with his big white paw, but when he settled for offering it to her, I could sense the impulse he was restraining. His slightest movements, the upward motion of his foreleg, the turning of his big head, revealed massive muscle, and the gentle warmth of his dark eyes plainly said that he was eager to share his strength, but Caprice merely took his paw as if it were a disembodied object and then quickly released it. To Kimi, whom she knew, Caprice simply said hello, but Kimi continued to train her intelligent eyes on the young woman as if waiting for a request that Caprice was unable to issue.

When I'd told Caprice to help herself to food, I let Rowdy and Kimi out in the yard and brought Sammy into the kitchen. Sammy had a hearty appetite, but he wasn't the horrendous food thief that Rowdy and Kimi were. Sammy, I should mention, was a vessel spilling over with joy. He curved his body around Caprice's legs and treated her to what really was a smile. He, too, got almost no response. In prescribing for his patients, Quinn Youngman probably had the same sort of experience I was having: when he'd had three drugs fail, he, too, probably tried a fourth. I replaced Sammy with India. Perhaps what Caprice needed was exactly the sense of safety, protection, and order so notably missing at home. India, ever dignified, approached Caprice, studied her, and stood calmly about a yard away. Caprice ignored her.

Not everyone loves dogs or even likes them. Take Dr. Vee Foote: phobic. But Caprice was not such a person. She did respond to one of our dogs, my fifth drug, the smallest of the dogs, our delicate, trembling little pointer, Lady. Anxiety is not a typical characteristic of the breed. The pointer belongs to the American Kennel Club's Sporting Group and, as the name suggests, was originally bred to indicate the presence and location of game by pointing. In the field, pointers also retrieve and otherwise perform as all-purpose hunting dogs. Because they should be able to run tirelessly through fields and woods from daybreak to sunset, they are supposed to be strong and athletic. A top-notch pointer from field lines may vibrate with energy in the manner of a Mercedes engine, but in both bench and field lines — show dogs and hunting dogs — it is undesirable to have a pointer, or any other breed, for that matter, quiver with apprehension in response to life itself. Viewed objectively, Lady was anything but a model of the breed. Exception: in pointers, any color is acceptable. Lady was what's unappetizingly called "liver and white ticked," that is, white with brown marks, including "ticks" or spots. As to her other physical features, love demands silence. Fortunately, Steve and I viewed her subjectively, and from our angle, she was a sweetheart. Do dogs feel gratitude? Lady had been left at Steve's clinic for euthanasia. She always acted as if she knew he had saved her life.

So, there was Caprice, weighing perhaps two hundred pounds, bleary-eyed and sluggish, newly bereft of her mother, and there was Lady, thin despite good nutrition, shaking like Jell-O, each needy, each hurt. Holding an English muffin in her right hand, Caprice allowed the left to dangle, and Lady took advantage of the unattended hand by placing her head under it and moving slowly forward so that the hand's owner, Caprice, involuntarily stroked the dog from crown to tail. To my astonishment, Caprice, observing this maneuver, burst into bubbly laughter.

"We call Lady 'the self-patting dog,' " I said.

"She is so sweet!"

"She is the perfect pet. She really is."

So, I got the medication right on the fifth try. Still, if I'd been offering one dog after the other as a sort of woofy projective test, a canine Rorschach, I'd have preferred a strong response to one of the big, strong, self-confident dogs. But any positive response was far better than none. There was hope for Caprice after all.

If I'd been designing a behavioral intervention for Caprice, she'd have spent the rest of the day with Lady. In particular, she and

Lady would have taken a long walk. As it was, as soon as Caprice finished breakfast, she called her human therapist, Dr. Missy Zinn, and arranged an emergency appointment for that same afternoon. When she went upstairs to shower and get dressed, Lady tagged along. Caprice could only have been flattered.

While Caprice was upstairs, Ted Green called to cancel our dog-training and canine-grief-counseling appointment. "Ai-ai-ai," he said, "the cops are making life hell for me. They're all over the house. Here I am, traumatized by the loss of my wife, and these schmucks are retraumatizing me."

"Ted, what I really think is that it's important for everyone to know exactly what happened."

"I know what happened. Eumie's trauma history clouded her judgment. She mixed up her meds. Wyeth and Caprice and I need a peaceful, loving environment to process our loss. So does Dolfo. And these dummkopfs won't listen. What they need is a program to sensitize them to trauma. That would be a fitting memorial to Eumie. But I'm not ready yet."

I bristled. What Caprice didn't need, of course, was the environment created by Wyeth and Ted. Furthermore, even before

Kevin Dennehy had sustained the indubitable trauma of being shot in the chest, he'd had an intuitive, if burly, kindness that no sensitization program would have been able to instill. And I damned well didn't like having him or his colleagues referred to as schmucks and dummkopfs. Fortunately, Ted ended the conversation quickly. He had to rush off to see Dr. Tortorello and, after that, Vee Foote.

When Caprice came downstairs, she looked awake. Her eyes had lost most of their puffiness, and her hair was a halo of pretty curls. She wore a long black linen skirt and top that had picked up only a few stray dog hairs. I offered to drive her to therapy, but she explained that Missy's office was actually a block away on Concord Avenue.

The location wasn't the coincidence it might seem. My stretch of Concord Avenue had an alarming number of buildings that appeared from the outside to be ordinary single-family and multi-family houses but were, in reality, psychotherapy office buildings. The discrepancy between appearance and reality struck me as underhanded and deceptive. I mean, if you were naively to start out at the corner of Concord Avenue and Huron and innocently walk a few blocks toward Appleton, you'd pass by house after house — hah! — that tried to pass itself off as the wholesome Cantabrigian abode of graduate students, Harvard faculty, families with children, and so forth, but was actually teeming with psychiatrists, psychologists, clinical social workers, and other practitioners who, instead of devoting themselves to writing dissertations, preparing lectures, and pursuing domesticity, were delving into the dark and impulse-ridden depths of the human psyche. Fact: those few blocks of Concord Avenue, from Huron to Appleton, contained fifty-four psychotherapy offices. Fifty-four! I didn't count them. Rita did — before she rented her new office, which was, I hesitate to say, in the very heart of those shrink-infested waters. So, the presence of Caprice's therapist, Missy Zinn, there in my own neighborhood was no coincidence. I have, by the way, a religious theory (*goD* spelled backward) about why psychotherapists have been drawn to the area near my house. It is my belief that the powerful, healing presence of my very own woofy, furry incarnations of the healing spirit, my beloved Creatures Great, acted like magnets in attracting human beings who charge money

142

to apply the mental balm that dogs freely and joyously give away all the time.

Anyway, once Caprice had left to see one of the fifty-four surrogate dogs, I tried to reach Kevin Dennehy. If, as Ted had told me, the police were conducting a full investigation of Eumie's death, Caprice was bound to be questioned again, and I wanted Kevin himself to do the interrogation. Having managed only to leave messages for him, I went next door to see Kevin's mother, who had more influence with him than I did. Kevin was fond of describing his mother as a religious fanatic, by which he meant that she had left Roman Catholicism for Seventh-Day Adventism and consequently wouldn't allow meat or alcohol in her house. In reality, I'm the religious fanatic, but the tenets of Canine Cosmology permit me to give refrigerator space to other people's meat and beer, and the provision of storage space was the original basis of my friendship with Kevin. It was also the origin of Mrs. Dennehy's prejudice against me, a bias that she abandoned when Kevin started dating Jennifer and I married Steve. In brief, Mrs. Dennehy, who dislikes Jennifer more than she used to dislike me, adores Steve, whose deep kindness she senses and respects and whom she views as a buffer between her son and my refrigerator. Kevin still keeps hamburger and Bud here, but he hesitates to drop in as often as he used to, and, in any case, his mother would rather have him eat meat and drink beer than breathe in the vicinity of Jennifer Pasquarelli.

Although Mrs. Dennehy had softened toward me, her appearance remained as severe as ever. In particular, her hair was pulled so tightly into a knot on her head that she must have had a permanent headache. When she opened the back door, I could see that she was busy. A vacuum cleaner sat on the linoleum, and by the sink were a bucket and mop.

"I'm sorry to interrupt you," I said, "but I need a favor."

Mrs. Dennehy tried to supply me with a cup of herbal tea, which I managed to weasel out of accepting. Still, at her insistence, I took a seat at her kitchen table and outlined my concerns about Caprice. "This was her mother who died," I said, "and I want Kevin to be the one who talks to her. He questioned her yesterday, just after the mother's body was found, but someone is going to want to talk to her again, and it really should be Kevin. Not that someone else would be brutal. But this young woman is very vulnerable."

" 'Suffer the little ones,' " said Mrs. Dennehy.

My face must have reddened. "Actually, that's part of the problem. Caprice is horribly overweight. I'm sure it's a response to the problems in her family." My manipulation was worthy of a malamute: Seventh-Day Adventism places a high value on health and on family life.

"The poor girl," Mrs. Dennehy said. "I'll have a little word with Kevin. Love thy neighbor. He's a good boy. He understands that."

"I've left messages for him," I said.

"He's being driven crazy! By these psychiatrists." She stretched out the word and put a heavy accent on the first syllable: *PSY-chi-uh-trists.*

"I've met them. They are a little . . . trying."

Two minutes after I returned home, the United States Postal Service thrilled and then disappointed the dogs, who were convinced that every package we received contained toys and treats and was thus theirs and not ours at all. The delivery wasn't a package. It was an overnight Express envelope, inside which was a second envelope, much smaller than the first, thick and cream-colored, with my name written on it in blue ink. Inside was a note in the same ink on matching paper. I recognized the handwriting and hence took offense at the most conventional of greetings, namely, *Dear Holly. Dear!* How dare that fiend call me *dear?* I read on. *I am very sorry for any harm I have caused, and I am willing to make amends even though I cannot think of a way to do it.*

Well, then, why mention it?

The note was, of course, signed *Anita Fairley.*

I was furious. *Make amends?* As if she'd broken a teacup and were willing to replace it but couldn't find one in the right pattern. I immediately acted on the agreement Steve and I had that either of us would let the other know if we heard from the Fiend. I caught him between patients. He had received an almost identical note. He told me to ignore the whole business. I couldn't. Consequently, I called the other person who seemed a likely recipient of one of these missives, my stepmother, Gabrielle, whom Anita had helped to defraud of a large amount of money.

Gabrielle, too, had received a note. "Something is up with her," she said in that warm, sultry voice of hers. "This nonsense isn't something Anita would ever have come up with her own. In fact, I'd bet anything that someone has put her up to it."

"Who?"

"Do you suppose she's become alcoholic? I don't remember that Anita ever drank, did she? Not to the point of alcoholism. But this business of apologies and amends is very AA."

"Yes, it is, now that you mention it."

"Maybe it's some other kind of recovery program. There are twelve-step programs for everything."

"Being a vile human being?"

"For all we know, yes. But whatever it is, Anita obviously hasn't committed herself wholeheartedly to the steps."

"The hypocrite! That business about amends made me want to throw up."

"She's obviously insincere," Gabrielle said temperately. "As usual. Making amends to you and Steve would be difficult of course. But to me? If she'd really wanted to make amends to me, it would've been easy. She'd have enclosed a check."

CHAPTER 14

I have an image of Johanna Green, Ted's ex-wife and Wyeth's mother, as she examines her face in what is all too accurately known as a *fright mirror.* The magnification confirms her sense that her lower lashes do an inadequate job of hiding the tiny scars from her eye job. Furthermore, in the four years since her last major cosmetic surgery, gravity has been at work. Jowls!

After resolving to recommit herself to aesthetic dermatology and cosmetic surgery, Johanna turns to her professional work, which at the moment consists of feminist linguistic research on grammatical gender in Hebrew, Verdurian, and various other languages in which verbs as well as nouns are masculine, feminine, or, in some instances, neuter.

Under Rita's influence, I am forced to wonder about the emotional meaning of Johanna's choice of topic. Does she find it nervy and greedy of languages to extend masculinity and femininity beyond the province of the noun to the vast territory of the verb? Or maybe the hidden source of Johanna's scholarly pursuit lies in her feelings about her ex-husband, Ted Green, who is forever saying that he wishes he knew Hebrew but has never bothered to learn its rudiments or to visit Israel. Or if she thinks about Ted, perhaps it is with regard to the third category of nouns and verbs, the neither feminine nor masculine group, the desexed or sexless one, so to speak: *neuter.*

CHAPTER 15

As soon as Caprice returned from her therapy appointment, she went upstairs to take a nap. Without Lady. Or any of the other dogs. I decided that her therapy hour had been a waste of time. Rita would've disagreed about the specifics, but she'd have agreed with the general proposition that if therapy doesn't teach you to give and accept love, what good is it?

While Caprice was napping, I took a break from work to check my e-mail and simultaneously to visit my cat, Tracker, who inhabits my study, in which I almost never write, never mind study. Tracker is mine because no one else wanted her. She has a torn ear, a birthmark on her nose, and, worse, a tendency to hiss at everyone but Steve and to scratch everyone but him, too. My efforts to teach Rowdy and Kimi to accept her had been less than the sort of success that would have made for a great article in *Dog's Life:*

"Malamute Lions Lie Down with Feline Lamb." Rowdy and Kimi were far calmer in Tracker's presence than they'd once been, but I still didn't trust them. Consequently, when they were loose, she was not. My study did offer her as much stimulation as one room could provide, including a tall cat tree and a myriad of toys, and she sometimes had the privilege of sleeping in our bedroom on Steve's pillow. Even so, I felt guilty about her and made a point of socializing with her, or trying, whenever I used my desktop computer.

Unfortunately, Tracker took the word *mouse* literally. She was asleep on it when I entered the room, and when my presence awakened her, she glared at me and hissed. When I finally got to sit at my own desk, I found my usual thousand e-mail messages from my malamute lists and dog writers' lists and an invitation from Ted Green to attend Eumie's memorial service at eight o'clock the following evening at his house. His message included this passage:

Eumie's mortal remains will not be available, but she is still and will always be very much with me in all possible senses and will be present in spirit at this gathering as we celebrate her life and especially her loving relationships with all of you. Each of you was very, very special to Eumie. Although her background was Protestant, her true religion was the nurturance of caring relationships. Consequently, I hope that each of you will speak to all of us and to Eumie herself about the memories of her that you cherish most and the lessons you learned from her.

I had met Eumie only twice — postmortem didn't count — and knew from experience in personal invitations to funerals that I was being invited only in case Dolfo acted up. If he did, I could be counted on to settle him down. My memories of Eumie weren't exactly cherished, so I had no intention of speaking about them, and, as for lessons she'd taught me, what could I possibly say? *Never buy a dog on the Internet?* I hadn't learned that one from Eumie. I'd known it for a long time. Still, although Thursday evenings were usually sacred to the training of the Sacred Animal, I e-mailed back an acceptance. Caprice would have to attend, and she couldn't be allowed to go unprotected.

Leah, who'd been up early, returned from work at five o'clock. Her face bare of makeup, her red-gold hair tumbling from a ponytail, she looked healthy and beautiful and was bubbling with exciting news about hyperthyroid cats, hypothyroid dogs, and two healthy ferrets who'd been at the clinic for routine exams but were nonetheless noteworthy because of their charm. Leah changed out of her green scrubs and into shorts and a T-shirt, and left to take Kimi for a run. Caprice was evidently still in bed. The contrast between her lethargy and Leah's energy was worrisome. If sleep was Caprice's means of handling loss and stress, it was preferable, I thought, to overeating and to a great many other possible coping mechanisms. Did she always go to bed early, sleep late, and nap for most of the afternoon? Or was the pattern a response to her mother's unnatural death? I had no idea. Did she have a chronic illness? Or, as I'd wondered earlier, could she be drugging herself into oblivion? I'd ask Rita, who was going to have dinner with us. Steve's clinic was open until nine on Wednesday evenings, so I'd be cooking for only four people. If it hadn't been for Caprice, we'd probably have had nature's most perfect food, pizza, but I couldn't bring myself to serve Caprice something so high in calories. On the other hand, tonight's vegetable would not be green beans, squash, or any other dog-weight-loss staple, either, even though Rita kept herself on a permanent diet. As I was about to leave for our local whole-foods market, Loaves and Fishes, Caprice made her way downstairs.

"I'm running out to get food for dinner. I thought we'd have a big salad with shrimp, if that's okay."

"Anything is fine," she said. "I think I might take another shower, if that's all right. It might help me wake up. And I need to check my e-mail."

"Whatever you want. Leah has gone running, so she'll want a shower, too, but she can use the bathroom on the first floor. If you want to use your notebook, there are a lot of phone jacks. Help yourself. Or you're welcome to use my computer, but it's in my study, which is where my cat, Tracker, lives, so please be careful not to let her out." I explained about Rowdy and Kimi, showed her where my study was, and warned her about Tracker's sour disposition and tendency toward aggression. "And our friend Rita will be here for dinner. She lives on the third floor. I'll be back in no time." I paused. "And you should know that Ted is planning a memorial service for tomorrow evening. Eight o'clock."

Caprice made a face. "I don't believe in death parties. And at eight o'clock? I'll tell you what he's doing. He's trying to drum up business for himself. Referrals."

"You don't have to go."

"I do."

"For what it's worth, I said I'd go. We can go together."

"Thank you."

I left for Loaves and Fishes, did the shopping, and returned to find that Leah and Caprice weren't going to be home for dinner after all. A friend of Leah's who was staying in Cambridge for the summer had called for help in moving to an apartment, and Leah had not only volunteered but was taking Caprice along. Pizza was part of the deal. Out of Caprice's hearing, I protested: "Caprice is in mourning."

But Leah said, "What do you want her to do? Hang around with you and Rita? Stay in her room? She needs to get out. It'll be good for her."

In fact, the prospect of doing anything seemed to energize Caprice, who helped Leah to move the crates out of my car, which Leah was borrowing to help with the move. Soon after Leah and Caprice left,

155

Rita showed up. I had just finished emptying the refrigerator, freezer, and cupboards of ice cream, cookies, chocolate, and other horror foods that I didn't want Caprice to know I was purging. I supplied Rita with a gin and tonic and myself with a glass of Australian Shiraz, and worked on the salad. Rita sat at the kitchen table with her feet propped up on a chair. She'd even taken off her bone-colored pumps. She wore a linen outfit in a shade of rose that brightened her cheeks. At my request, she was reading the note from Anita.

"Gabrielle got one, too," I said. "She thinks that the apology and the stuff about amends means that Anita is in some twelve-step program."

"A good guess. Or maybe she's in therapy. It does read as if someone told her to write it."

"I just can't imagine what she's supposed to be recovering from."

"It could be anything. The recovery movement covers a lot of ground. I think you should forget all about the note."

"Speaking of recovery," I said, "I could use some advice about Caprice." Rita already knew that Caprice was staying with us. I'd filled her in when we'd arranged dinner.

Rita sipped her drink. "Ethical considerations have arisen," she said. "I really can't say much about that family."

"No one has mentioned you," I said. "Caprice's therapist is Missy Zinn. You said she's good. Eumie told me the names of a lot of others. Ted has mentioned some. They were seeing Vee Foote, and she's seeing Ted now. It's exactly like her to do *couples* therapy with *one* person."

"He may need . . . why am I defending her? With someone else, there might be a good reason to see the surviving spouse, but knowing Vee, she'll probably keep on seeing him for years if he's willing to pay. Anyway, the reason is that I've just started supervising a young psychologist, Peter York, who's connected to the case, and this is a new patient of Peter's. I'm far from sure that I'm the best supervisor for Peter. He's more interested in families than in individuals."

I set the kitchen table, put the salad bowl on it, told Rita to help herself, and then resumed my badgering. "Rita, you aren't Caprice's therapist, so you have to listen. Her mother has just died. Either she committed suicide or she was murdered. The police are investigating her death. And even when Eumie was alive, Caprice was in trouble. She is horribly overweight. She's so overweight that her face is disfigured. If she were thirty, okay, then it would be her choice and so on, but it's simply a fact, whether we like it or not, that at her age, she cannot be obese and have any kind of half-decent social life. And she sleeps . . . it's normal for adolescents to sleep a lot. Leah used to, and she'll still sleep late sometimes, but this is different. It's not just how long Caprice sleeps, but when she wakes up, she seems drugged. Rita, look how Eumie died! And Ted and Eumie used to help themselves to each other's medications. For all I know, their medicine cabinets were open to the whole family, like refrigerators. What if . . . Rita, all I'm asking for is ordinary advice. There's nothing unethical about giving me that."

"Use your own judgment. Do what you're doing. She's seeing Missy. You are not her therapist. This is a good salad."

"Thank you. I've decided that salad is the new pizza. Almost. For women, anyway. Steve considers it a side dish."

I was interrupted by Kevin Dennehy's signature rapping on the back door. When he'd greeted both of us, I set a third place at the table and asked whether he wanted a beer. For once, he refused, but he did take a seat.

"Women and vegetables," he said, eyeing the salad I'd put on his plate.

"You're welcome," I said. "And you're welcome to pick out the shrimp and just eat those. And you have some hot dogs in the refrigerator, and there's some of your hamburger left, too, but it's turning strange colors."

"That's mold," Kevin said. "Excellent source of penicillin."

"Are you feeling sick?" I asked.

"In the head." Smiling at Rita, he added, "Not you, Rita, you're an exception, but I've got this theory about your profession. All it takes is one of you. And that one drives someone crazy. And then the victim goes to another one of you. And that one gets driven crazy and has to see another one. And so on. Like rabbits. Two of them are all cute and fluffy, and then a month later, it's thousands. Except with rabbits, you gotta start with two. With shrinks, all you need is one, and before you know it, there they are, all getting their heads examined, all stark raving mad."

Pointing to the lettuce on Kevin's plate, Rita said, "It's possible that the rabbit food is affecting your brain, Kevin. Maybe you should have some of that penicillin after all."

"Dogs," Kevin said. "You're not off the hook, Holly."

"Dolfo," I said, "is not my dog."

"Peed all over the scene. And did the first officer on the scene, O'Brien, remove him? And protect the scene? He did not. And did he permit Dr. Green, who was having quote-unquote an anxiety attack, to raid the bathroom and help himself out of the same medicine cabinets that should've been sealed up? He did. Is O'Brien an idiot? He is."

"Well," I said, "at least he's one of yours and not a shrink or a dog. Kevin, I am sorry. Your mother said you were being driven crazy by psychiatrists. I didn't realize it was this bad."

"And then there's my mother. And you."

I rounded up most of the shrimp that remained in the salad bowl and put them on Kevin's plate. "Protein may help," I said.

"Not according to Jennifer."

"Well," said Rita, "the theme for today is that the world is lined up on two opposing teams. One team consists of Kevin. The other consists of everyone else."

"You got it," Kevin agreed. "And guess who's winning." He paused to eat. When he'd swallowed, he asked, "Caprice Brainard is staying here?"

"Yes," I said. "That's why I left all those messages for you. But she isn't here right now. She and Leah have gone out."

Turning to Rita, Kevin said, "And you're in on this, too, aren't you."

"Indirectly," Rita conceded.

"The memorial service," I said, "is tomorrow."

"First I've heard," said Kevin. "The body hasn't been released."

"That's okay. It's not a funeral. It's a memorial service. No body required. We're supposed to share memories. And lessons Eumie taught us."

"Yeah. Don't get your head shrunk."

Sherlock Holmes fan that I am, I said, "As you value your life and reason, stay away from the shrinks. That's from *The Hound of the Baskervilles.* More or less."

"Enough, both of you!" Rita was genuinely put out.

"We don't mean you," I said.

"Do I make hostile jokes about cops and dog trainers?"

"There aren't any," I said, "or maybe you would."

"What's happening here," Rita announced, "is that the toxic environment of this horrible event is affecting all three of

161

us. Harry Stack Sullivan had what's really a contagion theory of emotion. He said —"

"Something about mothers," Kevin finished. "That's what they all say."

"Actually," said Rita, "now that you mention it, he was talking about mothers. 'Anxiety in the mother induces anxiety in the infant.' "

"Thus Caprice," I said. "Maternal overdependence on prescription medication induces —"

Kevin suddenly turned serious. "It's a homicide, you know. It's a homicide. Nobody could've taken that much by accident, and this crap in the refrigerator was loaded with it. You know stuff comes in liquid form? It was mixed with all this soy stuff and vegetable juice that no one else drank but her. It's gawdawful is what it is. I've been a cop a long time, and I've seen a wicked lot of drugs, but I gotta tell you, even after Dr. Green had been in that bathroom, there was so much there that I . . . it was . . . honest to God, it was like finding a meth lab on Avon Hill. It's a wonder there's anyone in that house still left alive."

Kevin likes exactly the kinds of heavy, creamy desserts I'd tossed out. When I offered raspberry sorbet and fresh strawberries, he looked disappointed but accepted anyway. As I was scooping the sorbet and hulling the berries, a phrase he'd spoken kept ringing in my head: *still left alive.* Maybe what triggered the ringing was the sight of the bird feeders outside the window over the sink.

When I was again seated at the table, I said, "This probably has nothing to do with anything, but, speaking of substances, there's one really odd thing at Ted and Eumie's."

"Yeah," said Kevin. "Ted."

"Kevin, you were in the backyard. When you talked to Caprice. I don't know whether you noticed, but there are a lot of bird feeders there." I ate some sorbet and continued. "And no squirrels. And the feeders aren't damaged. Squirrels will wreck feeders. They chew wood, and they ruin plastic perches. Those feeders are not damaged. And they don't even have squirrel baffles."

Rita cast a professional eye at me. "Are you suggesting . . . ?"

"I'm not suggesting anything. It's just that when I told Steve that there weren't any squirrels there, he said it was impossible. And then he said something about . . . he said that it was impossible unless someone

163

had killed them. But I'm not sure he was serious."

"Steve," said Rita, "isn't given to jokes about cruelty to animals."

"Of course not," I said. "He just meant that it was impossible. But it isn't. There are no squirrels there. No gray squirrels, no black squirrels, no squirrel damage. Period. No squirrels at all."

"Got it," said Kevin.

"Got what?" Rita demanded.

"The point Holly's making is that the place is some kind of Love Canal. It's polluted with shrinks and drugs and dog urine. You gotta wonder why anyone's left alive."

CHAPTER 16

When Steve got home that night, he was unhappy to find that I'd thrown out all the ice cream, and the next morning, he was even more unhappy to discover that I'd also tossed out all the bread and English muffins.

"Why stop there?" he asked. "Why didn't you get rid of all the butter? The jam?"

"Because there's nothing to put them on," I said.

"All of sudden we're becoming vegans?"

"We are not becoming vegans. It isn't what we are becoming. It's what we're not becoming. And that's enablers. If we have fattening food in the house, that's enabling Caprice to eat food she shouldn't eat."

"What about the rest of us? Are we supposed to starve?"

"Fasting is au courant these days," I said. "You subsist for days at a time on water, lemon juice, maple syrup, and hot peppers.

165

Or maybe it's chili powder. It's supposed to cleanse your system."

"Are the dogs being subjected to this regimen, too? They —"

"Of course not. All I did was remove temptation, and dog food isn't exactly tempting. Except to dogs, of course. Look, Steve, it's temporary. And it won't hurt us. If we took in a stray dog, we'd do everything possible to meet the dog's needs. This is exactly the same principle."

Leah's response was identical to Steve's. They made do with scrambled eggs and fruit. When they'd left for work, I reluctantly awakened Caprice. As I'd told her the night before, Kevin was going to arrive at nine o'clock to talk with her. That's how I'd phrased it. The whole idea was that she wouldn't be *interrogated.* When I'd broken the news that her mother's death was being treated as a homicide, she hadn't quite come out and said, "I told you so." But she'd come close.

Today, instead of staggering into the kitchen in her nightclothes, she first took a shower and got dressed, and when she came downstairs, her eyes were clear and focused. Without asking, I served her the same breakfast that Leah and Steve had had. As usual, she drank her coffee black. When Kevin rapped at the back door, she was still at the kitchen table.

"Hi, Lieutenant Dennehy," she said. "I'm glad it's you."

"You make it sound like I'm gonna take out your appendix," Kevin said.

Caprice looked astonished. After a second, she laughed.

Kevin informs me that modern guidelines for interrogation emphasize the importance of making the witness comfortable. In Kevin's view, the authorities in the field have now acknowledged what he knew all along, namely, as he phrases it, that nervous people clam up. So, confident that I was contributing to the relaxed atmosphere advocated by law enforcement experts, I dug out the Dunkin' Donuts coffee that Kevin likes, made him a cup, and served it with milk and sugar. The cream and the half-and-half had gone down the drain. As I was fixing coffee, Caprice asked Kevin whether he wanted to tape the interview.

"I got a whatchamacallit, audiographic memory." The smile on his big freckled face made it hard to tell whether he was or wasn't lying. "But thanks for asking. Holly, you out of cream?"

"Yes," I said flatly. Then, having refilled

my own cup, I took a seat at the table.

"You out of dogs, too?"

"Me? Never."

"Where are they? Or maybe Caprice is kind of fed up with them."

Caprice protested. "No! I like them."

"Leah and Steve took India and Sammy with them," I said. "Rowdy and Kimi are in the yard. Lady is around somewhere."

"On my bed, I think," Caprice reported. "She was the last time I saw her."

Our dogs are not allowed on beds unless they are explicitly invited. Unfortunately, they are astute about guessing who will or will not enforce the rule.

"Hey, good going," said Kevin. "It's not everybody she trusts like that."

Nonsense. How much trust does it take to sleep on someone's bed? Besides, what Lady mistrusted was life itself and not particular individuals. Exception: Anita. Lady was frightened of Anita — for good reason.

"Trauma history there," Kevin remarked. "You think so?"

It was a matter that Steve and I had discussed at length. Although environment had undoubtedly played a role in Lady's fearfulness, both of us thought that it had a strong genetic component as well.

"Have you been reading Ted's book?"

Caprice asked.

"No. Just listening to him."

"Have you talked to Johanna yet?"

"That'd be Johanna Green. The ex-wife."

"Ted divorced Johanna to marry my mother. Johanna was insulted. She still is. She hated my mother. She believes everything Baby Boy Wyeth tells her."

"Your stepbrother."

"My mother's husband's son. That doesn't make him *my* anything." Her face was expressionless. "We're not done with Johanna yet. One thing you might notice about her is that she kept Ted's name. Johanna Green."

"Some women do."

"Johanna is a feminist linguist. Supposedly. And she took her husband's name to begin with and then kept it after the divorce?"

"Your father."

It was as if Caprice became a new person. Her eyes brightened, and her face shone. "He didn't change his name. Before or after."

Kevin smiled. "How'd he react to the divorce?"

Caprice bought time by taking a sip of what must have been cold coffee. "Pragmatically," she finally said. "You see, Eumie was in therapy with Ted. While she and my father were still married, she went into therapy with Ted. And if you listen to them, they fell madly in love."

"And if you don't listen to them?"

"Ted slept with his patient. What else? Horrors! He violated the *taboo*." Her emphasis was heavy and cynical. "But they both tried to cover it up, of course. They pretended that she'd just been in supervision with him, but everyone knew that was bullshit. That's basically why we had to leave."

"And your father?"

"Are you planning a new career?"

"Hey, not me. It's mothers they ask about, anyway."

"Corny therapist joke. Definition of a Freudian slip. That's when you mean to say one thing and instead you say *a mother.* So, my father. Monty took it pretty well. He's mellow. He takes most things pretty well." With no prompting, she added, "He lives in Manhattan, but he travels a lot. He's a consultant. Otherwise, I'd've stayed with him."

"He was here this past weekend."

"Yes. At the Charles Hotel. That's where

he always stays. I had brunch with him on Monday. At the Charles. At Henrietta's Table."

"Did he and your mother see each other? This past weekend?"

"Not that I know of."

"Did he pick you up? Drop you off?"

"No. I took a cab there and a cab home."

"How about Ted and your mother? On Monday."

"They both saw a few patients."

"On Memorial Day?"

Caprice shrugged. "They did that. Saw people on holidays sometimes. And Monday night, they went out to dinner. To Rialto. That's at the Charles, too. That's why it's open on Mondays, because it's in a hotel. I guess they could've run into Monty there. You go through the lobby to get to Rialto. You'd have to ask Monty."

"Did Wyeth go with them?"

"No. He was at his computer. He didn't go out. He never does, except when he goes to Johanna's."

"Did they meet someone at the restaurant? Another couple, maybe?"

"I don't know. I don't think so. If they were going with other people, they didn't mention it."

"What time did they get home?"

"I don't know. I was in bed."

"Where was the dog all this time?"

"Eating mail. Chewing on books. Wrecking things. Where he wasn't was in my room." She paused. "I took him out to the yard before I went to bed. That was at maybe eight o'clock."

"Was the house locked?"

"My bedroom door was. The house probably wasn't. I told you when we talked before. Besides, half the world had keys."

"There's an alarm system."

"Dolfo jumps on things. Doors. Windows. He kept setting it off, so they quit using it."

Although Caprice was showing no signs of strain, I created a break by asking whether anyone wanted more coffee. Kevin and Caprice both accepted.

"The, uh, prescription bottles," Kevin said, "have the names of a lot of doctors. Maybe you could give me a sort of who's who."

Caprice gave a quirky smile. "It's a cast of thousands."

"Just the M.D.s. The ones who wrote prescriptions."

"Let's see. My mother had an internist. I forget her name. Salzman, maybe. Dr. Salzman. And a dermatologist. A man. I don't know his name. Her gynecologist. Dr. Cohen. Her therapist, Nixie Needleman. She's a psychiatrist. M.D. And her psychopharm guy, Dr. Youngman. He's Ted's, too. Ted's therapist is Dr. Tortorello. He's a psychiatrist, so he probably prescribes. Ted must have a primary-care physician, but I don't know who that is. Maybe he sees Dr. Salzman, too. And their couples therapist is Dr. Foote. Psychiatrist. I don't know whether she wrote prescriptions for them, but she could have. Wyeth supposedly goes to a pediatrician, which he hates, but mostly he pretends to go and doesn't actually see the doctor. His therapist is new. Dr. York. But he's a psychologist. A few of them can prescribe, but I don't know if this one does. My therapist is a Ph.D. She doesn't prescribe. I don't exactly have a primary. I just go to the University Health Services." She went on to name three dentists and her mother's endodontist. "She had a root canal last winter. He could've given her painkillers then. That's all I can think of. Unless you count my mother's herbalist."

"Is that the houseplant lady?"

"Oh, her. No. She's a houseplant tutor, to teach my mother to grow plants. Just for decoration. The herbalist prescribes medicinal herbs, not prescription drugs. My mother took a lot of supplements, too. She got most of them from Loaves and Fishes, not from a practitioner. Oh, I forgot the homeopath. But she wasn't seeing him anymore, anyway."

Kevin looked pale and wide-eyed. I felt sure that until he'd landed in the hospital with a bullet wound and had required a surgeon, he'd had a doctor and a dentist. And that had been it. "Did any of these, uh, practitioners talk to the others? Coordinate?"

"Probably not. Well, the psychopharm guy, Dr. Youngman, might talk to the individual therapists, I think. But otherwise . . . ? I don't think so."

"So, one hand didn't know what the other hand was doing. Hands. So, it was more like those Hindu goddesses, you know? Like what's her name, Colleen there, the lady with ten arms."

"Kali," Caprice said.

"Her. And all the hands got no idea about the prescriptions the others are writing."

"Precisely," said Caprice. "The perfect image."

"I got one last question, and you don't have to answer it if you don't want."

"Okay. If I don't want to answer it, I won't."

"Trauma. I keep hearing about your

mother's trauma history. You want to say anything about that?"

"It's no secret," said Caprice. "Ted wrote about it in his book. He didn't use my mother's real name, but it's her story. Her father was an undertaker. When her mother died, he did the embalming. Her father embalmed her mother. He embalmed his own wife. Or that's the story Ted tells, anyway."

CHAPTER 17

On the afternoon of Thursday, June 2, the day of her mother's memorial service, Caprice Brainard goes to the house on Avon Hill that she prefers not to think of as home. She has chosen the time because Ted has told her that this is when he'll be taking Wyeth out to buy something appropriate to wear to Eumie's service. Dolfo is next door at George and Barbara's. The only people in the house are six employees of a cleaning service that has accepted the job because it has never before been hired to clean this dog-dirtied abode. Caprice's previous departure was hurried; she had time only to grab her notebook computer and throw a few essentials into her backpack and a suitcase. This time she fills two suitcases, which she carries downstairs and out to the street, where I help her to load them into my car. When we reach Steve's and my house, where she is our guest, I drop her off and leave to run errands.

Alone in the house, Caprice goes to my study to take advantage of my invitation to use my desktop computer. Obeying the house rules, she is careful to shut the door so that Tracker does not escape. Startled at the entry of a stranger, Tracker leaps off the mouse pad and vanishes. Caprice seats herself at the computer in the hope that I have stored my password and that she will thus be able to read my e-mail without having to bother trying the guesses from her mental list of likely bets: *Rowdy, Kimi, Sammy, malamute, 256Concord, DogsLife,* our phone number, my license plate number, and so forth, all of which, I might add, would have been wrong. As it turns out, my password is stored, so she doesn't have to guess at all.

The rules of Netiquette, I might mention, typically concern the form, content, and tone of the messages the sender composes. If you WRITE EVERYTHING IN CAPITAL LETTERS, the message will look as if you're SHOUTING. In posts to e-mail lists, avoid obscenities and personal attacks. Remember that e-mail doesn't convey tone of voice, so if you don't want comments made in jest to be taken seriously, put in a smiley face or say that you are just kidding. Why do the rules fail to lay down as law the taboo that Caprice is now violating? Because they shouldn't have to, that's why. The rules of civilized conduct were written a long time ago, and it doesn't take a Harvard education to figure out that if you're a guest in someone's house, you're damned well not supposed to take advantage of her absence to read her e-mail.

Fair is, however, fair. As payback for her act of ungrateful snooping, Caprice sees before her on the screen of my computer about ten gazillion messages devoted to one single subject, the subject being, of course, dogs, dogs, and more dogs. Pack animal that I am, I subscribe to the list for members of the Cambridge Dog Training Club, to lists about Alaskan malamutes, and to lists for dog writers and dog trainers. Since all the other subscribers are pack animals, too, and are therefore given to frequent woofing and wooing and yapping, the lists are very active, and Caprice has the chance to read message after message that has nothing to do with me and can be of no interest to her. Indeed, she doesn't even bother to read the list mail. She does, however, come upon a piece of personal e-mail that she opens and reads.

Subject: Cartoonbank.com E-card from Steve
From: SDelaney@hightailit.com
To: HollyWinter@amrone.org

You've just been sent an E-card from Steve, care of Cartoonbank.com, the Internet's premier cartoon Web site and source for *New Yorker* cartoons.

There follows a hyperlink that takes Caprice to an E-card meant only for me. It shows a Booth cartoon from the *New Yorker* depicting a man seated at a typewriter in the midst of scruffy, disoriented-looking canines. The caption, spoken by the lady of the house is, "Write about dogs." To the right of the cartoon is what E-card sites always call the "personalized greeting." This one reads: "Dear Holly, I love you. From Steve."

When Caprice finishes with my e-mail, she carefully marks the Cartoonbank message as unread. She would have been welcome to read messages from the lists to which I subscribe. But Steve's message is personal. It is private. Or it should have been. Steve and I make a little game of sending each other *New Yorker* dog cartoon E-cards with love notes. We order the same cartoons on T-shirts when we want presents for each other. We are united by dogs and laughter and love. And our union is none of Caprice's business.

CHAPTER 18

At five-thirty on Thursday afternoon, Monty Brainard called Caprice on her cell phone to say that he was flying in from New York for Eumie's memorial service. Leah and I were with her in the kitchen when she got the call, which was brief.

"You don't have to," she said. "I mean —" After listening, she said, "It's okay. Really. It's fine. Don't worry about it. I'll see you there. I love you." And then, "Bye."

"My father's coming," she announced with a smile of relief. "Holly, you really don't have to go. I won't be there alone."

"We're both going," Leah said.

"Please! Leah, it'll be gross. Please don't. Ted will pretend she's there in spirit. He'll speak to her."

"I can handle that," Leah said.

"It would be embarrassing to have you hear it. *Please.*"

Leah conceded. In case Caprice tried to

discourage me, too, I shifted the conversation to another topic. "We need to get organized. Caprice, you have your appointment with Dr. Zinn at six, don't you? Steve will be home any minute, and he'll be going to dog training. Leah, are you going with him?"

"I'll take Kimi. For rally."

"I got takeout from Loaves and Fishes. Roast chicken, eggplant, asparagus, some other stuff." I didn't mention the green bean salad, which I'd chosen out of habit and should probably have fed to the dogs once its significance dawned on me. What stopped me, I suppose, was the knowledge that greens beans really were an excellent weight-loss food. "We'll all have to forage. Rowdy, Kimi, and Lady have been fed, and Steve can feed Sammy and India when he gets home with them. I'll need to get ready for the service." I have an old-fashioned streak. In Cambridge, you can wear anything to anything, but when I go to anything even remotely like a funeral, what I wear is a dark dress.

An unsettling little event had made me suddenly eager to pay my respects. About forty-five minutes earlier, when I'd been checking my e-mail, I'd been interrupted by the delivery of a small package from a company I'd never heard of. My work for *Dog's Life* sometimes included product evaluations, and now and then an enterprising company would send samples directly to me, usually with a note expressing the optimistic certainty that my dogs and I would be so enthusiastic about the items that I'd recommend them in my column. Shamelessly lacking in even the most rudimentary sense of journalistic integrity, the dogs would have had me write a rave review of every edible bribe I was offered, but I stuck to my ethics. My product reviews were fair, and when I recommended toys, equipment, and treats in my column, it was never because I'd been bought off. For example, I bought the Buster Cube myself; my fabulous Chris Christensen 27mm pin brush with the T handle was a present from my stepmother, Gabrielle; and as to the Bil-Jac treats, for which I regularly shopped, the dogs loved the liver, peanut butter, and pizza flavors, and I liked being able to break the soft morsels into little pieces when I trained. Anyway, this package was too small to contain anything for the dogs and, in fact, turned out to hold a CD titled *Guided Imagery for Performance Anxiety.* My dogs weren't the ones with ring nerves; the CD was meant exclusively for me. The gift receipt in the package included this note: *I will help you to do your own personal version, but this will get you started. Gratefully, Eumie.* Although the notion of a message from beyond the grave was a bit gothic for me, I still found it unsettling to realize that Eumie had taken an active step to help cure me of ring nerves. When she'd said she could help, she had not been making a vague promise, on the contrary, as soon as she'd heard of my problem, she'd ordered the CD. If she'd lived, I now saw, she'd have followed through. I had no intention of thanking her aloud at the memorial service, but I did want to attend.

That was before we got there. Once we did, I realized that Caprice had been right: Ted Green was throwing a death party. What's more, he must have invited everyone he and Eumie had ever known. The closest parking place I found was three blocks away, and by the time I snagged it, I was wishing we'd left the car at home and gone on foot. All the lights in the big house were on, and the front door stood open. The porch was so crowded with people taking off their shoes that we had to wait to get in.

"Your mother had so many friends," I said softly to Caprice.

"Most of these people weren't her friends, and they aren't Ted's. Some of them are people he wants referrals from. A lot of them are people they both wanted to impress, mostly parents from Avon Hill. They're here out of curiosity." A second later, her cynicism vanished. "There's my father! Monty! Monty, I'm here!"

When I saw Monty Brainard, I realized that I'd been expecting him to have the human equivalent of the real Monty's malamute splendor. In reality, the only obvious resemblance between the false Monty, Monty Brainard, and the real Monty, Ch. Benchmark Captain Montague, was that both were muscular. Monty Brainard was a short, balding man with straight, medium-brown hair and small brown eyes. His only outstanding physical characteristic was a deep tan, probably natural, possibly chemical. He wore a conservative gray suit. Forcing his way through the crowd, he wrapped Caprice in his arms and said, "Daddy's here, baby girl."

Baby girl. Only when Monty Brainard spoke the phrase did I take a hard look at Caprice, who was swathed in a voluminous dress of pale lavender. Her pale blond curls were held back with little white barrettes. Baby girl, indeed. Daddy's plump baby girl.

"Holly, this is my father, Monty," Caprice said. "Daddy, this is Holly. She's the one I'm staying with, Holly and her husband. Holly is my friend Leah's cousin."

"I'm very grateful," Monty said as he shook my hand. His late ex-wife, I suspected, would've thrown her arms around me, gushed about her gratitude, and told me how special I was. By comparison, Monty's ordinary civility felt . . . I am tempted to say that it felt special. After all, if everything is special, what's left to be truly special? Ordinariness.

Caprice, her father, and I exchanged a few words. I said that Steve and I were happy to have Caprice stay with us. Monty said that he was going back to New York tomorrow after he'd taken Caprice out to lunch. Ted came rushing up to me, threw his arms around me, and told me how glad he was to see me. He wore a sage green linen suit with a shirt of what looked like unbleached, unironed muslin. "You were so special to Eumie," he said. Diverted by the arrival of yet more people, he hurriedly pointed toward the dining room, told all three of us to help ourselves to food, and moved away to greet the new visitors.

If I were entirely human instead of half malamute, I'd have been driven toward the dining room by my sensitivity to Caprice's desire to have time alone with her father. In fact, the driving force was my quest for food. The dining-room table and a long sideboard held an almost incredible spread that was being neglected by most of the other guests, who, I assumed, lived the kinds of unappetizing lives characteristic of people who fail to receive daily infusions of big, hungry dog DNA. The offerings were characteristic of Jewish rites of passages but combined the typical dishes of a big Jewish wedding with those of a big Jewish breakfast. Tremendous platters contained delectable arrangements of chicken, roast beef, and grilled vegetables. There were baskets of bagels, bialys, and black bread, bowls of cream cheese, plates of lox, tomatoes, and cukes, dishes of half-sour pickles, and two supersize green salads. My initial survey also identified noodle kugel, a gigantic poached salmon, and — oh, bliss! — blintzes, which are the Jewish version of crepes, thin pancakes filled with ambrosial cheese and served with sour cream and jam. To convey my appreciation of this display of gustatory generosity, I should mention that I come from a New England WASP background and have yet to shake the expectation that the so-called food offered to fifty or a hundred mourners will consist of one small plate of 1/2-by-1/2-inch brownies and another of 1/2-by-1/2-inch lemon squares accompanied by your choice of watery tea or see-through coffee.

Anyway, filling their plates were two people, one of whom I was surprised to recognize as Rita's psychopharmacologist date, Quinn Youngman. The other was a young woman with long, straight dark hair, Asian features, and a rather tall, athletic build. When I approached, Quinn was telling her that his choice of psychopharmacology had been a natural extension of his previous interest in drugs of all sorts, if she knew what he meant. After I'd interrupted, he introduced us, and that's how I met Missy Zinn, Caprice's therapist, whose plate held a bagel with cream cheese and lox, a chicken breast, and roasted eggplant. As I ate blintzes with sour cream and blueberry jam, we were joined by a lanky, sandy-haired guy who turned out to be an adult rather than the teenage boy I'd taken him for. In fact, he was Peter York, Wyeth's therapist. Fortunately, I didn't have to mention Wyeth. Instead, I said, "You're in supervision with Rita. She's a good friend of mine."

"And mine," said Quinn Youngman.

As we ate, we said flattering things about Rita. A pleasant-looking fortyish woman I'd never seen before overheard and misunderstood us. "Eumie was a dear friend to a lot of people," she said. "Eumie changed my life."

I didn't know what to say. *That's nice* would've felt hopelessly inadequate. Luckily, Ted spoke up to ask everyone to move into the living room and the family room. Brushing past me, he murmured, "Damn Johanna. I invited her, and I expected her to have the decency to turn up."

Following the crowd, I found that the wall between the two big rooms was actually a pair of sliding doors that had been opened to create a long, wide space that held folding chairs arranged in rows. At the front of the makeshift theater was a small table intended to serve as a podium. Or maybe the idea was a chapel with an altar. In any case, since the gathering had been described as a service, I expected family members to take seats in the first rows, with close friends occupying seats toward the front and with acquaintances and such toward the rear. Dog trainers presumably belonged in the last row. As I was settling myself there in the family room, Dolfo came galloping up to me with a piece of paper in his mouth.

"Where have you been?" I whispered. "And what do you have? Give! Trade!"

Like every other dog trainer in the world, I find that I automatically speak to all dogs as I do to my own and to other educated canines. There wasn't a chance in a trillion that Dolfo had been taught *give,* our household's formal obedience command for requesting a dumbbell, or *trade,* our everyday order to relinquish an object. The remarkable feature of foolish lapses like mine, however, is that evolution has bequeathed to the domestic dog an astonishing capacity to decode even the most seemingly incomprehensible messages of Homo sapiens. Dogs perform the miracle of penetrating the unfathomable by using all available cues: the direction of the human gaze, tone of voice, subtle movements of the body, slight changes in respiration, and, I suspect, minute variations in the scent we emit. So, in apparent response to words he didn't know, Dolfo handed over his treasure, which proved to be a page torn from an L.L.Bean catalog.

"Good boy," I whispered to Dolfo. "Did you want one of these Bean dog beds? Is that why you brought me this?"

"Talking to dogs," a male voice said. "A sure sign of sanity. Holly, good to see you." The speaker was George McBane, who was, in his own way, as Irish-looking as Kevin Dennehy. George had the same bright blue eyes and pale skin, but he had curly black hair shot with white, and he lacked Kevin's freckles. According to Rita, George McBane was so handsome that in shrink circles, he was called Gorgeous George — never, of course, to his face. With a hint of condescension, Rita said that he had a reputation for doing rapid, effective work with difficult patients. As far as I could tell, a lot of the most prestigious shrinks did what struck me as slow, ineffective work — ten years of nothing but insight in patients suffering from nothing worse than existential malaise — but what do I know? I'm a dog trainer. Canine self-understanding is never my primary goal.

"We'll sit with you," said Barbara. "And then George will behave himself."

Barbara was, if anything, more gorgeous than George. The phrase "person of color" actually fit her well. Her vividness made almost everyone else look washed-out and almost sickly.

"Please do sit with me," I said.

"Where we can escape," George muttered.

"You and I," Barbara told him quietly, "have agreed to say a few words about Eumie. Remember? Hi there, Dolfo. Are you being a good boy?" Barbara took the seat next to mine, and George sat beyond her. Dolfo did a silly, bouncy dance of welcome and would have ended up in their laps if Barbara and I hadn't stopped him. "He's a loveable idiot," she commented.

"I thought he was staying with you," I said.

"Just off and on."

"To the detriment of all our possessions," George said. "It's eight-thirty. Isn't this ever going to get going?"

As if in response, Ted stepped up to the little table at the front of the room, cleared his throat, and said, "I want to thank all of you for being here tonight. Each and every one of you was special to Eumie, who is here with us and is grateful for your presence."

Someone in back of me groaned softly. Turning my head, I saw Wyeth leaning against one of the glass doors. His groan had clearly not been one of agonized grief for his departed stepmother. He was making faces and shifting his weight from foot to foot. I was again struck by how extraordinarily flabby he was. In fact, he reminded me of a freshly opened oyster, pale and invertebrate.

"Our beloved Eumie," said Ted, "has, to quote the Bard, 'undergone a sea change into something rich and strange.' "

George McBane peered past Barbara to catch my eye, and when he did, I had the uncanny and unmistakable sense that he and I were suffering from the same dreadful thought, namely that Eumie had been rich before her death, although probably not so rich as she'd have liked, and, by most people's standards, more than a little strange. I could feel nervous laughter rising in my chest and was terrified of making a spectacle of myself. Fortunately, as so often happens, I was saved by a dog. Dolfo, who'd stationed himself in front of Barbara and me, squeezed past my knees and began to sniff and circle. I was all action. With Ted presiding over his wife's memorial service, there was no one to object to my restraining the dog, so, having stashed a few essential tools of my trade in the pockets of my dress, I leashed Dolfo, helped myself to a pair of sandals from a supply by the door, and unobtrusively led the dog out onto the deck and down the steps to the yard. The trip outdoors was justified. I had wanted somehow to express my gratitude to Eumie for the CD and for her desire to help me. No one's memorial service should be interrupted by canine bodily functions. My thanks were heartfelt, if peculiar and even grotesque. Still, I had offered posthumous dignity.

CHAPTER 19

In the manner of a public park, the Brainard-Greens' yard was equipped with a small covered trash can and a weatherproof metal box that dispensed doggie clean-up bags. Having availed myself of one of the bags, used it, and deposited it in the trash can, I walked Dolfo around for a few minutes. Probably because he'd been spending time next door with Barbara and George, his demeanor was calmer than usual, which is to say that he wasn't acting like a yo-yo at the end of the leash or trying to jump on me. Since Dolfo was for once in a highly trainable state, I couldn't resist taking him to the far end of the yard and working with him for a few minutes. I started by "charging the clicker," as it's called, clicking and immediately treating him to a tiny snack of liver as a reminder that the click meant that food was on the way. Then I used a bit of food to lure him into a sit, and I reinforced the behavior with a click and treat. We practiced for a few minutes. He didn't hold a sit for more than about five seconds, but I felt proud of him anyway.

When Dolfo and I got back inside, Ted was talking about Sylvia Plath. Like Plath, he said, Eumie was beautiful, sensitive, and gifted. Within my hearing, at least, he didn't refer explicitly to suicide, but he didn't need to; it was sufficient to mention Sylvia Plath at all. I half expected Caprice to stand up and protest, but she didn't, and Ted moved immediately to a new topic, which was the special role that each of us had played in Eumie's life. "Let's get started by going around the room and introducing ourselves and saying a few brief words about who we are in Eumie's life," he said. *A few brief words.* I hate that phrase. At best, it's redundant. But what irritates me is that it's misleading. What are brief words? Words that take less than a second to speak? Words under three syllables? But there's another phrase I hate even more. "In your own words," Ted said, "tell us about your role." I mean, whose words would we be likely to use? Wouldn't our own be the likely choice? Or was there some weird warning embedded in the phrase? *Don't quote T. S. Eliot or else!* Anyway, Ted assured us that we'd have time to speak at length after the introductions, and he got us started by saying, as everyone already knew, that he was Ted Green, Eumie's husband.

As a person who has attended hundreds or maybe thousands of classes, workshops, seminars, and other gatherings, I'm used to the initial ritual of having participants introduce themselves by saying their names and a few words — of any length — about themselves: *I'm Holly, this is Rowdy, and we're just getting started in rally obedience.* Those are my words, obviously. Rowdy's principal spoken word is the syllable *woo,* often melodiously repeated — *woo-woo-woo* — and thus, now that I think of it, laudably brief and his own, unless he filches it from other malamutes, many of whom do, I concede, say exactly the same thing. I am, however, used to relatively small groups, even when you count the dogs, as I certainly do, whereas there must have been eighty or a hundred people in this one. Fortunately, the introductions moved speedily along. Here in the People's Psychotherapeutic Republic of Cambridge, therapists had no hesitation about presenting themselves as such: *I'm Vee Foote, Ted and Eumie's couples therapist. Nixie Needleman, Eumie's therapist. Alex Tortorello, Ted's therapist.* Missy Zinn used the phrase "part of the team." Quinn Youngman said that he was "one of the helpers." Not everyone was a therapist. Patients of Eumie's presented themselves as such, as did some patients of Ted's. Some used the word *client.* Some were "seeing" Eumie or Ted. We heard from Eumie's personal shopper, her personal trainer, and her Reiki healer. Quite a few people were, as Caprice had told me, parents from the Avon Hill School. George McBane and Barbara Leibowitz described themselves as friends and neighbors. I just said that I helped with Dolfo. With the exception of Caprice, not a single person there was a blood relative of Eumie's, and the only relative of Ted's was his son, Wyeth, who was, in effect, excused from participation in the introductory ritual. When the boy's turn came, Ted spoke for him: "And Wyeth, of course. Eumie's beloved stepson, right, boy-chick?"

Now that the introductions were complete — it was twenty minutes after nine — Ted invited all of us to share our memories of

Eumie. "My Eumie," he said, "*mayn bash-erter,* my soul mate, is what we call a yenta, a busybody, in the best sense of the word. She meets somebody, anybody, she cares. She's got to know the person, got to know everything, understand everything. That's who she is. Bubee, we love you for it and . . ." When he'd finished going on at considerable length, he finally invited people to speak to and about Eumie.

The first person to accept the invitation was a frail young woman with a beatific smile who'd been Eumie's muscular therapist and who described the tension locked in Eumie's body and the progress she'd made in releasing herself from the bonds of her armor. But, she concluded, trauma had triumphed. A parent from the Avon Hill School talked about Eumie's love of children and her commitment to excellence. Another parent praised her generosity. George, who'd been grumbling almost inaudibly about having an eight o'clock patient the next morning and wanting to get to bed, took Barbara's hand and walked with her to the front of the room. Far from addressing Eumie, they spoke of her in the past tense, but their remarks were fond and, by my standards, appropriate to the occasion. They took turns talking about her love of life, her enthusiasm, and her curiosity. "Barbara and Eumie," George said, "shared a love of birds and the great gift of being able to see them through the eyes of a child. What Eumie saw weren't so much birds as magical creatures, delightful visions with feathers. She had the great good fortune not to take the magic for granted." Barbara spoke of Eumie's pleasure in giving presents. As it turned out, my experience was typical. She'd had a habit of sending flowers, food, books, music, and films only because she'd sensed what her friends would like and had wanted to offer happiness.

When Barbara and George had finished, they made their way to the back of the room and slipped out through one of the glass doors to the deck. Although someone else had stepped forward and had begun to eulogize Eumie, I followed Barbara and George outside and caught up with them as they were about to go through a gate in the fence that separated their yard and the Brainard-Greens'. Dolfo was, of course, with me. When we reached Barbara and George, he wiggled all over and then cuddled up to Barbara, who stroked his side.

"I just wanted to tell both of you that that

was lovely," I said. "This gift giving was a part of Eumie that I didn't know at all. Until today. She'd ordered something for me that was delivered this afternoon."

"Eumie had many good qualities," Barbara said.

After Barbara and George had wished me good night, I took a few minutes to do a little more work with Dolfo on his sit. This time, I began to cue the behavior ("Dolfo, sit!" plus a signal with my left hand), and Dolfo succeeded in staying for eight seconds. When we got back inside, a woman was testifying to Eumie's commitment to helping her patients overcome the effects of trauma. As the woman spoke, she began to choke up and then to sob. In horrible pain, she eventually cried, "How could she have abandoned me? How could she?"

Three people hurried to the heartbroken woman and, with their arms around her, led her away. I fervently wished that Kevin Dennehy were there and that he'd stand up and assure Eumie's patients that she had not committed suicide.

The person who actually moved to the podium was Caprice. "My mother did not kill herself. Not deliberately and not accidentally. She placed a high value on herself and her own life. She was not self-destructive." And that was all she said.

Before Caprice had even taken a seat, she was replaced at the podium by the woman who had introduced herself as Nixie Needleman, Eumie's psychiatrist. I remembered who she was because of her distinctive appearance: mountains of platinum hair, heavy makeup, and a black dress with a neckline that plunged almost to her navel. By *distinctive,* I mean that she looked radically different from everyone else at the service. On certain street corners, her appearance wouldn't have been distinctive at all; if the police had been present, they'd probably have kept an eye on her in case she started soliciting. When she spoke, however, it wasn't to offer the wares she was displaying but to repeat what others had said, namely, that Eumie placed a high value on life. "Furthermore," Dr. Needleman said, "she had no history of suicide attempts or gestures and no suicidal ideation. Any loss touches off fantasies of primitive abandonment and betrayal, with concomitant grief and rage. In some cases, it arouses powerful feelings of guilt. All of those emotions can be traced to sources far back in our own lives. They have no basis in present reality. We need to remind ourselves that no one, including Eumie, could have foreseen her death."

Dr. Needleman's definitive tone had a simple, obvious effect on Dolfo, who spontaneously sat. I did not, of course, interrupt the proceedings by pulling out the clicker and startling everyone with its sharp metallic sound. Rather, I just slipped Dolfo a treat and rubbed his chest.

As I was doing so, Vee Foote stepped forward to second everything that Dr. Needleman had said. "Eumie made no preparations," she declared. "There was no note. There were no warnings. There was, in fact, nothing to hint at self-destruction."

Behind me, someone softly exhaled. Turning around, I saw that Quinn Youngman was now standing at the back of the room. Out of nowhere came the realization that he was not just exhaling; rather, what I'd heard was a sigh of relief. As Eumie's psychopharmacologist, he had prescribed for her. Dr. Needleman, an M.D., might well have written prescriptions, too. Vee Foote was also a psychiatrist, an M.D. The picture I had been given by Kevin and by Caprice was of a family with a pharmacopeia of psychoactive drugs, presumably including the prescription medications that had caused Eumie's death. The cynical thought came to me that

Eumie's doctors were not "sharing memories," as Ted's e-mail had phrased the purpose of the memorial service, but were using the occasion to make self-serving, self-protective claims that had nothing to do with Eumie and everything to do with themselves. Were they afraid of lawsuits? Were they simply protecting their reputations? I had no idea.

The service continued. Other patients of Eumie's spoke of their attachment to her. I took Dolfo out. And brought him back in. More than once. Eventually, I returned to find that Ted was concluding the service by reading Tennyson's *In Memoriam,* which I'd read in a college English course. It consisted, if I remembered correctly, of 133 incredibly long poems in memory of a dear friend of the poet's, Arthur Hallam, who, I'd thought at the time, was lucky to have been the subject of the lamentations instead of what I felt myself to be, namely, their bored-to-death victim.

Ted couldn't possibly have read the work in its entirety. But he did read a lot of it. Dolfo and I found it tedious. We left. We returned. At eleven-thirty, when the service finally ended, Dolfo was sitting and staying on command. In a small way, I had kept a promise to Eumie: I had used exclusively positive methods to train her dog.

CHAPTER 20

It is five minutes after nine on Friday morning, and Rita is in her office seeing her second patient of the day. Rita and her patient are sitting in expensive and extraordinarily comfortable chairs designed to minimize back strain. The chairs are upholstered in a pale beige fabric that is neither sensuous nor scratchy. They are identical. Rita's hair is newly trimmed — it always is — and lightly streaked with blond highlights. She is almost certainly wearing a linen suit and high-heeled leather shoes. So far, I am limiting myself to facts and to near certainties. For example, I know everything about the chairs in Rita's new office because she agonized over them. When she rented this new office on Concord Avenue, she decided that her old chairs were shabby and had to be replaced. Because she spends so much time sitting down, she had to have a chair that would protect her back from the chronic strain that is an occupational hazard of doing therapy. Or so therapists think. It's my observation that one of the hazards of the profession is hypochondria. But maybe I'm being harsh. Still, it does seem to me that a great many therapists are valetudinarians. But to return to my knowledge of facts and near certainties, as opposed to the fantasies and reconstructions that will follow, I know about the chairs because Rita dragged me along when she shopped for them and used me as a sounding board in long debates about them. If she chose a large, imposing chair for herself and a lesser chair for the patient, wouldn't the difference create a sense of hierarchy that Rita wanted to avoid? I said that in my layperson's opinion, it was a good idea not to enthrone herself while making the patient feel small. My professional opinion was, of course, that a clearly defined hierarchy was an ideal arrangement, providing that the high-ranking individual was the handler rather than the dog. In fact, my goal in training was to secure for myself the position of benevolent despot. Still, many dogs find it threatening and unpleasant to have people loom over them, and I suspect that psychotherapy patients feel the same way. So, Rita ended up with identical chairs, three of them, in fact, because she sometimes treated couples, an act of madness, if you ask me. Breaking up a dog fight now and then is one thing, but voluntarily doing it all the time as a way to earn a living? With or without identical chairs, that's just plain nuts.

This Friday morning, however, Rita is seeing an individual patient, a woman. Having spent a great deal of time watching Rita as she listens to me, I know for certain that Rita's expression as she listens to her patient is at once calm and alert. Rita is remarkably easy to talk to. She possesses the gift of being able to make sense of the senseless. So, Rita looks calm and alert as her patient briefly discusses the effectiveness of the medication that Dr. Quinn Youngman has prescribed for her bipolar illness.

The patient then talks about Eumie Brainard-Green, who was her previous therapist. "I should never had confided in her. Never. That was terrible judgment on my part."

Rita thinks about pointing out that Eumie was, after all, the patient's therapist, so passing along private information was perfectly appropriate. But Rita reconsiders and decides to wait before either speaking as the voice of reality or interpreting the concern about confidences as a question about the safety of confiding in Rita herself.

"I do have an excuse," continues the patient, "in the sense that I wasn't on lithium, but goddamn it! That was half her fault, too. One hundred percent, she recast everything about me as trauma. One hundred percent."

Rita refrains from informing the angry patient that the emotion she feels is anger. Instead, she says, "I wonder whether it might be useful to take a moment to look at things from her point of view. How she might have viewed you and your situation."

"Clever, aren't you? Well, yes, okay, that's how she really saw it. She didn't say to herself, well, here's a bipolar person who needs lithium, but I'll try to fool her into thinking she's been traumatized. Oh, okay. She was perfectly genuine. Not too bright. And wrong. But genuine. And that's why I told her things I wish I hadn't. That's why I trusted her."

"I'm wondering whether there's anything else. Anything in addition to your bipolar disorder. Maybe something else that you sense was missed. Or misread."

After a moment of silence, the patient says, "Yes, she could've realized that sooner or later, I'd hear about her husband's book, and I'd hear the rumors about it. She knew the contacts I have. It should've crossed her mind that I was one patient she should've shut up about. That I'm not the kind of person who wants to end up half disguised in someone's husband's pop psychology self-help book. It's possible that she *did* realize that. Maybe she never said a word to him about me. Or to anyone else. But I know she talked about other clients. Not only to her husband. To Avon Hill parents, among others. And I know why she did it. She wanted to feel important. Who doesn't? So, if someone's name came up, a big name, obviously, she'd let it slip that she couldn't talk about him or that she knew things she couldn't say, stuff like that. Not that she came right out and said that these people were in treatment with her. But she might as well have. And then there was this conference where Ted Green, her husband, gave a talk, maybe two months ago, and supposedly the cases he described were composites or some such — he didn't use real names, at least — but the mother of a friend of my daughter's, the mother of one of her classmates, told me that these people were very easy to identify. At least for people in

Cambridge. And that one of them was a patient of Eumie Brainard-Green's. Not Ted Green's. Hers. And Ted Green is apparently writing a second book."

Rita says nothing about the narcissism evident in her patient's fantasy of being so interesting that Ted Green will be unable to resist the temptation to write about her case, of which, in reality, he may or may not have secondhand information blabbed by his wife. It should also be noted that Rita is not given to corny statements of the form *You haven't mentioned your mother lately.* Even so, she does notice crucial omissions. What she says is casual and quite vague: "And Eumie Brainard-Green's death?"

"It's all I've been thinking about."

Without making even the most oblique reference in this session. But Rita doesn't say that, either.

The patient continues. "When I heard she'd died, the first thing I felt was this incredible relief. That my secrets would go to the grave with her. Unless she'd told her husband. But, really, why should he write about me? I mean, for one thing, I was hardly one of their success stories. My therapy with her was a total failure. I didn't embrace the concept of trauma and use that to revolutionize my life. I quit therapy with her, I started seeing you, you sent me to Dr. Youngman, and we're working on how I learn to live with my illness. That doesn't exactly make me a likely candidate to star in Ted Green's next book. But I felt relieved anyway. And then I felt guilty. She dies, and my only reaction is that my secrets are safe. What kind of person does that make me? But now I have to wonder. All I did was wish that I'd never told her a thing. But there must be other clients of hers who were more worried than I was. The police think she was murdered, you know. There's a little paragraph in today's paper. And I have to wonder whether someone didn't regret confiding in her even more than I do."

It's all fantasy, of course. Well, most of it. What I know is that Rita had a patient, male or female, who'd been in treatment with Eumie Brainard-Green and who passed on the rumor that Ted Green gave a conference presentation in which two cases were readily identifiable to Cambridge cognoscenti as patients of Eumie Brainard-Green's.

CHAPTER 21

It was after midnight when Caprice and I got home from Ted's. The malamutes, Rowdy, Kimi, and Sammy, were asleep in their crates. Caprice asked whether Lady could stay with her. I was delighted and eventually found Lady, as well as India and my cat, Tracker, on the bed next to Steve, who had left my bedside light on for me. As quietly as possible, I led Lady into the hallway, and she happily trailed after Caprice. When I returned to the bedroom, India was on the floor next to Steve, and Tracker was on his pillow. Her eyes were ever so slightly open and, miraculously, she was purring. When I climbed in bed, instead of turning off the light, I took a few moments to enjoy the rare sight of Tracker relaxed and happy. She trusted no one but Steve. My love for him was so strong that I wanted to stroke his face: to feel his cheekbones under my fingertips, to trace his strong jawline. It seemed a magical opportunity to touch the impalpable: although I scoff at the idea of mystical emanations, Steve possessed a magnetism that made even the most frightened creatures feel safe. It seemed to me that he must be emanating the kinds of forces that don't exist and that if I could have physical contact with him, I'd enter his energy field and be healed in places I wasn't even wounded. Tracker, however, needed him more than I did. If I awakened Steve, he wouldn't mind and would be able to go instantly back to sleep, but my hand would scare Tracker away. I settled for using my eyes in place of my fingertips. Within a few minutes, I felt peaceful and sleepy and overwhelmingly fortunate. I turned off the light and slept until eight the next morning.

I almost never sleep that late, but it was the kind of dark, rainy morning that almost anesthetizes dogs, and, in any case, Steve had left me a note to say that he'd given the dogs a quick trip out before he and Leah, together with Lady, India, and Sammy, had left for work. Now and then, I enjoyed a morning of regression to my unmarried life with my two original dogs. (*Unmarried?* With dogs, you're not exactly *single*.) At nine-thirty, Rowdy and Kimi were dozing on the kitchen floor, and I was writing a column about custodial pets, as I called them, Tracker being a good example. I'd rescued her from a horrible life that had been about to come to a cruel end when I'd intervened. After restoring her to health, I'd done my best to find her a good home. Rowdy and Kimi had made my own far from ideal, but no one had wanted her, in part because of her disfiguring birthmark and torn ear, in part because of her unfriendly behavior. People want cute, sweet cats, preferably kittens. I'd reconciled myself to keeping her. Her life was, I believed, far better than none at all — and death *was* the alternative. The column was about what I'd learned from Tracker. The main lesson was humility: after a lifetime spent with dogs — and a few cats — I'd finally learned that I'd been taking far more credit than I deserved for sweet temperaments and loveable behavior. I'd have denied it. But I'd been doing it all along. By comparison with most other people, I am still a Higher Power when it comes to dogs, but I now know in my heart what I previously knew only in my thick head: that there are animal behaviors I can't modify. Damn it all. But there are. I'd learned other lessons, too: provide vet care, food, grooming, physical safety, and emotional availability to even the ugliest and nastiest animal, do it all out of a sense of responsibility and none of it out of affection, and damned if you won't end up feeling loyalty and even a weird kind of love for the custodial pet.

"People aren't going to like this," I told the dogs. "My readers are going to e-mail a lot of complaints about what a lousy cat owner I am. Even people who read *Dog's Life!* But there are *dogs* like Tracker, and they deserve to live, too, and I'm not going to apologize for saying so." The dogs' beautiful brown eyes shone with eagerness and admiration. I sometimes wish that *Dog's Life* were for dogs and not just about them. If that were the case, the publication would have to be edible to be popular. We could offer it in different flavors: liver, beef, or peanut butter. The canine subscribers, however, wouldn't care what was printed on the delicious pages, so I'd be out of a job.

At noon, when Caprice appeared in the kitchen, I'd completed the first draft of the column. Her hair was damp from the shower, and she was dressed up for lunch with her father. Her outfit, like the one she'd worn the previous night, bore what I found to be a disquieting resemblance to a little girl's dress. It was pale blue, and her shoes were white Mary Janes. Her weight, I thought, didn't account for the voluminousness of her clothing, and it certainly didn't explain her preference for pastel colors. Leah, with her red-gold curls, would've looked great in the pale blue traditionally recommended for redheads, but, in the hope of being seen as a young Simone de Beauvoir, she favored black, which really is slimming. I'd have been happy to see Caprice in black linen, which she did own. Holly Winter, fashion consultant: specializing in faded jeans, dog-themed T-shirts, and kennel clothes. I was no one to talk.

Although I offered Caprice a ride, she insisted on calling a taxi. After she left, I made myself some chicken salad and looked through the newspaper, which had one short paragraph reporting that Eumie Brainard-Green's death was being treated as a homicide. A husband who organizes the kind of big memorial service I'd attended the previous night might be expected to run a long obituary for his wife, but there hadn't been one before, and there was none in today's paper. After lunch, I would've walked both dogs, but it was still raining. Walking Rowdy in wet weather is quick and easy because he considers water to be a threat to his survival: he takes two steps out the door, relieves himself, turns around, and comes back in. Instead of arguing with him, I left him in the dry house and walked Kimi. When we returned, I decided to listen to the CD that Eumie had sent. Imagery was nothing new in obedience handling. I owned a couple of old tapes and had been to a workshop about envisioning yourself standing tall with your dog in perfect heel position at your side. With my last golden retriever, the imagery had been simple to use: Vinnie was such an outstanding obedience dog that with her glued to my left side, I couldn't help standing tall and proud. Then I got Rowdy, who was my first malamute. Let's settle for saying that he introduced a major discrepancy between my mental picture of ideal performance and malamute actuality: it just isn't useful to see pictures in your head of Velcro heeling if your dog is zooming over the baby gates and out of the ring, is it? It's worse than useless. And worse than demoralizing. It's clinically delusional. So, I quit imagining things and learned to train dogs who weren't golden retrievers.

The new CD was nothing like the old tapes, which were all about maximizing potential and achieving the perfect performance. When I'd listened to the introductory section of Eumie's gift, I decided that it would be safe for me to continue. For one thing, the woman on the CD didn't speak in the voice of my late mother, which is to say, in the internal voice that was principally responsible for my ring nerves, the maternal whisper in my ear that corrected me for handler errors before I'd even had a chance to make them. In her day and, especially, from her perspective, dog training was mainly about catching the dog doing something wrong and making an unambiguous correction. When I was first training Rowdy with food, an instructor pointed out to me that I was hunching my shoulders and bending over him when I slipped bits of meat and cheese into his mouth, and I immediately knew that I was making a futile effort to block my mother's view. In contrast, the woman on the CD didn't seem to care whether I won or lost, or even whether I played the game well or badly. As I heard her, she wanted me to treat myself as I treated my dogs: with patience and kindness, and, incredibly, with the goal of having fun. My mother, I might remark, took a dim view of fun. I quote: *"Fun?* Anyone can have *fun!"*

So, following the instructions, I chose a quiet, comfortable place, namely, our bed, and stretched out on my back and listened. Because the imagery exercises weren't specifically about showing dogs, the woman neglected to instruct me to have Rowdy and Kimi next to me, but I knew she'd approve. We, that is, Rowdy, Kimi, the woman, and I, began by taking deep breaths and then progressed to relaxing our bodies from head to toe. After that, we imagined ourselves in a secure, beloved place. We addressed our anxiety by breathing into it and breathing it out. And so it went. In saying that *we* did these exercises, I don't mean to suggest that Rowdy and Kimi had anything remotely like ring nerves or that they complied with the woman's suggestions. In fact, their true contribution was to share with me their calm, steady breathing, their loving presence, and their relaxed self-confidence. When she called us back to the real world, I felt hopeful about showing my dogs. And I shed a few tears for Eumie, who had wanted to help.

"Things can be corny and therapeutic at the same time, guys," I told the dogs. "I'm in no position to sneer. I feel better now. That's all that matters."

When we got back downstairs, not just one but two squirrels were gorging themselves at one of Steve's feeders, and not the black squirrels that I persisted in seeing as exotic and charming, but plain gray ones. Damn it! Steve deserved ivory-billed woodpeckers! Or failing that, Baltimore orioles. If there were any in Cambridge? If they visited feeders? Or cardinals, robins, nuthatches, downy woodpeckers, chickadees, anything but these thieving rodents. I rapped on the window. And was ignored. Out of love for Steve, I went to my computer, did a search, and printed out some pages about foiling squirrels. Steve was already using one kind of baffle, but the pages included a couple of potentially useful suggestions for new efforts. One was to use two different baffles, one above the other, on a pole. Another was to use a PVC pole or to put an ordinary pole in a length of PVC pipe.

Returning to the kitchen and looking out the window, I saw that one of the feeders had been emptied of seed and that the other was occupied by guess what — and not an ivory-billed woodpecker. This time, I simultaneously tapped the glass and hollered, thus managing to drown out the sound of Caprice letting herself and her father in through the kitchen door. I'd given Caprice a key and wanted her to use it, but I was embarrassed to be caught threatening a squirrel with destruction by malamute. The threat was idle, but I felt like a dope, especially because Monty Brainard was so irritatingly suave and urbane.

"No apologies necessary," he said. "I can't stay. I just wanted to thank you again."

He was dressed in a conservative summer suit, this one dark navy — how many did he own? — and his tan hadn't faded at all. Rowdy and Kimi wouldn't, of course, induce pallor, but if they brushed against Monty, their hair would be all over that navy suit, and I'd feel obliged to remove it. Or try. The easiest way would be to don a pair of ordinary rubber gloves and, using moderate pressure, run my hands repeatedly downward on the fabric while saying . . . I could just hear myself: *Now, Monty, it may seem as if I'm using dog hair as an excuse to give you an intimate massage, but this method really is very effective.* Plus, the rubber gloves would make him think I was some kind of pervert.

Fortunately, instead of greeting Monty in

their usual hair-depositing fashion, the dogs behaved oddly. They sashayed up to Caprice and gave her the big-brown-eyes treatment, but what they did with Monty was . . . nothing. Specifically, Kimi did not drop to the floor, roll over, tuck in her paws, fix her gaze on her victim, and await a tummy rub. What's more, she remained silent. Rowdy, for his part, did not stack himself as if he were showing off for a judge. Like Kimi, he failed to present his underbelly, and he issued not a single *woo.* Although one of his fleece toys was right there, he did not offer it to Monty, and he did not vanish and reappear with other fleece tokens of welcome. I also want to note that neither dog showed any sign of perceiving Monty as a threat. Those signs are subtle, but I wouldn't have missed them. Kimi didn't station herself at my side and move her eyes back and forth between Monty and me. Rowdy didn't position himself between Monty and me as if to create a canine barricade. In brief, the dogs did nothing. For malamutes, especially these two, to ignore a visitor was peculiar and unsettling. Still, for once, a dark suit escaped unfurred.

Monty Brainard, seeing nothing, noticed nothing.

"You don't need to thank us," I said.

"I wish I could stay to help out," Monty said.

"He's due back in New York," Caprice explained. "I need to go to Ted's to get some stuff. There's not a lot there that's actually mine, but I'll feel better if I can get it out."

"The cellar here is dry. There's plenty of room." I couldn't recall having invited Caprice to move in with us for the summer, but Leah might have issued the invitation for an extended stay. Steve would have consulted me first, but, always with good intentions, Leah could be high-handed. "If you need help, I'll go with you, or Leah will. She finishes early today. She'll be home soon."

"Caprice would be better off not going there alone," Monty said. "Thank you." Then, after kissing Caprice good-bye, he left.

Monty Brainard knew that his daughter shouldn't go to Ted's alone. And what was his response? To leave for New York. If Rowdy had decided that I was threatened, he'd have used his massive body to place a barrier between me and the source of danger. If I'd had to enter a place I feared, Kimi would have stayed right by my side. Rowdy and Kimi were, in fact, better dogs than Monty Brainard was a father. Indeed, when the occasion demanded it, they were excellent parents.

CHAPTER 22

If you're stuck with inadequate parents, the situation is more hopeful than it might seem. There's always psychotherapy, but it has its limits, including what are called "boundaries," which good therapists set and maintain. Your fifty-minute session is your time, and unless you are in a dreadful crisis, you are supposed to express and satisfy all your psychotherapeutic needs in your therapy hour, and you are definitively not supposed to keep pestering your therapist with phone calls or otherwise to encroach on time that doesn't belong to you. The relationship is supposed to be professional: the therapist is the therapist, you are the client, and that's that. In contrast to therapists, dogs have a limitless mind-set. A dog never decrees that a small, fixed period of time, a fifty-minute hour, is all you get, and as to the boundary between your life and the dog's, the dog sees the two lives as a richly intertwined unity. Indeed, one of the challenges of raising and training dogs is to convince these fusion-minded creatures that certain places and things are off-limits: *my* kitchen counters, *my* dinner, *my* cherished possessions, which are for *my* use only and are not to be mistaken for dog toys. It is also necessary to set and enforce the rule of nonreciprocity: whereas *my* belongings are exclusively *mine,* yours are mine, too, including your food bowl, your toys, and even your body, which I will handle whenever you need grooming or veterinary care. But once those rules about what belongs to whom have been suitably clarified, *we* are free to become a joyful plurality that offers in place of the fifty-minute hour a boundless flow of twenty-four-hour days and a limitless exchange of love.

And then there's friendship. You can pay a shrink for it. Your dog will give it freely. But sometimes you need a human friend. When Caprice's father deserted her, Leah and I stepped in. I wouldn't have allowed Caprice to go alone to Ted's, but soon after Monty's departure, Leah got home and promptly organized the expedition to retrieve Caprice's possessions. There are, I might mention, two people responsible for Leah's bossiness. I am one of them. I introduced her to dog training and dog-show handling by putting her in charge of Kimi, who practiced a militant form of radical feminism and canine liberationist activism that would have challenged even an experienced dog person and did, in fact, challenge one, namely, me. Leah responded by rapidly learning to set and enforce strict limits and high standards. The second person responsible for Leah's bossy streak is Maria Montessori, whose contribution was to found the educational movement in which Leah received her early schooling. The Montessori method, as I understand it, is supposed to produce self-directed children. In Leah's case, it instilled the conviction that besides directing herself, she was supposed to direct the rest of us, too.

"Holly, we need your car," she said. "I'm going with Caprice. There won't be room for all three of us, so you're staying here. She can't go alone. Wyeth is horrible to her, and who knows what Ted might do? Try to get her to move back there? And she's not doing that. Caprice, change into jeans or something, or you'll ruin your dress."

Caprice obediently went upstairs and returned in jeans and a tunic-length T-shirt. "Woof woof," she said. "Click? Treat?"

Leah had the grace to blush and apologize. Then she hurried Caprice out to the car. When they returned an hour later, they were in high spirits.

"Caprice's mother has left her all of the china and silver and stuff at Ted's house," Leah reported. "If he isn't maximally polite and considerate to Caprice, we're going to auction it all on eBay."

"And let him eat off paper plates," said Caprice. "With plastic forks."

"He was there?" I asked.

"We only saw him for a second," Caprice answered. "Between patients. Wyeth wasn't home. We lucked out."

"Was Dolfo there?"

"He was eating the mail," said Leah.

Caprice added, "A while ago, Dolfo ate Ted's passport, which he's going to need when he and Wyeth go to Russia, and then when the new one came in the mail, he ate that, too. Mail is his favorite food."

"It's one of Sammy's, too," I said. "Paper and plastic. He likes to think of himself as a canine recycling facility."

The convivial mood boosted my hopes. It lasted as the three of us unloaded the car and carried boxes to the cellar. Steve got home, and we fed the dogs and got ready to go out to the restaurant where we were meeting friends. Four of Leah's friends from school turned up, and the group decided to go to a movie. Although everyone urged Caprice to go along, she declined by saying that she'd had a rough week and wanted to go to bed early. It had been a terrible week, of course, so no one leaned on her to change her mind. When Steve and I left, the household was peaceful: India was in her crate, Tracker was in my office, Rowdy and Kimi were in the living room with the door closed, and both Sammy and Lady were in Caprice's room. We started to remind Caprice about who could and could not be loose with whom, but she rattled off the rules practically word for word. "And if Sammy starts to act wild, he goes to his crate," she finished.

"Sammy always wants to be a good boy," I said. "But he doesn't always succeed. Right, Sammy?" His eyes had a glint that concerned me a bit. "Remember! He's a big puppy. Don't trust him! He gets into things."

"I'm used to Dolfo," Caprice reminded me. "Compared to Dolfo, Sammy is an angel. And he's so sweet."

In response, Sammy curved himself around Caprice and leaned gently against her. Then he stretched his neck, raised his big, gorgeous head, and gazed lovingly at her.

"If he has a fit of flying around and bouncing off the walls, put him in his crate," I said. "No matter how cute he is." I paused. "Where is Pink Piggy?"

Sammy replied by dashing under a table and emerging with the battered toy in his mouth. He gave it three firm squeezes, thus producing three distinct squeaks.

"We'll take all the dogs out when we get home," Steve said. "They should be fine until then."

We had a so-so dinner at a restaurant in Inman Square. Our friends had to get up early the next day and didn't want dessert or coffee, so Steve and I stopped at Christina's and bought ice cream to take with us. Despite the hideously cold winters in Greater Boston, everyone here eats a lot of ice cream all year round, and everyone has an opinion about the major contenders for Best of Breed. When I'm judging, Christina's wins.

We got home at about ten, and since the weather was now dry, we decided to take the dogs out to the yard and to have our coffee and dessert there. As I was making coffee and dishing out white chocolate ice cream, Steve let India out and, after her,

Rowdy and Kimi. His optimism about harmony in the pack didn't extend to foolhardiness: he trusted Kimi to behave herself with India only if the two were supervised. Consequently, he stayed outside. When the coffee was ready, I put our mugs, bowls of ice cream, spoons, and napkins on a tray. (Short on household items? Get married! We now have everything, including, for the first time, items without depictions of dogs.) As I was carrying out the tray, Lady came prancing into the kitchen and followed me to the yard. The big question — the fateful one, the crucial one, the one that should have been paramount and obvious — did, of course, occur to me: where's Sammy? I have no excuse for failing to answer it. I should immediately have gone back inside to look for him. What's more, Steve should have asked himself or me exactly the same question and should have seen to it that one of us acted on it. India and Lady were Steve's dogs, Rowdy was mine, and Kimi belonged to Leah and me. But Sammy was *our* dog, Steve's and mine, sired by Rowdy, bought by Steve, and, since our wedding, owned by both of us: my co-ownership had been Steve's wedding gift to me. I had a ring, too, but as the wedding ceremony itself says, a ring is a *token,* and what's a token, really? A trifle, an arbitrary sign, an object that's a mere nothing by comparison with what it represents. Sammy, in contrast, was no bauble or trinket or symbol of love given and received; Sammy was love itself.

But as I set the tray on our wedding-present picnic table, the familiar voice of Kevin Dennehy called from the gate to the driveway: "Hey, Holly? Steve?"

With a six-pack of Budweiser in one of his big hands, Kevin entered the yard and was immediately surrounded by dogs. "Any thirsty boys here?" he asked. "Dry throats, huh? Hey, Rowdy, she still keeping you on the wagon?"

"Permanently," I said.

"Hey, don't yell at me. I didn't teach him that trick," Kevin said. "Did I, big boy? It came natural to you. Like singing. Some people are born being able to carry a tune like a songbird, and some aren't. Knowing how to chug beer's just like that. A God-given gift. And you got it."

"Kevin, besides being a talented beer drinker, Rowdy does happen to have a spectacular voice, so why don't you work on developing that talent and quit giving him alcohol! It is not good for him. Or for Kimi, either."

Disloyally, Steve said, "A sip or two of beer now and then isn't going to hurt them."

"I don't see you feeding them beer," I said. In fact, neither India nor Lady had any interest in it.

"They don't ask me," Steve said. "They ask Kevin. Kevin, take a seat. You want some ice cream?"

He turned down the offer in favor of popping the top off a beer, sipping, and then accidentally-on-purpose holding the can at the level of Rowdy's mouth. Even I have to admit that Kevin's claim about Rowdy's talent was justified. Strictly behind my back, Kevin had also taught Kimi to sip beer, but she performed the trick without Rowdy's air of mastery. Also, she seemed to me to dislike the taste, whereas Rowdy obviously loved it.

"Enough!" I said. "Steve said a sip or two now and then. He's had a sip or two. Enough!"

After giving Kimi her turn, Kevin rested the can on the table. "They do a good job of sharing," he remarked. "You ever thought about writing to Budweiser about them? They could be on TV instead of those Clydesdales."

"The Clydesdales haul beer around," I said. "They don't drink it."

"That's what I mean. What kind of ad is that? If you want to sell beer, you should show people drinking it. Or dogs. The head honchos at Budweiser could work out some kind of deal with Purina or Eukanuba or whatever. Brew Team Dog Chow. Just add water, and it makes its own beer."

"Or the other way around," I said. "All Natural Lamb and Rice Premium Performance Budweiser for Large Breed Adults." I paused. "With small brains. But speaking of food, do you want a sandwich or something?"

"No, thanks. I can't stay. I just wanted to tell you about those squirrels." Kevin's expression was uncharacteristically grim.

"They were at the feeders today," I said. "Steve, I meant to tell you. I printed some pages from the Web. You need to add baffles. Two squirrel baffles on each pole. And PVC pipe for the poles to go in."

"There's a quicker way," said Kevin. "That's what someone did over there. Over at the Greens'."

Steve and I waited in silence.

"I took a look at the feeders," Kevin continued. "Like you said, no squirrels. And no squirrel damage. And in Cambridge, that's not normal. My mother's got that feeder you gave her, Holly, and half of what's there are squirrels. They eat the birdseed, and the perches are all chewed up. And over there at the Greens', there are a dozen of these feeders, all kinds, fancy ones, with no squirrel baffles. No nothing. So I start looking around and . . ." He shrugged. "And I call this bird feeder company, On the Wing, and ask if they're doing something, putting something in the birdseed, and they say no, they're not. They used to add some kind of hot pepper, but it turned out to be bad for birds, and they quit. There's some kind of feeder that gives electric shocks, but the clients didn't want one. So, then I get a bright idea. I send a guy up a tree. And there it is. Rat poison. A lot of it. In that tree and two others. Not all that high up, either. And that's your answer. No squirrels."

I reached for Steve's hand and squeezed it. "Kevin, that's monstrous. It makes me sick. No one *wants* squirrels at feeders, but —"

"It's sick," Steve said. "And dangerous."

"There are dogs there!" I said. "Dolfo. And next door, Portia. George and Barbara's dog. There are probably other dogs in the neighborhood. And cats. If one of them had eaten a poisoned squirrel . . ."

"And if kids found a dead squirrel," Kevin added. "When I was a kid, we used to have these funerals for dead animals if we found them. Bury them, flowers on the little grave." He crossed himself. "Kids do that. Handle the dead squirrel, put your hands in your mouth. And kids climb trees."

"Have there been any reports?" I asked. "Reports of anything . . . ?"

"No. And we asked around. It's luck is all it is."

"Kevin, who did this?"

"I don't know. But I'll tell you something. Homicide, that's a lot of people's business. But this — this one's Cambridge. Hey, a few years back, I could've been the kid that climbed one of those trees or buried a dead squirrel. This one's mine. And so's the bastard that did it."

CHAPTER 23

As soon as Kevin left, I suddenly and belatedly thought of Sammy. "I'll go get him," I told Steve. "You stay here with the others."

Neither of us was alarmed. Sammy was probably in Caprice's room. The privilege of staying with her was new to Sammy, who was probably curled up on the bed next to her. Still, he was a sociable dog, and it was unlike him not to have come dashing down the stairs to greet us when we'd arrived home. Furthermore, he must have heard me dishing out ice cream, and any sound even remotely suggestive of food, the alpha and omega of malamute existence, usually sent him flying toward its source. It did not, however, occur to me that Sammy was in serious trouble. I casually checked the downstairs rooms and did not run upstairs, but tiptoed to avoid awakening Caprice, whose bedroom door turned out to be ajar. The room itself was dark. I heard her snoring lightly. Still on tiptoe, I checked the other rooms and then waited outside Caprice's for a moment as I tried to decide whether to leave Sammy to keep her company or to make him have one trip outside before he settled in for the night.

Just when a rustling noise made me resolve to inch my way in and lure Sammy out, his big head emerged from the room. In his mouth were the damp remains of a bag of Pepperidge Farm cookies. His formerly white face was smeared with what I at first mistook for dirt. A second later, the smears registered on me as chocolate. Chocolate contains a substance called theobromine that is toxic to dogs. A large amount of dark chocolate can kill a small dog. To a dog Sammy's size, a small amount of chocolate, especially milk chocolate, isn't usually fatal, but dogs vary in their sensitivity to chocolate. Without hesitation, I snatched the bag out of Sammy's mouth. To my relief, it had contained oatmeal raisin cookies. Having examined the bag, I turned my attention to Sammy and immediately saw that he was simply not himself. His characteristically bright eyes looked at once wide and dopey, and his expression was puzzled and unhappy. Bending over, I ran my hands over his belly, which was frighteningly enlarged.

"Steve!" I screamed. "Steve, get up here now! Steve, help me!"

Before I'd even finished yelling, Sammy provided his own veterinary treatment by lowering his head and vomiting copiously on the hallway floor. Kneeling at his side, I rested my hands on his heaving abdomen and whispered gently to him. "Good boy. Poor Sammy. Good boy. Get it all up." Reaching out a hand, I banged Caprice's door open and shouted, "Caprice, get up! Sammy is sick. Get downstairs this second and tell Steve to lock up the other dogs and then to get up here. Go get him! Now!" Hearing Steve at the bottom of the stairs, I called, "Steve, Sammy is sick. Don't let the other dogs up here. Do something with them, and then get up here. Please! I need you!"

In the light that spilled from the hall into Caprice's room, I saw that the floor was littered with torn food packages and crumbs. The scene told the whole story: Sammy had raided a stash of food. And a big one at that. Strewn around were torn bags that had held potato chips, tortilla chips, candy, and yet more cookies. I was enraged. When Steve and I had welcomed Caprice, we'd carefully explained the house rules, most of which were about dogs. Caprice had understood those rules perfectly. Only this evening, she'd recited the ones that governed the safe and unsafe combinations of loose dogs. She'd been explicitly warned about malamutes and food, and she'd seen the precautions that Steve, Leah, and I took to prevent them from devouring every edible morsel in the house. Damn it! In return for our hospitality and our generosity, she'd done *exactly* what she'd been told not to do! I kept my temper only by thinking of Eumie's death.

Steve was cool. He calmly led Sammy a few feet away from the stinking puddles and lumps on the floor and slowly checked him out. Caprice had finally appeared at the door to her room and was leaning against the door frame. She wore a gargantuan red T-shirt. Her skin was blotchy, and tears ran down her face. She looked drugged with sleep. Or maybe just drugged. In a child's voice, she said, "You're angry with me."

Before I had the chance to tell her that she was right, Steve said, "Caprice, splash some cold water on your face. Right now, please."

"I feel so —" she started to say.

"Wash your face in cold water," said Steve. "Now. If I'm going to help Sammy, I'll need some information."

I had the sense to leave things to Steve. Here was Sammy, standing a few feet from the hideous mess he'd brought up, still looking ghastly, and what did Caprice have to say for herself? *I feel . . .* If I'd opened my mouth, it would've been to inform her that no one gave a single sweet goddamn about her feelings. I was right to keep quiet. Still crying, Caprice made her way to the bathroom and emerged about a minute later with her face and her baby curls wet.

"First of all," Steve said, "I don't see anything about Sammy that's got me worried. At least not yet." He sounded as if he were speaking to a distraught pet owner instead of to the person who could've killed our dog. "But I need to know what he swallowed. And there are three categories of things I need to know about. One is chocolate. Another is medication. Sedatives, antidepressants, marijuana, anything. Anything at all. And the third is foreign objects. Things. Socks. Underwear. Anything that could get lodged in his digestive tract."

"Nothing," she said.

Without showing a hint of impatience, he said, "Let's start with an inventory of what's on the floor of your room. Put the light on. Good. Okay, there's a wastebasket in there.

I want you to pick up everything, one thing at a time, tell me what the package or the wrapper was for, and then put it in the wastebasket."

"There's a bag that had oatmeal cookies," I said. "It's here."

"Tortilla chips," Caprice said thickly. "Potato chips. Corn chips. Pralines. Butterscotch." She paused to blow her nose. Then she continued to name the junk she'd kept in a cache in her room. Eventually, she said, "Chocolate chip cookies."

Steve must've heard me take a sharp breath. "Probably not enough chocolate to do any harm. Is that it?"

"Yes," she said.

"Medications. Do you take anything? Ever."

After a pause, Caprice said, "Sometimes. For sleep."

"Take a look where you keep anything like that. Your purse. Anywhere you could've put any sleeping medication."

I was watching Sammy, who was beginning to perk up. From Caprice's room — our guest room — I heard a drawer open and close and then the sound of a zipper. "It's all here," Caprice said.

With endless patience, Steve said, "Objects. Anything missing? Any scraps of fabric

243

on the floor?"

"Nothing."

"Check whatever you were wearing today. Socks. Underwear."

"All here."

"Then we're probably out of the woods," Steve said. "We'll need to keep an eye on you, Sammy, and watch out for dehydration. Or further developments. But it looks like you're doing fine." To Caprice, he said, "I'd like you to come on downstairs with us. There are a few things we need to go over. You want to get dressed? Or get a robe. Before we talk, there's a mess here to clean up. I'll get you what you'll need."

My first thought was a Ted-like one: *chutzpah!* The nerve! And how uncharacteristic of Steve! Then I realized that he was simply telling Caprice that fair was fair: since her carelessness had made Sammy sick, she was the one responsible for mopping up after him. Still, I took pity on her and helped out. Even for me, the task was challenging. In a lifetime with dogs, I'd developed a strong stomach. That night, I needed one. I have to admit, too, that I had a selfish motive, which was to make sure that Caprice didn't damage the floor. When Rita had moved up to the third-floor apartment and we'd redone the second floor, we'd had the hardwood sanded and refinished. In the normal course of things, dogs who realize that they are on the verge of puking all over the place will immediately hasten to the spot where they'll do the maximum amount of damage to valued human possessions. If a dog is seized with queasiness while he's in the kitchen, will he considerately upchuck on the linoleum or tile? Never. Why? Because linoleum and tile are easy to wash. So, rather than create a mess that can be cleaned up at no expense and with no permanent harm done, he overcomes his nausea for the few seconds it takes to dash into the living room and leave an ineradicable splotch in the center of a light-colored rug, and not just any rug, either, but one that will be wrecked if you try to shampoo it yourself and thus requires professional cleaning, with an extra charge for the removal of pet stains. Sammy, of course, found himself in a situation somewhat different from that one. Once he'd realized that he was on the verge of bringing up what he'd wolfed down, he'd eyed our guest room and said to himself, *This won't do at all! Nothing here but a cheap area rug that can go through the washing machine!* So, he'd shoved his muzzle and the cookie bag out into the hallway, where he'd spied our newly refinished hardwood floor, which was perfect for his purposes, since it couldn't be scrubbed with hot water and assuredly couldn't be bleached.

I made Caprice do her share of the work, and a disgusting share it was, I'm sure. When we'd finished, she washed her hands and face, put on a second and even larger T-shirt over the first, and joined Steve and me in the kitchen. To my relief, Sammy was his perky self again. Steve had even allowed him to sip water. Steve had made fresh coffee, caffeinated for himself and decaf for me. Caprice accepted a cup of decaf, and we sat around the table.

"Sammy is going to be fine," Steve told her. "All he did was overeat. But the consequences could've been serious." He patiently described chocolate toxicity, gastric dilatation and volvulus syndrome, and the hazards of ingesting foreign objects. For him, he was remarkably succinct. "And if there'd been medication in the same place as the food . . . I don't have to tell you about that."

"There wasn't," Caprice said.

"From now on," Steve said, "prescription medications belong strictly out of the reach of dogs. Not in your purse or your backpack that you leave lying around. Food belongs in the kitchen."

"I understand," she said.

"You *understood* before. This time, from now on, you follow the rules. Part of my job is dealing with the results of carelessness. And that's what we don't want here. No matter how careful you are, dogs are going to get into things. All we're trying to do is minimize the chances of those episodes. Now, about the food. You might've noticed that in this house, we eat nutritious food. And that's what we feed our animals. Treats are treats. And most of them are nutritious, too. You've seen the book that Holly and I wrote. *No More Fat Dogs.* The reason we wrote it is that most dogs in this country *are* fat. They're overfed and underexercised. Now, if you want to eat junk and overeat junk, that's your business, but I don't want it happening here."

To my amazement, Caprice hadn't burst into tears when Steve had mentioned overeating. When he'd said the word *fat,* I'd felt blood rush to my face. Caprice hadn't reddened. She'd just kept watching Steve's kind face.

He continued. "Prescription drugs. If you've got medication prescribed for you, take it the way you were told to take it. You got anything else? Anything prescribed for Ted? Or your mother?"

"Yes," she said. "Over there, at Ted's, that was the house rule. Share your meds. But all I have is Ambien and Sonata. And some Valium. And a little . . . I think it's Xanax."

"Anything prescribed for you?"

Caprice looked almost shocked at the notion of taking pills that weren't meant for someone else. "No. Nothing. My therapist is a psychologist. Missy Zinn. She doesn't prescribe." After a little pause she added, as if Missy were guilty of an oversight, "And she hasn't sent me to anyone."

I finally spoke. "Does Missy Zinn know about the pills you're taking?"

Caprice lowered her eyes and shook her head. "I didn't want her to be angry with my mother. It was just something we always did. Shared." I saw no sign that Caprice made any connection between the *just something we did* and her mother's death. "With Dr. Zinn, I did a little work on my feeling needy. The divorce. The divorce was hard. Everyone was angry at everyone else. And hurt. Monty blamed Ted, and Johanna hated my mother."

Here, I cannot resist drawing attention to the verb *to work* as used by therapists and their clients. *Work,* as I understand it, means putting out a lot of effort and then having something to show for it: a ditch that's been dug, a book that's been written, a class of first-graders who've learned to read, a cat who's been cured of a urinary tract infection, or a dog who's learned to heel so accurately and gracefully that when you're his partner, you know that with your voice, your treats, your footwork, your timing, and, most of all, your relationship with the other half of the team, you've performed a damned miracle — what you started out with was a dog, and what you've ended up with is the honest to doG reincarnation of Fred Astaire. And that, let me tell you, takes work. But talking about your mother? Your father? Your parents' painful divorce? To my mind, that's just not work. It's talking, isn't it? Rita vehemently disagrees. In fact, when I told her about the miracle of Fred Astaire, she said that it was a pretty good analogy, except that it described patients who started out in pieces and ended up whole. But then, Rita has never trained a dog to heel like a dancer, and I, of course, have never practiced psychotherapy.

"I'm sorry to hear about the divorce," said Steve, "but if you're going to lose weight, you're going to need to decrease calories and increase exercise. It's real simple. Eat less. Do more."

If you're a dog, it is simple! Get an owner who decreases your calories and increases your exercise. In fact, as I hoped Caprice didn't realize, Steve was delivering exactly the same lecture he'd given a million times before . . . in a slightly different context. Fortunately, he stopped before he reached the part about obesity's contribution to the clinical signs of canine hip dysplasia.

"There's a group," I said hesitantly. "It's called Overeaters Anonymous. OA. There are meetings in Cambridge. I know someone who goes. If you're ever interested, I know she'd be glad to have you go with her." The someone was a member of the Cambridge Dog Training Club, but I didn't say so. Caprice wouldn't necessarily have been flattered by the canine nature of our concern for her. To prevent any misunderstanding that might ever arise, let me say outright that if Steve and I treat you as we'd treat a stray mutt, if we phrase our advice in veterinary terms and refer you to dog trainers for help with your human problems, please don't be insulted. You should, on the contrary, feel honored: if we treat you like a dog, it means that we've peered into the depths of your soul, recognized a familiar essence, and are fulfilling the religious obligation to worship the goD within.

Caprice groaned. "Twelve steps."

"I'm afraid they're unavoidable," I conceded.

"This'd be more than twelve steps," Steve said with a smile, "but you could try walking Lady. She could use the attention. And before we all get some sleep, let's go over what you're doing this summer. If you don't have a job, you should get one."

Vets rush in where shrinks fear to tread.

Caprice looked stunned. "A job?" She sounded as if he'd suggested that she drop out of Harvard and start panhandling in the Square.

"Paid employment. Or you could volunteer. Or take a course somewhere. What's your, uh, field of concentration?" Harvard doesn't have majors, and not because it's a bastion of antimilitarist liberalism. The real reason is that *majors* would suggest the pos-

251

sibility of *minors,* whereas at Harvard, everything, simply by virtue of being at Harvard, is always preeminent.

"Physics," Caprice said.

"You could tutor physics," I said. "Or math. Paid or volunteer. But no one has to decide anything now. Your eyes are drooping."

"Have you taken any medication tonight?" Steve asked.

Caprice was silent for a moment. Then, addressing Steve, she said, "No. I ate myself to sleep. But I'm okay now. I'm actually tired."

"Hey, this isn't going to be hard," Steve told her. "We live real well. We eat well. We sleep well. We work hard. We have fun. We're glad to have you here. Now, go to bed. You want Lady with you?"

"If you trust me with her," Caprice said. We did.

CHAPTER 24

Tellers of entomological tales may long to be flies on walls, but I dislike insects and have no desire for even the briefest metamorphosis into one. What I'd like the power to become is an invisible dog on the floor, preferably a golden retriever, a peaceful, ancient creature given to snoozing and eavesdropping. If Monty Brainard had owned a dog, visible or otherwise, I'd have mentioned it by now; he did not. Even so, if others may imagine themselves as flies on walls, I am entitled to listen in on Monty through the ears of that old golden, who is startled awake at 3 A.M. on that same Friday night.

So, curled up on an area rug on Monty's bedroom floor, I hear the ring of the phone. Monty utters a monosyllable that no self-respecting golden would repeat. He clears his throat, picks up the phone, and grumbles, "Yes." The rug, as I see it — I,

Holly, the fantasizer — is an ethnic one of some sort, perhaps Polish or Afghani. I, Holly the invisible dog, cannot see it; Monty does not bother to put on his bedside light.

After listening for what I, the golden retriever, find to be a frustratingly long time, he says, "I know the middle of the night's your pattern, but it's a pattern you're going to have to start breaking." And I, Holly, she who is conjuring up the dog, make a mental note to myself: like therapists and dog trainers, participants in twelve-step programs need to establish boundaries and set limits. And just how do I, Holly, know about the twelve-step program? The golden tells me. She is very intuitive.

"What you're doing," Monty continues, "is that you're not going to meetings and calling me instead. The meetings are the heart of the program. If you show up at them and then you still need to call someone, okay. But you're not doing that. There's no substitute for the meetings. And I know we're in the same dilemma. And not everyone else is. But close enough."

Monty listens and resumes. "Look, it's not just guilt. It's shame. It's both. And it's easy to think that it's people like us, parents, who really feel it. Take me. The idea is that I go to my daughter and say, 'Well, honey,

Daddy needs to tell you that he knows he's been shortchanging you on time and attention and everything else, but he's got a good reason. He's hooked on Internet pornography, and he's been protecting you from knowing that Daddy's a pervert.' And then I undo the harm I've done? Then I make amends? I'm not there, and I'm not going to get there. I'd do anything to protect my daughter. But it's hard for everyone else, too. Show up at the meetings. You'll see. We've all got the same problem."

Well, okay. I have to confess that on that Friday night, the actual one, I had no idea about Monty's secret and that I later learned it from a human being and not from an invisible dog. The admission is disappointing. Still, I did learn it in time to credit the elderly golden with intuiting it, and I'm always happy to do a favor for a dog.

CHAPTER 25

"We had quite a scene here last night," I told Leah at nine o'clock on Saturday morning. She had the day off and had slept late. She was standing at the kitchen counter buttering an English muffin. Her red-gold curls were spilling from a knot on her head. She wore at least two black tank tops and had more earrings in both ears than I wanted to count. Sammy had plastered himself to her left thigh and was drooling so profusely that he was leaving a spot on her jeans.

"I know. Caprice told me. She heard me come in, and we talked for a while."

"Steve was . . . he was quite blunt with her. He said things I wouldn't have."

Leah poured herself some coffee and took her mug and the muffin to the table. When she sat down, Sammy was her shadow. "Oh, she's ready to drop out of therapy and see a vet instead."

"I wouldn't have mentioned her weight. But it's strange. I think it bothers me more than it does Steve. It's not that . . . what I really want . . . I do *not* think that everyone has to be thin and good-looking. I don't. It's the way her face is distorted. That bothers me because it's just such a tremendous disadvantage."

"You get used to it."

"Easy for you to say! Leah, what I want is for her to have your advantages."

"I sweat over chemistry. She takes physics courses for guts." Harvard slang: easy courses.

"That's not what I mean."

"Maybe it should be."

"Look, before Caprice gets back . . . that was one of the effects of Steve's, uh, directness. She got up at eight, and she's out walking Lady. And she had boiled eggs and cantaloupe for breakfast. But while she's out, I want to tell you . . . Kevin says that the police found rat poison in the trees in Ted and Eumie's yard. Someone put it there to kill the squirrels."

Leah's face fell. Her eyes filled with tears. "Who?"

"I have no idea. Someone who wanted to keep the squirrels out of the feeders, presumably."

"That's vicious! It's monstrous!"

"Yes."

"Ted? Or Eumie?" She paused. "Holly, Caprice would never do that. Never."

"There's also Wyeth, not that he'd care about bird feeders, but —"

The conversation ended abruptly when Caprice and Lady entered through the back door. Lady was wiggling all over and tossing happy looks to Caprice, who was flushed and damp. When Sammy ran up and greeted her with a deep *woo-woo-woo*, she said, "You're still speaking to me, huh?"

"Sammy will love you forever," I said. "He'll remember the feast and forget everything else."

"I wish I could."

"Consider yourself redeemed," I said.

As I was refilling the water bowl that Lady had emptied, Kevin Dennehy's signature rap sounded on the back door, and Leah let him in.

"I heard voices in here," he said.

"Maybe you should see someone about that," Leah told him.

"Ha-ha. The three of you were chirping like birds. I thought maybe Rita was here. It's a semiofficial visit."

"What's she done?" Leah asked.

"Nothing. A building up the street was

entered last night. One of those places crawling with shrinks. It's near where her new office is, and I thought she ought to know. If she's got patient records there, she ought to get them out."

"I'll go get her." In seconds, Leah's feet were pounding up the back stairway.

"Coffee?" I asked. "Kevin? Caprice?"

They both accepted, and I went ahead and made Dunkin' Donuts for Kevin, Bustelo for me, half caffeinated and half decaf Peet's House Blend for Rita, and Trader Joe's French roast for Leah and Caprice. Cambridge! On the one hand, we're affected and precious, but on the other hand, we're wildly considerate. Kevin took cream, and Leah and I liked milk foamed in a clever pitcher-cum-plunger gadget that Steve had given me. Caprice usually drank her coffee black, as did Rita when she was dieting. But there were limits. I hate the bitter aftertaste of artificial sweeteners, and I won't serve them with coffee unless someone asks or unless a guest has diabetes. Also, I'd recovered from the all-things-French phase I'd gone through after our honeymoon in Paris and thus was no longer buying those rough lumps of brown and white sugar that look ever so continental but won't dissolve in liquid.

As I look back at the five of us who were soon sitting around my kitchen table drinking coffee and talking about the neighborhood burglary, I realize that a stranger would have seen us as an ill-assorted group. Kevin and Caprice were about twice the size of anyone else. Kevin had the height and bone structure to carry to his bulk, but there was nonetheless a lot of him, as befitted his personality and, I suppose, his occupation. A frail cop? Dandy. On someone else's block. Rita was the smallest of us, in weight and build, and although Kevin was wearing fresh chinos and a starched oxford cloth blue shirt, Rita was the only one who'd bothered to *dress*, in her sense of the word. By her standards, the black linen pants and top were informal, as were the flat-heeled black sandals she wore. Leah was an artist's model from the Pre-Raphaelite era anachronistically costumed as a Parisian existentialist in hot weather, while Caprice wore a floor-length cotton dress that suggested membership in an agricultural commune of the 1970s. In my battered jeans, their pockets filled with clickers and treats, and my Alaskan Malamute Assistance League sweatshirt, with our motto, *We Pull for Them*, lettered across the back, I was unmistakable: a contemporary dog trainer and breed-rescue devotee. Sammy and Lady were timeless and, need I say, well-groomed.

"There are twelve of them in the building." Kevin sounded as if he were describing an infestation of alligators, maybe, or some other unexpected and unwelcome species of animal. "It looks like the front door got left unlocked. They're confused about who was supposed to lock up for the night. No alarm system. The door to this particular office was locked, but the guy kept the key on the door frame just above the door, so it didn't take a genius to work out where it was."

"Whose office was it?" Rita asked.

"Guy named Hershberg. Myron Hershberg. You know him?"

"I've heard of him. I don't know him."

"Anyways, there's minor vandalism, stuff tossed around. All that's missing are some old diskettes and CD-ROMs."

"With patient records," Rita said. "Oh, shit."

"Most secrets are online, anyway," said Leah.

Caprice nodded.

"The information that patients confide in their therapists is very definitely not online," said Rita. "Kevin, thank you. I'll have to take precautions I should've taken anyway."

After Kevin left, the discussion continued.

"Maybe the aim was to find information to discredit someone for some other reason," I said. "Something to use in a divorce, maybe." I thought of Anita the Fiend. Hiring some thug to obtain personal information about Steve was exactly the kind of thing she'd have done during their divorce. Fortunately, he hadn't been seeing a psychiatrist. Besides, marrying Anita was the only discreditable thing Steve had ever done, and it was public record.

"The aim might not have been practical," said Rita. "The more I think about it, the more it feels symbolic. Penetrating a presumed repository of secret knowledge? It was probably more a plea for help than anything else."

"Some people just like knowing other people's secrets," Caprice said. "My mother was like that. She teased Daddy. She'd tell him to remember that she knew all his secrets. She did that with other people, too. Maybe that's what got her —" To my astonishment, Caprice broke into tears.

Ever so gently, Rita said, "Maybe this is a thought you need to finish, Caprice."

Between sobs, Caprice said, "She used to get me to help. On the Web. I'm good at that. It was stupid stuff, really. If people were older than they said they were, how much they paid for their houses, whether they owed back taxes . . . nothing anyone would've murdered her for knowing."

Leah took her hand. "But you still wish you hadn't helped."

"It made me feel . . . dirty."

"You probably didn't have much choice," Leah said.

"I did. I just didn't know it."

Leah hugged Caprice, and then Rita and I did, too. Lady and Sammy crowded in. I like to think that the dogs were sympathetic. What I know is that if there's one thing dogs hate, it's being left out. Not that human beings like it. I, for example, had a disquieting thought that raised a question in my mind, and the question made me feel isolated. When Kevin had come here to question Caprice, she'd greeted him as Lieutenant Dennehy. Her use of his rank had struck me because I'd remembered that on the day of Eumie's death, in the Brainard-Greens' yard, I'd wanted to soften everything for her and consequently had introduced Kevin just as Kevin Dennehy. Furthermore, none of us ever called him Lieutenant Dennehy. So, how had Caprice known his rank? The answer was obvious: Google. She'd checked him out on the Web. Since she'd met Kevin only after Eumie's death, she'd done the search for herself, not for her mother. Kevin's rank was an entirely public matter; there was nothing even remotely secret about it. Furthermore, it was becoming common practice to use Internet search engines to find out who was who, hence the transitive verb *to Google,* as in *She Googled him.* The point wasn't that she'd done it, though; the point was that she'd put the blame for using the Web in that fashion entirely on her mother. Eumie, Caprice claimed, had liked knowing things about people. Eumie, I thought, wasn't the only one.

CHAPTER 26

On Saturday evening, Rita sits across the table from Quinn Youngman, who is eating a grass-fed organic baby duckling with farro, ramps, favas, cardoons, and guanciale, or so the menu promised. Rita's dish, also described quite grandly, tastes to her like a plain roast chicken with mashed potatoes. Next to the chicken is a tiny puddle of violently red liquid. She wonders whether the puddle is, in fact, a sauce or whether it is blood that accidently dripped from the cut finger of someone in the kitchen. Consequently, she avoids tasting it.

"Pleasant little bistro," Quinn remarks.

"Very," says Rita, who thinks that Quinn probably likes this overpriced establishment because it is in a cellar and thus reminds him of the coffeehouses of his radical youth. Her own youth, which was thoroughly conformist, took place twenty years after the time of Quinn's turbulence, so she has only his word for what that era of his life was like. Their age difference, she tells herself, means nothing. Quinn Youngman, M.D., is an attractive older man, an appropriate choice for her. Of his rebelliousness, nothing remains except the memories on which he dwells at some length. These days, his political activity consists of donating to the ACLU, Amnesty International, and the Democratic National Committee. He reads the *New York Times* and listens to National Public Radio. He is almost too appropriate for her.

When they have discussed the food for a few moments, Quinn says, "Oh, there's Nixie Needleman over there, just coming in."

Rita has seen Dr. Needleman before and is not surprised by the mountains of platinum hair, the thick makeup, and the cleavage. "She has quite a good reputation," Rita says demurely.

Happily for Quinn and Rita, Nixie Needleman and the nondescript man accompanying her are shown to a table at the opposite end of what Rita continues to view as this expensive basement.

"Have you heard, uh, anything . . . let me start again." Quinn refills Rita's wineglass with the Argentine Malbec that he and the waiter made such a show of selecting. Rita considers it unsuitable for her chicken, but for all she knows, connoisseurs consider it utterly gauche to consume ramps and farro with any wine other than a Malbec. As an aside, I might mention that when Rita reviewed the restaurant for all of us, Caprice remarked that the ideal accompaniment to the menu was an unabridged dictionary.

Rita smiles at Quinn, who has, she reminds herself, many good qualities. In particular, there is nothing fringy or alternative about his practice of psychopharmacology. On the contrary, he is solid, knowledgeable, and compassionate.

Encouraged, he says, "This has to do with, uh, payment." He exhales audibly. "Let me just say it. I have a new patient who's been in treatment with her and also with" — his voice drops to a whisper — "Ted Green. What my patient has to say about him is nothing new — I've heard it before — and that's that he expects to be paid at the beginning of each session. Preferably but not necessarily in cash."

"I've heard that, too," Rita says.

"Have you heard anything about . . . ?" He nods in Nixie Needleman's direction.

"About patients paying her under the table? No. Would she be so stupid?"

"What my patient has to say, and this is a credible woman, is that our, uh, silver-haired friend over there wasn't happy to settle for the co-pay that my patient's insurance allowed. My patient thought it was standard practice."

"Well, it certainly is not standard practice! It's very stupid. If the insurance company finds out, she'll get nailed for fraud."

Quinn nods. "It's a dangerous game."

"So is unreported income. If Ted gets audited, it's the first thing the IRS will look for."

"Eumie must've known," Quinn points out. "Ted? Her husband? Of course she knew."

"That was safe enough," Rita says. "She'd hardly have turned him over to the IRS."

Quinn laughs. "Don't you treat couples?"

Rita looks chagrined. "I see what you mean. I definitely see what you mean."

CHAPTER 27

Ted Green had the nerve to call me at eight-thirty on Sunday morning to demand that I make an emergency visit to treat Dolfo's posttraumatic stress. Instead of arguing with Ted about the diagnosis, I asked him to describe what Dolfo was doing. Could he give some examples of worrisome behavior?

"He's restless. He can't settle down."

"Does he seem to be in pain?"

"Pain! I knew you'd know. The dog maven! Dolfo is in pain."

"Angell has a twenty-four-hour emergency service. The Angell Animal Medical Center. It's on South Huntington Avenue in —"

"Emotional pain. He is suffering. But he has no words."

For all I knew, Dolfo was suffering from a torn cruciate ligament or a nail bed infection or some other physically painful condition. It would be just like Ted, I thought, to focus on the dog's mental state while failing to notice that he was limping or bleeding. Consequently, I agreed to take a look at the dog. Steve was, for once, sleeping late, and I had no intention of dragging him out of bed. Furthermore, if Dolfo needed veterinary care, I'd send Ted to Angell or tell him to call his own veterinarian's emergency number. Steve and I had plans to take all the dogs to Gloucester for a hike and a picnic, and I wasn't going to see our day together spoiled because of a dog who wasn't even Steve's patient. Leah and Caprice were still asleep, too. With luck, I'd be home before the human household was awake.

My previous semiprofessional visit to Ted's had ended so sadly that I felt a superstitious sense of unease as I parked in his driveway, made my way up the stairs, rang the bell, and slipped off my shoes, but it immediately became apparent that the residents of the house, Ted and Wyeth, were noisily alive. As Ted was thanking me for remembering to remove my shoes, Wyeth was shouting from another room. "Stingy bastard!"

"Separation from parents," Ted informed me in an undertone, "is an essential component of normal adolescence." Then he called to Dolfo, who turned out to be in the kitchen, where Wyeth was slouched at the table eating a bagel. His hair was greasy. He wore a torn short-sleeved white T-shirt with yellow sweat stains. As I had on the day of Eumie's death, I noticed the peculiarity of his body. Although he wasn't overweight, he had the kind of potbelly that usually develops only in adulthood. His bare arms showed such an absence of muscle that his flesh seemed held in place by skin alone. The sink was filled with dirty dishes. Everything stank of old food and dog urine. On the floor was a gigantic dog dish filled with stale-looking kibble.

"Coffee?" Ted offered. "Bagels. Cream cheese. Nova lox."

"No, thanks," I said. "I don't have a lot of —"

As if I weren't even there, Wyeth said, "The store opens at ten. The one I have is a piece of shit. And you promised." He pouted like a two-year-old.

"I keep my promises," said Ted, "and I never promised you a new computer."

"You did so."

"If I did, I've forgotten it."

"That's not my fault."

"Wyeth, Holly has gone to the trouble to come here to help Dolfo. She is performing a mitzvah. You're going to need to wait a

271

few minutes, and then we'll discuss things."

"With a monitor and a printer," Wyeth said. "And a router, too." I wanted to tell him that what he could really use were manners, exercise, and a bath. If he'd stopped with the request for a router, I'd have controlled myself. As it was, he persisted. "Pig Face has a new notebook," he said, "and an iPod and a new cell phone, and what've I got? I've got shit." Before the insult to Caprice had registered on me, even before Wyeth had stopped speaking, he stretched one of his sausagelike arms over the table, grabbed a slice of lox, and held it above Dolfo's head. Lox is, of course, smoked salmon, a treat that most dogs find irresistible. In that respect, Dolfo was a typical dog. His eyes lit up, his nose twitched, and he rose on his hindquarters. His foolish face was the picture of delight. And Wyeth raised the slice of lox.

Even then, I didn't get it. In our household, we never feed dogs at the table, but we do train with food. That's exactly what I assumed Wyeth was doing: teaching Dolfo to sit up or maybe to jump in the air.

Dolfo bounced upward, and Wyeth rose to his feet and dangled the slice of lox just out of the dog's reach.

My temper snapped. I stood up, snatched

the lox from Wyeth's hand, told Dolfo to sit, and, when he obeyed, fed him the whole slice. I then addressed Wyeth. "Get something straight — you don't tease this dog or any other dog ever again as long as you live. In particular, you don't tease this dog with food. In fact, if I ever again even begin to suspect that you are thinking about teasing Dolfo or any other dog with food, I am going to put a choke chain around your spoiled neck and I am going to yank until your Adam's apple bursts." I turned to Ted. "And *you.* You're supposed to be the grown-up here. What the hell is wrong with you? You heard what your son called Caprice, and I have no doubt that he's called her that to her face. You saw him tease your dog with food. And you did nothing. And you've had the nerve to call me here on a Sunday morning to treat your dog's post-traumatic stress? Let me tell you something! The stress afflicting your dog is you! If I thought that anyone would adopt him, I'd tell you to find him a new home, but you've made the poor dog unadoptable. You've ruined a perfectly sweet dog, you've let Caprice get so fat that her face is deformed, you've turned your son into a cruel, insufferable, demanding brat, God only knows what happened to your wife, and if I'm traumatizing you by telling you the truth, good! It's about time someone did. You deserve it."

With that, I walked out.

CHAPTER 28

"The more I see of men, the more I prefer or love or admire my dogs, *men* meaning fellow human beings, of course. Mark Twain," I said to Steve. "Pascal. Frederick the Great, Madame de Sévigné, and a few dozen other people. I've seen it attributed to all of them, probably because all of them said it. Or something to that effect. But if you want to quote me, the statement right now is that the more I see of *myself,* the more I prefer my dogs. Our dogs. All dogs. Any dogs. Even Dolfo was better behaved than I was! I am completely disgusted with myself."

That was on Sunday afternoon during our hike, which was not entirely ruined by my self-recriminations, but only because of Steve. He patiently pointed out that it was perfectly all right to stop someone from teasing a dog with food. Among other things, he said, the behavior was dangerous: Dolfo could have bitten Wyeth. Steve also said that it was probably high time that someone spoke bluntly to Ted. My only big mistake, in Steve's view, was telling the brutal truth in front of Wyeth. I agreed.

"You were trying to protect everyone," he said. "Dolfo, Caprice, and Wyeth. There's nothing wrong with kindness to animals and children."

"Oh, my impulses were admirable. But in front of Wyeth! He is so pitiful. And at the same time, he's so cruel. My temper just snapped."

"You lost it," Steve agreed. "It happens."

"It doesn't happen to you," I said.

"It does. Go easy on yourself. Look, Holly, it was a one-shot deal. You don't go around making scenes all the time. It's not like you make a habit of it. Let it go."

And I did, at least for the moment. Even the weather seemed determined to lift my spirits. The New England climate is notoriously changeable: it typically changes for the worse by making abrupt leaps from freezing to sweltering and back to freezing again. The temperature that afternoon was, for once, seventy degrees. As if to compensate for my uncivilized conduct and my consequent shame and guilt, the dogs were at their best during the hike through the wilds of Dogtown, a large wooded area in Gloucester that Steve and I both liked. Kimi refrained from growling at India, and not once did she crowd Lady or loom over her. Kimi, Rowdy, and Sammy wore their red two-piece Wenaha packs, and Sammy managed not to detach the saddlebags that were Velcro-fastened to the yoke. When we stopped to give water to the dogs, no one tried to steal anyone else's folding bowl. On wet stretches of the trail, Rowdy kept his head up instead of indulging his revolting appetite for mud. Lady moved with a bounce in her step that showed, we thought, unusual self-confidence. When we got back to the van and were loading in all the dogs, India, whose dignity usually prevented her from begging for treats, paused for a moment to nuzzle my pocket, and I had the pleasure of slipping her a piece of cheddar. We arrived home to find a note from Leah and Caprice to say that they'd gone to a concert at a nearby church and were going to hang out with friends afterward. Our house and our evening were ours.

Sunday's hike and the evening with Steve restored my equilibrium. Monday morning started off well. After finishing my usual chores, I took a shower and, contrary to the instructions on the CD that Eumie had given me, listened to the guided imagery while I shampooed my hair and bathed. Just as promised, I ended up feeling strong and relaxed. Better yet, I felt hopeful that showing my dogs could become fun again. That afternoon, I decided, Rowdy and I would go to a park to work on rally obedience. When we got to the park, I'd keep taking deep, smooth breaths in and out, and Rowdy and I would play. The happy thought came to me that the cure for my ring nerves wasn't so much guided imagery as it was Rowdy, whose performance of the required exercises in obedience had always been maddeningly unpredictable, but who, I now realized, had reliably enjoyed every second in the ring and who was more than willing to allow his joy to replace my fun-killing pride and competitiveness.

Writers are dreadful opportunists, and malamute-owning writers are the worst. Having experienced renewed optimism about my ring nerves for all of twenty minutes, I sat at the kitchen table with my notebook computer and rapidly drafted a column about the cure that I felt certain was going to work. The first half of the column, I must point out, was about methods that had failed or had made me more anxious than ever. For example, bursting into song to make sure I kept breathing had been dandy during practice sessions, but what was I supposed to do as I stood just outside the ring? Make a spectacle of myself by loudly caroling an off-key "Happy Birthday" or "Amazing Grace"? Or sing to myself under my breath when I was too terrified to have a breath to sing under? So, the first half of the column was based on experience, and only the second half was derived largely from my imagination. After all, a draft was a draft. I'd eventually do a few reality-based revisions.

Caprice, I might mention, had roused herself at what was for her the early hour of nine o'clock. She'd eaten a nutritious breakfast of fruit and yogurt, taken Lady for a walk, and cleaned her room before going to see her therapist. After her therapy hour, she was going to Rita's office to help Rita with her computer. As I hope I've suggested, Rita was a brilliant therapist — despite never having trained a dog. Rita's present dog, Willie, a Scottish terrier, was no one's idea of a promising candidate for competition obedience, but Rita had refused to take him to Canine Good Citizen classes or basic pet obedience. He walked politely on leash because he'd known how when she'd adopted him. He was house-trained. I had made notable progress in teaching him to quit yapping during her absence and to stop flying at my ankles. Rita was fully satisfied with him, as she'd been with her previous dog, Groucho, an amiable dachshund who, by virtue of walking pleasantly on leash and never using the indoors for outdoor purposes, was as educated as Rita expected a dog to be. Rita always argued that she spent her professional life helping people to change and that the last thing she wanted to do when she got home was to start again with her dog. I, on the other hand, said that anyone setting up in the therapy business should be required to have spent a minimum of two preparatory years training a dog; a clinician who lacked the prerequisite was merely *practicing,* whereas someone who'd learned first on a dog might actually be able to *do* human therapy. Rita excepted. But when it came to computers, she exemplified yet another radical difference between dog trainers and shrinks: dog trainers, who are fully accustomed to exchanging clear, unambiguous messages with intelligent beings different from themselves, easily transfer their skills and attitudes toward computers, whereas a lot of shrinks get irritated at computers on the grounds that computers fail to have deep feelings, never appreciate the complex nuances of anyone's life history, and are aggravatingly reminiscent of unsatisfactory parents. Leah had tried to convince Rita that just as dogs were companion animals, computers were companion machines, but instead of buying the argument, Rita had hired Leah to help her. Leah, who was endlessly patient with dogs, hated the job and did it only out of pity for Rita. Leah was, however, working all day, so the pressing task of transferring Rita's files from her computer to a CD that she could bring home, and deleting the sensitive material from her computer, had fallen to Caprice. Rita had taken Kevin's warning seriously. She'd be right there as Caprice copied and deleted, and there'd be no need to open files, so there was no concern about access to anyone's secrets.

So, while Caprice was presumably at Rita's office, when I'd finished my work, I gathered together the rally obedience signs I'd printed out from the Web, selected the ones I wanted, packed some dog treats, and made a shopping list. I intended to take Rowdy to the big park behind the Fresh

Pond Mall and to buy food for dinner on the way home. By my malamute standards, the day was even better than the previous one — sixty degrees and overcast — so Rowdy would be safe in the car with the windows lowered and a padlock on his crate.

Sammy was at work with Steve. Before leaving, I needed to make sure that the dogs left at home would be comfortable. I gave Kimi a turn in the fenced yard, then India and Lady. While they were still wandering around, I picked up the pooper-scooper and was engaged in what Leah calls "the unaesthetic task" when India suddenly began to growl. The German shepherd dog is, of course, supposed to be a watchdog. Fortunately, India recognized the background noise of our neighborhood as just that and never sounded pointless alarms. Indeed, her watchdog vocalizations often struck me as primarily expressive rather than communicative: when India barked, she sometimes seemed less interested in frightening off intruders or in warning us of potential dangers than in voicing her observations of changes in the environment. *I've noticed something new,* she seemed to say. *And I'm curious about it!* If she perceived a threat, especially a threat to Steve, she sounded serious and even menacing rather than simply alert.

But on the rare occasions when India growled, she meant business. A few seconds earlier, she'd been meandering around our little yard. Now, she faced the driveway and was approaching the wooden gate with slow, deliberate steps. Lady cowered next to her. I was less concerned about India than I was about Lady, who was clearly caught between the desire to flee and the equally strong wish to plaster herself to India, her powerful protector: Lady's entire body trembled as if set in motion by the almost inaudible rumble emerging from India's throat.

"That will do," I told India. "Enough. Whatever it is, it's my job and not yours." As I moved ahead of India to reach the gate, she obediently stopped growling, but I could now see that her lip was lifted and that her dark eyes were ablaze.

It was typical of Steve's horrible ex-wife to reply with an accusation: "You aren't answering your phone!"

"I have nothing to say to you," I told Anita in what I hoped was a tone of calm control. I didn't care what Anita thought of me, but I wanted to assure India and Lady that I had the power to keep the Fiend out of their lives. Although India had obeyed me, her intelligent face wore an expression of what I am forced to describe as skepticism.

"We need to talk," Anita said loudly.

"Go away." I took pride in keeping my voice firm and quiet.

"I don't like yelling through this gate."

"Then don't yell. Just go away." If I'd been alone, I'd simply have gone into the house and ignored Anita, but I couldn't bear to sink in India's opinion. Ludicrous though it may sound, I wanted India — and Lady, too — to see that I could make Anita turn tail.

"I have to undo the wrongs I've done," said Anita, a sliver of whose face was now visible through the narrow gap between the gate and the fence. The statement sounded rehearsed.

Peering at Anita, I realized with sudden and foolish embarrassment that the pooper-scooper was still in my hand. Indeed, my fingers were gripping its handle tightly, as if my body intended me to use it as a weapon. With as much dignity as I could summon, I rested the implement against the fence. "Down," I told India. "Stay." Then I un-latched the gate, slipped out, and latched the gate again.

Anita looked as beautiful as ever: tall, slim, and elegant, with even features and long, silky blond hair. She wore a beige trouser outfit and simple gold jewelry.

"Make it quick," I said. "India and Lady are on the other side of that gate, and your presence is bothering them."

"I need to make up for hurting people," she said.

"And dogs?"

"What?"

"Dogs."

"You must be joking."

"How do you intend to make amends to Lady?"

Anita nearly spat. Truly, I'm sure that her mouth filled with saliva. She settled for saying, "If I knew of some way to undo the pain I've caused you . . ."

"You haven't," I said. "I don't know why you're targeting me, but it doesn't matter. I've seen what you did to Steve. To Gabrielle. And to Lady, who couldn't defend herself. I hope you rot in hell. I never want to see you near me or near our dogs again. If you aren't off my property in exactly sixty seconds, I am calling the police."

As I'd hoped, Anita retreated. I returned to the yard and led India and Lady up the stairs to the house. To my surprise, Caprice was in the kitchen.

"I couldn't help overhearing some of

that," she said. "Is there anything I can do?"

"Yes. If she shows up again, don't let her in. That's Steve's ex-wife."

"Anita Fairley," Caprice said.

"Please sit down." I pointed to a chair, took one directly across from it, rested my elbows on the table, and put my chin in my hands. For once, I didn't offer coffee, tea, or food. Caprice was now directly across from me. I looked her straight in the eye. "Fairley," I said. "No one here ever calls her Anita Fairley. We seldom mention her. When we do, we use her first name."

"Leah must've used her last name. It stuck with me." Caprice wasn't gazing at the ceiling or shifting around. Her eyes continued to meet mine.

"Or possibly you looked her up. On Google? Or somewhere else. On one of the Deep Web sites? Let me guess something else. You looked me up, too. And Steve."

The facade broke. Tears ran down Caprice's face.

"Hey," I said, "it's okay! I'm sorry! Caprice, I don't care. What's there to find out about Steve and me? Nothing!" I got up, found a box of tissues, and handed it to Caprice. "If you looked me up, all you found was more than any sane human being has ever wanted to know about dogs."

A smile crossed her face.

"It's okay. I mean that. What's getting to me isn't that you checked us out. I use Google, too, you know. What's making me uneasy is this feeling of secrecy. Not that I expect you to come right out and say, 'Hey, I see that you've published forty thousand articles about flea control, and they all say the same thing.' It's —"

"It's that I was sneaky."

"We would've told you, you know. All you had to do was ask. But for all you knew, we had something to hide. I did. Or Steve did."

"If you do," said Caprice, "it's not on the Web."

CHAPTER 29

Caprice apologized, and I ended up giving her a big hug. I then repeated my request not to open the door to Anita, and Rowdy and I left. Even though I was relieved to have confronted Caprice and even though I felt justified in having ordered Anita off my property, I needed time to commune with Rowdy.

As planned, I drove Rowdy to the park behind the Fresh Pond Mall. Newcomers to Cambridge probably wonder how many trees were felled to create so large an area of grass. The answer is none: as I prefer to forget when I'm there and as you'd never guess to look at it, the place was once a dump. My only objection to it was the occasional presence of dog-aggressive off-leash dogs. That afternoon, there were no dogs in sight. The sky had clouded up, and the temperature had dropped. More to the point, there was no wind to blow away the rally signs I was placing here and there on the rough grass. At rally events, the signs are fastened to wooden stakes in the ground, and the particular signs are chosen to mark off a varied course, but my signs had no stakes, and I chose the particular exercises more or less at random. At the Novice level, rally offered no challenge to Rowdy or to any other dog with experience in competition obedience, but the shift was as difficult for me as it was easy for Rowdy. Learning to interpret the rally signs was like learning to decode traffic signs. I was becoming accustomed to the rules of the rally road, but I was still finding it hard to shake the high-pressure attitude of competition obedience, which is to say, the attitude responsible for my ring nerves. My reflexive response was to say, *Well, perfect heeling doesn't cost points, and scoring is scoring, so don't settle for less than perfection!* Worse, when I mulled over the idea that rally was supposed to be fun, I thought, *Fun? Oh, we'll be good at that. We'll be better than everyone else!*

Anyway, once I'd finished laying out the course of stations marked by signs, Rowdy and I moved to the first station, marked by the start sign, where I automatically said, "Place," and raised my left hand to signal

Rowdy to get into flawless heel position and focus on my face. Losing myself in his all-but-black eyes, I said, "Rowdy, habits are hard to break. We don't need to do this, buddy. In fact, we're allowed to rush hell-for-leather-leash into the rally course. You get to bounce around. I get to clap my hands and talk and whistle and cluck my tongue. And not just here, either. At real rally trials. If, that is, I have it left in me to loosen up. You do. So please remind me of how it's done, chum. I need you." I paused to take deep breaths in and out, and I released Rowdy: "Okay!" Then we started all over by running to the first station, a left turn, easy enough, and on to a moving side step right, into a fast pace, on to three spirals with Rowdy on the outside, and so forth, and all the while, I chattered and whistled and kept going so fast that precision was out of the question, and when we finally reached the finish sign, I was overjoyed at our success in having performed the exercises with admirably sloppy exuberance. Then we dashed through the course again and were even worse, which is to say better, that time than we'd been the first, and at the finish sign, I held out my arm and had Rowdy rise up in all his wolf-gray-and-white magnificence, his massive paws on my forearm, his face in my face, and I said, "Thank you, Rowdy. I love you with all my heart."

Fundamental principle of dog training: end on a note of success. If we kept practicing, we might wreck my recovery by getting good at the new sport. If that happened, we'd be forced to take up a canine activity so unsuitable for malamutes that we'd be kicked out and probably banned for life. Herding came to mind. Confronted with a flock, Rowdy would reduce the sheep to racks of lamb. At least he wouldn't do it in any sort of sneaky, duplicitous fashion. He didn't have secrets, and he didn't ferret out other people's. If he caught a whiff of a puzzling scent, he acted openly and directly by sticking his nose in its source. I felt overwhelming gratitude to him for restoring me to myself.

Forty-five minutes later, after shopping for food, I returned home to find a note from Caprice, who was taking Lady for a walk. I was just putting a pound of sliced roast beef, my thank-you gift to all five dogs, in the refrigerator when the phone rang. The caller was Gabrielle, my stepmother, who wanted to talk about Anita.

"She was here today," I said. "I didn't invite her in. We talked in the driveway.

She's still on that kick about undoing wrongs."

"Well, she called me." Whenever Gabrielle began a conversation by saying *Well, . . .* in that particular tone of voice, she made me feel that she was about to confide an observation or insight that would give us both great satisfaction. "We were right," she continued. "Anita has become involved in the recovery movement. She's been to a place called CHIRP. It sounds like an Audubon sanctuary, doesn't it? But it's some kind of spa or luxury mental hospital. Or both. So, someone *did* put her up to making amends."

"There was a hollow ring to it. What she said to me sounded rehearsed. Or maybe memorized. But CHIRP isn't a mental hospital. It's . . . as I understand it, it's more like a retreat. Or sometimes a detox place. And maybe a spa, too. Healing and recovery."

"She's been in therapy," Gabrielle announced.

"Are you sure?"

"With someone named Ted Green. I want you to ask Rita about him."

I sighed and poured out everything. When I'd finished, Gabrielle said, "He sounds worse than anyone deserves."

"No. Rita says that a lot of people find him helpful. And I honestly can imagine that he would be very sympathetic. Not that Anita deserves sympathy, if you ask me."

"She is a terribly unhappy person," Gabrielle said.

"She is a sadistic crook."

"If she's trying to change, she deserves to be encouraged."

"When she starts writing you checks, maybe I'll be convinced," I said.

Oddly enough, the call left me feeling unusually mellow, possibly because I'd had the chance to vent my spleen at and about Anita in a single day. I was, however, aware of somehow having contracted a case of contagious sympathy for her. Gabrielle, who always thought of every friend or acquaintance as the equivalent of a family member, persisted in speaking as if Anita were a difficult relative. In a way, Anita was a member of my network, if not of my family, and it suddenly occurred to me that when she spoke about making amends, she just might be serious and genuine.

But I had my own amends to make. I owed an apology to Ted and Wyeth, and in storming out, I'd deprived Dolfo of help. The approach I'd taken with Ted and

Eumie, and then with Ted alone, had done nothing for the poor dog. My major error, as I saw it, had been to impose my viewpoint on the Brainard-Greens instead of discovering theirs and working from within it; I'd accepted their desire to use positive methods, but I'd failed to adapt my positive methods to their framework. From every dog I'd ever trained, indeed, from every dog I'd ever watched, I'd learned the importance of tailoring training to fit the individual animal. Even so simple a matter as what constituted positive reinforcement differed from breed to breed and from individual to individual. For the typical Border collie, the glorious opportunity to retrieve a tennis ball was wildly reinforcing. In contrast, if I tossed a tennis ball for Rowdy, his superior and scornful expression would inform me that if I insisted on throwing my toys on the ground, I shouldn't expect him to pick up after me. Sammy, however, flew after balls and brought them back with the enthusiasm of a golden retriever. Rowdy worked for treats; his attitude was that if it wasn't edible, it wasn't really reinforcement, was it? When I told Rowdy and Kimi what good dogs they were, they might as well have come out and said, *Oh, is that what you think? How nice for you. Now where's the liver?* Sammy simply ate up *Good boy.* So, which breed was Ted? What motivated him? And what kind of reinforcement did he want?

I went to the computer and read up on Ted's book and on his theories about trauma. As I'd heard, he had a broad definition of trauma, and in his view, trauma led to addiction, by which he meant almost any kind of dependency. Trauma required healing, and addiction required recovery, mainly by means of twelve-step programs. In evaluating what Ted had to say, I searched for examples in my own life. Naturally, I started out and ended up thinking about dogs: alpha and omega. The death of every dog I'd ever owned had, in Ted's view, been traumatic. My losses had certainly felt traumatic. How had I responded to each such "ordinary trauma," as Ted phrased it? By getting another dog. Was I hooked on dog love? Oh, yes. Indeed, my interpretation of the Serenity Prayer was a measure of the strength of my addiction: the serenity to accept behaviors I couldn't change, the courage to change those I could, and the wisdom to know the difference was just what every dog trainer needed.

So, having prepared myself, I called Ted

Green. "I want to apologize for losing my temper," I said. "And I feel terrible about saying what I did in front of Wyeth. If you still want my help with Dolfo, I'd like to give it another try."

"Something was going on with you," Ted said gently. "Your reaction felt overdetermined. Out of proportion to the situation, so to speak."

"Yes," I agreed.

"So, what's with you?"

"I guess you don't know. I, uh, I had a head injury a couple of years ago . . . a little less than that." I was using the truth to tell a lie, so to speak. Losing my temper had nothing to do with head trauma. "And just afterward, I had a major emotional shock." True. To my horror, Steve had married Anita Fairley, whose name I certainly wasn't going to mention to Ted, who was, as I'd just learned, her therapist. "Anyway, as I was mulling over the way I overreacted at your house, I was thinking about grounding. And containment. In other words, grounding myself in present realities and containing my reactions to triggers. Setting boundaries. And I knew I'd let myself get sucked into the past. And so on. So, I had to call you."

"I understand," he said.

"I thought you would."

Ted said that he had a cancellation at five o'clock, and we agreed that I'd visit then.

In my defense, I have to point out that my mendacity and, worse, my trivialization of life-shattering trauma was in a good cause, namely, Dolfo. What's more, sustaining a whopping whack on the head and then finding out about Steve and Anita hadn't exactly been fun, and in struggling to recover, I honestly had found it useful to ground myself in the here and now and so on. That is, beneath my palaver about true events, there actually lay some truth.

CHAPTER 30

At quarter of five, equipped with baby gates, leashes, and treats, I was ready to set off for Ted Green's when Caprice decided to accompany me. "I left my winter clothes," she said. "They're in a cedar closet. I forgot about them when Leah and I were there. I want all my possessions out of that house, and I don't want to have to go back alone. But if I'll be in the way, I can go another time."

"No, it's fine."

As I was backing out of the driveway, I was again delayed, this time by Kevin Dennehy, who greeted us and made what sounded like an offhand inquiry about where we were going.

"To Ted Green's," I said. "I'm having another go at helping with the dog, and Caprice is picking up the last of her belongings. We'll be —"

"Hey, Caprice," he said. "I gotta have a

word with Holly. Personal matter."

Kevin opened the driver's side door of my car, and we walked back toward the house.

"Personal matter?" I asked.

"Personal safety," he said. "I didn't know you were still going over there."

"I haven't been. Except for the memorial service. And Sunday morning, but not for long. Leah and Caprice went to get Caprice's things. Otherwise —"

"This is homicide we're talking about."

"Kevin, I know that, but it's not *my* homicide. I'm alive, obviously. It had nothing to do with me. Eumie wasn't killed because I was training her dog."

"Her daughter's living with you."

"Visiting us," I corrected.

"Get him to bring the dog here."

"It won't work. For one thing, I said I'd be there. And for another, I need to work on restructuring the dog's environment. I can't do that here."

"Get Steve to go with you."

"No. Absolutely not. Kevin, you know how hard Steve works. I'm not asking him to put in time as my bodyguard. I don't need one. If I did, I'd take a dog."

"Look, do me a favor. Don't eat or drink

anything. You or the kid. As a personal favor."

"I'm going there to train a dog. If I swallow anything, it'll be liver out of my own pockets, and that'll be by accident. Okay? And I'll tell Caprice. Am I excused now?"

Kevin nodded. He waved to Caprice and walked off looking glum.

On the short drive to Ted Green's, I passed along Kevin's order, which I explained to Caprice by saying that Kevin was given to fits of paranoia and that the malady was an occupational hazard of being a cop.

"He's not being paranoid," she said. "I hate walking into that house. If I could go in there and not breathe the air, I'd do it."

When we'd parked in Ted's driveway and were heading for the steps to the front door, I caught sight of George McBane, who was emerging from his driveway on an expensive-looking racing bike. I expected him to stop and say hello, but he whizzed past and sped away without even nodding to us. He looked horrible. His face was pale, and his expression was sad and almost dazed.

"George looks ghastly," I said to Caprice. "I wonder if he's sick." We'd reached the porch and were dutifully removing our shoes.

"He was probably the one who poisoned the squirrels," Caprice said. "I saw him in one of those trees between their house and ours. He had a ladder. He probably got caught."

I was stunned. Only a few days earlier, I'd been looking through a large glossy mailing that Steve and I had received from the MSPCA-Angell when I'd spotted a photo of George McBane and Barbara Leibowitz, who were spotlighted because of a gift to the Boston Capital Campaign. The official slogan of the MSPCA-Angell was Kindness and Care of Animals. And George had been poisoning squirrels? Did Kevin know? Had Barbara found out and confronted him?

Before I'd composed myself, the door opened, and Ted tried to give Caprice a welcoming hug. "Home at last," he said.

"I've come to get my winter clothes." Caprice held up a box of trash bags she'd brought with her. "Holly, I'll meet you in the car."

I handed her the keys. "You'll need these. And you might want to listen to the radio."

"That girl," Ted said with a dramatic shrug.

Eager to get to the point, I said, "I have some fresh thoughts about Dolfo. Ted, who really knows what happened before you got him? It's occurred to me that he may not feel safely grounded and that what he needs is a clear sense of boundaries. I'm worried that in the absence of them, he's experiencing anxiety. It's even possible that he's having flashbacks." As I was wondering whether I'd gone too far, I glanced around in search of the dog. "Where is he?"

"Dolfo, here! Dolfo!" To me, Ted said, "He was here a minute ago when I came up from my office. Maybe I forgot to close the door, and he's downstairs."

Ted headed for the kitchen, but before reaching it, he vanished through an open door. I followed him down a flight of carpeted stairs to an attractive waiting room with a couch, two upholstered chairs, and end tables that held magazines and boxes of tissues. Everything was off-white and had remained so. In other words, the waiting room appeared to be a Dolfo-free zone. From an open door, however, there emerged a soft thump. Cursing in what I took to be Yiddish, Ted dashed into what proved to be a small, windowless business office rather than the spacious psychotherapy office I expected. Crammed into the room, which had an ugly fluorescent ceiling light, were a desk that held a computer and printer, an office chair, and three filing cabinets. The bottom drawer of one filing cabinet was wide open. The floor space was occupied mainly by Dolfo and the manila folders and papers with which he was playing.

"Jesus Christ! Damn it all!" Ted yelled.

Dolfo responded by dropping the single sheet of paper he'd been chewing and turning his attention to what at first registered on my writer's eye as the manuscript of a book, a thick stack of paper bound with one large clasp.

"Boundaries," I said calmly. "You see? He's begging for boundaries. It's in the nature of dogs to search for them, to force us to set limits by a process of trial and error. *Is this a violation? Is that?*"

"Goddamn it, Dolfo, give me that!" Ted shouted.

Enough. I had to shove past Ted to squeeze all the way into the little office. As I did so, I filled my left hand with treats from one of my capacious pockets. Instead of trying to persuade Dolfo to trade the manuscript for liver goodies, I took the expeditious course of tossing the food on the floor a foot or two away from the dog's head. Predictably, he released his grip on his booty and turned his attention from the merely interesting to the irresistibly delicious. Pushing past Ted, I swooped down and quickly grabbed what I was embarrassed to recognize not as a book manuscript but as a copy of a thick federal tax return. There's nothing wrong with *my* sense of boundaries: books are intended for publication, but tax returns are private. Still, I'm a rapid reader. The same quick glance that had enabled me to identify the return had also shown me a gross adjusted income that was impossibly low for someone living as Ted did; at a guess, Ted was reporting less than half the amount of money he actually took in. The responsibilities of a dog trainer, I decided, did not include the obligation to inform the IRS that her client was cheating on his taxes. Furthermore, this was not the time to tell him that if he underpaid, I therefore ended up overpaying because of his dishonesty. Etiquette having triumphed over ethics, I put the thick return facedown on the desk. By then, Ted was on the floor gathering up loose papers and folders. Dolfo, having wolfed down the treats, helped him by licking his face. When Ted stood up, I realized that he was, for once, angry at something Dolfo had done. Instead of psychologizing, Ted said, "Point made, Holly. Enough is enough."

"It's like the end of *Portnoy's Complaint*," I agreed. "Maybe now we can begin."

Five minutes later, Ted and I sat at the kitchen table. Dolfo, on leash, sat at my side. Ted took notes on a yellow legal pad.

"Doors will be kept closed," I dictated. "Dolfo will be loose in, at most, one room at a time. If you can't watch him every second, he will be either outdoors in your fenced yard or in a crate. I will leave one of the crates I have in my car. Dolfo will be taken out once an hour. If he produces, he will be given praise and food. He will be fed twice a day. You will put the bowl down for ten minutes. At the end of that time, you will remove it. You will hire a trainer. Not me. I will give you her name."

"You sure you don't want coffee?" Ted asked. "Something to eat?"

"Nothing, thanks. I can't stay, and we have work to do." The remaining work actually took only a few minutes. Ted helped me to carry a big folding crate from the car to his kitchen. I dug in my purse and found the number I'd promised, and I added the name and number of a reliable dog walker. Then I apologized. "You don't have the time to train Dolfo by yourself. And so on. I should have known that from the beginning. I'm sorry." I really should have. Ted and

Eumie did things by hiring other people; it was a way of life, and I should have recognized and accepted it as such.

To my astonishment, Ted began to cry. "I can't do much of anything without Eumie."

"I'm sure you can learn. Ted, I'm really very sorry."

"Caprice hates me," he said.

As I was on the verge of mendaciously assuring him otherwise, Caprice walked into the kitchen carrying a big trash bag that presumably contained her winter clothes.

"What we've got here," he said to her, gesturing to me, "is a real mensch."

"Keep the Jewish shtick to yourself," she said. "I just ran into your un-bar-mitzvahed son, who's a prize piece of dreck, and all the Yiddish and all the knishes going aren't going to get you the Jewish family warmth you're after, Ted, so lay off."

"Wyeth's mother isn't Jewish. That's the only reason —"

"Don't tell me! I know! There's a Yiddish word for it: *meshugass*," she said. "You and your Yiddish. You are such a phony. You put a mezuzah by the door and a menorah in the dining room, and on the High Holidays, you don't go near a temple. But the main thing, the important thing, is that you don't know a mitzvah when you see one. Or when you benefit from one. Holly's trying to save your awful dog. Steve and Holly took me in. Mitzvahs both. So shut up." She stomped out.

I made as graceful a departure as I could manage.

CHAPTER 31

On the way home, Caprice and I stopped at Loaves and Fishes for takeout. For most of my adult life, preparing my own meals had consisted mainly of walking to pizzerias. My lackadaisical attitude toward my own diet had been in total contrast to the care I devoted to making sure that my animals received optimal nutrition. As a dog writer, I was bombarded with information about canine nutrition and was forever changing or combining brands of commercial food and introducing or discontinuing additional ingredients and supplements. Meanwhile, genetic luck and my high metabolic rate let me get away with eating whatever was convenient. As usual in my life, the impetus for change was dogs. Specifically, I wrote a dog-treat cookbook called *101 Ways to Cook Liver,* the research for which had filled my house with such nauseating odors that I'd developed a temporary aversion to hot food and a craving for salad. Once the book was done, my normal appetite returned, but by then, I'd not only learned to make salad but had actually learned to cook. Then Steve and I began work on *No More Fat Dogs,* and when I started to read about human and canine obesity, I lost my taste for junk food. We ate good pizza now and then, but when we wanted convenience food, we relied mainly on Loaves and Fishes.

Even before I opened the back door, I could hear Rita's voice and was glad I'd bought a lot of food. She was usually soft-spoken. Now, her tone was agitated. I assumed that she would want company and would stay for dinner. I was correct. She was seated at the kitchen table with Steve and Leah. Steve was always an excellent listener. Leah, however, had a tendency to finish other people's sentences and to offer her own conclusions and interpretations before she'd finished hearing facts. At the moment, she didn't stand a chance of interrupting Rita, who was sputtering with outrage. "Nothing was taken! Nothing that I can see. But how do I tell what was read? Caprice, you know that everything was . . . whatever you did so that no one could open those files. How I hate computers!"

"Hi, Rita," I said as Caprice and I put the shopping bags on the counter.

Rita didn't even greet us. "Shit. Someone broke into my office. I feel so damned violated!"

"Your computer is password protected," Caprice said. "So are the individual files."

"I should've thrown the damned computer in the trash and kept good old ordinary files at home. Damn it! I hate computers! And why didn't I get a new lock for my office door? Two of them! A hundred! What kind of vile human being sneaks around . . . I have spent my entire professional life trying to help people, trying to assure them that here, in my office, they're safe, that nothing terrible will happen, that this is a temporary refuge, and now this! I could strangle that stinking piece of scum! I am outraged! I am . . ."

Without consulting Rita, I set the kitchen table for five people. As Rita continued to vent her rage, Caprice and Leah silently helped to put out the barbecued chicken, eggplant parmigiana, and green salad we'd bought, and Steve opened a bottle of wine. I noticed a new bandage on Leah's left hand, but Rita was still talking, so I didn't ask what had happened. When the four of us took seats at the table, Rita finally paused for breath.

"When Rita got to her office this morning," Steve said, "she found that the building had been entered. And her office."

"Two others," Rita added. "Both psychotherapy offices."

"The second building on your block," I said. The temptation was strong to remind her that after the first incident, she'd maintained that breaking into therapy offices was a symbolic act and a plea for help.

"What happened to the symbolism?" Leah asked. "Penetration? Wasn't there something about a plea for help?"

Rita almost choked, but then she smiled. "Yes, what about that? That's when someone else's office is entered. When it's mine, my attitude does a volte-face."

Laughter relieved the tension. We began to eat, and over dinner, we heard the details, of which there were few. Despite the recent entering of the nearby therapy building, the last therapist to leave Rita's building on the previous night couldn't remember whether he had locked the outer door, and he was sure that he hadn't set the alarm. It had a password that he could never remember, and he hadn't wanted to lock himself out in case he'd forgotten something.

"I've done the same thing myself," Rita admitted. "But not this week."

"You did change the passwords on your computer," Caprice said. "We went over that. No names of pets. Nothing in the dictionary. Not your phone number. Combine letters and numerals."

"Yes," said Rita. "But my Rolodex was there."

"How private is that?" Steve asked. "It isn't, is it?"

"No. And it has the names of colleagues, too. Friends. There's nothing to identify people as patients."

"What did the police say?" I asked.

"Not much. They dusted for prints. They told us to lock the doors and set the alarm. That was about it. I didn't have the sense that we were being dismissed, really, but from their point of view, it wasn't a major crime. Nothing was stolen from any of our offices. Nothing that we noticed, anyway. One of the offices was a psychiatrist's. She had some drug samples in a drawer, and even those weren't taken." She paused. "But I still hate computers!"

After the meal, Rita went upstairs to her own place, and Leah and Caprice took Sammy and Lady for a walk. Leah, who was between serious boyfriends, usually walked

Kimi, and I felt convinced that she'd chosen Sammy instead because he was such an attention grabber. Malamutes are tremendously showy showoffs. Furthermore, they create occasions for talking to strangers. You don't just hear the usual *What a beautiful dog,* either. Rather, you get comments that absolutely require correction, such as *Nice husky!* Incredibly, you even get asked, *Is that an Alaskan Malibu?* So, Rowdy and Kimi were more than adequate as dating service representatives, but Sammy's combination of gorgeous looks and puppyish demeanor was irresistible. I tactfully refrained from uttering the phrase *man magnet* lest I raise Leah's feminist hackles.

As Steve and I were loading the dishwasher and cleaning up the kitchen, he said, "Anita showed up at work today."

"And bit Leah," I said. "I noticed a bandage on her hand."

Steve laughed. "You're closer than you know. When she showed up — I was busy. I didn't even see her — Leah happened to be carrying a cat from one of the exam rooms to another, and the cat sank his teeth into Leah's hand. He's never done anything like that before. Passive, mellow cat."

"I hope you got Leah to a doctor. Cat

bites can be very serious."

"No kidding?"

"Sorry."

"Yes, she's on antibiotics."

"She showed up here this morning. Not Leah. Anita. Anita did. She's on some kick about undoing wrongs. She called Gabrielle, too. When she got here, I was in the yard with India and Lady."

"I hope you ignored her."

"I told her to vaporize. She was outside the gate. I didn't let her in. India probably wouldn't have let me even if I'd wanted to. Lady was cowering."

Steve stopped wiping the table. Losing his usual air of calm, he almost threw himself at me, and instead of holding me gently, he wrapped his arms around me so hard that I could barely breathe. "I am so sorry," he said. "I am so sorry."

"Steve, it is *not* your fault that she showed up here. I can take care of myself. She is no threat to any of us. Yes, she scares Lady, but so do a lot of other things, and Lady trusts India."

"For good reason," Steve said. "She trusts you, too. Also for good reason. You know, I can begin to forgive myself all the rest, but I can never forgive myself for how she treated

Lady. I just didn't see it. Until it was too late."

"It isn't too late. Lady is fine. She really is. She has all of us. You, me, Leah, India, Rowdy. And Sammy! He's so lighthearted that he can't imagine why Lady worries. Even Kimi! And now Caprice. Steve, I swear it. Anita is no threat to any of us."

"I love you," he said. "I love you with all my heart."

CHAPTER 32

On that same Monday evening, Ted Green is congratulating himself on his success in the matter of limits and boundaries. Ted is pleased that over a wild mushroom fricassee delivered by his new cook and heated up according to her written directions, he calmly yet firmly refused to grant Wyeth's irate demand for a new computer. Ted is now in the backyard with Dolfo, who is sniffing a shrub and beginning to raise his left leg. Clicker and treats in hand, Ted is prepared to reinforce a behavior heartily desired outdoors and outdoors only. He enjoys, I suspect, a sense of manly control over his environment. In my opinion, there's nothing intrinsically masculine about his situation or his behavior, but if a gratifying illusion motivates him to train his dog, who am I to nitpick? As to Ted's parenting, it's outside my field of expertise, and when I think about what happens next, I'm glad of that.

What happens is that Wyeth opens his bedroom window all the way and, without even glancing down to the backyard beneath, hurls his desktop computer, his monitor, and his printer, one right after the other, through the open window, which he then slams shut. As wood bangs against wood, howls and screams erupt from below, and Wyeth belatedly looks down to see Ted and Dolfo, both of whom have been struck. Wyeth grabs cash and his cell phone, races downstairs and out the front door, and runs away.

Ted has had the bad luck to be hit by the computer itself, the heavy CPU, but the good luck to have been struck on his right leg and foot rather than on his head. Dolfo is racing around in mad figure eights. It is clear to Ted that something, either the monitor or the printer, hit Dolfo, who howled in pain; perhaps the damage is internal. Fortunately, Ted's cell phone escaped injury. After hauling himself to a sitting position, he unhesitatingly calls Dr. Tortorello. He is, however, disappointed to reach his psychiatrist's answering machine and not the man himself. Still, he leaves a message.

CHAPTER 33

If my dogs and I ever suffer the misfortune of being injured by heavy objects descending from above, I'll have the sense not to call a mental-health professional, even Rita. These people have no common sense. I won't call a dog trainer, either, but that's exactly what Ted did. When I'd finally elicited a few facts from him, I realized that calling our number had actually been sensible, if unintentionally so: Dolfo needed an immediate veterinary exam. Consequently, Steve and I got into his van, where he always kept basic veterinary instruments and supplies. By then, Leah and Caprice had returned. Leah insisted on accompanying us, mainly in case Steve needed help with Dolfo, and Caprice tagged along, too, perhaps because of an unexpected sense of loyalty to a family that wasn't quite one.

When we arrived at Ted's, he and Dolfo were still in the yard, but Barbara Leibowitz and George McBane were with them. As psychiatrists, they'd both gone to medical school, but I doubted that either one had treated a nonpsychiatric problem in decades. Even so, George was trying to examine Ted's right leg and foot. Ted was lying on a teak bench, and someone had cut the fabric of his trousers and removed his shoe and sock. His foot and ankle were purple and swollen, but instead of groaning about physical pain, he was barraging George with complaints about his anxiety and pleading for Valium.

Barbara had taken charge of Dolfo. "Steve, thank God you're here," she said. "I can't find anything wrong, but Ted says something must've hit Dolfo. I heard some yelping and howling. As far as I can tell, Ted had Dolfo out here, and Wyeth threw this stuff out the window."

"Not intentionally," said Ted.

"Of course not," Caprice said. "Wyeth merely opened a window, and then his computer flew out all on its own."

"Has anyone called an ambulance?" I asked.

Ted was vehement. "No! Don't call anyone! If you call nine-one-one, the police will come, and Wyeth didn't mean any harm. It was an accident."

"Ted," George said, "I'm rusty, but I think your ankle's fractured and probably some of the bones in your foot. I can't treat you."

Meanwhile, Steve was kneeling next to Dolfo and running his hands over the dog. Dolfo's ridiculously long tail was waving in the air, and his oversized tongue was hanging merrily out of his mouth. Steve and Barbara were speaking in undertones. Steve then produced a leash from his pocket and had Barbara gait Dolfo back and forth across the yard. I noticed a slight limp, as Steve undoubtedly did, too.

"Caprice," Ted called out, "do me a favor. Go up to the medicine cabinet and get me some Valium. Or Ativan."

George intervened. "Ted, it's not a good idea to take anything right now."

"I'm hyperventilating! I can feel a panic attack coming on."

"George, do you want me to call an ambulance?" I asked. "Or I could drive Ted to the hospital. And does anyone know where Wyeth is?"

Everyone looked at everyone else.

"Caprice, go look for your brother," Ted said.

"I'm an only child. Besides, he probably ran away when he saw what he'd done."

"Enough of this!" I said. "Caprice, it's just

not the time. Steve, what's the story on that limp?"

Steve nodded. "Looks like something grazed his right front foot. That's probably why he yelped. There's no sign of anything else, but he ought to be kept under observation."

Leah, whose absence I hadn't noticed, appeared from the house with a plastic bag of ice in her hands. Without consulting anyone, she went to Ted and wrapped the ice pack around his ankle. "That'll help with the swelling," she said. "And the pain."

"Leah, thank you," I said. "Steve, could you and Caprice see whether Wyeth is in the house? If he isn't, we need to find him."

"I didn't see anyone," Leah said.

"Caprice, please go with Steve. You know where Wyeth's room is, and he doesn't, but check everywhere."

Ted was now sitting up. He punched a number into his cell phone. To all of us, he said, "Caprice is probably right — Wyeth has run off somewhere, running from his own irrational guilt. I tried his cell phone before. No answer." In a few seconds, he added, "No answer now."

Steve and Caprice had gone up the back stairs and were presumably searching the house. George said, "Barbara, do you want to take Ted to the ER? Or do you want me to do it?"

Without answering her husband, without even turning toward him, Barbara addressed Ted. "Mount Auburn?"

Ted nodded.

"George will drive you. I'll stay here by the phone in case Wyeth turns up or calls, that is, if he really has taken off somewhere. In fact, if he isn't here, let me be command central. For a start, we need to exchange phone numbers. Dolfo can stay here with me. I'll keep an eye on him. If he shows any distress, I'll call Steve, or George can drive him to Angell. Leah, would you go find a pen and paper so we can deal with phone numbers? And once everything's a little more clear, I'll take Dolfo home with me. Ted, you're not going to be in any shape to manage him for a few days."

Leah carried out her assignment. Caprice and Steve returned to the yard with the news that Wyeth seemed to be nowhere in the house. It belatedly occurred to Ted that someone should call his ex-wife, Johanna, in case Wyeth had fled to his mother's house. Instead of placing the call himself, he tried to foist off the job, first on Caprice, then on Barbara. Caprice refused, but Barbara agreed and immediately borrowed and used Ted's cell phone. It seemed to me that Barbara showed exceptional tact in describing matters to Johanna Green. Instead of bluntly informing Johanna that her son had tossed his computer and peripherals out a window and might have killed Ted and Dolfo, Barbara said that a difficult situation had arisen. Was Wyeth there? With a glance at Ted, Barbara said that maybe Wyeth had gone to a friend's house. Could Johanna think of people who should be called? Ted shook his head. I heard Caprice mutter that Wyeth didn't have any friends. As Barbara was telling Johanna that it seemed a little premature to call the police and as Leah was helpfully writing down phone numbers for everyone, George and Steve helped Ted to hobble toward the gate in the yard and thus toward George's car. As Barbara was saying that Wyeth really couldn't be considered a missing person, my eyes wandered to the computer that lay on the lawn. What drew my attention was, I suspect, the recognition that the piece of trash that Wyeth had thrown out was a newer and more powerful desktop computer than my own. As I was pondering that observation, I noticed that a drive door was open and that a CD or DVD remained in it. If the disc had been a commercial one,

I'd have left it in the drive; it would never have occurred to me to steal a computer game, a movie, a music album, or a software program. Close inspection, however, showed me that the drive held the same brand of CD I used when I backed up documents. My only excuse for what I did is that the absence of appropriate boundaries somehow infected or seduced me. That's no excuse, really, and I don't want to add to my list of transgressions by lying or whitewashing. Let me just spit this out: when no one was looking, I slipped the disc out of the drive and into my jacket pocket. I wanted to know what Wyeth was up to.

CHAPTER 34

Of the many sneaky psychotherapeutic distinctions that Rita is always trying to slip past me, the most galling is the supposed difference between what she calls *historical truth* and *psychological truth.* By *historical truth,* she means what I call truth plain and simple, or sometimes tortuous and complex, but truth nonetheless, in other words, the facts of what really happened. Rita, however, does not call it *truth plain and simple.* Worse, she is alarmingly inclined to demean and dismiss it and even to cast doubt on its very existence. In contrast, she places a high value on *psychological truth,* which in my opinion refers to the imaginative and inevitably distorted reconstruction that all of us have to make do with when truth itself, real truth, is unavailable. Whenever Rita and I get into an argument about truth, she always ends up saying, "Well, it's a good thing that you're not a psychotherapist!" On that point, we agree.

So, since I'm not a psychotherapist, thank heaven, I have to preface the following by stating that since a transcript of Rita's phone conversation with Peter York is nonexistent and therefore unavailable to me, I am reluctantly settling for the most accurate version of their exchange that I'm able to reconstruct.

Fact: at about the time I was filching the disc from Wyeth's computer, Peter York calls his supervisor, Rita, to consult with her about a patient of his who is in a crisis. The patient is, of course, Wyeth, who has called his therapist, Peter, from his cell phone to say that he almost killed his father and is now wandering the streets of Cambridge with nowhere to go.

Rita calmly asks Peter what he said to Wyeth. Peter, it emerges, told Wyeth to go to his mother's house. Peter expresses his concern about the boy's potential for violence, both intentional and unintentional. Remarkably, or so it might seem, Rita's response is more practical than psychological: assuring the boy's physical safety comes first; Peter must maintain contact with Wyeth until the situation is stable. "He'll probably go to his mother's," she says.

She then asks what precipitated the crisis. After listening closely, she says, "Okay, the father makes a sudden unilateral change in the rules. Until tonight, the rule was that sooner or later, Wyeth got anything he wanted. Then all of a sudden, with no negotiation and no real warning, the father said no. And apparently meant it. There was obviously a need to modify the old rule, but with an adolescent, there has to be negotiation. The son needs to participate in the process and not just have this radical change sprung on him."

After again listening, Rita says, "Frank Farmer. Yes, I agree. They're his speciality — these families with individual therapists and couples therapists, and everyone's on meds, and everyone's acting out, yes. When it comes to impossible families, he's the court of last resort. He's a legend. But Frank may not be willing to see these people." She listens and then replies, "Okay, I could run it by him. He might do it for me. But in the meantime, see if the son is at the mother's by now. And then you're going to need to see the father and son together. If the rules are changing, the two of them need to work on how that happens."

CHAPTER 35

When Steve, Leah, Caprice, and I returned home, Rita was in the yard, where she was talking on her cell phone and letting Willie, her Scottie, run around. Leah and Caprice went upstairs to watch a video. I felt like going to bed, snuggling up between Steve and a couple of dogs, and losing myself in a novel written before the invention of computers, psychotherapy, twelve-step programs, or cell phones. *Pride and Prejudice. The Moonstone. Our Mutual Friend.*

As it was, our dogs needed their evening outing, and we had to listen for the phone. Furthermore, although Steve was always happy to let all five of our own dogs run together, neither of us wanted to take our dogs to the yard while Willie was there lest Willie display his excess of what's called *real terrier character.* His feistiness always terrified Lady, and Lady's terror aroused India's protectiveness. Under my tutelage,

Rowdy had become more than decent with other dogs, but not to the extent of calmly tolerating a noisy terrier challenge. As to Sammy, like sire, like son? I didn't want to find out. Weirdly enough, Kimi, my alpha malamute feminist, reacted to Willie only by regarding him with an expression of utter disdain; in Kimi's view, he was an upstart pipsqueak incapable of constituting a serious threat to her supremacy.

So, I opened the door to the yard and stood at the top of the steps in the hope that Rita would hurry up. She met my gaze and gestured that she'd be off the phone in a second. "Well, crisis over for the moment," she said into the phone. "We'll talk about this at our next meeting. Look, before managed care and all the insurance problems, there were family systems therapists who would've met with everyone involved. Everyone. Parents, children, relatives, neighbors, friends, all the therapists, the household help. Even the dog trainer! The whole network. No one does that these days. Frank Farmer is probably the only therapist around who'd know how to do it, and even he doesn't want to do it anymore. No one does. It's not just the question of how you bill the insurance companies. It's exhausting." She listened. "Well, I wouldn't go so far as to say that individual psychotherapy is a complete waste of time with this boy, but I do agree, Peter. Now, does the father know that the boy is at his mother's?" She nodded and, after a few concluding words, ended the conversation.

"Wyeth is at Johanna's?" I asked.

"You know —"

"You said 'even the dog trainer.' We've just come from Ted Green's. As you apparently know, Wyeth threw his computer and monitor and printer out the window when Ted had Dolfo in the yard. They got hit. Ted probably has a broken ankle or foot. Steve went to check out Dolfo. Wyeth had taken off. When we left, just now, George McBane had taken Ted to the emergency room, and Barbara Leibowitz was staying at Ted's in case Wyeth came back. George and Barbara live next door. You know them. They're psychiatrists. I need to call her. She offered to let everyone know what was going on."

While I was updating Barbara and then telling Steve, Caprice, and Leah that Wyeth was at his mother's, Rita took Willie to her apartment. Then she came back down and joined Steve and the dogs and me in the yard. She greeted me by saying, "These boundary violations make me very uncomfortable."

"Rita, Barbara needed to know that Wyeth was safe. So did the rest of us. And if you think that Caprice's presence here is a boundary violation, you're wrong. What are we supposed to do? Throw her out? Besides, you're the one who said 'dog trainer.' "

"It was only a figure of speech."

"*Dog trainer* isn't a figure of speech. You meant me, and you meant it in a disparaging way, as if my efforts to help Dolfo didn't really count. He is a member of that crazy family, and I have to say that getting everyone together sounds like a wonderful idea. Like one of those . . . What do you call them? Confrontations? Interventions? To persuade people to go into drug treatment centers. That kind of thing."

"That's not what I was talking about. The idea isn't to confront any one person. It's to treat the entire system instead of identifying any one person as the locus of pathology."

"In this case," Steve said, "you could flip a coin about which one to choose. Rita, you want a drink?"

Rita was concerned that the crisis might not actually be over, so she wanted to stay sober, and Steve and I were thirsty, so all of us ended up drinking lemonade.

"I think that you should organize one of these systems interventions," I told Rita.

"Not me! I don't even know how. The only person who could do it is a guy named Frank Farmer. He specializes in these complicated families. Why I am talking to you about this? I'm not!"

"He specializes in basenjis," I said.

"What?"

"If it's the same Frank Farmer. Sixty or so? With a mane of white hair? Good-looking. Very athletic."

"Frank's a client of mine," Steve said. "He's a psychologist. Nice dogs. One of them went Best of Breed at Westminster a couple of years ago."

"Dogs!" Rita exclaimed. "I should've known."

I wasn't surprised at all. Anything but. "Of course you should've known. As the hymn says, *All nature sings, and round me rings, the music of the spheres.* It's obvious that the universe is sending us a message, namely, that Frank was meant to intercede."

"I told Peter I'd speak to him, but I don't think he'll do it."

"Frank owes me," I said. "I'm the one who sent him to the handler who showed that dog for him at Westminster. Frank is grateful to me. Besides, we go way back. He knew my mother."

"Every dog owner over the age of forty knew your mother," Rita grumbled.

"Those who did thought very highly of her. She has posthumous clout. But go ahead and talk to Frank on your own. Then if he says no, tell him I said to ask."

CHAPTER 36

At seven o'clock on Tuesday morning in the house next to Ted Green's, Barbara Leibowitz and George McBane are having breakfast. Although they are sitting at the same kitchen table and listening to the same National Public Radio program, they are not exactly eating together. Indeed, it might be said that they are eating apart or that George is having breakfast with Barbara; and she with the half-Westie and entirely adorable Portia and with Dolfo. In deference to Barbara's desire that he lower his cholesterol level, George is sprinkling granola on a bowl of low-fat Total yogurt. Barbara is indulging in an Iggy's croissant, on which she is spreading sweet butter. The well-trained, civilized Portia, loose in the kitchen, is munching on the contents of a white ceramic dish that bears her name in ornate blue letters. Since Barbara wisely views Dolfo as precivilized, he is in a nearby wire crate. He does not envy Portia her personalized dish but is happy to make do with a stainless steel bowl. The dogs are eating together in the sense that they are having the same meal, a mixture of Eukanuba, safflower oil, grated carrot, diced chicken breast that Barbara cooked herself, a small quantity of filtered water, and two powdered supplements, Nupro and Missing Link. Although the dogs are silent right now and are attending exclusively to their food, each would be willing to woof pleasantly at the other, whereas Barbara is not speaking to George.

"Barbara, they're rodents, for God's sake," says George. "They're rats with furry tails. Try thinking of it that way. We had rats. I poisoned them. I didn't tell you because I didn't want to upset you. I know how softhearted you are. The only thing I'm guilty of is pest control."

CHAPTER 37

On Tuesday morning, Caprice astonished me by getting up early with the rest of us and leaving to meet with a physics teacher at Cambridge Rindge and Latin High School to discuss tutoring. It soon emerged that the teacher was a client of Steve's and that Steve had been the matchmaker. As a romantic matchmaker for human beings, Steve was all but useless; he failed to share my interest in fixing people up, and whenever I suggested that So-and-so and So-and-so might make a good couple, he'd shrug his shoulders and offer no opinion on the matter. Need I add that he refused to read Jane Austen? He did, however, have a good eye for a dog and a particular talent for prophesying the outcomes of particular breedings. For instance, when he'd learned about the Emma-Rowdy breeding that had produced Sammy, he'd known right away that he'd want a puppy. So, I assumed that he'd regarded Caprice as in physics season, so to speak, and had applied his talented eye to identifying a suitable mate.

Once the animals and I had the house to ourselves, I did my usual morning chores and then settled down at the kitchen table with my notebook computer and the disc I'd lifted from Ted Green's yard. My guilt about the pilfering took the form of a conviction that the disc was going to contaminate my notebook with a virus that would wipe out my hard drive and e-mail itself to all my friends, who'd blame me for the epidemic, and rightly so! What do thieves deserve? The worry about a virus was justified, but since I used the notebook only for writing and never for e-mail, even the worst infection couldn't have spread itself to my Internet contacts. Still, my guilt-driven fears led me to go online with the notebook and update the virus definitions before slipping the CD into the drive and scanning it for infection. It was clean.

All my guesses about its contents were wrong. I expected music, a movie, or maybe pirated software or games. My hope, of course, was that in preparing to transfer files to the new computer he'd been demanding, Wyeth had backed up his documents on the disc and that somewhere in his files there'd be something — anything — about Eumie's murder. The notion now seems nuts. Wyeth was about as likely to keep an intimate diary as he was to pen sonnets or to execute delicate watercolor paintings of flowers. Still, there was an off chance that he'd taken an English course that had required him to keep a journal and that he'd continued the habit of making entries. In fact, the files on the disc weren't Wyeth's at all; rather, they were what I quickly recognized as a therapist's notes about patients. I opened and quickly closed several files after reading only the first few sentences. To my shame, I then read one brief file in its entirety.

Youngman, Quinn. Initial interview. Psychiatrist, psychopharm. Pt. grew up in small town in Montana, conservative family, sent to college to become minister. Attended U. of Mont., superstraight Young Republican, no sex, drugs, alcohol. Took science course, encountered evolution & scientific method. Result: internal revolution. Switched to chem, biology, physics. Excelled. Applied to med schools in East. Went to Cornell, where he rewrote his past, now seen by self as embarrassing and absurd. Recast self to peers as having been radical outsider among political

conservatives and religious fundamental-
ists at home. Now complains of sense of
fakery and emptiness, with false presentation of self that in own opinion impedes
ability to form genuine relationships.

"Rowdy," I said to my most trusted confi-
dante, "I have done a bad, bad thing. I have
learned things I have no right to know."
Therapists are taught to be nonjudgmental.
If a patient is on the verge of murdering
someone, the therapist is obliged to warn
the intended victim. But in most instances,
no matter how despicable, rotten, disgusting, irritating, boring, or unlikable the
patient, the poor therapist is supposed to
listen and help rather than to judge. Such
idealism! I ask you, just how capable is even
the most highly trained and self-disciplined
professional of squelching inevitable human
feelings? It's possible, I suppose, that Psychotherapy 101 includes a unit on keeping
a poker face, and I'm sure that skilled,
experienced therapists manage to keep their
judgments from leaking into their behavior
with patients, but imagine the effort! In
contrast, consider dogs, all dogs, any dog,
Rowdy, for instance, dog of dogs, primus
inter pares, he of the deepest dark eyes, the
most heartily wagging of heavily furred

white tails, he of the heavy bone, the massive muscle, and the oldest of souls, he who knew all my sins, judged not, and effortlessly loved me with all his heart. "What," I asked him, "am I supposed to do now? These notes weren't made by Ted Green or Eumie Brainard-Green. That's not where Wyeth got these files. Quinn Youngman is Ted's psychopharmacologist, and he was Eumie's. He isn't Ted's patient, and he wasn't hers. Those break-ins up the street? That's where this disc came from. Quinn Youngman and all these other people whose records are on this disc are patients of one of those therapists. So, take a wild guess about who broke into those offices. Absolutely. Wyeth Green."

I got down on the floor and wrapped my arms around Rowdy's neck. In his profoundly nonjudgmental opinion, I hadn't done anything wrong. Consequently, I can't actually say that he sympathized with my moral dilemma. He did, however, respond to my hug by lying down and presenting his belly in the hope that I'd rub it, as I did. The interchange isn't, I hope, typical of therapist-patient interaction unless, of course, one or the other is a dog. But being a dog, Rowdy was extremely helpful. "Yes," I said. "About Quinn, what I do is nothing.

The information isn't mine and therefore isn't mine to pass along. Wyeth? What I don't do about Wyeth is turn him over to the police. Or I don't rush into doing that, anyway. Maybe what I do is talk to Rita. Because, you know what? Once in a while, human therapists do have their uses."

CHAPTER 38

That same Tuesday afternoon at about four o'clock, I got another pleading call from Ted Green. His previous pleas had been merely alarmist. This time, his ordinarily pleasant, calm voice sounded weak and thick. He said that his ankle was in a cast and that he wasn't supposed to put weight on it. His new housekeeper hadn't shown up. At his insistence, Barbara had returned Dolfo. He'd managed to get down the back steps to take Dolfo out, but the exuberant dog had jumped on him and knocked him to the ground. He'd had to crawl back upstairs to the house. It seemed to me that he hadn't been thinking straight: the yard was fenced, and if he was unable to manage stairs, he should just have let Dolfo out and then in. Ted went on. He was out of dog food, the milk was sour, he'd had to cancel all his patients, and he was on so much pain medication that he belonged in bed. Barbara and George weren't home. He didn't know what to do. *Oy vey iz mir!* The cry was merited. He really needed help.

Caprice was there when I took the call. "What's true is that Ted has no real friends," she said when I'd hung up. "He has people he sucks up to, people he wants to impress, that kind of thing. There were people who cared about my mother, but they were her friends, not Ted's. They know what a poseur he is. He called you because he knew you'd feel sorry for him."

Mindful of Kevin's warning, I said, "Look, I'm not crazy about the idea of going there alone, but he sounds terrible. I do feel sorry for him. But . . . Caprice, bad things happen in that house. I don't have to tell you that."

"They probably won't happen to you," she said.

"I'll just take over milk and dog food. I'll drop it off. I won't stay. Or maybe Barbara and George are home by now. They'd help. I'm sure Barbara would take Dolfo."

"She tried to talk them out of buying him," Caprice said. "She said there was no such thing as a golden Aussie huskapoo and that if they wanted a mixed-breed dog, they should go to a shelter."

"She was right. But at least there's nothing wrong with his temperament, why, I can't imagine. According to everything I know about dogs, it's a miracle that he isn't biting people. Anyway, let me try Barbara and George. If they aren't there and if I really think that safety is an issue, I'll get Steve to keep Dolfo at the clinic. I can't have him here, not with our five."

I had no luck in reaching Barbara and George, and reluctantly decided to make a quick trip to Ted's. I didn't ask Caprice to accompany me. It was her idea. She insisted. "After what happened last night, Wyeth won't be there. Really, I don't mind. I want to go with you."

I filled a couple of heavy-duty food-storage bags with dry dog food. In case Barbara and George were out of town and Ted insisted on keeping Dolfo with him, I also took two stuffed Kong toys from the freezer to keep Dolfo happy in his crate. On the drive to Ted's, I stopped for milk and, on impulse, also got eggs, bread, and cheddar cheese; for all I knew, the housekeeper wasn't the only one who'd failed to show up, and if the milk had turned, Ted might be short on other perishables, too. When we arrived, one of the three parking spots in the paved area next to Ted's house was empty. Instead of pulling into it, I backed into a space on the street, as if to remind myself that I was just dropping off supplies and not really paying a visit. Caprice helped me to carry everything in. We left our shoes on the porch, of course. When I rang the bell, I heard Ted call out, and Dolfo barked, but no one came to the door, so Caprice used her key.

The house reeked of urine, and I made the mistake of putting one stocking foot on a dark carpet only to feel moisture seep through. Dolfo greeted us by running madly up and down the stairs to the second floor, but at least he didn't manage to jump on either of us. We found Ted on a couch in the family room. His hair was greasy, and his skin was pale and waxy. I was used to seeing Ted in the kinds of trendy clothes that Steve would never have bought, and he'd always looked as if his clothes were brand new or fresh from the cleaner. Now, he wore an unfashionably wrinkled lime-green shirt with a coffee-colored stain on the front. Instead of trousers, he had on baggy maroon shorts that he must have chosen because he'd been able to pull them on despite the cast that covered most of his right foot and extended up his calf. A pair of crutches lay on the floor beside the couch.

"Hey, thanks for coming," he said in the

weak, groggy voice I'd heard on the phone. His eyes looked heavy and unfocused. "Wyeth would've helped me, but he's at his mother's."

Caprice and I exchanged a glance. In spite of her cynical and suspicious attitude toward Ted, she had the frightened, bewildered expression of a child forced to confront parental weakness.

"Ted, you can't be here by yourself," I said.

"It's the pills," he said. "You ever broken a bone? It hurts like hell, and this, uh, thing, the cast . . . I can't get ice on my ankle, and it hurts like shit. Can you help me get up? I need to go to the bathroom."

For building strength, big dogs have it all over health clubs. Ted outweighed my malamutes, but I didn't have to take his full weight, and I easily helped him off the couch and onto his crutches. At my direction, Caprice leashed Dolfo to prevent him from barging into Ted. Through the big glass doors of the family room, I caught sight of Barbara, who was in her backyard with Portia.

"Ted, Barbara's home. She's in the yard. I'm going to ask her to take Dolfo," I said. "Don't argue about it."

Ted began to work his way toward the

kitchen and presumably toward the powder room where we'd once discovered Dolfo. He managed the crutches surprisingly well. I opened a door to the deck and called out to Barbara, who readily agreed to take Dolfo. "Just bring him over," she called.

"Let's just get Dolfo to Barbara before Ted comes back," I said to Caprice. "Could you walk Dolfo over there right now? I'll put the milk and stuff in the refrigerator, and then I'll be right over. I want to talk to Barbara about Ted. At a minimum, someone should keep checking on him."

"He's stoned," Caprice said.

"His judgment is clouded."

"Permanently."

"Take Dolfo out the front door before Ted has a chance to see him leaving. I don't want him looking out and seeing you in the yard, or he'll give us a hard time."

"Dolfo, let's go! Go visit Barbara and Portia? Good boy!" She patted her thigh and led Dolfo toward the front hall with the self-confidence of a dog person. You know those total immersion programs for people who want to learn foreign languages? The ones where you live with a family and have to communicate exclusively in their language? It occurred to me that Steve and I could take in people who needed to become fluent in dog. *Converse with native speakers! No boring grammar drills! Rapid mastery guaranteed!*

When I'd finished putting the milk, eggs, and cheddar in the refrigerator, I glanced down the corridor toward the powder room and saw that the door was still closed. Although I felt a duty to see to it that Ted was safe, I had no desire to spend yet more time with him. Consequently, I grabbed the dog food and the Kong toys I'd brought with me and hurried to the front door and out to the porch. Caprice, who was wearing running shoes, must have stopped to tie them. As I was slipping on my own shoes, she and Dolfo were beginning to walk along the sidewalk in front of Ted's wide driveway, which lay between Ted's house and Barbara and George's. This off-street parking area was beautifully paved in cobblestone to create what looked like a patio. The space nearest Ted's house was occupied by the silver Lexus SUV that Ted and Eumie had driven on the night I'd first met them. Parked next to it was a silver BMW sedan. The third space, the one closest to Barbara and George's property, was empty, as it had been when we'd arrived. As usual, the neighborhood looked more suburban than urban, and at the moment, it was exceptionally quiet: no lawn mowers, no leaf blowers, not even a passing car.

As I was starting down the front steps, Dolfo stopped to sniff one of the tires of the BMW. Sounding eerily like Leah, Caprice said, "Not there! No man-made objects! Fire hydrants excepted. And that's not a fire hydrant. Good boy, Dolfo. This way!"

As I descended the steps, I looked down to avoid losing my footing. At the precise moment I reached the bottom, when Caprice and Dolfo were on the sidewalk in front of the empty space next to the BMW, a big, shiny black SUV came tearing down the street, slowed abruptly, turned, and headed directly for that same parking space, which is to say, directly at Caprice and Dolfo.

"Caprice, run!" I screamed. "Get out of the way! Run!"

I had a clear view of the driver: Wyeth Green. Even if he somehow hadn't seen Caprice and Dolfo, he'd have heard my desperate warning in time to put on the brakes. As it was, he ran that gigantic car into Caprice. His expression left no doubt that he had deliberately hit her. By the time he came to a halt, I was banging on the driver's side window of the monstrous vehicle, which reminded me all too much of a hearse: long, wide, black, and deathly.

I'm unsure of the exact sequence of my next actions, and my memory of the details has a weirdly kaleidoscopic quality. I wrenched open the car door and must have thrown myself on top of Wyeth as I made sure that the transmission was in park and as I yanked the key out of the ignition. Logic suggests that I first prevented the car — and its driver — from doing further harm and only then knelt on the cobblestones next to Caprice, who lay in a fetal position and was groaning in pain. Amazingly, she retained a tight grip of Dolfo's leash. I took it from her.

"It's just my knee. I'll be okay," she managed to say. "Dolfo broke my fall. I fell on him. Is he all right?"

I remember that Dolfo was leaning over Caprice and licking her face. I had to push him aside, perhaps before she spoke, perhaps after. I have a vivid image of the front wheels, the massive tires, and the oversized chrome bumper of the car, and of Caprice on the beautiful stone paving only a few feet away.

"He's fine." I pulled out my cell phone. "I'm calling an ambulance."

I know that she told me that she didn't

need one. "I just have to catch my breath," she said.

After that, the sequence is clear to me.

A small beige sedan pulled off the street and parked behind my Blazer. Out of it stepped a familiar-looking fine-boned woman with short blond hair and pale skin. She wore beige linen pants and a pale linen top. I recognized her as Johanna Green not only because she fit the description I'd been given of Ted's ex-wife but because I knew that Johanna had a papillon, and this woman had one tucked under her left arm. The little dog's bright, eager expression was in marked contrast to Johanna's. The woman had dark circles under her eyes, and her whole face seemed to droop.

"Mom, it wasn't my fault," I heard Wyeth say.

Only when Ted replied did I realize that he was on the front porch of his house. "What the hell is going on?" he demanded.

"Wyeth," said Johanna, "has apparently had a little incident. We were coming here to get his belongings."

"Mom got me my Land Rover," Wyeth said, "and I'm not all that used to it. I accidentally bumped into Caprice."

Ted's voice was suddenly strong. "Johanna, did you buy him that car?"

"Ted, you and I have joint custody. I'm perfectly within my rights to mother him as I see fit."

"You are ruining him! He needs limits! Boundaries! He has to learn that there are consequences to his behavior! He threw his computer out the window and broke my ankle, and the consequence you've provided is a fucking Land Rover? Johanna, I'm going to see you in court for this. You are a vicious, destructive person and a terrible mother."

"Don't talk to her like that!" Wyeth shouted. "Shut up! Just shut up!"

Johanna ignored him and hollered at her ex-husband. "Ted, let me tell you something. What happened was that as usual, you blamed Wyeth for what was nothing more than an accident. He would never, ever have deliberately done what he's accused of doing. He was heartbroken, and he was terrified. When he showed up at my door last night, he was shaking all over. I'll see *you* in court, you abusive son of a bitch!"

Ted remained on the porch, and Johanna had now moved to the open door of the extravagant gift Wyeth had received for breaking his father's ankle. Wyeth was in the driver's seat. Johanna reached in and rested a hand on his shoulder. Had Johanna and Ted been right next to each other, their voices would have been raised. As it was, they were a considerable distance apart, so they were shouting to be heard as well as to vent rage.

"Johanna," Ted bellowed, "you are a vain, selfish monster! I should've known! This is what I deserve for marrying the ultimate shikse! I've brought it on myself, and I've brought it on my son. Ai-ai-ai!"

"I'm a shikse? You're calling *me* a shikse? What do think your precious Eumie was? Well, I'll tell you what she was! A marriage wrecker! A conniving bitch! A dirty little sneak!"

With an exaggerated shrug, Ted said, "The truth comes out, Johanna. Holly, I hope you're paying attention, because you might have to testify to what that woman is saying. She hated my Eumie. She was consumed by jealousy and envy. So she —"

"You are such a bullshit artist, Ted! She was a dirty sneak, and you know it. She knew all your little secrets, didn't she? But you couldn't trust her. Is that why you killed her? To keep her loud mouth shut?"

Caprice had pulled herself to her feet. She was resting one hand on the hood of the car, the other on Dolfo's head. When I turned to her, I was horrified at myself. She should never have heard any of this fight. Tears were running down her face.

"We're leaving," I whispered as I took Dolfo's leash. "I'll be back in a second."

In no more than twenty seconds, I was handing Dolfo's leash to Barbara, who must have been next to her front door when I rang the bell. "Just take him. Please!" I handed her Wyeth's keys. "Could you return these once we've left? I'm in a hurry. Caprice shouldn't have to listen to what's going on out there."

"Of course not," Barbara said. "Go!"

As I led Caprice to my car, Ted and Johanna continued to trade vicious accusations at top volume. They had returned to the dispute about which of them had ruined their son. The son, Wyeth, was, of course, right there. Although he was the subject of the fight, neither parent seemed aware of his presence. I knew that I was witnessing one of the final battles in an epic war between love and hate. The forces of love were in retreat; they were nowhere to be seen. Hate fought hate. There could be no victor.

CHAPTER 39

On that same Tuesday afternoon, Anita Fairley marches triumphantly out of Dr. Vee Foote's office. Anita feels vindicated and liberated. No more of that trauma and healing shit! No more relationship addiction and no more making amends! All along, she has been depressed. Depressed! She has been suffering from depression! What a beautiful revelation! Rubbing the prescription between her fingers, she can barely contain her joy. Once she reaches her car and settles into the driver's seat, she reaches into her purse, extracts the samples that Dr. Foote so generously gave her, and dry swallows one capsule. Then she repeats the action: a double dose.

She'll fix that Ted Green! She'll hire a private investigator and sue him for malpractice! He misdiagnosed and mistreated her. She'll get him. She'll ruin him. She'll grind him into the ground.

Could the magic capsules already be at work? Now? Within seconds? She is perhaps the happiest depressed person on earth. She is delighted. She savors the prospect of revenge.

CHAPTER 40

That same Tuesday evening, I pinned Rita in her lair, which is to say in the newly renovated apartment that occupied the third floor of my house. *Our* house. It's probably a good thing that I kept my original last name instead of taking Steve's. If marriage can make such a hash of trivial little parts of speech such as personal pronouns, just imagine the mess that matrimony could make of big, important proper nouns. I mean, those things are capitalized! Anyway, my marriage — our marriage, Steve's and mine — had meant a radical shift in living arrangements. To compensate Rita for the inconvenience of moving to the third floor and, in fact, to lure her into staying in the house at all, we'd done a thorough and expensive revamping of the top-floor apartment: The walls and ceilings were freshly plastered and painted, the windows and sills were new, the bathroom was a veritable spa, and the kitchen was all granite and wood and weird foreign appliances with unpronounceable brand names. The range, as the brochure had persisted in calling it, was so complicated that it had taken Rita two weeks to figure out how to use the oven and the broiler; until then, she'd used nothing but the burners. Far from complaining about this miserable stove, Rita had repeatedly expressed her delight with it. It was almost impossible to use, but so what? It was foreign and magnificent, like some European gentleman whose enchanting accent and continental demeanor more than compensated for a crabby disposition and an inability to hold a job.

Anyway, on Tuesday night after dinner, I climbed to the third floor, rapped on the door, protected my hearing from Willie's barking by putting my hands over my ears, and subsequently distracted him from my ankles by tossing a rawhide flip chip across the room.

"Rita," I said, "we have to talk. I respect your professional and personal ethics, I really do, but when a threat to life is involved, you're allowed to make exceptions. Stop! I'm not asking you to say anything. But you do have to listen."

"Cold sober?" she asked. "I've had a long day." For once, she was less than perfectly groomed. Her navy linen suit was wrinkled, her face was shiny, and her mouth showed faded traces of lipstick. She had, I thought, been running her hands through her usually neat cap of carefully streaked hair. "I had emergencies with two patients. I just got off the phone."

"Have you had dinner? We have leftovers. I'll —"

"Thanks, Holly, but I had a snack, and I'm really too tired to eat."

"Gin?" I suggested. "Gin and tonic? Scotch? Vodka? A Manhattan. Let me fix you a Manhattan. Or a Rob Roy." In giving a precise report of what I said, I do not mean to suggest that Rita is some sort of lush. She isn't. On the other hand, she's no teetotaler, either.

"I'd keel over."

"Hot chocolate?"

"Ugh. I'm not that far gone."

"Wine," I said. "A little therapeutic glass of wine. I'll go downstairs and get some. Red or white? Rita, I'm sorry, but this is important. Otherwise, I wouldn't bother you."

"You're not bothering me. I'm sorry to be

so frazzled. And I have wine."

"I'll be succinct. I promise. I'm not asking for advice. All I need is to pass along some information. I'm worried. I think that Wyeth is dangerous."

Five minutes later, we were settled in Rita's living room. In moving, she'd kept only her best pieces of furniture, mainly end tables and lamps. The upholstered couch and two chairs, all three new, were upholstered in fabrics that looked tweedy but didn't itch. It occurred to me that if Sammy were locked in that living room, he could easily do $20,000 worth of damage in the first ten minutes.

Rita was stretched out on the couch with her stockinged feet propped up. Eager to show that I'd be quick, I perched on the edge of one of the armchairs.

"Wyeth," I said. "You already know about the episode with the computer. Ted's ankle is broken. If the computer or the monitor or the printer had landed on his head? In just the wrong spot? Well, the latest is that Johanna, Wyeth's mother, felt so sorry for him after what he'd been through in that episode that she bought him a new car. A Land Rover. Brand-new, I think."

"You can't tell one make of car from another."

"I can if I read what's written on them. Anyway, Ted said it was a Land Rover. I think they're expensive."

"An understatement."

"I'll spare you the details. What happened late this afternoon is that Caprice was walking Dolfo from Ted's to Barbara Leibowitz's. Ted can't manage anything. Barbara is taking care of Dolfo. So, Caprice and Dolfo were on the sidewalk in front of Ted's driveway, an empty spot in this sort of parking area he has, when Wyeth came zooming down the street in his new car, turned in, and ran into Caprice."

"Dear God! Is she all right?"

"Yes. Her knee is sore. Fortunately, she fell on Dolfo, and he broke her fall. But the point is, Rita, that when I saw what was about to happen, I was screaming and running, but I got a good look at the expression on Wyeth's face, and, Rita, I swear to you, he deliberately ran that car into her. For all I know, he intended to hit Dolfo, too. It was no accident." I was tempted to tell Rita about the contents of the disc I'd removed from Wyeth's computer. If she hadn't been so exhausted, I'd probably have broken my vow to ignore information I had no right to possess. Besides, sneaking into therapy offices wasn't an act of violence, and I was principally concerned with just that: violence. "After it happened," I continued, "Ted and Johanna got into a raging fight about Wyeth. They were accusing each other of ruining him. With him right there! That was the word they used: *ruined.* So, if he wants to kill people, it's no wonder. And the fight was verbal violence, if there is such a thing."

"There is," Rita said.

"Wyeth is on his mother's side. She hated Eumie. So did Wyeth. And Eumie was inviting trouble in a family filled with rage and violence. She collected people's secrets. She was married to Monty, Caprice's father, and then to Ted. She knew their secrets. Eumie enlisted Caprice in ferreting out information about people. Including Johanna? Why not? So, I'm worried. Someone murdered Eumie. We know that Wyeth could easily have killed Ted and that he ran his car into Caprice. I'm worried about what's going to happen next."

"I am, too," Rita said.

"Wyeth could kill someone." I paused. "Maybe he already has."

CHAPTER 41

With considerable difficulty, Wyeth Green parallel parks his Land Rover on Concord Avenue near Dr. Peter York's office building, which is a three-story wood-frame house similar to mine. It, too, is set close to the street and has a small porch. At four o'clock in the morning, the streetlights are on, but Wyeth has no feel for the dimensions of his new car and ends up bumping the car behind it. When he gets out, he notices that he has parked more than a foot from the curb.

Wyeth is unarmed; the bottle of Poland Spring water he carries doesn't count as a weapon. Although he ends up on the front porch, my reconstruction shows him first making his way to the back door, checking it, finding it locked, and then checking windows, which are also locked. Only then does he return to the front of the building, climb the short flight of stairs, and uselessly try the front door. After that, he settles himself in a corner of the porch, removes the prescription bottle from his pocket, and swallows six ten-milligram tablets of a generic version of Valium. In twenty minutes, he falls asleep.

About two hours later, he is discovered there, still asleep, by my cousin Leah, who is accompanied by Kimi. The two are returning from an early-morning run and have slowed to a walk to cool down before returning home. Never having seen Wyeth before, Leah does not recognize him; the young man whose shoulder she shakes is a stranger to her. "Are you all right?" she asks. "Kimi, leave it!" In using the word *it*, Leah does not, I should note, intend to refer to Wyeth as an object; the command is her equivalent of the musher's *On by* and simply tells Kimi to mind her own business. Kimi, however, thrusts her wet nose in the boy's face and begins to lick vigorously. Leah reconsiders. Dog saliva is, after all, a potent panacea. She allows Kimi to continue her ministrations.

CHAPTER 42

"Kevin was right about making me take my cell when I go running," Leah said over breakfast. "I was glad I had it." She took a bite of scrambled eggs and swallowed. "You should've seen Kimi! She was just determined to help him. And I must say that he wasn't very grateful. When he started to come to, he shoved her away."

"Did you get any explanation?" I asked. "I mean, what was he doing there? Was he a street person? Was he drunk?"

"No, he wasn't drunk. There wasn't any smell. There was a bottle next to him, but it was Poland Spring water. And he was wearing good clothes. Lands' End or something. Good shoes. When the police and the ambulance got there, someone said something about pills."

"Good thing you had the sense to call nine-one-one," Steve said.

"Of course I did! I could see that he was

breathing, but I couldn't get him to wake up. And he was really pale. He was all flabby. I think maybe he has some kind of chronic illness, and he collapsed and crawled up onto that porch. The pills could've been something he was supposed to take if his illness suddenly struck." Her tone was dramatic. "Maybe he felt his heart starting to flutter, but he took the medicine too late, and he fainted."

Caprice came downstairs just as Steve and Leah were leaving, so she missed the details of Leah's account. I simply told her that Leah had been coming back from a run with Kimi when she'd found someone who'd collapsed on a porch down the street. Leah had called an ambulance, I said. After that, I went to my study to work, and Caprice left to do some tutoring.

At ten minutes of eleven, Rita called from her office. "I thought you should know," she said. Her tone was hurried and vaguely prissy. "Someone will probably call Caprice. Peter York tells me that Wyeth Green made a suicide gesture last night. Or early this morning."

"How is he?"

"All he took was Valium. And not that much of it. If he'd been in bed, he'd probably have slept it off, and no one would've known. But what he did was go to Peter's office. Someone found him there, on the front porch."

"Leah," I said. "Leah found him. She didn't know who it was, but it must've been Wyeth."

"What a weird coincidence."

"Not really. Peter York's office must be right near here."

"It is."

"She'd taken Kimi for an early run, and she was on her way back when she saw someone curled up on a porch. She stopped to see whether he was okay, and when she couldn't get him to wake up, she called an ambulance."

"He's at Mount Auburn. This really was a gesture. To kill yourself with Valium, you have to take it with alcohol, maybe, or something else, and then fall asleep with your face in a pillow and suffocate. But the meaning of the suicide gesture is very serious, of course. Anyway, this is a heads-up. First of all, let Caprice know. And you need to be aware that Peter is knocking himself out to avoid having this boy hospitalized long term. I've been on the phone with Frank Farmer."

"I haven't seen Frank for a few months," I said. "The last time I saw him, one of his dogs went Best of Breed at —"

"This is not about dog shows!"

"I know that."

"Look, I have a patient any minute. Frank has agreed to meet with everyone on Thursday evening. This'll be at Ted Green's. Seven o'clock. You and Caprice will need to be there."

My Thursday evenings are sacred to dog training, but I knew better than to say so and, in fact, didn't even want to say so. "We'll be there," I said. "Both of us. But Rita, there's just one thing you might —"

"My patient's here. I've got to go. I'll be at the meeting, too. Frank has roped me in. Holly, I've really got to go."

What I didn't have a chance to say concerned Frank Farmer — well, not so much Frank himself as his basenjis. The basenji is, in my opinion, a short-haired, pint-sized African malamute, which is to say, a breed with a wild streak, intelligent, alert, energetic, and, as is said euphemistically, challenging to train for the obedience ring. Few handlers rise to the challenge of showing basenjis in obedience, and it's probably an indication of the splendid state of Frank's mental health that he was not among those few. He had shown dogs for ages, but strictly in conformation, where dogs are not judged on the extent to which they obey their handlers' commands, which in the case of basenjis as well as Shiba Inus, for example, and, indeed, Alaskan malamutes, tends to be not at all. Furthermore, in saying that Frank showed his basenjis, I do not mean that he handled them himself in the breed ring; he used professional handlers. And it was a good thing, too, because his dogs never listened to a single word Frank said and, in their daily lives with Frank, were always flying around all over his house and bouncing off people. They didn't bark. Basenjis don't, or not exactly. But they sure can yodel. And Frank's did. They were, however, perfectly beautiful and won a lot, deservedly so, and also had excellent temperaments, so Frank didn't care how wild they were, and they were, after all, his dogs. Anyway, what I didn't have a chance to mention to Rita was that although Frank was a legendary clinician, a genius with human beings, he was not, according to my own observations, any kind of expert in bringing a pack of wild creatures to heel. Rita would have dismissed my remarks anyway, and as it turned out, the point I'd have tried to make didn't matter at all.

But I am leaping ahead of myself. It wasn't yet Thursday, the day of the great meeting of the Brainard-Green network, but Wednesday, when it was still being planned. I intended to tell Caprice about the meeting, but when she returned home at two in the afternoon, she already knew about it. After doing her tutoring, she'd kept an appointment with her therapist, Missy Zinn, who was planning to attend and who considered it vital that Caprice be there.

"I hate the whole idea," Caprice said. "I hate it!"

For someone whose mother had just died, Caprice had, I thought, been peculiarly self-contained. When my own mother died, I cried for days. For weeks afterward, waves of grief would roll over me, and I'd again be in tears. My father had been in no condition to help me. As always, I had turned to our dogs, who needed me as much as I needed them. The joy and energy had gone out of them. All of us clung to one another. It was as if we'd all had an identical surgical operation that had removed the same vital organ from our bodies. The release of crying was, of course, unavailable to the dogs, but they found solace in simple physical contact, as I did, too.

That Wednesday afternoon, Caprice had obviously been crying. Her fair skin was blotched, and her eyes were puffy. Still, resentment about the family meeting was triumphing over grief. After saying that she hated the idea, she went on to complain that instead of pooling resources to help Wyeth, everyone should pool resources to figure out who murdered her mother. "This is just one more way to let Wyeth make himself the center of attention."

"Caprice," I said, "from what Rita tells me, the idea isn't to focus on any one person. The point is to make the whole family system and the whole network the center of attention."

"The family system didn't murder Eumie," Caprice said, "and it isn't fair that I have to go to this awful meeting because of" — she took a deep breath and spat out the name — *"Wyeth."*

"I haven't had lunch yet," I said. "Have you? There's leftover chicken. You want a sandwich?"

She accepted the offer. As I was making sandwiches — lettuce and tomato, no mayo, and no tactless green beans on the side — I thought over her angry assertion that the family system hadn't murdered Eumie. In one sense, she was right: Caprice, Wyeth, Ted, Monty, Johanna, and, indeed, Dolfo had not held some secret conclave in which they'd schemed to administer an overdose of multiple medications to Eumie. In another sense, the entire way the family operated had set the stage for murder. Medicine cabinets were packed with prescription drugs, everyone had access to everyone else's medication, interior and exterior doors were left unlocked, secrets weren't kept secret, and so forth. Even the family dog, Dolfo, hadn't been taught the distinction between indoors and outdoors and the corresponding rule about what was kept inside his body in one place and released only in the other.

"Missy sounds nervous about it, too," Caprice said.

"Really?"

"I think it's this visiting conductor. Dr. Farmer. She's in the position of some second violinist who joined the orchestra last week, and she's afraid she's going to play a sour note and have him single her out for ruining the music."

"Is that what she said?"

"No! Not at all. That's just the feeling I get. But I *am* glad she'll be there."

"I'll be there, too, Caprice, and I've known Frank Farmer for ages. He has dogs. I'm not afraid of him. He's a perfectly nice man. And Rita will be there."

Caprice's lips were trembling.

I asked, "Is there something else?"

She almost slapped her sandwich onto her plate. "It's not supposed to be just about Wyeth. Of course! Let's not make Wyeth take any responsibility for anything he's done! God forbid! So, since it's not going to be about Wyeth, it's going to be about the rest of us. Including —" As she broke off, she reached down and stretched out the voluminous shirt she was wearing. Dropping it, she raised her right hand to her face, squeezed a substantial mass of flesh between her fingers and thumb, and pressed so hard that I couldn't bear to watch.

I grabbed her arm and gently removed it. "Caprice, I have never been to a meeting like this one. But I know Frank, and I know Rita, and neither one is going to let the focus shift to your weight. I don't know anything about Frank's professional life, but he has a fabulous reputation, and you can bet that it isn't founded on letting people get away with that kind of ploy. And Rita? Rita is brainless about computers, and she's brainless about dog training, but that's because all her intelligence is devoted to understanding and helping people. If Wyeth or anyone else tried to transform this meeting into some hostile confrontation about your weight, Rita would see it coming, and she'd stop it."

At that inopportune moment, Caprice's cell phone rang. She dug it out of her purse and answered. "Daddy?" She listened. "I don't want to go," she said. "I wish —" This time, she listened for at least thirty seconds. "Okay. If you're going to be there, then I will. But I don't want to." After another pause, she said, "Yes, I understand. No one is going to chain me up and drag me there. It's my decision. But you'll be there? For sure?" Monty must have said yes. Caprice's face brightened. Then she changed the topic. "I need you to talk to Ted. About Eumie. Mommy. He wants to do something so awful. She's being cremated." Another pause. "Yes, I know. It's what she wanted. But then he has this awful idea about turning her into a coral reef. It's grotesque. He e-mailed me. I can't even manage to answer his e-mail. It makes me feel sick." After that, she listened and murmured. The call ended.

"Your father's coming," I said.

"He doesn't want to either. Dr. Zinn talked him into it. But I can change my mind. Even at the last minute. And I can always walk out."

"That's true. And if things somehow get out of control or hurtful to you, Caprice, I will walk out with you. I promise."

"I have an idea," Caprice said.

"Yes?"

"Could we take Lady?"

"Lady?" I was thrown, so surprised that my voice registered my feelings all too accurately. India, Rowdy, or Kimi, yes. Any of the three would have been a solid choice as a symbol of protection and a source of powerful support. Sammy? I was starting to wonder whether his puppy brain would ever catch up with his maturing body. In the midst of a serious gathering intended to address the horrendous problems of the Brainard-Green family — problems including a murder and a suicide attempt, not to mention prescription drug abuse, obesity, and breaking and entering, to name a few — Sammy was more than capable of interrupting the proceedings by hurling Pink Piggy in the air, catching him, and repeatedly biting on Pink Piggy's loud squeaker. So, Sammy would have offered the promise of comic relief. But Lady? She was the vulnerable one, the one least able to offer protection, the one in unremitting need of it herself. Still, Lady was the one Caprice loved most. "Of course," I said. "We may not be able to have her in the meeting with us. I don't know. But she can come with us. If you want her, she'll be as close as my car."

"I know she's fragile," Caprice said. "I really do know that. I've been talking to Dr. Zinn about her. But Lady is a survivor."

"Yes, she is."

"And I am, too. Or I'm going to be."

"Yes," I said. "Yes, you are."

CHAPTER 43

If I could travel back in time, I know exactly where I'd choose to go: without hesitation, I'd pick the 1939 Morris and Essex Kennel Club Dog Show, which was held at the New Jersey estate of Geraldine Rockefeller Dodge. All of Mrs. Dodge's shows were spectacular, but the Morris and Essex show of shows was the one in 1939. The pageantry! The bright banners, the tents, the rings, the sterling silver trophies, the famed foreign judges, the proud exhibitors, the 50,000 spectators, and the 4,456 gorgeous dogs! The goal of the newly revived Morris and Essex Kennel Club is the rebirth of the legendary Morris and Essex in all its glory, and it looks as if the club will succeed if it can do in its only serious rival, which, I regret to report, offers whopping competition. The pageantry! The splendid tents, the famed foreign academics, the proud parents, and the thousands of canine stand-ins resplendent in their flowing caps and gowns! Indeed, Harvard University Commencement!

So, Harvard Commencement being the closest Cambridge offers to the Morris and Essex Kennel Club Dog Show, I make a habit of taking Rowdy and Kimi to the Square each June to enjoy the annual spectacle. Since we aren't actually entered in the show, we are not allowed to wander in the show grounds proper, namely Harvard Yard, during Commencement Exercises, but we saunter around and take in the scene. The dogs sniff. I gape, especially at the famed academics, foreign and domestic, who, in their brilliantly colored and elaborately embellished caps and gowns, put even the best-dressed dog show judges to shame.

So, on the afternoon of Thursday, June 9, Rowdy, Kimi, and I walked down Concord Avenue to Garden Street and into the Square, which was satisfyingly crowded with distinguished-looking people in flamboyant academic costumes. Obedient to tradition — it supposedly never rains on Harvard Commencement — the day was sunny and still, and the three of us had a lovely time, as we'd had in previous years. The only unusual event was minor, or so it seemed at the time. It was this: when we'd finished sniffing and gaping in the Square itself, I decided that instead of retracing our route, we'd go through Brattle Square and then take Brattle Street to Appleton, which would lead us home. When we reached Brattle Square, we crossed to the far side of the street and were approaching an emporium of expensive women's clothing, a favorite of Rita's, when Anita Fairley emerged from the store. I wasn't at all surprised to see that she'd been shopping there; she always dressed in coordinated outfits that gave her a polished look. Furthermore, it was no surprise to see that she'd been spending money; extravagance was one of her characteristic vices. At the moment, she was carrying three large shopping bags emblazoned with the name of the shop. In several other ways, she did not, however, seem quite like herself.

For one thing, her long blond hair was in disarray; there was no breeze at all to muss anyone's coiffure, and it was entirely unlike Anita not to have restored herself to perfection after trying on clothes. For another thing, her eyes looked oddly bright. My first thought was that she'd visited an ophthalmologist earlier in the day and that her pupils remained dilated after an exam. I immediately realized that I was wrong: the brightness wasn't limited to her eyes, but included her whole face. Her expression was, of all things, animated. But the strangest thing of all was that as she emerged from the store carrying those big bags, she immediately accosted a dark-skinned couple, a man and a woman from Africa, I guessed, both of whom wore flowing academic gowns trimmed with vivid colors that signified, in some fashion I couldn't decode, degrees or honors conferred by institutions of higher learning. Even on Commencement Day, with all its pageantry and finery, these people were exceptionally striking, tall and eye-catching in a distinctly exotic fashion. I must also mention that they were obviously engaged in intense conversation with each other while self-confidently hastening to some destination that they knew how to reach; they were clearly not hanging around hoping to strike up a conversation with a stranger, and I saw no sign whatever that they were lost and in need of directions. On the contrary, Anita the Fiend, Miss Uncongeniality, the personification of coldness and distance, had forced herself upon this couple, to whom she was now speaking with insistent friendliness. To describe my curiosity as piqued would be an understatement; I had an almost uncontrollable itch to know what was going on. In opposition to that fervent desire was an even stronger wish to avoid having Anita turn her attention to me. Consequently, before she had the chance to notice our presence, the dogs and I turned around and took a little detour to Mount Auburn Street that led us to Brattle, which took us to Appleton and eventually back home.

When we got there, Caprice was pacing around in the kitchen talking to Leah, who was merely stopping in after attending the Commencement events at one of the Harvard houses and before dining out with a new graduate and his family.

"If you seriously don't want to go," Leah was saying, "just don't go!"

"I feel as if . . . as if Eumie would want me to," Caprice said. "Or as if I owe it to her. Or as if someone has to be there to represent her. Or her interests, somehow."

"Why?"

"Because she can't be there herself, Leah!" With that, Caprice started to cry.

"Oh, shit," Leah said. "I'm sorry. I didn't mean it that way. Caprice, I am so sorry." She gave Caprice a big hug and then got a fistful of tissues out of the drawer where they're kept to protect them from the malamutes. Handing the tissues to Caprice, she said, "Well, if you go, don't take any crap from anyone."

"I want to remind both of you," I said, "that this meeting is not going to be some free-for-all in which people are allowed to attack one another. It's meant to help everyone and not to cause further pain."

"What it's meant to do and what it actually does could be two different things," said Leah.

"If Caprice needs to leave, we'll leave," I said. "But I don't think that's going to happen. And Caprice is going to have lots of support. It isn't as if she'll be there all alone."

"Caprice," said Leah, "I know you love Lady, but the one you really ought to take is Kimi. Lady is a pushover. Kimi is tough."

I was losing patience. "Leah, really! Kimi is not some kind of attack dog! You know that. And even if she were, that's hardly what Caprice needs. Aren't you leaving soon?"

"As soon as I get dressed."

"Then get dressed, and stop badgering Caprice."

"She isn't," Caprice said.

After that, I fed the dogs and washed greens for a salad. Leah, of course, was eating out, and Steve was going to a veterinary meeting that included dinner, so there'd be only two of us to feed. After that, since Caprice's anxiety seemed to have infected me, I took a shower and simultaneously listened to the CD that Eumie had given me. The imagery was becoming more and more effective each time I listened. Of course, it was one thing to feel peaceful and calm in a relaxing shower and quite another to feel equally comfortable during a performance event with a potentially wild-acting and therefore humiliating Alaskan malamute. Still, I was learning to pretend that something wonderful was just about to happen, and the resulting happiness was beginning to make headway against my recollections of what I'll euphemistically call malamute reality. I got out of the shower feeling grateful to Eumie for her gift and clear about the need to attend this meeting as the ally of Eumie's daughter and of Eumie's dog.

After getting dressed, I checked my e-mail. So much for my feeling that something wonderful was about to happen! As if to teach me the distinction between fantasy and reality, a message from a friend with malamutes conveyed the sad news that Monty had died — not Caprice's father, I hasten to add, but the real Monty, as I thought of him, Ch. Benchmark's Captain Montague, ROM, Phyllis Hamilton's great dog. *ROM* stands for Register of Merit. The title, highly coveted by breeders, is conferred by our national breed club, the Alaskan Malamute Club of America, on a dog with eight or more champion offspring or a bitch with five or more. I called Phyllis immediately.

"I just heard about Monty," I said. "I had to call. I am *so* sorry."

Phyllis thanked me. In spite of her grief, her voice was as clear, warm, and musical as ever. "He was fine until a week ago. He'd just celebrated his fourteenth birthday. Every one of my dogs is special, but maybe just once, we breed that extra-special one. I am so grateful that God gave this one to me."

It's an unwritten rule of the Dog Fancy that breeders must take pride in the accomplishments of their dogs. Few breeders, however, possess the grace to give credit where it's due, as Phyllis had just done.

"I remember Monty so well," I said. "He had incredible bone. And everyone said, 'Nobody moves like Monty.' He had such presence, such great dignity. Phyllis, he really was majestic."

"Monty knew who he was," Phyllis contin- ued. "He was so *defined*. He had a con- sciousness, a deep sense of who he was."

The same, I thought, could not be said of Sammy. "Was he always like that?" I asked.

"No! His sense of who he was, the wave, really, began building when he was six or seven. Like with some men." We both laughed lightly. "It's only when they're middle-aged that they begin to be defined."

We talked for a few more minutes before Phyllis's sorrow overcame her ability to focus on the fourteen years of joy that Monty had given her. When I hung up, I had tears in my eyes, in part because I was sharing Phyllis's grief, but in part because I was moved by the difference between my own extended family in the world of dogs and the network of the Brainard-Green fam- ily. In our malamute community, we shared passionate love for the breed and for our individual dogs, and we reached out to sup- port one another in times of pain and loss. I felt terrible sadness at the contrast between the talk I'd just had with Phyllis and the meeting I was about to attend.

CHAPTER 44

Loyal as I am to the canine cosmological faith of my parents, I reject the notion of coincidence: delve deeply into any apparently haphazard phenomenon, and you'll find evidence not merely of a governing principle but of an archetypal being whose all-pervasive presence reveals to the eyes of the devout the wondrous order hidden beneath seeming chaos and the joyous meaning of what nonbelievers misinterpret as muddled pointlessness. In brief, when the Almighty plays dice with the universe, they are dog-loaded dice. Such were the thoughts that filled my mind when I arrived at Ted Green's and was filled with the awe-inspiring realization that twice in a single day was I to be blessed with the heaven-sent opportunity to wander in precincts patterned on the template revered by my forbears, all of which is to say that just as Harvard Square on Commencement Day had testified to celestial design, so too the therapeutic family meeting proclaimed its spiritual origins in that paradigmatic Event of Events, the dog show.

That the meeting was to be modeled on the dog-show archetype became apparent to me when I pulled Steve's van into Ted's parking area, which I unhesitatingly recognized as a variant of the unloading areas available to exhibitors so that they don't have to haul crates, grooming tables, and other show paraphernalia, as well as dogs, of course, all the way across big parking lots to the show sites where they are going to set up. At actual shows, parking in the unloading zones is strictly temporary, whereas I had arranged with Ted to occupy a spot close to the show site for the whole evening. Also, I had nothing to unload. I did, however, have two dogs with me, Lady, who was there for Caprice, and Sammy, whom I was hoping to take to at least a few final minutes of dog training at the Cambridge Armory, and I'd wanted them near the house. Parking in Cambridge is notoriously terrible, but on Commencement Day, it can be impossible, and the point of having Lady with us was to have her available to Caprice, not in a car parked two or three blocks away. Besides, I hate leaving a dog in a car on the street, especially a dog like Sammy, who'd go anywhere with anyone.

By so-called coincidence, Caprice, Lady, Sammy, and I arrived in Steve's van rather than in my Blazer, my own car having supposedly just so happened to develop a flat tire. I'd discovered the flat before Steve had left, and since neither of us had wanted to be delayed by tire changing, Steve had arranged a ride to his veterinary meeting with friends, and I'd taken his van. The van was a battered old vehicle to which Steve was greatly attached, less because of its convenience, I suspected — it easily held five dog crates and was outfitted with compartments for veterinary supplies and fishing gear — than because of its ineradicably canine and thus homey and comforting odor. In fact, on the short drive to Ted's, it was the redolence that reminded me of the afternoon's odd little episode involving Anita, who had hated Steve's van and had incessantly nagged him to replace it with a two-seater sports car with no room for even one of his dogs.

But I digress. As I was saying, when I pulled Steve's van into the parking spot at Ted's, I was aware of using an exhibitor space, but was distracted from meditations on universal paradigms and such by Caprice, who said lightly, "The scene of the crime."

"No one is going to run you over tonight," I assured her.

"There's my mother's Reiki healer," Caprice said. "What's she doing here?"

"Part of the network, presumably."

"What time is it?"

"Ten to seven. We're a little early. Do you want to take Lady in now? Or leave her here for the moment?"

"I think maybe she can stay here for now. Can I give her one of the Kongs you brought?"

To keep the dogs happy in their crates, I'd packed a cooler with four stuffed Kong toys from the freezer. Caprice eased open Lady's crate, hugged her, slipped in the Kong, and latched the door. Meanwhile, I gave Sammy his Kong. "You be a good boy," I said. "Keep Lady company. We'll be back to check on you." Then, leaving a couple of windows slightly open, I closed and locked the van, and Caprice and I made our way up the steps to the porch of Ted's house and added our shoes to a row of twelve or fourteen pairs.

Before I'd even rung the bell, Ted opened the door and, without mentioning Rita, made her influence apparent. "I hate to start out by kvetching," he said, "but they won't let me serve food. Not even coffee. Nothing. So, my apologies." Ted was on crutches, but he looked freshly showered, and he wore clean, new-looking clothes, a greenish-yellow shirt and chinos with the right calf neatly slit to accommodate his cast.

"It isn't a social occasion, Ted," Caprice told him.

"The ultimate shikse, that's what you are. Everything's a social occasion."

A female shriek interrupted us. "Dolfo!" Ted yelled uselessly. "Dolfo!" To me, he said, "He's taken a liking to Vee Foote, and she's allergic."

My foot! I wanted to say. *She isn't allergic. She's phobic.* I restrained myself. Not everyone appreciates puns. I said, "Dolfo should be on leash. And I thought he was with Barbara and George."

"They aren't speaking," Ted whispered. "Well, he's speaking to her, but she isn't speaking to him. To George, I mean."

For the second time in less than a minute, I tactfully kept quiet. "Awkward," I said.

"But they're here. Barbara brought Dolfo with her. They're in the living room. Frank Farmer isn't here yet. Dr. York and Dr. Youngman and the others are in the family room."

"What's the Reiki woman doing here?" Caprice asked.

"She was very special to Eumie," Ted said. "I thought she ought to be here. And my acupuncturist. She's here, too. I'm waiting for Wyeth. The hospital is sending his social worker with him. It was all a misunderstanding, but they're —"

"Wyeth tried to kill me," Caprice said, "and he could've killed you, and there's every chance that he killed Mommy. Now, where's the misunderstanding?"

"Caprice," I said, "let's let that wait for the meeting, okay?"

She might not have listened to me. Luckily, her father, the false Monty, as opposed to Phyllis's dog, arrived at that moment, and Caprice and Ted competed for his attention. Competed. As I've said, a dog show. Caprice won. Like the real Monty, Caprice's father was a gentleman. His polite acknowledgment of Ted struck me as especially civil and admirable; Ted had, after all, stolen Monty's wife when she'd been a patient of Ted's. Even so, Monty Brainard nodded to Ted and said hello. Then he wrapped Caprice in a bear hug and greeted her with his favorite term of endearment: "Hi, baby girl."

Caprice, I was happy to notice, looked far less babyish than she had at Eumie's memorial service. She wore a black linen dress with only a few of Lady's hairs clinging to it, and her blond hair was curling back from her face on its own, with no childish barrettes or bows. Monty's tan had faded a little since the last time I'd seen him, but he looked hearty and strong, and his thinning hair had been cut very short.

It must now have been about five minutes before seven. I heard people at the door. Eager to spare Caprice a face-to-face encounter with Wyeth in the absence of a protective coterie of mental-health professionals, I said, "The meeting should be starting soon. Let's move to the living room." As she, Monty, and I started to make our way there, I looked back and saw that Wyeth was, in fact, among the new arrivals. With him were his mother and a woman I'd never seen before. As Johanna entered the hallway, the light from an overhead fixture seemed briefly to zoom in on her and to illuminate her face in an unflattering way, as if she were being photographed for the *before* picture in an impending makeover; her short blond hair showed a quarter-inch of white roots, incipient jowls appeared, and she acquired a vaguely ravaged look. The accompanying woman, whom I assumed to be the social worker Ted had mentioned, was a comfortingly familiar Cambridge type. At the age of fifty-five or sixty, she had waist-length gray-streaked black hair tied at the nape of her neck with an ethnic-looking scarf. Her flowing skirt and tunic had been handwoven in some Third World country. She had weathered skin and wore no makeup. I was willing to bet that the shoes she'd left on the porch were Birkenstock sandals. It seemed to me that she should occupy a place of honor in some living museum of Cambridge. I wanted to clone her.

The living room, apparently intended as the site for the meeting, was all pale green and silk. It had a large fireplace that held a massive display of fresh flowers. In front of the fireplace, two long couches, a love seat, and a glass-topped coffee table formed what I thought was called a conversation area. Unfortunately, Dolfo's activity there had not consisted of conversation. As one of the world's leading experts on pet stain removal, I accurately diagnosed the cause of the yellow marks on the silky upholstery materials and knew that they were permanent. The urine splotches did, however, look dry, and the odor in the house was less pronounced than usual, in part because several windows were open and in part because Nixie

Needleman, Eumie's psychiatrist, was exuding a nose-assaulting scent of musky perfume. As on the night of Eumie's memorial service, Dr. Needleman's platinum hair was tumbling down her back, her makeup was heavy, and the neckline of her black dress plunged toward her solar plexus. She was perched on one of the couches next to Vee Foote, who had gray-streaked brown hair and wore a rather dowdy gray jersey outfit. The contrast between the flamboyant Dr. Needleman and the conservative Dr. Foote, together with their positions on the silk couch and the intensity with which Dr. Foote was whispering to Dr. Needleman, suggested an old-fashioned tableau in which a female reformer, played by Vee Foote, visits a brothel to try to convince a prostitute, played by Dr. Needleman, to abandon her sinful, lucrative ways in favor of a respectable life of poverty in domestic service. Seated opposite them was the person Caprice had referred to as her mother's Reiki healer, a small, wiry woman with short black curls who was talking to a tall, brown-haired man in a conservative suit. "You don't touch them?" I heard him exclaim. "Then how does this procedure supposedly work?"

Seated in armchairs outside the central

area by the fireplace were George McBane and Barbara Leibowitz, with Dolfo at her side. With them was an attractive red-haired woman in a navy business suit. Leaving Caprice with her father, I joined George and Barbara. George looked far better than he had the last time I'd seen him: his color had returned and, with it, his handsome looks. This time, too, he greeted me in his normal, friendly way. Then he introduced the red-haired woman. "Holly, this is Oona Sundquist," he said.

"George's lawyer," Barbara explained.

Oona and I shook hands. "Holly Winter," I said.

"The police are here," George said.

"Where?" I asked.

"There," Barbara said.

I turned to see Kevin Dennehy, who was just entering the room. He wore a light summer suit and looked perfectly at ease. Catching my eye, he nodded and gave me a mysterious little smile before stationing himself against a wall. At a big show, you can expect to find a representative of the American Kennel Club, and I had no difficulty in identifying Kevin as our AKC rep.

Then a small crowd poured in: Wyeth, Johanna, the clone-worthy Cambridge woman who'd arrived with them, Ted Green on his crutches, and four people I didn't know. The door to the family room opened, and in stepped Rita, who was followed by Peter York, Quinn Youngman, and Missy Zinn. I looked around in search of Frank Farmer, our show chair, so to speak, or perhaps the judge for the breed about to be shown in this ring, but he was nowhere in sight.

With an air of authority, Rita stepped in front of the fireplace, introduced herself, and said, "I've just had a call from Frank Farmer. I'm sorry to say that Frank called me from the emergency room. He's there with a broken leg, and he won't be able to join us."

For a second, Rita's eyes met mine. What I saw in her gaze was accusation. No, worse than accusation. Blame! Irrational, mindless blame! Directed toward me! The cause of Frank's broken leg, I immediately realized, must be an incident with one of his utterly gorgeous, top-winning, and wild-acting basenjis. At a guess, the dogs had been bouncing around in a frenzy, and instead of ordering them out from underfoot, Frank had tripped and taken a hard fall. I am certainly not responsible for the misdeeds of all naughty dogs in the entire universe. But Rita tends to assume that I am. Hence the gaze of blame.

"We've talked this over," Rita continued, with a gesture that included Peter, Quinn, and Missy, "and we've decided that since everyone is here, we'll go ahead with the meeting, and we'll reserve the possibility of getting together a second time once Frank has recovered."

A central tenet of canine cosmology: doG works in a mysterious way. Delve into any seeming coincidence, and what you'll find is woofy purpose. Rita absolutely, positively had not wanted to lead this family meeting. She'd never have done it if Frank had not, purely by dog-driven coincidence, broken his leg. With renewed faith in the comforting orderliness of the universe, I took a seat near Barbara and George in one of Ted's upholstered armchairs, leaned back, relaxed, and smiled at Rita. I knew she'd do a good job. After all, she was meant to.

CHAPTER 45

"To begin," said Rita. "The purpose of this meeting is to bring together the Brainard-Green family and the family's support system so that everyone is working together. This is a family that has experienced considerable conflict and considerable stress, including the recent loss of a family member. We need to pool our resources to relieve some of that stress."

Caprice interrupted. "My mother didn't just wander off somewhere! She wasn't *lost*. She was murdered."

Before she'd finished, Ted said, "*Traumatic* stress."

Without uttering a word, Rita nodded at Caprice and then at Ted in some clever psychotherapist way that conveyed nothing about the content of what either had said, but nonetheless seemed to make both feel acknowledged. What's more, she didn't let the interruptions interrupt her. "In other words," she continued, "we're going to work toward a cohesive, integrated approach." Vee Foote was almost bouncing on the couch in her eagerness to say something, but Rita was too quick for her. "Here's our general framework. We're going to start by clarifying who's who and who does what in this system."

Here, I just have to take a second to express my admiration for Rita. In the words of the AKC's *Guidelines for Conformation Dog Show Judges,* "As the judge, you have full authority over all persons in the ring." I was happy to see that Rita not only intended to exert her authority, but to do so in the thoughtful and considerate manner that the AKC advocates in that same publication.

Probably because Dr. Needleman was shamefully unfamiliar with AKC guidelines, rules, and regulations, she failed to share my appreciation for Rita's skill. "Roles," she said with high-toned condescension. "I, for one, am not concerned with all these superficialities of social psychology. I treat introjects" — she paused dramatically — "and not objects!"

Although I didn't understand the distinction, I got her point: *I breed top-winning show dogs, not mutts.*

Addressing everyone, Rita said, as if performing a routine introduction, "Dr. Nixie Needleman. Dr. Needleman was Eumie Brainard-Green's individual therapist." Dr. Needleman, who clearly considered herself to be a high-ranking member of the Professional Handlers' Association, had tried to use her presumed clout to undermine the judge's authority. Rita, however, had dealt with the challenge by incorporating it into the ordinary process of checking the presence of all dogs in all classes to be judged. "So," Rita went on, "once we've finished clarifying who's who here, so everyone knows everyone else, we'll break up into subgroups, and we'll come up with some recommendations and guidelines to share with everyone about preventing recurrences of some of the recent difficulties and about helping each member of the family and the family as a whole to thrive."

I practically expected Rita to start handing out armbands. If I'd been chosen as one of her stewards, I'd have been tempted to do just that. At a show, the armbands display only the numbers that appear in the show catalog, but at this special event, names would've been acceptable. Dr. Needleman's armband would have identified her as the late Eumie's handler. Peter York would've been prominently labeled as Wyeth's, Missy Zinn as Caprice's, and so forth. Still, with a relatively small entry like this one, perhaps armbands weren't strictly necessary after all. In particular, anything remotely like those "Hi, I'm So-and-so" name tags would've mocked the seriousness of the gathering. By the way, as a little aside, I might mention that the Cantabrigian woman was indeed the hospital social worker and was wonderfully named India Cohen. India! What's more, this India had exactly the same air of calm yet alert self-confidence, intelligence, and protectiveness that characterized Steve's German shepherd bitch. I use *bitch* strictly in its technical and hence entirely inoffensive sense; there was nothing even remotely bitchy about India Cohen or, for that matter, Steve's female dog.

"Family members," Rita said. As she named them, she gestured toward each person in a welcoming way that didn't even hint at finger pointing. "Ted Green. Ted's first wife, Johanna Green. Their son, Wyeth. Monty Brainard, Eumie Brainard-Green's first husband. Their daughter, Caprice Brainard."

"And Dolfo," Ted interjected. "Dolfo is a full member of this family."

With a friendly little wave of her hand toward the tall, brown-haired man seated on the couch opposite Nixie Needleman and Vee Foote, Rita said, "John Tortorello. Dr. Tortorello is Ted's psychiatrist." The AKC enjoins its judges not to make what it calls *theatrical movements*. Rita's little hand motion was admirably subtle. "Dr. Peter York, Wyeth's therapist. Dr. Missy Zinn, Caprice's therapist. Dr. Quinn Youngman, Ted's psychopharmacologist. And Eumie's. Dr. Vee Foote, their couples therapist." She then introduced Eumie's Reiki healer, her herbalist, Ted and Eumie's acupuncturist, Ted's massage therapist, and Ted's primary-care physician, Dr. Salzman, who had been Eumie's as well. "Neighbors. Dr. George McBane and Dr. Barbara Leibowitz, who live next door. And Holly Winter, with whom Caprice is now staying."

Ted, I could see, was itching to add that I was the family dog trainer. In fact, he stood up and, using his crutches, moved toward Dolfo, who had been lying peacefully at Barbara's side. As Ted approached, Dolfo leaped to his feet. Out of the corner of my eye, I saw Dr. Foote shake a tablet or capsule into her hand and swiftly toss it into her mouth. "Ted," Barbara whispered, "not right now, I think."

"And," Rita said, "Lieutenant Kevin Dennehy, who is our representative of the larger society." She looked fleetingly embarrassed about the pretentious phrase. "Lieutenant Dennehy is with the Cambridge police. There have been legal ramifications to events in this family. And Oona Sundquist, who is an attorney."

"George," Barbara whispered to me, "is the only person here who felt the need for legal representation. What does that tell you?"

"Barbara," George said none too quietly, "I love you. There is not a more repentant person in the world than I am."

"Murderer," said Barbara, who continued to address me rather than her husband.

"I think that's everyone," Rita said.

Johanna rose to her feet. "I have to say that I'm not part of this psychobabble. I'm here because my child was threatened. I was told that my presence here was a condition for my son's release from an institution that was trying to strip him of his identity. But I am here against my will, and I deeply resent the accusation that I am a bad mother."

No one had said that she was. Ted rapidly

made up for the omission. "What else would you call yourself when Wyeth is out of control, acting out all over the place, and your response is to go out and buy him a new car? And a new computer? And God only knows what else by now? *Meshugass!*"

"Someone has to do something to compensate for what a cold, selfish son of a bitch he has for a father," Johanna said.

"This meeting," Rita said, "is about the family as whole. We are going to —"

"Rita," said Caprice, "let's cut the crap. We're here because Wyeth is dangerous, okay? He tries to kill people. With my mother, he succeeded. With Ted and me, he failed."

Barbara stood up. "I understand that the intention is to avoid focusing on one person," she said with dignity. "To address the system. But Caprice has a point. After all, no one else has made a suicide attempt, and it's plainly true that Ted and Caprice were injured as a direct result of Wyeth's actions, as was Dolfo."

"Leave the goddamned dog out of it," Wyeth said.

"Barbara," said George, "is fair and sympathetic almost to a fault. If she's suggesting that we deal straightforwardly and directly with a troubled young man, we need to listen to her."

"And so we will," said Rita. "But at the
—"

"This so-called meeting is degenerating
into a melee," said Dr. Needleman. "I find
it highly unprofessional."

"Shut up!" Caprice told her. "Who are
you to talk about other people being unprofessional? First of all, you look professional
all right! You look like a, uh, a harlot! A, uh,
demimondaine! And what did you ever do
to help my mother? Did you ever try to get
her off all those prescription drugs? You did
not! You prescribed and prescribed and
prescribed, and if she hadn't been pumped
full of . . ." Here, Caprice broke off and
began to sob. Monty wrapped an arm over
her shoulders. I could see that he was speaking to her.

"What did I tell you?" Johanna said. "Psy-
chocrap!"

"Johanna," Monty said, "you're awfully
eager to lay the blame for Eumie's death on
anyone except yourself, aren't you? Well, I
know better. Your rage and your bitterness
—"

"Who really understands bitterness,
Monty?" Johanna demanded. "You're the
one —"

"Lay off," said Wyeth. "Monty, let my

mother alone."

"Alone? What else is she?" Ted added. "Ever? Johanna is forever alone and always was, with no room in her narcissistic little shell for —"

"Enough," said Rita. "We're not here to —"

"We're here to get Wyeth locked up," said Caprice. "Safely behind bars. That's why Kevin's here. He's a homicide detective. He doesn't care about Wyeth's piddling little petty crimes."

"You sick, fat bitch!" Johanna charged. "You've got *matricide* written all over you."

As unobtrusively as possible, I stood up. To my mind, Caprice's weight was off-limits, and if she showed any sign of wanting to leave, I was prepared to accompany her.

"Look," said Monty, "let's get something out in the open. Eumie, who was my wife, went into therapy with Ted. Therapy. That's a joke. And from the first session on, he had her pay in cash at the beginning, and we all understand that there's only one reason for that, don't we? So, Ted, what did Eumie threaten to do to you that made you kill her? Was she going to turn you over to the IRS for unreported income?"

"Monty, you don't know a damned thing

about therapy," Ted said. "Some patients don't pay. They bounce checks. And Eumie and I filed joint returns. She'd hardly have sicced the IRS on herself. And I loved Eumie! Look at me! *Oy vey!* I'm lost without her!" His cry and his claim struck me as pitifully genuine. For all of their pretensions, for all of their self-absorption, for all of their inadequacy as parents, not to mention as dog owners, they'd been remarkably compatible.

"Let me summarize," began Rita in what I saw as a valiant attempt to impose order. "We're seeing a pattern of alliances and, uh, conflicts within the family."

"Which, I have to say," interjected Monty, "were all made a million times worse by every person here who ever wrote a prescription for anyone involved in this mess. Caprice is right, as usual. You, Dr. Needleman, and you, Dr. Foote, and the rest of you, you started out with unhappy people, people who came to you looking for help, and what the hell did you turn them into? Addicts! And you did it knowing that they didn't just dose themselves. Oh, no! They shared! If you want to know who's to blame for the mess Wyeth's in, look to yourselves. This poor slob of a kid, an empty human being, got his hands on *your* —"

To my surprise, Wyeth spoke up. "Yeah, addicts. Starting with you."

"Daddy is not —" began Caprice.

Wyeth spoke a single syllable that made everyone in the room freeze in place: "Porn."

"Wyeth, you —" Caprice began.

"Internet porn. Your dumb mother knew everybody's secrets. She told me. Right, Monty?"

Monty's tan vanished. Then his face turned crimson. After that, he lowered his head and held it in his hands. Caprice wrapped her arms around him. "It's okay," she said. "If it's true, it's really okay."

"We could all use a short break," Rita said. "Monty and Caprice, stay here with me, please. The rest of you, take five."

CHAPTER 46

I took advantage of the intermission to check on the dogs, which is to say that I used the dogs as an excuse to escape. Although Sammy and Lady were both quiet and content, I added spring water to the buckets in their crates and spent a few moments stroking each dog. Physical contact with a beloved animal lowers blood pressure: yours and the dog's, too. As I began to relax, it occurred to me that if I, one of the most peripheral people at the meeting, had a racing pulse, damp palms, and a tight stomach, then the central members of the group must be in danger of stress-induced heart attacks. Monty Brainard! Wyeth's revelation had been like a bullet fired at close range. For all that I sympathized with Monty, I couldn't help realizing that in wounding him, Wyeth had revealed a powerful motive for Eumie's murder. Eumie *had* collected secrets. She'd certainly known that

Caprice idealized and even idolized her father, who must have reveled in his daughter's esteem. Had Eumie resented it? After all, she was the parent with whom Caprice lived. If she had threatened to tell Caprice about Monty's addiction, wouldn't he have done anything to maintain his baby girl's admiration? Then there was what I now saw as Johanna's outright viciousness, especially her cruelty to Caprice. It was now easy to see that Johanna had modeled cruelty for her son, Wyeth. Either of them, mother or son, could have killed Eumie, and either could now be lashing out to protect the other.

I reluctantly stepped out of the van. As I was locking it, I realized that I stood on the exact spot where Caprice had been when Wyeth had run his car into her. I retained a clear memory of the expression on his face. That recollection jarred with everything about Eumie's murder, which had been indirect and, as I'd never before quite realized, sneaky. In contrast, Wyeth's dangerous acts had been altogether forthright. For example, he hadn't placed his computer and peripherals on a windowsill where they'd fall into the backyard; he'd actively thrown them out the window. He'd run his car right into Caprice, and he'd done it while I'd been there to see him. As to his violence toward himself, his suicide gesture, he hadn't tried to make the overdose look like an accident, and he hadn't set someone else up to take the blame for it. In fact, I suddenly realized, the sneaky person in the family was Caprice. Her binge eating was a secret activity, as was her use of medication. She'd found out Anita's last name by researching all of us on the Web, and when I'd confronted her, she herself had used the word *sneaky.* What's more, her own mother, Eumie, had enlisted her as a fellow sneak, a Web-savvy assistant in ferreting out information about people.

With these depressing and worrisome thoughts in mind, I made my way back to the house. In the front hall, Dr. Foote and Dr. Needleman were speaking with Dr. Tortorello. In passing, I heard Vee Foote say, "Well, I assume we'll be paid for all this time! I'm not here for my own pleasure!" Vee Foote, ever the helping professional! When I entered the living room, Rita was again in front of the fireplace. Caprice and Monty, I saw, were deep in muted conversation, each with a hand on the other's arm. I wanted to think well of both of them. If, as seemed to be the case, this Monty, the false Monty, was truly addicted to Internet pornography, he was hardly alone; the addiction was common. At a guess, he had nonetheless allowed it to act as a barrier in his relationship with his daughter. He visited occasionally, took her to restaurants, and left, thus protecting his baby girl from knowledge that he assumed would destroy her golden image of him. And what was the consequence for Caprice of having her father keep his distance? I didn't want to think about it and looked away. In a corner, the capable-looking Cantabrigian social worker from the hospital was conferring with Wyeth and Johanna. Kevin remained against a wall, as if he hoped to be mistaken for a piece of furniture. Ted was now seated with Barbara, George, and George's lawyer. Like me, Ted had sought the solace of a dog. He had his hands wrapped around Dolfo's head. As I watched, he lowered his face to the dog's so that two pairs of eyes met only inches apart.

"Let's reassemble," said Rita. As people drifted back to their seats, she said, "Let me summarize. We're dealing here with two sets of alliances that were ruptured. Ted and Johanna's marriage, and Monty and Eumie's. The divorces left a great deal of anger. Monty's anger at Ted, Johanna's at Eumie, and anger of each former partner at the other. The anger of the children. Wyeth's at Eumie and at his father, Caprice's at Ted. And the conflict between the stepchildren. This is a family, I think, in which it's difficult to see the alliances, but they're here. Ted and Eumie had a strong alliance, really, a kind of enmeshment, as it's called, so that they were, as I see it, aimed at becoming the same person. In that unit, they even included their dog, Dolfo. As we all know, Eumie's death suddenly disrupted that enmeshment and, with it, the whole family system. Each child has a powerful alliance with the parent of the opposite sex, Wyeth with Johanna, Caprice with Monty, even though that's also a distant relationship. And we find powerful alliances with therapists, each individual with one or more people outside the family. Another unit in this family is, as I see, prescription medication. In effect, the people living in this house had attachments of a sort to that unit, which really functioned as a member of the family, a member about which everyone agreed, a member with which every person was deeply involved. Now, we'll separate into four subgroups. And what we're going to do in these groups is try to come up with recommendations to share with everyone, guidelines for this family and its support system to use in planning what we can do to promote healthy, normal alliances where those are possible and to avoid some of the painful conflicts we're seeing."

"All one big, happy family," Caprice said cynically.

"Not at all. One source of difficulty here has to do with boundaries. It may be that the outcome you decide on will be to set strict limits about involvement with other members of the family, including severing some relationships entirely."

"Individuation," said Ted. "But before we separate, I'd like to say a word about the role of trauma here. And a few words about Eumie, who is still with us in spirit. We need to acknowledge the part played by her trauma in our family life."

"Bullshit!" The speaker was Caprice. "Ted, if you're talking about that undertaker story —"

"Caprice, it's no story. Your maternal grandfather was an undertaker, as you know, and you also know that when his wife, Eumie's mother, died, he himself —"

"He himself," said Caprice, "was an electrician! Eumie's father was not an undertaker. Therefore, he was hardly in a

414

position to embalm his own wife."

"Denial," said Ted, "is a normal phase, Caprice. We don't want to believe that these terrible events really happened to ourselves or our loved ones, so we deny that they did."

"Genealogy sites on the Web," said Caprice, "happen to include a lot of city directories. Old directories. They usually have information about occupations. Professions. Repeat! Mommy's father was not an undertaker. He was an electrician. Electricians do not embalm people. Therefore, her father did not embalm her mother."

"Caprice, every family has its secrets. It's normal. Johanna doesn't tell people about her eye job. Ai-ai-ai! Johanna, I've let it out! Not that you ever needed cosmetic surgery."

Before Johanna could respond, Rita intervened. "We're about to break into subgroups, and I want to say with regard to family secrets that this is a family with what appear to be a great many. On the one hand, this family has a lot of blurring going on, blurring of boundaries between parents and children, therapists and patients, even people and dogs. And complicating all that is this business of who knows what about whom, and those secrets create their own unhealthy kinds of boundaries and unhealthy alliances. So, in these meetings, the

415

rule is going to be that everyone will refrain from telling secrets that can't be shared with this entire group. Okay. Everyone who has prescribed medication for anyone in the family is going to meet with Dr. Youngman in the kitchen, please. The three parents, Monty, Ted, and Johanna, are going to meet here with me. Ms. Cohen and Lieutenant Dennehy, you're going to meet with us, too. The children, Wyeth and Caprice, are going to be with their therapists, Dr. York and Dr. Zinn. Perhaps you could use the family room. And those of you concerned with Dolfo, maybe you could meet in the back-yard. That's you, Holly, and Dr. Leibowitz and Dr. McBane. And those of you who don't fit into these subgroups, just stay here in the living room, please."

For once, I was frustrated to find myself in the dog group, which felt like the dog-show class known as American-Bred, which draws a small entry and is thus less competitive than the big Open class. Furthermore, it lacks the prestige of Bred-by-Exhibitor, which is, as its name suggests, limited to dogs handled by the people who bred them. American-Bred, I reminded myself, had its uses; for instance, a dog who might be overlooked among all the others in Open could win American-Bred and subsequently defeat the winners of the other classes to go Winners Dog, then maybe Best of Winners and even Best of Breed. Indeed, all the world is a dog show, and all the men and women . . . except that we weren't actually here to compete, were we? Anyway, by the time Barbara, George, Dolfo, and I were in the backyard, I felt that I was where I belonged. Oona Sundquist, George's lawyer, had remained in the living room; George hadn't even tried to get her to accompany us. Barbara and I took seats on one bench, and George sat opposite us on another. Dolfo was sniffing the grass in the area between the benches.

Barbara smiled at me and said, "Dolfo. Oh, my. Dolfo. Well, aesthetic considerations aside, there's nothing inherently wrong with him. He wants desperately to be a good dog."

"Don't we all," said George. "Me, for example."

Looking at me, Barbara said, "The touching thing about Dolfo is that his lovely temperament has somehow survived, triumphed, really. He loves other dogs. He's sweet and friendly with everyone. And he's perfectly trainable."

"That's my impression, too," I said. "He doesn't jump on me. He sits for me. Have you had him in a crate?"

"He's fine! Give him the least little thing to occupy him, and he's perfectly happy in his crate. And at my house, where I watch him every second, he's had only one accident."

"*Our* house," said George. "Where *we* watch him."

"There are two problems here." I pointed to Ted's house. "Well, more than two. But one is that it would be almost impossible to remove the odor. It's everywhere. Wherever Dolfo sniffs, there's a stimulus that prompts him to overmark. It isn't as if you could completely deodorize a few areas where he's gone before. You'd have to steam clean everything and spray the whole house with enzymes and air it all out. And the other problem is habit. Housebreaking is so easy if you can *prevent* the dog from ever going in the house."

"Habits," said Barbara, "are the worst! But with Dolfo, the habit is established here, at Ted and Eumie's. He doesn't transfer it to my house as much as you'd think. So, there's a lot of hope for Dolfo. The problem is Ted."

"Barbara, there's hope for all of us," said George.

"Ted is very motivated," I said.

"So am I," said George.

"He really loves Dolfo."

George said, "Barbara, I worship you."

"I hate to say this," I said, "but Ted and Eumie were basically colluding to block any effort to change Dolfo's behavior. Without Eumie, there's a better chance of making progress than there was when she was alive."

Barbara nodded in agreement. "And Ted would pay whatever it took. There must be a decontamination company he could hire, the kinds of people who clean up after industrial accidents, environmental disasters, that sort of thing."

I said, "And a dog trainer other than me. Someone who has no connection to the family."

"A fresh start," said George. "Decontamination. Barbara, I'm an environmental disaster, but I'm very motivated."

"Look," I said, "could the two of you possibly talk about what you're talking about? To each other? I'm a dog trainer. I'm out of my depth."

"The squirrels were driving her crazy," George said. "Barbara, they were. You complained about them all the time. You kept running out yelling at them. You were banging on the windows. They chewed up the window frame when you put that feeder there."

Barbara said, "If a living creature bothers me, that doesn't mean that I want it poisoned. It just means that I wish it would stop bothering me. Ted bothers me. Eumie bothered me. I don't like to see a dog being ruined. But am I going to poison Ted? Did I sneak into their house and poison Eumie? Of course not!"

"Eumie wasn't poisoned," George said.

"What do you call an overdose?" Barbara demanded. Her tone was sharp, but she was addressing George. "Maybe his lawyer should be here after all," she then said to me, "instead of back inside where she can keep an eye on Lieutenant Dennehy."

"Barbara, I did not murder Eumie. Squirrels are not human beings."

"They are living things."

"So are rats. Cockroaches. Fleas. Mosquitos."

"Squirrels," said Barbara, "don't transmit disease."

"Neither do rats."

"Yes, they do."

"Barbara, the point is that everyone draws the line somewhere. Now, I knew you wouldn't approve, and that's why I didn't tell you, but I did it for you. I love the pleasure you take in feeding birds. I watch you when you're filling the feeders and keeping your lists of the species you see in our yard, and you're so beautiful. The squirrels were your enemies. That's how I saw it. They were like fleas on a dog. Barbara, I know I never should've done it. It was stupid, stupid, stupid."

"It wasn't just stupid. It was cruel."

"This is none of my business and totally outside my field of expertise," I said, "so please tell me if I'm out of line. But I can't help noticing that the two of you are still living together. That's a good sign, maybe. And we've mentioned decontamination. A fresh start. George, I honestly think that your perspective has changed and that you really are sorry. Barbara, I'm sure he really will never do anything like this again."

"Never," said George. "Barbara, if there were anything I could do . . ."

"Such as what? To the best of my knowledge, even the best intentions won't restore life to the dead, George."

"What I've been wondering," I said hesitantly, "is whether there's a possibility of redemption. And room for some compromise. Barbara, maybe if you agreed to some new policy about the squirrels at your feeders. Tolerate them? Even feed them. And

George, you just said that if there were anything you could do . . . well, I wonder whether the two of you might be able to think of something."

George said, "Barbara, you need new bird feeders. With baffles. And we can get squirrel feeders. It's what I should've done instead."

Barbara looked eager to speak. The second George finished, she said with great emphasis, "Urban wildlife." She paused and then repeated the phrase in a tone of surprise and wonder as if it were a treasure she had discovered and was eager to display. *Look what I've found! Urban wildlife!* "George, the urban wildlife groups always need volunteers. In fact, I've thought about volunteering, not just donating, but —"

George rose from his bench, stood in front of Barbara, and held out both hands.

She took them in hers. "We could," she said. "We could both volunteer." Tears were running down her cheeks. George began to sob.

I know when to disappear. I did.

Chapter 47

In my eagerness to give the reconciling couple the privacy they needed, I made straight for the steps to the deck. Only as I entered the family room did I realize that I'd given no thought to where I was going. In any case, I couldn't stay where I was. Wyeth was slumped down in one of the big leather chairs, and Peter York, Missy Zinn, and Caprice were engaged in an intense discussion. As I passed through the room, I caught only fragments.

". . . no reason the two of you ever need . . . ," Missy was saying. Then Caprice spoke angrily about the trip to Russia that Ted and Wyeth were to take in July.

It happens now and then that two dogs in the same household or kennel come to hate the sight of each other so violently that they must be kept completely apart. At a guess, this group would offer the recommendation that Caprice and Wyeth have no contact with each other. I gave the matter only a moment's thought. My attention belonged elsewhere, as did I.

By *elsewhere,* I refer, of course, to dogs and specifically to Sammy and Lady, who had suddenly started to make noise. Pointers can and do bark in the normal fashion usually rendered as *woof-woof* or *ruff-ruff.* Alaskan malamutes are capable of barking, but they also produce yips and growls and howls, weirdly feline purrs, and the long strings of syllables that malamute fanciers refer to as "talking" because intonation marks these utterances as assertions, questions, exclamations, interjections, or commands. The most characteristic malamute syllable, *woo,* attains its maximum aesthetic potential when emitted repeatedly and operatically in an ecstatic *woo-woo-woo-woo!*

At the moment, Sammy was not delivering himself of the malamute *Ode to Joy.* He was speaking rather than singing, but I couldn't tell what he meant. *Something's up,* perhaps? Lady was adding high-pitched, nervous barks that expressed agitation, excitement, or fear. I was more puzzled than alarmed. Both dogs were crated. Steve's van was locked. It was hard to imagine what was triggering the outburst. Another dog? Maybe a loose dog had decided to sniff around the van or even jump on it. In any case, the dogs needed to be quiet. Peter and Missy were already throwing me questioning glances.

I hurried out of the family room and through the kitchen, where the prescribing physicians were meeting. Vee Foote was once again shaking a pill from a prescription bottle into her hand. "Dander," she explained in a thick voice.

"Vee, are you sure you're not overdoing it?" Quinn Youngman asked. He began to say something about antihistamines.

When I'd passed through the front hall and reached the porch, I paused for a second not only to put on my shoes but to prop the door open with someone's leather clog so that I wouldn't lock myself out. From my vantage point, I saw no sign of a roving dog or of anyone or anything else near Steve's van, but my view was blocked by the gigantic Lexus and the BMW in Ted's cobblestoned parking area.

"Hey, guys!" I called out as I rushed down the stairs. "Enough! I'm coming." I wasn't worried. My only concern was that the dogs were annoying people; I want my dogs to be a source of pleasure to everyone or, failing that, to refrain from being a source of even the slightest displeasure. By the time I was in back of the van, the dogs were silent. I stopped for a second to get the keys out of my pocket and heard what sounded like a woman's voice coming from inside the van. The radio? The van was old, but the radio worked. It had certainly never turned itself on.

And it hadn't this time. When I reached the side of the van, I saw that the sliding door was open about three inches and that the interior lights were on. I had locked that door. I *knew* I had. Could Steve have inexplicably left his veterinary meeting and for some unknown reason decided to come here to Ted's and . . . ? The explanation made no sense. And a set of keys dangled from the lock in the van's door. Steve never left his keys in the lock. I slid open the door to discover the last person I expected to see, namely, Steve's horrible ex-wife, Anita the Fiend, who was kneeling on the floor in front of Lady's crate. Anita, who hated this van, despised dogs, and really had it in for helpless little Lady!

"What the hell are you doing?" I demanded.

She turned to face me, and even before she spoke, I realized that there was something wrong with her. Well, there had to be. She hated dogs, yet here she was in Steve's van with two of our dogs. But she looked peculiar, too. Her eyes had that brightness I'd noticed when I'd seen her in the afternoon, and her long blond hair was wild and tangled. She was dressed entirely in white: white silk shell, white canvas pants, white shoes with three-inch heels. Even I, with my limited fashion sense, saw that the dressy sleeveless top and the high heels didn't go with the casual pants. Furthermore, although the evening was cool, the silk shell had sweat stains at the armpits. It's said of tall, slim, beautiful, fashionable women like Anita that they look like models. Anita really did; she always looked ready to be photographed for *Vogue.* Or she always had.

When she spoke, her speech was so rapid that I had to listen closely to understand her. "I'm thinking about getting a dog. A dog! I'm seeing them with new eyes. The eyes have it! The ayes! Ai-ai-ai! With green eyes, like Steve's. How lucky that I kept his keys! On key and off key. Tequila. Steve doesn't like it. But he loves me. He lusts after me. I'm beautiful, you see. I have the face that launched a thousand ships. Helen!

Why the hell didn't my parents name me Helen? From now on, I am Helen of Troy. No! A hair dryer! It's a brand of hair dryer. I don't need it. My hair is beautiful as it is. It reaches out to catch the vibrations of the universe."

To my horror, Anita turned back to face Lady's crate and fiddled with the latch. Lady, I should explain, was in the kind of solid plastic crate you see at airports. It's common for dogs to show marked preferences for one kind of crate or another. Lady liked the security of an opaque crate. Sammy tolerated plastic crates, but he greatly preferred the kind of open metal crate he was in now. His crate latch was a simple horizontal bar that slid back and forth, but Lady's crate had a more complicated vertical latch that I hoped would defeat Anita. It did not. She had, after all, been married to a veterinarian. She opened the crate, reached in, grabbed Lady by the collar, and dragged her out. Lady's eyes were huge with fear, and she was trembling all over.

"Hey, Lady," I said gently. "It's okay." To Anita, I said, in the same soft tone, "Now, maybe you could explain what you're doing here."

"Everything!" Anita cried. "There's so

much to be done! And I have the strength and talent for all of it!" She bestowed a big smile on me. "Where's Steve? Need to see Steve. Gorgeous Steve!"

Sammy, who'd been standing in his crate, chose that moment to bang the door with one of his big snowshoe paws.

"What a beautiful one this is!" Anita exclaimed. "Stunning!"

Maintaining her grip on Lady's collar, she rose to her feet and opened Sammy's crate. He came bounding out. While Anita's attention was diverted, I closed the van door to prevent the dogs from escaping. The van was now crowded. The five crates occupied a fair amount of space; there'd been just enough room for Anita, Lady, and me. The addition of Sammy squished us together. The confinement made me a little claustrophobic; in every way, I needed room to maneuver, and here I was, squeezed against the back of the passenger seat with no way to get between Anita and the dogs. I could've moved to the front of the van, and I could even have slid open the door and stepped out, but what about Lady and Sammy? I couldn't abandon them to a madwoman, especially to a madwoman who, when sane, hated dogs as fiercely as Anita did. Everything about her was strange and driven and frighteningly unpredictable. What if she kicked Lady? What if she somehow provoked Sammy and then accused him of attacking her? What if she . . . ?

Damn! What if Rowdy were here instead of Sammy! For all his exuberance and playfulness, Rowdy was a mature, well-trained dog. As Phyllis had said of her beloved Monty, he was defined. Furthermore, Rowdy was a certified therapy dog. If it somehow became expedient for me to give a hand signal, Rowdy would understand and obey it. On visits to nursing homes, he'd become accustomed to erratic behavior. He'd take Anita's frenzied manner in stride. If she snatched at his ears, shoved against him, or even fell on him, Rowdy would remain calm while accurately assessing the situation and doing his cool best to protect Lady and me. But Sammy? Sweet, rambunctious, baby-brained Sammy? I didn't know.

In fact, Sammy surprised me: gently shoving his way between Anita and Lady, he used his massive body to create a protective barrier between the menace and her probable victim. Did Sammy know that Anita would then let go of Lady's collar? Kimi would have predicted the result; if malamute chess ever catches on, she'll be a grand master. Sammy, I thought, lacked her capacity to foresee the result of each move. Still, Lady was now free. Better yet, she was on my side of Sammy and out of Anita's immediate range.

Totally misinterpreting Sammy's shove, Anita cried, "You see? He knows I'm beautiful. All creatures respond to astounding physical perfection."

The more fools they, I thought. Then I reconsidered. What about my own reaction to the beauty of dogs and especially to the physical perfection of my own? But at the moment, Sammy's stunning appearance was the least of his virtues. As Anita fixed him with an unblinking stare, I unobtrusively reached into my pocket, extracted a leash, and snapped it onto Lady's collar. One dog under my control! One dog safe from escape and thus safe from traffic. If I could get a leash on Sammy, I could slide open the door, and the dogs and I could bolt. Lady was now pressed hard against me, her entire body vibrating with fear. I had to get her out. I'd been carrying only one leash. A half dozen others hung from pegs at the rear of the van, beyond the crates, beyond Anita, hopelessly far away.

Sammy had distracted Anita. In the hope

of doing the same and with the dim hope of making Anita decide to leave, I said, "Anita, is there some reason you're at Ted Green's house? What made you come here?"

Kimi might have predicted Anita's reaction. I'm not Kimi; I didn't. Far from being harmlessly distracted, Anita abruptly shifted from euphoria to rage. She was talking so fast that I missed most of what she said. One word that I did catch was *kickbacks.* Her attitude to Sammy changed with her mood. "Get off!" she yelled. "Get off!" She bent down. I couldn't imagine why she'd want to grab his feet.

The last time I'd spoken, Anita had reacted so wildly that I was afraid to speak aloud. Instead of calling Sammy, I silently patted my thigh. He took one step toward me. If he'd only move next to me, I could transfer the leash from Lady's collar to his, hold Lady by her collar, and get the three of us out of this increasingly hellish van. If need be, I'd hold Sammy by his collar alone, but I was far from sure that I'd have the strength to maintain my grip if he took a dive out of the van, as he'd be likely to do. As I was trying to work out a plan either to get both dogs back in their crates, or to coax Lady to exit first so I could block the door and force Sammy to leave slowly, Anita stood up. In her hand were perhaps four sheets of paper. I'd been wrong. She hadn't been after Sammy's feet; her object had been the papers on which he'd been standing.

In her glee at having retrieved the papers, she shook them rapidly back and forth. "No one cheats Anita Fairley!" she crowed.

Sammy was fascinated; he was tantalized; he was impelled to respond. Bouncing with happy excitement, he bit into the papers Anita was waving right in front of his face.

"Goddamned dog!" she shrieked.

Lady was huddled next to me, but Sammy was still close to Anita, who moved her right foot backward and eyed Sammy in a way that terrified me. I'd once seen Anita kick Lady, and I could see exactly what was coming now.

No one cheats Anita Fairley, huh? Well, no one but no one under any circumstances kicks Holly Winter's dog!

Taking a lesson from Rowdy and now from his son, I barged forward and wedged myself between Anita and Sammy. With Lady's leash still in one hand, I filled my other hand with liver treats from my pocket. "Sammy, trade! Trade, buddy! Oh what a good boy! Good dog!" Giving Anita no time to think and no time to act, I hurled treats into Sammy's crate. He went after them, and I latched the door.

"Step to the back of this van, Anita, or I tear up these papers," I said.

She obeyed. I'd had a little practice in getting creatures to do that, of course. Losing no time, I crated Lady and stationed myself in front of the two occupied crates. Now that the dogs were safe, I'd have been happy to hand over the papers that Anita had determined to keep safe, but she'd taken yet another abrupt shift and was now raging at Ted Green. "Big phony! Cheat! CHIRP, CHIRP, CHIRP!"

For a second, I thought that she'd switched to birds. Then I made the connection.

"You've been there," I said. "To CHIRP. The Center for —"

Before I could even remember the name of the place, Anita, still clutching her precious papers, flew past me, slid open the door, and ran off.

I removed the keys that she'd left in the door and locked us in.

"Good riddance to her!" I told the dogs. "Both of you handled yourselves with admirable grace. Lady, you were frightened, but you didn't panic. Sammy, you are your father's son in every way." I gave each dog a frozen Kong. "Now, I have to check on things, but you are going to be fine. I'll be back as soon as humanly possible. Then we'll go home. Anita isn't going to bother us anymore."

CHAPTER 48

I never lie to dogs. I believed, which is to say hoped, that Anita had gone flying off far away. She had not. While I was still on the sidewalk on my way back to the house, I heard banging and looked up to see her on Ted's porch. I'd had more than enough of her and intended to avoid the front door by using the gate to the yard and then the entrance to the family room. That was before I saw what she was doing. Her action was so bizarre that it froze me in place: having removed one of her spike-heeled shoes, she was vigorously whacking at the door frame with a three-inch heel. Approaching, I saw that she was pounding on the mezuzah mounted by the door. A mezuzah is a sacred object. I couldn't stand by and watch her commit desecration.

"Stop that!" I yelled as I ran up the steps.

As I reached the porch, Anita succeeded in removing the mezuzah. At the same time, the door opened, and there stood Kevin Dennehy, who'd undoubtedly been attracted by the hammering. Without hesitation and without apparent effort, the willowy Anita rammed him aside — and that's saying something. It was like watching a gazelle slam a full-grown male gorilla out of its path.

"Kevin," I said, "that's Anita Fairley, Steve's ex-wife. There's something radically wrong with her."

He rolled his eyes. "So you've said once or twice."

"No, not . . . I'm serious. She's having some kind of episode."

Anita spared me the need to elaborate. Having charged into the living room, she began to berate Ted Green. "You're going to lose your license, you son of a bitch! Kickbacks! You got kickbacks for sending me and a lot of other people to that goddamned CHIRP, and that's unethical!"

This from Anita, who was a disbarred lawyer? I had to suppress nervous laughter. Kevin and I had followed Anita, but we were lingering near the door, whereas she had positioned herself close to Ted, Rita, Johanna, Monty, and the hospital social worker, all of whom were seated on the couches near the fireplace. In armchairs in a corner of the room were the participants in the meeting who hadn't been assigned to any of the subgroups: the Reiki woman, the acupuncturist, the massage therapist, the herbalist, and George McBane's lawyer, Oona Sundquist. Anita had startled everyone into silence. Tall and thin, dressed entirely in white, her long blond hair disheveled, she'd have stood out if she'd done nothing more than stroll quietly into the room. Like everyone else, I was staring at her. Weirdly enough, she'd respected the custom of the house by removing both shoes, not just the one she'd used as a hammer. In her right hand was the mezuzah. In her left, she still held the sheaf of papers that Sammy had snatched.

"Anita," said Ted Green, "you need to get control of yourself. You're not feeling well."

"I have never felt better in my life!" she shrieked. "No thanks to you! I'm going to sue you! You misdiagnosed me, and you mistreated me, and you duped me into making apologies for things I didn't do! You and your goddamned trauma! I have never been traumatized in my life! I have been depressed! And I want my money back!"

While my attention had been focused on Anita, Kevin had slipped out of the room and returned with all the physicians who'd been meeting in the kitchen. Although I only glanced at them, I noticed that Vee Foote looked asleep on her feet. Her eyes were heavy, and her head was almost lolling.

"That wonderful doctor," said Anita, pointing to Dr. Foote, "understands my depth and my strength and my creativity!"

Dr. Foote summoned the energy to mumble something.

"What did she say?" I whispered to Kevin.

"She said, 'Oh, shit'," he informed me.

"What have you done to my client?" Ted demanded. "What did you give her?"

"Pills!" replied Anita. "Beautiful pills! Who thought they'd work so fast?" Stretching out the syllables, she almost sang, "Selective serotonin reuptake inhibitors. See-lec-tive! See? See Dick run! Dick!"

As Anita was elaborating in an obscene fashion that there is no need to report in detail, I finally realized that we were witnessing a psychiatric emergency and that someone, damn it, should do something about it. Rita must have had the same thought. She stood up. At the same time, the door to the family room opened, and in came Caprice, Wyeth, Missy Zinn, and Peter York, followed by Barbara, George, and Dolfo.

In a moment of sanity, Anita said, "Christ,

what an ugly dog!"

"Dolfo," said Ted. "My beautiful boychick! Come to Daddy!"

"Cut the Yiddish," Anita ordered him. "You phony!" She frantically waved the papers. "You're as Jewish as I am."

Ted shook his head sadly. "You? Anita, I don't think so. Now, Dolfo? We talked about having a bark mitzvah, Eumie and I did, but . . . Anita, listen to me. You're having a reaction to your medication." He shrugged elaborately. "These wonder drugs? They do this now and then."

"I know everything about you!" Anita hollered. "Arkansas!" She brandished the papers. "My PI got the dirt on you! And you're a big fat liar! You're from Arkansas, you dick! Dickhead! *Gentile* Arkansas dickhead!"

Since Barbara and George had been in my dog group rather than in the doctors' group, I'd almost forgotten that they were both psychiatrists. Fortunately, Rita remembered, as did they. Rita, who was ordinarily too much of a lady ever to point at anyone, now pointed directly at them. They nodded. Barbara handed Dolfo's leash to Ted and moved slowly and calmly toward Anita. George followed her. The other psychiatrists, I might note, were standing uselessly

440

around or, in Dr. Foote's case, snoozing around. She had dropped into a chair and fallen asleep. If Dolfo had hung around or gone to sleep, or if Ted Green had maintained control of his dog, Barbara and George might have succeeded in leading Anita away or persuading her to go to a hospital, which was where, as I now realized, she belonged.

But that's not what happened. As Ted was explaining that his was the only Jewish family in their little town in Arkansas and that his mother's maiden name was Epstein, for God's sake, and as Anita was saying that *O'Flaherty* was a funny was to pronounce *Epstein*, Dolfo acted exactly as Sammy had done: when Anita shook the papers in her hand, Dolfo was so tantalized that he shot up, grabbed them, tore his leash from Ted's hand, and dashed out of his reach. Caprice, I recalled, had once remarked that mail was Dolfo's favorite food. And mail was made of paper.

Ted made the mistake of hauling himself up on his crutches and trying to chase Dolfo. Run after a dog, and guess what? He'll run away. My supply of dog treats was low, but my pocket held enough bits and crumbs to provide bargaining power. Dolfo had taken refuge behind the armchair occupied by the Reiki healer, who cooperatively moved when I approached.

"Dolfo, trade," I said casually. "Give." The trick is to avoid asking the dog a question. Don't invite resistance by making a rough demand, either. Your voice has to sound as if you're stating a happy fact that both of you take for granted. I kneeled on the floor and slipped my hand behind the chair. "Here you go! Trade." I scattered the bits and crumbs. The second Dolfo went for the goodies, I picked up the papers he'd dropped. "Good boy," I said.

As I've just said, don't invite resistance. If Ted Green had done nothing, I might have handed him the papers. As it was, he lunged toward me and, balancing precariously on his crutches, grabbed for them. It's vital not to reinforce undesired behavior. I considered Ted's behavior highly undesirable. I moved the papers behind my back and, in what was probably doglike fashion, scurried out of the living room, into the front hall, and up the stairs. When I reached the landing at the top, I sat down and read the papers that Anita had prized so highly and that Ted had been so determined to capture. They were exactly what Anita had said: a private investigator's written report about

Ted Green. As he'd said, he'd grown up in a small town in Arkansas. According to the report, he'd spent his high school years as a social misfit and an academic achiever. His father died when he was sixteen. In part because he'd somehow come across the work of a Brandeis University psychologist named Abraham Maslow, he'd then gone to Brandeis, where, for the first time, he'd found himself among others who read avidly and who discussed ideas. At Brandeis, he told his friends that he'd been born in New York City and that his parents had left for political reasons. His mother died during spring break of his senior year.

Activity in the hall below drew my attention. Barbara and George were escorting Anita out the door. George was in the lead. I'll say tactfully that Anita was following him. She was still talking a million words a minute, mainly to and about George, who was, as I've mentioned, known in the psychiatric community as Gorgeous George. Barbara was, of course, a dog person and was thus familiar with the use of lures. The usual lure is a tasty tidbit rather than a handsome husband, but Anita wouldn't have been all that interested in liver treats. Barbara was using what worked. Good dog trainers are flexible pragmatists. So, I suppose, are good psychotherapists.

Before descending the stairs, I took a moment to revisit the bedroom where I'd found Eumie Brainard-Green's body. The same multicolored duvet and matching pillows were still on the bed. They must have been laundered. I was surprised that Ted had kept them at all. Perhaps they reminded him of Eumie. I, at least, found them evocative. "Eumie, thank you," I said softly. "Thank you for your gift. I am listening to the imagery. It is helping. You were selfish, greedy, vain, pretentious, and incredibly kind. You cared about my trouble. If you were still alive, I would thank you by helping you to train your dog. I have faith that you could have learned. I know that you deserved the chance. Good-bye."

With that, I folded the PI's report, stowed it in my pocket, ran down the stairs, paused briefly in the hall to say a few words to Kevin Dennehy, and walked boldly into the living room, where Rita was struggling to reconvene the meeting, presumably so that she could bring it to an end. I did not take my dog trainer's seat on the periphery, but marched to the front of the room.

"Rita believes in dreams," I said to everyone. "She explains them to me. Among other things, she distinguishes between their manifest content and their latent content." Dr. Needleman's eyes opened wide. She opened her mouth, but before she had a chance to speak, I went on. "If I dream about dogs, as I always do, Rita makes me ask what the dogs mean, what they symbolize, what message the dream dogs are conveying to me, and what message I am sending to myself. I think that besides the manifest content of our meeting tonight, there's also latent content. And the latent content is about who murdered Eumie Brainard-Green. I now know who murdered her. And I know why."

My heart was pounding exactly as it did when I was entering the ring. My palms were drenched. But in the back of my mind, I could hear echoes of Eumie's gift to me. I took a strong, deep breath and went on.

"The woman who has just left, Anita Fairley, was a disgruntled client of yours, Ted, as well as a more recent client of Dr. Foote's. It was Dr. Foote who prescribed the antidepressants that are causing what I've heard Rita call a hypomanic reaction. Anita wasn't making a lot of sense about quite a few things, but she did, in fact, hire a private investigator. The papers that Ted was so eager to get his hands on are the PI's report."

It's possible that if I ever somehow get stuck handling Rowdy or Sammy all the way to the competition for Best in Show, or if we're ever in a runoff for High in Trial, I'll overcome my ring nerves well enough to do a decent job. If it happens, though, I'll have a calming presence at my side: a dog. As it was, I had my imagination, which I put to good use by conjuring the image of Rowdy at my left side, India to his left, Sammy at my right, Lady beyond him, and Kimi in front of me, her fearless eyes on my face. I smiled at Kimi and summarized: Arkansas, Brandeis, psychology.

"Public knowledge," Ted commented.

"O'Flaherty," I said. "Anita was raving, but she didn't make that up."

"Epstein," Ted insisted.

"When you got to Brandeis, you got mistaken for a Jew. Why not? Green."

"Shortened from Greenberg."

"Is that what you said? Why not? There must've been other people there whose families had shortened their names. Or changed them. You probably never even lied outright, Ted. You just didn't correct people's assumptions. And you picked up the Yinglish. Yiddish phrases. That's not hard. I mean, I'm a shikse, and I can understand your Yiddish expressions. I know what a mezuzah is. I can recognize a menorah. It couldn't have taken you too long, and plenty of the Jewish students at Brandeis must've come from assimilated families. Why not you? You belonged! You fit in. And your parents weren't around to set people straight. Your father died when you were in high school. Your mother died just before you graduated. Who was to know? So, no one did."

"My mother," said Caprice.

"Did Eumie tell you?" I asked.

Caprice shook her head. "Mommy knew everything."

Awakening briefly from her stupor, Dr. Foote mumbled, "A Jewish profession."

"Not exclusively," said Dr. Needleman. "Look at Dr. Zinn."

"My father is Jewish," said Missy Zinn.

"In Israel," Wyeth said unexpectedly, "if your mother's not Jewish, you're not."

"Freud!" exclaimed Dr. Needleman.

"Wasn't his mother Jewish?" asked Dr. Tortorello.

"Of course she was," said Dr. Needleman. "No one knows anything anymore."

"But how did Eumie find out?" I asked rhetorically. "The sad part is, really, that Dolfo told on you, Ted. Or he might as well have. We just saw a demonstration. Dolfo steals things. He especially steals paper. As Caprice once told me, mail is his favorite food."

"Your passport, Ted," said Caprice. "Dolfo ate it. You had to get a new one for the trip to Russia. And you had to send in your birth certificate. And Mommy saw it. Was your mother's name really O'Flaherty?"

"Have you ever heard of a Jew named O'Flaherty?" Ted's voice, however, had lost its strength, and tears were running down his face.

"Neither had Eumie," I said. "So, she made a fatal mistake. She teased you."

"Like she did me," Monty said. "She taunted you, didn't she? She threatened to tell everyone. She threatened to tell Wyeth what a jerk his father was. Eumie did that. She did it to me."

"You're not a jerk," Caprice said.

"I'm a liar," Monty said.

"You're not lying now," Rita told him. "And your daughter loves you."

"Dylan," said Quinn Youngman. "The themes, the images, the raw sense of being where you belong!"

"No one is going gentle into anything," said Dr. Needleman.

"He means *Bob* Dylan," said Peter York, "not Dylan Thomas."

"The poet and prophet," said Quinn. "You can't imagine what he meant to all of us. You know, Ted, it might help you to listen to Dylan. Being where you belong. He gave voice to —"

"Cut the bullshit," said Wyeth.

"You don't understand what he meant to us," Quinn said.

"Liar," said Wyeth.

I, of course, had read the notes taken by Quinn's therapist that were on the disc Wyeth had stolen and then left in his computer. I, however, considered the information confidential.

"Ted, you acted in self-defense," I said. "When you discovered being Jewish, you found yourself. Eumie threatened to kill your identity. She threatened to kill you." I thought of Phyllis's Monty and of what she'd said about him. Once Ted defined himself as Jewish, he knew who he was.

Ted was sobbing. "She said I was a goy," he managed to say. "Me! That's what she said. *Oy vey!*"

Kevin Dennehy stepped forward. He picked up Ted's crutches in one hand. With the other, he helped Ted to his feet. With no protest, Ted went with him. On his way out, Ted asked whether he could call someone.

"A lawyer," Kevin said.

"No," said Ted. "A rabbi."

CHAPTER 49

I like a happy ending. The ending to this story is happier than I might have imagined and certainly happier than I feared when Kevin Dennehy took Ted Green into custody and Ted made his ridiculous demand for a rabbi. It's clear to me that I underestimated Kevin, whose network in Cambridge rivaled my network in dogs and who was thus able immediately to summon the kind of psychologically minded rabbi Ted needed. The rabbi somehow succeeded in getting Ted to accept that he'd been born gentile. I recently had e-mail from Ted on that very topic. He said that he'd at first found the full realization quite traumatic. After that, he'd hurled himself into the study of Judaism. With no encouragement from the rabbi, he intended to convert. As to his legal situation, he has a good criminal lawyer, Oona Sundquist, as it happens, and the evidence against him isn't all that strong. Among other things, it turns out that Vee Foote had been overprescribing for both Ted and Eumie. Their other physicians had been irresponsible in failing to coordinate with one another. As I understand it, Ted's defense is going to rest on the contention that if Eumie hadn't been loaded with prescription drugs to begin with, then the overdose that killed her wouldn't have been a fatal one at all. I don't buy the argument, but I'm no lawyer, so what do I know? If the jury shares my view, justice will be served, I think, and not only with regard to Eumie's death. That business about Ted's mother having died during spring break in his senior year of college? About the former Ms. O'Flaherty having conveniently perished just in time to miss his graduation? Just how did she die, anyway?

Speaking of lawyers, including the disbarred, Anita Fairley recovered from the hypomanic episode that was induced by an antidepressant prescribed by Vee Foote. Anita does not confide in me, but Rita heard that the Fiend was threatening to sue Dr. Foote for putting her on an SSRI known to pose a risk of hypomania and failing to monitor her condition; and that Dr. Foote was insisting that instead of taking the drug as prescribed, Anita had taken twice the correct amount. Furthermore, Anita's rapid and extreme reaction had been very rare. For what it's worth, I believe Dr. Foote.

Although Rita says that the Brainard-Green family meeting was the worst effort she has ever made at a therapeutic intervention, it had one outcome that even she admits is worthwhile. In their meeting in the kitchen, the physicians were surprised and appalled to discover the quantities and varieties of psychoactive drugs they were collectively prescribing for the Brainard-Greens. Furthermore, although Rita maintains that Quinn Youngman did not make himself obnoxious, the psychopharmacologist's superior knowledge evidently made the other doctors aware of the extent of their own ignorance. They responded by hiring Quinn for a series of teaching sessions to be followed by group supervision.

Rita is still dating Quinn Youngman, who, she informs me, confided to her that he had been making a distorted presentation of self and now wanted to establish a genuine relationship with her. Far from devoting his youth to sex, drugs, radical politics, and Bob Dylan, he'd conformed to the expectations of his conservative family, at least until he'd discovered science. After that, he'd concentrated on getting into medical school and then on graduating at the top of his class. Rita reinterpreted his confession. In her view, he had a truly radical past in the sense that beneath the conformist self imposed on him by his parents, there existed a rebellious part of himself even in his adolescent years. Thus he hadn't really lied to her; rather, he'd liberated himself from a false persona.

Adolescence. Oh my. Wyeth. With his father in jail, one source of money was cut off. Then the foundation that had been funding Johanna's research on feminist linguistics failed to renew her grant. These misfortunes had unexpected consequences. First, Johanna lucked into a position with the national office of a chain of day spas specializing in facials, laser treatments, and the like. She plans advertising campaigns, writes brochures, and maintains Web sites. Her original field was feminist linguistics, women and words, so the departure is less radical than it might at first seem. Second, Johanna's brother, someone I'd never heard of before, took an interest in Wyeth and even accompanied Wyeth to a few sessions with Peter York. As Rita explained to me, in many matrilineal societies, the mother's brother plays a powerful role in a child's life. Anyway, this mother's brother, who lives in

Cambridge, almost forcibly removed Wyeth from Cambridge for a month and took him on a backpacking trip in the Sierras. The idea, I guess, was to make a man of Wyeth, to give him a sort of WASP bar mitzvah. I hope the ritual works.

About Caprice and her father, Monty, I have nothing but good news. With the secrecy about his Internet porn addiction dispelled, they are spending a lot of time together. They cemented their new bond by going to CHIRP for two weeks. Its former director was fired during a scandal about kickbacks, and Rita says that the new one is uncorrupt and excellent. Monty continues to participate in a support group for people with his addiction, and Caprice attends meetings of Overeaters Anonymous as dutifully and fervently as I go to dog training. She is losing weight. As part of her new approach to diet and exercise, she still walks Lady. Also, she read and claimed to enjoy *No More Fat Dogs,* which she kindly credits with helping her to follow the principles of building muscle while decreasing calories. I can see the book's influence: she certainly does eat an awful lot of green beans. She continues to see Missy Zinn, who, by the way, is seeing Peter York in the romantic rather than the therapeutic sense of the word.

Barbara and George have gone into couples therapy with Frank Farmer, whose broken leg is healing well. His dogs are as naughty as ever, but they're still winning. Dolfo now lives with Barbara, George, and Portia. He is housebroken. Barbara is taking him to obedience classes and feels confident that he will pass his Canine Good Citizenship test within a few months. As planned, Barbara and George volunteer with an urban wildlife program. George is very enthusiastic about the work he is doing there. In fact, he and Steve are doing a project together. It's about Cambridge black squirrels.

I still listen to Eumie's gift now and then, but it has done its work. Rowdy and I went to a rally event. It wasn't an official trial. So what? Rowdy was wonderful. My heart was pounding for the first minute or so on the course, but then I got lost in my dog, and I had fun. Indeed, everyone is benefitting from therapy of one kind or another. Rita isn't in therapy with Frank Farmer, but he is supervising her. Dr. Foote is reputed to be consulting a hypnotherapist about her dog phobia. According to Rita, Missy Zinn is in treatment with India Cohen, the social worker who accompanied Wyeth to the meeting. One evening when Rita and I were going to have dinner out together, I was supposed to meet her at her office. I arrived early. Rita's door opened, and out walked her last patient of the day. She was Oona Sundquist, formerly George McBane's lawyer, now Ted Green's. In my world, dogs are never left out. Lady is seeing, in the therapeutic sense, the Reiki healer and the massage therapist I met at Ted Green's. Both of them treat dogs as well as people. Lady adores them, and her anxiety seems to be decreasing.

I do have some final dog news that was passed on to me by Barbara Leibowitz, who found it on the Web. Dolfo's breeder is being sued by irate puppy buyers because she misled them into believing that they were paying high prices for golden Aussie huskapoos, whereas her breeding stock actually consisted of mixed-breeds she had adopted from shelters that lacked the funds to spay and neuter animals before placing them for adoption. She has repeatedly inbred her stock, so her lines do have a certain consistency, but her puppies were not precisely what she said they were.

Which of us is?

ABOUT THE AUTHOR

Susan Conant is a three-time recipient of the Maxwell Award for Fiction Writing given by the Dog Writers Association of America. She lives in Newton, Massachusetts, with her husband, two cats, and two Alaskan malamutes.

HPL

V. V.